HEATHER SONG

A sequel to *Angel Harp*

Also by Michael Phillips

Angel Harp

Available wherever books are sold.

HEATHER SONG

A Novel

MICHAEL PHILLIPS

New York   Boston   Nashville

Copyright © 2011 by Michael Phillips

FaithWords
Hachette Book Group
237 Park Avenue
New York, NY 10017

www.faithwords.com

Printed in the United States of America

First Edition: September 2011

10 9 8 7 6 5 4 3 2 1

FaithWords is a division of Hachette Book Group, Inc.
The FaithWords name and logo are trademarks of Hachette Book Group, Inc.

Library of Congress Cataloging-in-Publication Data

Phillips, Michael R., 1946–
Heather song / Michael Phillips. — 1st ed.
        p. cm.
ISBN 978-0-446-56772-5
1. Scotland—Fiction. I. Title.
PS3566.H492H43 2011
813'.54—dc22
                    2011023226

To

Those hundreds of aspiring musicians, young and old,
and their parents, relatives, and friends,
who through the years have enjoyed and marveled at
the music from the harp studio of my wife, Judy Phillips.
The harp is indeed a magical instrument whose music,
touching us on so many levels, cannot but remind us a little
of God's angels and their invisible work among us.

Contents

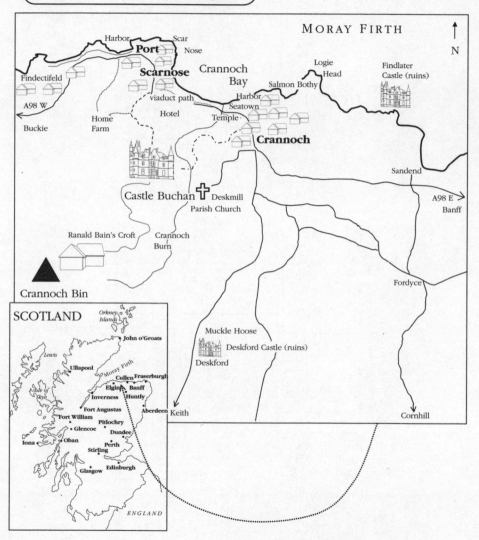

Map of Port Scarnose Region

MORAY FIRTH

N

Harbor · Scar · Nose
Port
Scarnose · Crannoch Bay

Logie Head · Findlater Castle (ruins)

Salmon Bothy

Findectifeld

viaduct path · Harbor · Seatown

A98 W

Hotel · Temple

Buckie

Home Farm

Crannoch

Castle Buchan ✝ Deskmill Parish Church

Sandend

A98 E Banff

Ranald Bain's Croft · Crannoch Burn

Fordyce

Crannoch Bin

SCOTLAND

Orkney Islands

Muckle Hoose

John o'Groats

Deskford Castle (ruins)

Lewis

Deskford

Ullapool

Moray Firth

Cullen · Fraserburgh

Isle of Skye

Elgin · Banff

Inverness · Huntly

Fort Augustus · Aberdeen · Keith

Fort William

Pitlochry

Iona · Glencoe · Dundee

Oban · Perth

Stirling

Glasgow · Edinburgh

Cornhill

ENGLAND

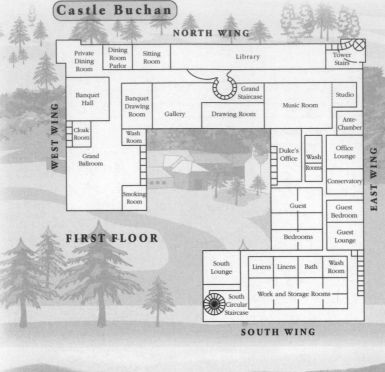

Castle Buchan

NORTH WING

Private Dining Room | Dining Room Parlor | Sitting Room | Library | Tower Stairs

WEST WING

Banquet Hall | Banquet Drawing Room | Gallery | Drawing Room | Grand Staircase | Music Room | Studio

Cloak Room | Wash Room | Ante-Chamber

Grand Ballroom | Duke's Office | Wash Rooms | Office Lounge

Smoking Room | Conservatory

FIRST FLOOR

Guest | Guest Bedroom

Bedrooms | Guest Lounge

EAST WING

South Lounge | Linens | Linens | Bath | Wash Room

South Circular Staircase | Work and Storage Rooms

SOUTH WING

NORTH WING

Formal Dining Room | Cloak Room | Entry Hall | Sitting Room | Great Room

Family Dining Room | Formal Lounge | Piano Room | Grand Staircase | Withdrawing Room

WEST WING

China Room | Wash Rooms | Drawing Room | Courtyard Sitting Room | Small Library | Guest Lounge | Coat/Hat Closets

Kitchen | Pantry | INTERIOR COURTYARD | East Parlor | Wash Room | East Sitting Room

Food Storage | Housekeeping Supplies

EAST WING

Breakfast Room | Larder | Laundry Room | Ironing Room

To Basement

GROUND FLOOR

Work Rooms

Maintenance and Work Rooms | Gardening Workshop

Garages | Tool and Equipment Room

SOUTH WING

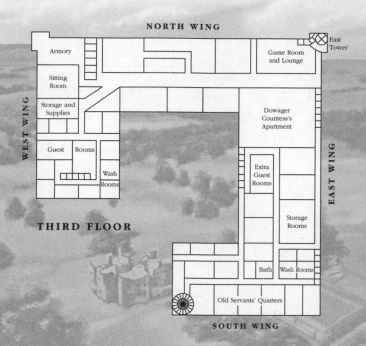

NORTH WING

Armory

East Tower

Game Room and Lounge

Sitting Room

Storage and Supplies

Dowager Countess's Apartment

Guest Rooms

Wash Rooms

Extra Guest Rooms

Storage Rooms

WEST WING

EAST WING

THIRD FLOOR

Bath

Wash Rooms

Old Servants' Quarters

SOUTH WING

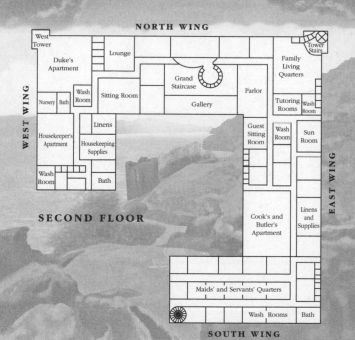

NORTH WING

West Tower

Lounge

Tower Stairs

Duke's Apartment

Family Living Quarters

Wash Room

Grand Staircase

Parlor

Sitting Room

Gallery

WEST WING

Nursery

Bath

Tutoring Rooms

Wash Room

Linens

Guest Sitting Room

Wash Room

Sun Room

Housekeeper's Apartment

Housekeeping Supplies

EAST WING

Wash Room

Bath

SECOND FLOOR

Cook's and Butler's Apartment

Linens and Supplies

Maids' and Servants' Quarters

Wash Rooms

Bath

SOUTH WING

HEATHER SONG

Chapter One

The Dream

Could I but sojourn with thee only
In some green glen, secure and lonely,
Then neither glory, fame, nor treasure,
Could ever bring me half such pleasure.
—"My Pretty Mary"

There was a time in my life when a dream of mine almost died.

I was forty years old and alone in the world. I had been married but was widowed six years before. My mother was dead, and though my father was still living, we weren't close. I had no children, no brothers, no sisters, and sad to say, not even any close friends. Life had begun to progress as a gray drudgery of year following year.

Turning forty woke me out of my lethargy. I realized I didn't want the rest of my life to just drift by without ever doing anything...having an adventure.

That's when I remembered my dream.

It wasn't anything spectacular, not something anyone couldn't have done. It was just to take a summer trip to Scotland. I wanted to travel and see places I had never been. I wanted to play my harp on a high mountain or maybe on a cliff overlooking the sea. So before I suddenly realized I was *fifty*, I decided to do something about it.

Music in general, and especially the music of the harp, was one of the most important ingredients to the dream. It was the music of the Celtic countries that had through the years gotten under my skin, creating a longing that I wanted to fulfill. I had a vague sense that I possessed Celtic blood. Maybe that's why I liked the music.

Something about the melancholy nature of Celtic harmony probes the soul in a way other music cannot. The melodies and themes of its folk songs and ballads draw you in. At that phase of my life, the haunting melancholy of Celtic music resonated with a loneliness that was stirring inside me. It is music you *feel*, not just hear. You want to *be* there.

I'd always thought that one of the reasons music gets so deep into the human consciousness is that people are "tuned" in different ways like musical instruments. Some have talkative, frilly personalities like a flute. Others are natural leaders like a trumpet. Others are full and complex like a viola or cello.

I also thought that all men and women possessed an innate personality that was tuned in either a major or a minor key. Not that some were always happy and others always sad. Some of the world's most triumphant and joyous music is composed in minor keys. But an inherent difference exists between the sound and the texture of the two that I think is replicated in people as well.

My personality was one that vibrated to the rhythms of life in minor keys. Celtic music stimulated the melancholy harmonies of those chords. Its melodies resonated within me in ways I could not explain. And I wanted to allow that inner resonance to take place where the music originated.

That's how my adventure in Scotland began.

I packed my small harp as one of my two allowable bags and flew from my home in Alberta, Canada, to London, took the train north to Inverness, and there rented a car and drove around, staying in B and Bs and getting to know Scotland. My name is Angel Marie. But because I play the harp, and to avoid the inevitable jokes about harps and angels and heaven, I have always gone by just the *Marie*.

After a week, I realized I *wasn't* getting to know Scotland. I was learning a few isolated facts about its colorful history. But I was getting to know only tourist stops where busloads of people stopped to buy souvenirs. That wasn't what I'd had in mind. I didn't want to be a "tourist," I wanted to connect in a deeper way with places and people. I wanted to *feel* the reality of Scotland.

Therefore, purely at random, while driving through a quaint little seacoast village, knowing not a soul but liking the look of the place, I booked a bed-and-breakfast and decided to stay for a week, maybe if I liked it even two. The name of the village was Port Scarnose. It was situated on the most gorgeous headland overlooking the Moray Firth of the North Sea, where I had heard that if you were lucky, you might see dolphins swimming in the temperate waters of the Gulf Stream.

That's where my Scottish adventure began. It turned out to be more of an adventure than I imagined would ever happen to me!

While playing my Celtic harp a few days later on an overlook above the sea, a voice startled me. I was surprised to see a red-haired man appearing from amid the shrubbery, raving about my beautiful music. I quickly learned that he was the energetic curate of the local parish church—Iain Barclay. We talked and hit it off, and a friendship developed. He invited me to play my harp for his church, which I did.

It may not seem like such a big thing to meet a minister and then accept an invitation to play for his church. But it was a big deal to me. I didn't consider myself a religious person, a "Christian," if you like. I had once been active in church but had drifted away after the death of my husband, and I gradually quit believing much of anything. I wouldn't have called myself antagonistic to spiritual things, but I wasn't really interested either.

The trouble was, I liked Iain Barclay. He wasn't pushy or religious, he was accepting and gracious . . . and fun. But I have to admit it seemed a bit strange the first time we had dinner to realize I was having a date with a *minister*!

But I liked him. There it was. I couldn't help it.

Out on the same path I also met the most enchanting little red-headed girl walking along the path above the sea. Immediately I fell in love with her and she fell in love with my harp. Even as I let her strum a few notes, I could tell she had the gift of music inside her. She was a little odd, in both mannerisms and speech, and it crossed my mind whether she might have savant tendencies. Her name was Gwendolyn. The woman with her, whom I took for her mother, was in fact her aunt and legal guardian.

After running into her a second time, I made inquiries about where she lived and offered to begin teaching her to play the harp. Gwendolyn's aunt Olivia was cool and distant and did not warm to my involvement. But she agreed to let me bring my harp to their house so that Gwendolyn could learn to play.

I was enthralled. The music Gwendolyn made was ethereal and otherworldly, like nothing I had ever heard in all my years of teaching harp. It wasn't long before the idea came to me that I should record her playing.

Unknown to me at the time, the church where I had played happened to sit across a high stone wall from the estate and castle of the local duke, enigmatic recluse Alasdair Reidhaven. The duke had overheard my playing in the churchyard one day from over the wall and was mesmerized. As a result, I received a written invitation to play at the castle. When I arrived at the castle, however, the duke never showed himself. I played for an hour in solitude, wondering what was going on. I would later learn that the duke was listening to me from behind a room divider.

I wasn't as alone as I thought!

From both my experience at the castle and negative talk around the village, I couldn't help forming an "attitude" toward the duke, building up an image of him in my mind as heartless and rude.

Meanwhile, more local relationships developed as my stay in Port Scarnose lengthened—particularly with an eccentric sheepherder and "crofter" by the name of Ranald Bain who lived on the slope of a nearby mountain. Ranald was a fiddler as well as a shepherd. After several more visits, we began making music together and had the greatest time! Ranald's wife, Margaret—he always called her "Maggie"—had been dead six years, the same as my husband, and though he didn't talk about it, there seemed to be something mysterious about her death. They had lost their only daughter, Winny, many years before, when she was still in her teens. Her death, too, was a mystery no one talked about.

Out of the blue, another invitation to the castle appeared—this time to dinner! In spite of my attitude about the duke, whom I still had never seen, I accepted. What I was not prepared for was to find him shy, awkward, apologetic for what had taken place earlier, and, though a little peculiar, altogether likable.

I was especially not prepared, after seeing Curate Barclay several more times and realizing that something was beginning to click between us, for Duke Reidhaven to appear at the door of my cottage in person. According to everyone I'd talked to, he *never* showed himself in the village.

Now there he was, standing in front of me, inviting me out for a walk!

The duke, no less! Had my simple three-week vacation to Scotland turned into an adventure or what?

But actually the walk was nice. I liked the duke, too. He began to loosen up and told me stories of his boyhood. That's when I first learned that he and Iain Barclay had been childhood best friends. They hadn't spoken in years, however. Something serious had come between them. I had no idea what.

By this time I had developed several friendships. Because of Gwendolyn's harp playing I felt a sense of purpose in what I was doing, and I decided to stay for a while longer.

I couldn't go home yet.

My decision obviously also had to do with the two men I was seeing regularly, though I'm not sure I was able to admit it to myself right then. But whatever I was ready to admit or not admit, I postponed my return flight to Canada, left the bed-and-breakfast, and rented a self-catering cottage in the village.

How long I would stay, I had no idea.

My life now began to get complicated. My long talks with Iain

Barclay about spiritual things were penetrating deep into my heart. I began to think about God in new and liberating ways. This could not help deepening the bond I felt with Iain. At the same time I was seeing more and more of the duke.

Though I didn't fully recognize what was happening at first, eventually it began to dawn on me. That's when I knew I had a problem—I was involved with two men.

An even bigger shock awaited me. I learned that Gwendolyn was the duke's daughter, raised after his young wife's death by the duke's sister, Olivia Urquhart. Here, too, something strange was going on. The duke never saw his dear little daughter. When I asked about it, Olivia gave me plausible enough reasons. She said the duke was dangerous, that she was protecting Gwendolyn from him. She told dreadful stories about the duke, insinuating that he may have even killed his own wife.

None of these tales squared with what the duke told me, nor with the character of Alasdair Reidhaven as I was getting to know him. *Someone* wasn't telling the truth.

The longer I was in Port Scarnose, the more intertwined became the relationships in which I had become entangled. Complexities hinted at murders, madness, jealousies, and hatreds from the past.

What was I in the middle of? I felt like I'd landed in the middle of a Gothic novel.

I also gradually learned that Gwendolyn was seriously ill, with only a few years to live. It was a shocking thing to find out, but I determined to do all I could to make her life as rich as possible. I hoped my harp would bring her solace and peace.

Gwendolyn's illness, the events surrounding her birth, the death of the duke's wife . . . all of it deepened my questions about the mysterious Reidhaven family. Somehow Olivia seemed to hold the key to everything. Bad blood obviously existed between her and all three of the principal men who had become my good friends—Ranald Bain, Olivia's brother, Alasdair, the duke, and Iain Barclay, the curate. In spite of much I did not understand, however, the music of my harp seemed to be exercising a healing influence in the lives of the people who heard it. For that I was grateful.

Though I still did not know what was at the root of all the mysteries, Iain Barclay and I went one day to the Urquhart home and insisted that Olivia allow us to take Gwendolyn to see her father. In silent fury—and uncharacteristically . . . I couldn't figure out why she gave in so quickly—she reluctantly consented.

The reconciliation between father and daughter was one of the most wonderful things I have ever witnessed. Gwendolyn was clearly frightened as she and I approached the castle hand in hand. Despite my reassurances, she could not escape her thoughts of the terrible things her aunt had told her about Alasdair, the duke.

"You don't think I am mean, do you?" I asked her.

"Oh, no, Marie!" replied Gwendolyn. "You are the nicest person in the whole world."

"You can trust me, can't you?"

"Oh, yes!"

"Well, I know your father, Gwendolyn. He is not so very different from me. I know that he loves you very much. He wants you to know him just like I know him," I said. "So I have come to take you to him, so that you can know him just like I know him. Can you trust me, Gwendolyn?"

"I will try, Marie."

"Then trust me that your father loves you, too."

We stopped in front of the great oak door. I looked down at her and gave her a smile of reassurance.

"Would you like to ring the bell or use the knocker?" I said.

She stretched up on her toes and turned the bell-knob. Then we waited.

After several minutes we heard heavy steps approaching. When Alasdair appeared, the look of joy on his face was such that no one could possibly be afraid.

It was the expression of a father's boundless love.

When his gaze settled on the red-haired girl beside me, his eyes were misty. He stooped down and smiled.

"This is your father, dear," I said.

"Hello, Gwendolyn," said Alasdair in a soft, husky voice.

"How do you know my name, sir?" said Gwendolyn timidly.

"Because I am your father," replied Alasdair, smiling and blinking back tears. "I have known you all your life, though I have not seen you for many years. You do not remember, but you have been here before."

"In this castle?"

"Yes."

"When?"

"You were born here."

"I was?"

"Would you like to see where?"

"I think I would."

As I left father and daughter alone, I was crying my eyes out in happiness.

I saw neither of them for over half an hour. I was sitting on a bench in the garden and heard a happy shout followed by footsteps. I looked up to see Gwendolyn running in her awkward gait toward me, followed by Alasdair hurrying to keep up.

In Gwendolyn's eyes was a look of radiance such as I had not seen on her face before. She ran straight into my arms.

"Daddy is nothing like what Mummy said," she said excitedly. "He is as nice as you, Marie. I sat in his lap and he told me stories. He told me about my real mother. I think my real mummy must have been nice. I saw her picture."

The joyous reunion was the beginning of happy times for father and daughter. I had never seen Gwendolyn so full of life. Meanwhile, Olivia was furious at being coerced into allowing Gwendolyn to visit her father, and she took no joy in the blossoming relationship between Alasdair and his daughter. By this point I think she hated me, and my music, too, for my part in bringing Gwendolyn and Alasdair back together.

Sadly, the reunion came too late. Almost immediately Gwendolyn took a turn for the worse. It soon became obvious that she was dying. As the day she first saw Alasdair was one of the happiest days of my life, the last day of her life, as Alasdair and I sat at her bedside, was surely the most heartbreaking.

"Will you play for me on the angel harp?" Gwendolyn asked me. Her voice was so soft I could barely hear it.

"Of course, sweetheart," I replied.

I began the song that had been inspired by the first sounds to come out of her playing on my harp, which I called "Gwendolyn's Song." Though I played softly, the sound seemed to fill the room. The moment Gwendolyn heard the familiar melody, she leaned her head back on the pillow, a smile of peace on her lips.

"One of the angels told me she heard you when you were playing once in the church," she said. "She said she wants me to play for her, too."

Gradually the tiniest sound came from the bed. My fingers stilled and I listened. Gwendolyn was gazing up out of the pillow into Alasdair's face. She was singing.

"*A baby came to Mummy and Daddy. I had just begun to be . . .*"

She stopped to take a breath. Her voice was faint.

"*Mummy and Daddy,*" she tried to go on. "*Mummy and Daddy . . . loved baby. That baby . . . was me.*"

The tiny voice fell silent.

I stood and went to Alasdair's side. As I glanced down upon the bed, Gwendolyn's eyes were closed. The light had faded from her face, though the remnant of a smile lingered on her lips.

She had taken her music to share it with the angels.

They say death brings healing and renewal, if only you know where to look for it. Though the whole community mourned Gwendolyn's passing, no one could deny the new life everyone felt as a result of the reconciliation between Alasdair Reidhaven and Iain Barclay that took place during Gwendolyn's final days.

With Gwendolyn gone, I suddenly had to face reality. Whether I had been completely clueless all this time, or whether it was a slow-dawning realization that only now became obvious, it was at Gwendolyn's funeral that a shocking truth finally broke over me:

I was in love with two men!

The worst of it was that these same two men had already been separated by their love for a woman years before—Fiona, Gwendolyn's mother. Now that they were finally reconciled and their friendship restored, I could not let such a thing happen again. I cared too much about both of them to run the risk of allowing either relationship to go further.

I had no choice but to bring my adventure in Scotland to an end.

The good-byes were poignant. I had the sense that either man might propose to me if I gave them the chance. My heart was especially torn as I saw Alasdair for the last time. I just couldn't find the words to tell him. While I was stalling, he reached into his pocket and pulled out a small oblong black box.

"This necklace belonged to my mother," he said. "I was saving it for Gwendolyn, hoping that...Well, she will not be able to wear it now, and...I would like you to have it, Marie."

Alasdair opened the box, then reached out and set it across the table in front of me. It must have contained twenty or more diamonds!

"I...Alasdair, it's...I've never seen anything so lovely," I said, fumbling for words. "It's so kind...I mean, but...I can't accept a family heirloom."

Alasdair looked away. The open box with the necklace sparkling on a black velvet bed sat on the table between us.

"It's Iain, isn't it?" he said after a minute.

The words jolted me.

"I've seen it all along," he continued, smiling a little sadly. "I knew you loved him. And I...You need have no worry about me. He is a fine man...You could not do better. Even so...even if you wear it as Iain's wife...I would like you to have this necklace...as a reminder of . . . of happy times . . . times you once spent with a man who cared for you very much, and—"

He drew in a deep breath and smiled again. "And to remember Gwendolyn," he added.

"It is not because of Iain," I said softly.

"What, then? Please . . . ," implored Alasdair. "Say you will accept the necklace, as a token of my—"

"Oh, Alasdair," I said, at last bursting into tears. "I am leaving to-morrow!"

I was crying in earnest now. I couldn't look at him.

For a moment all was silence.

Then I heard his chair slide across the floor. He got up and his footsteps came around the table to where I sat. I stood, and the next moment I was swallowed in his embrace.

"I knew this day would come," he said. "It had to eventually."

"I'm sorry I didn't tell you sooner," I said through my tears.

"I know you were thinking of me," he said. "I tried to pretend there would not have to be a day of farewell. Inside I knew I was just fooling myself. This will be the most painful parting of my life. But you needn't worry. Things are different now. I am a changed man. I have known you and loved you and I will never forget you. And," he added, "if you can . . . I hope you won't forget me either."

I burst into sobs as I pulled back and gazed deeply into his eyes.

"Oh, Alasdair!" I said. "How could you even think I would forget you! Some of the most wonderful memories of my life will be of this place."

I embraced him again, tight and long, then stepped back. I took his arm and we walked downstairs and outside without another word.

I left to return to Canada the next day.

Chapter Two

Beginning of Auld Lang Syne

Farewell to the bluebells, and welcome the new bells,
The bridal bells, pealing o'er the valley and hill;
Sweet bells that betoken love's link never broken,
Though time bring the cloud and the chill.
  —J. S. Skinner, "The Cloud and the Chill"

After a few lonely months in Calgary trying to resume my former life, I realized it was no use.

Love never just goes away. It has to be done something with, brought to a resolution. Many people, of course, interpret this need wrongly by thinking of it in physical terms. Nothing could have been further from my mind. Nevertheless, I knew the uncertainty of the situation had to be "resolved" and brought to completion—emotionally, personally, spiritually.

Even though I had done so to protect the two men from pain, I could not "run away" from the love, or *loves*, in my heart.

I had to face my destiny, whatever it was. I had to return to Scotland. I had to decide where my deepest love truly was.

I made plans without telling a soul. Even as I arrived by bus in Port Scarnose, I still wasn't absolutely sure what my decision would be . . . or whether either man would even want me. But I had to find out.

Whom did I *really* love?

After several long, prayerful walks, at last my soul-searching came to an end. I knew my decision. Immediately I set out on a long walk that took me on a familiar route out of town.

When I reached my destination and saw the huge door in front of me, I paused, drew in a deep breath of final resolve, then reached out my hand and lifted the knocker.

A minute later footsteps came from inside. Slowly the door opened.

"Hello, Alicia," I said to the duke's housekeeper. "Would you please tell Mr. Reidhaven that he has a visitor who has come to inquire about a certain diamond necklace?"

When Alasdair saw me a minute later, his face went pale.

The look of joy flooding his eyes was so childlike it took my breath away.

"*Marie!*" he said in wonder, almost as if I were a specter from his imagination.

At the sound of his voice, all my fears vanished and I hurried toward him. He received me with open arms. We stood for what seemed like forever.

"I think perhaps I am now ready," I whispered at last. "That is, if you still want me to . . . to wear the diamond necklace you wanted to give me."

"Oh, Marie!" he said. "There is nothing I want more. But what about . . . I mean, have you seen—"

"Alasdair," I said, stopping him before he could say it. "I have seen no one else. I came back . . . to *you*."

It was agony to walk up to Iain's door later that same day. But he had to hear it from me.

The moment he saw me standing on his porch, his eyes swam, but he did not allow whatever he might be feeling to spill over. He saw the expression on my face, and I knew he knew.

I told him that I had come from the castle, where Alasdair had proposed to me and that I had accepted him.

Only then did Iain approach and hug me warmly, as a brother now, and congratulated us both. I knew his words were utterly genuine, and I knew all over again why I had loved him.

The day after my visit, Iain called on Alasdair to personally congratulate him and to offer his services, if Alasdair and I so desired, for the ceremony. He was sincerely and honestly happy for us—I think for Alasdair most of all. The whole thing fit no Hollywood script where men compete for a woman's affections. Iain *loved* Alasdair in the full sense of brother loving brother. Alasdair's happiness meant more to him than his own.

Alasdair and I were married in the gardens of Castle Buchan the following spring, just as the rosebuds were starting to come on. Tulips were in profusion, and rhododendrons. The earth was everywhere alive and bursting forth with the renewal of spring.

Iain performed the ceremony. Everyone within Deskmill Parish was invited to the wedding, and indeed, so many came that the grounds were overflowing. Ranald Bain, in the full Highland costume of his clan, added the haunting strains of ballad after ballad to the afternoon from the annals of Scottish legend and lore.

Midway through the afternoon, Alasdair made a speech and toasted the good health of his friends one and all, culminating in inviting the entire community to the harbor that evening to send him and his bride on the newly christened yacht *Gwendolyn* off into the gloaming on the tide.

Several hundred people or more accepted the invitation and came to see us off.

As the *Gwendolyn* slowly slipped out of the harbor, Alasdair and I stood on the deck returning the waves and shouts of the townspeople. From somewhere in their midst a bagpipe was playing.

As we cleared the thick cement harbor walls, slowly a familiar tune began to blend in with the pipes. The high, clear tone came unmistakably from Ranald Bain's violin—the fiddle and the pipes intermingling with the mysterious harmony one hears only in Scotland.

Within seconds, hundreds of voices joined in unison. The words of the Scottish anthem of memories and hopes drifted across the evening waters toward us:

> Should auld acquaintance be forgot,
> And ne'er brought to mind.
> Should auld acquaintance be forgot,
> In days of auld lang syne.

Alasdair looked at me, smiled, and stretched his arm around me. We stood at the rail, gazing back at the harbor and crowd, as both slowly faded into the distance.

Over and over the strains repeated themselves, the sounds growing ever fainter...

...auld acquaintance...to mind...forgot...in days of auld lang syne...

...days of auld lang syne...

...auld lang syne...

—until we could hear them no longer.

Gradually Ranald's violin also faded from hearing.

Finally only the skirl of the pipes remained, and that for but another few moments. At last the pipes, too, were gone, and we were left alone.

Still we stood, gazing back over the *Gwendolyn*'s wake, until land and sea and sky faded into a purply haze behind us, and we were left surrounded by the reds and oranges of a slowly dying gloaming sunset over the widening Moray Firth of the North Sea.

Chapter Three

The Vast Sea of God's Fatherhood

The wind is fair, the day is fine, and swiftly, swiftly runs the time;
The boat is floating on the tide that wafts me off from Fiunary.
We must up and be away! We must up and be away!
We must up and be away! Farewell, farewell to Fiunary.
—Norman MacLeod, "Farewell to Fiunary"

Alasdair and I planned a voyage of about a month, perhaps six weeks, for our honeymoon—to Malta, Crete, Italy, and the Greek Islands. For someone who had never been anywhere—except to Scotland, of course!—I was so excited.

Talk about an adventure. Maybe my adventure was still just beginning.

Alasdair only laughed at my girlish enthusiasm. I was now forty-one, but I felt eighteen.

"You can go anywhere you like, my dear," he said. "I will take you anywhere in the world it is your heart's desire to see."

"Really—do you mean it, Alasdair?"

Again he laughed.

"Of course," he said. "Marie, you are a duchess now. You can do whatever you like."

"Me? I'm no duchess!"

"You certainly are. What did you think you would be, marrying a duke?"

"But the agreement . . . I thought—"

"I don't want to hear any more about that silly prenup of yours! Against my better judgment, I went along because you were so in-

16

sistent that I was afraid you wouldn't marry me otherwise. But I managed to sneak in a few private discussions with my solicitors when you weren't around."

"Alasdair, you didn't . . . not really?"

"I did indeed."

"But you didn't change it?"

"Only in one or two points. I made absolutely certain that as long as I am the duke, *you* will be the duchess. I know you didn't care about the title, but I did. It's done and legal and there's nothing you can do to undo it. So eat cake, my dear—you *are* the Duchess of Buchan."

"Oh, Alasdair," I sighed. "You are so good to me! But you do understand, don't you—we don't have aristocracy in Canada. It's hard for me to get used to. I am just so fearful of people misunderstanding my motives. That's the only reason I insisted on the agreement. I wanted no doubt in anyone's mind that I was marrying you because I *loved* you—nothing more. Not even your suspicious sister can spin that into some nefarious design."

"Don't be too sure." Alasdair smiled wryly. "Olivia is a clever woman. We will doubtless have to contend with her wiles for the rest of our lives. There is no telling what mischief she might yet concoct. In any event, you are the Duchess of Buchan and I hope you can get used to it, because from here on people will treat you differently. They will bow and curtsy and call you *my lady* or *Your Grace*."

"I'm not sure I can take all that."

"It is expected. Besides, with someone who has as many names as you, what's one more?"

"Alasdair!"

"I still haven't decided whether to be angry with you or not for keeping your *Angel* from me for so long."

"I explained all that." I laughed. "And what about you? You didn't exactly come clean with your whole name either."

"But I had good reason. I wasn't keeping a beautiful name like

Angel under wraps. The British aristocracy and their long names...
Alasdair Timothy *Fotheringay* Reidhaven—goodness! With a name like
Fotheringay stuck in there, who wouldn't try to keep it a secret?!"

"So we were both holding out on each other. That makes us
even."

"But no more secrets between us," Alasdair said, laughing. "I
still contend that your list has a more aristocratic ring to it than
mine...Angel Dawn Marie Buchan Lorcini Reidhaven of
Buchan...*Duchess* of Buchan. You could compete with a king or
queen with all that!"

"It is truly amazing," I said, "the Buchan as much as the duchess.
Now I am a Buchan twice."

"Don't think that fact has escaped me!" rejoined Alasdair. "It's one
of the reasons I knew we were meant for each other. The double
Buchan has a ring to it, don't you think, and qualifies you for the
'duchess' all the more—with *two* Buchan names, you surely have a
full complement of Scots blood in your veins. They call the Brodies
Brodie of Brodie. We shall call you *Buchan of Buchan*!"

"But doesn't the fact that I'm Canadian prevent my *really* being
the duchess? It is just an honorary title, isn't it?"

"I am having that all looked into by my people in Edinburgh. And
to be certain of your legal standing...papers will be awaiting us
when we reach home with which to file your application for joint
citizenship."

"Can I really do that?"

"Being married to a UK citizen, and a duke besides, with all the
legal firepower I will bring to the case—absolutely. You will have a
UK passport with full citizenship within the year. No, my dear, your
standing will be anything but honorary. You are, as I believe they
say in the States, the *real deal*."

"Will this fairy-tale dream that I landed into the middle of never
cease?"

"Not if I can help it."

* * *

The first several days at sea were magical. I had never experienced anything like it. And on my honeymoon, no less.

We were alone on the yacht. Alasdair knew every inch of her, knew what to do, and was as skilled a captain as I could have hoped for. When darkness came each night we weighed anchor and put the *Gwendolyn* to sleep for the night. Captain Travis flew on ahead to Lisbon, where he met us. After that he took command.

Alasdair was a little quiet when we passed the place off Spain where Gwendolyn had taken ill. But the next afternoon, with Gibraltar looming like a sentinel of history over us, we passed into the Mediterranean and the magic, if anything, increased. We put to shore at Morocco, Barcelona, and Marseilles, then set a course for Sicily and Malta.

Alasdair got sick as we sailed down the west coast of Italy. Remembering what had happened to Gwendolyn, I was concerned. I wondered if we should put in somewhere, or even return home. But Alasdair wouldn't hear of it.

"I have never been seasick a day in my life," he said. "It's just a flu bug, or food poisoning from that fish market in Marseilles. I'll be fine in a day or two."

He was right. He recovered, though it took three days and I confess I was more than a little worried. I didn't like the pale look on his face. I was glad Captain Travis was at the helm with Alasdair free to rest. By the time we reached Crete, he was himself again.

The Greek Islands were fabulous. It was so warm, the water so clear and blue, the coastline and rocks so white—completely unlike Scotland. We swam off the *Gwendolyn* almost daily, and put in at dozens of little towns and villages, where we walked the streets and marketplaces and hiked in the hills and toured old ruins and churches and monasteries and obscure family wineries. I must have taken five thousand pictures! Everything was lovely, different, old, historic, picturesque. Europeans have no idea what it is like for an

American, whether from the US or Canada, to find oneself in the midst of such antiquity. If Britain's sites are old, some of the places we saw in Greece and Rome were *thousands* of years old. It was more than I could comprehend.

We rounded Buchan Ness and Rattray Head in early July, then passed Fraserburgh and headed again into the dolphin-filled Moray Firth for home. We had been gone almost two months—seven weeks, to be exact. You'd think such a long time at sea would be tiring. But the trip was so leisurely, and the yacht so roomy and cozy and with every comfort imaginable, that it was positively relaxing and restful. Not only did I see more historic sites than I ever dreamed I would see, I read a half-dozen books besides.

Home!

I can still hardly believe I was calling a village in northeast Scotland my home.

Both Alasdair and I were quiet most of the day, reflecting on the voyage and what lay ahead for us. As I stood on the bow of the *Gwendolyn*, drinking in the tangy warm salt air, a delicious occasional light spray reaching my face, Iain's words from my first visit to Port Scarnose returned to me:

"*I view God in the way that Jesus spoke of him,*" I could hear his voice saying like it was yesterday, "*as a good Father waiting with open arms to receive us back home.*"

"Thank you, Lord," I whispered quietly, "that you are indeed a God to call Father, and that you are helping me grow as your daughter."

I heard Alasdair's steps behind me. He came up and stood beside me.

"I can tell even from behind that you are lost in thought," he said.

"The ocean is like that," I said. "From the first day I came to Port Scarnose, the sea got inside me."

"And now?"

"I was thinking of something Iain once said, about the goodness of God's Fatherhood. That's what the sea always makes me think of now—the vastness of God's love waiting to fill all men."

"*Waiting...?*" repeated Alasdair with a questioning expression. "Waiting for what?"

"For them to be ready to receive it."

Chapter Four

Shock in the Pulpit

Once o'er the wide moor wending, or round the green hill bending,
Gay words and wild notes blending, spread far my good cheer,
For then my heart, light leaping, in waking, in sleeping,
Had no dubh ciar-dubh keeping, its joys far from here.
—"The Dark, Black-haired Youth"

It was hard to get used to the idea that I was a duchess. Alasdair had long since ceased to be a duke to me. He was just who he was, Alasdair Reidhaven.

But as much of it as had been thrown out with the march of modern times, the people of Britain still valued their traditional past. In that sense, I suppose Canada and the United States were more alike as a united "America" than Canada was with Britain, despite its long association with the British Commonwealth. The idea of "aristocracy" was still a foreign concept to me. In my mind, people were people. But there remained in Scotland a consciousness of kings, queen, dukes, earls, lairds, titles, and royalty. I would be listed in the book of peers. Even if this truly were my ancestral home, I still wasn't sure I would get used to it.

Wherever I went now, women smiled and nodded and sometimes curtsied, men paused and tipped their hats. Along with this, of course, was the natural politeness of the British. Perhaps the gracious treatment I received was simply because the villagers were being nice. But I had the feeling it also stemmed from the fact that I had married a duke...their duke.

I would never be anonymous again. I may have been an "incomer," but I was now *their* duchess, too.

After my spiritual "awakening," I could not help but be interested and attuned to Alasdair's spiritual outlook as well. We had talked about our perspectives, ways we had changed, ways we were still changing. But we had not explored it in great depth. I knew he was thinking about things in new ways. For now, that was enough. Alasdair had come awake, in a different way perhaps, but even more dramatically than I had. Iain once told me that God and ministers were in the business of waking people up. Thanks to him—and God!—Alasdair and I were not only together, we were *awake*...personally, relationally, emotionally...yes, and *spiritually*.

Yet I knew Alasdair might never relate to God in the same personal way I had learned to. After knowing Iain Barclay, however, I had learned to value the individual journey of growth and development and faith that is bound up in each man's and each woman's personal life story. I could not expect anyone else's journey to be like mine, nor for mine to be like theirs...not even Alasdair's.

As long as he was *awake*, God himself would lead him on that journey, without my interfering or trying to nudge it along.

The subject had come up in preparation for signing the marriage license.

"When they ask about religion on the license application," I said to Alasdair, "what will you say?"

"Church of Scotland, of course," he replied.

"I wasn't certain whether you would identify yourself with a specific affiliation."

"I was baptized as a child," said Alasdair. "That's as near as half the people inside church get to God in their lives, and I suppose as close as I ever got to him until I heard the angel harp."

I smiled. I was still amazed at the impact my harp had had, not only in Alasdair's life but in Gwendolyn's life and other people's lives, too.

"But I just could never take everything about the church as seriously as Iain does," Alasdair went on. "And you, too, for that matter," he added.

"But you ... you believe in God?"

"Of course. But I can't go along with all the theology and doctrine the church teaches. It's one of the reasons I have trouble with the church—the teaching is so complicated, I hardly know what to make of it. But do I *believe* in him, yes. What about you—how will you answer the question on the license form—Church of Scotland, or your church from Canada?"

"I wasn't part of a church in Canada before I came here."

"What church will you list, then?"

"None," I answered. "I will just say that I am a *Christian*."

We arrived back in Port Scarnose late on Thursday afternoon. Friday we rested at the castle and I began the process of "moving in." Most of my things that had been shipped across the Atlantic were still in boxes. Some of the crates from Canada had arrived during our honeymoon voyage on the *Gwendolyn*. I was still anxiously awaiting the arrival of my harps.

It would take me months to sort through everything. But I was in no hurry.

Most people would find themselves thinking, *Hmm, where will I find room to put everything?*

But not me.

I now lived in a castle!

Mostly I was dying to go out, to walk the streets and headlands and see people. Yet I knew everything was different now. I couldn't just *go* where I liked, or *do* what I wanted, without thinking of the consequences.

I wasn't sure I liked that. Actually, I *didn't* like it—knowing that for the rest of my life I would be a center of attention, that people would be looking at *me*. But that was one of the price tags associated with being Mrs. Alasdair Reidhaven ... the *Duchess* of Buchan.

I remained "home" at the castle all day on the Saturday after our arrival. I thought that the church service on the following morning would be the best time for us to make an "appearance" again after our return, and to greet the many people I was dying to see.

Alasdair agreed to accompany me, even though I wouldn't be playing my harp for the service.

"I can't promise to go *every* Sunday," he said with a smile. "But I'm not opposed to a little spiritual food now and then from Reddy. I have to admit, he has a way of putting things that cuts sufficiently across the grain as to appeal to the nonconformist in me."

"I don't think anyone would accuse either you *or* Iain of being conformist!" I laughed.

Alicia had piled dozens of cards and letters and gifts high on a table as they had poured in during our absence. She said that Olivia had been to the castle a couple of times, but, not surprisingly, there was nothing from her.

Sunday morning came. We made the two-mile drive around to the church parking lot, which sat only some two hundred yards from our front door. I couldn't wait till the gate was completed through the stone wall as Alasdair had planned. Then we would be able to walk through and be in the churchyard in two minutes.

We arrived about ten minutes before the start of the service and had a little time to visit and be seen by those making their way down the lane and clustered about the church door.

Everything was so changed. The first service I attended here, without my harp, I'd snuck in through the back, hoping to be seen by no one. I had also crept out before the end so I wouldn't be seen by Iain.

Now as we walked through the door, I was seen by *everyone!*

Greetings and smiles and nods and a tumult of whispering spread from one wall of the church to the other as we made our way inside.

I would much have preferred to sit in the pews along with everyone else, but Alasdair convinced me that it was best for us to sit together up in the "duke's box." People expected it, he said.

We climbed the creaky stairs as the organ played its final Introductory, and sat down to await Iain's appearance. By the time the service started, the hubbub from our presence was settling down.

This time, unlike the previous occasion when Alasdair had unexpectedly appeared, I knew that Iain would look up at us from the pulpit and smile. If I knew him, he would also probably mention our presence and greet us formally on behalf of the church.

So long an enigma, Alasdair was now part of the community.

I heard the door of Iain's office open. The beadle appeared carrying the Bible, but as she mounted the steps, she was not followed by Iain.

Another minister walked up into the pulpit in his place!

His greetings and few words and introduction of the opening hymn passed like a blur. Alasdair and I glanced at each other with questioning expressions.

Was Iain sick, or on holiday? Neither of us knew. No one had mentioned that he would not be present.

At last came the minister's announcements.

"Good morning again, my friends," the minister began. "It continues to be a great pleasure and privilege to become gradually more intimately acquainted with your community and its lovely villages and people. I see the duke and the duchess have returned and are with us this morning—welcome back to you both!"

He glanced toward us with a smile, which we returned as heads throughout the church turned up in our direction. But we were bewildered.

"I look forward to meeting you both personally and getting to know you," the minister went on, "and hopefully of finding ways I can be of service to you in any way possible."

We smiled back and nodded appreciatively. But speaking for myself, I wasn't paying much attention to his words.

"And to the rest of you," the minister went on, turning back toward the congregation and glancing in the direction of each of the four alcoves of pews, "I repeat that same desire. I look forward to meeting each one of you personally, though it may take some time. As new minister of the Deskmill Parish, it is my commitment to each one of you to—"

I heard nothing more. My head was spinning.

The new minister!

Where was Iain Barclay?

Chapter Five

Departure of a Friend

I may not hide it—my heart's devotion
Is not a season's brief emotion;
Thy love in childhood began to seize me,
And ne'er shall fade until death release me.
—Dr. MacLachlan, "O My Boatman"

I can't give an accurate report of what the sermon was like that first Sunday after Alasdair and I returned from our honeymoon. I sat in a stupor, hearing scarcely a word of what the minister, a forty-seven-year-old newly arrived from Edinburgh, Rev. Charles Gillihan, had to contribute to the spiritual well-being of the flock of Deskmill Parish. It might have been a great sermon; it might have been a better sermon than Iain ever preached. But I was too distracted to have any idea what he was talking about.

Whatever there might once have been between us, and in spite of the fact that I was now Alasdair's wife, Iain Barclay was one of my closest friends. *And* Alasdair's.

It would have been unseemly to begin a barrage of questions the instant the service was over. We smiled as we shook Reverend Gillihan's hand and introduced ourselves. Alasdair complimented him on his "fine sermon." Then we made our way outside where clusters of people waited to greet us as if we were royalty. Mrs. Gauld and so many other acquaintances from the village hugged me and cried and shook Alasdair's hand. It was a wonderful reunion. I was pleased all over again at how the community so thoroughly took us into their hearts.

28

It must have been well after noon before the enthusiastic Sunday crowd had dissipated and the two of us walked back to the BMW. We got in, closed the doors, glanced over at each other with stunned expressions, then both said at once: "What happened to Ian?!"

Shaking his head in bewilderment, Alasdair reached for the key to start the car. Then, glancing out the side window, he hesitated.

"Just a minute," he said. "I'll have a word with Leslie."

He got back out of the car and walked toward Leslie Mair, an elder in the church who was usually one of the last to leave and was now walking toward his own car. I didn't know him well, though we had met. All I knew was that he, too, had grown up knowing Iain and Alasdair and was now one of the leaders in the church and community. The two men shook hands again, and I lowered my window to listen.

"Leslie, my friend," said Alasdair, "if anyone can tell us, it is you . . . Where is Reddy—on holiday or a sabbatical or what?"

Mr. Mair stared back at Alasdair, seemingly puzzled by his question.

"What div ye mean, Duke?" he said after a moment.

"Please, Leslie—just *Alasdair*, if you don't mind. We've been through enough together, even though it's been a few years, to dispense with the *Duke*. And what I mean is, where is Iain Barclay? When will he be back?"

"Back?"

"Yes, man!" Alasdair laughed. "How many ways must I ask it? Where is Iain? How long will he be gone . . . and when will he be back in his pulpit?"

"The lad's nae comin' back, Alasdair," replied Mair. "I thocht ye kennt."

"Knew what?"

"Reddy handed in his resignation till us the day ye sailed—"

As I listened, I felt myself going faint a moment.

"—We a' thocht ye an' the lass kennt as weel."

Alasdair stood motionless staring into Leslie Mair's face. I sat in the car staring at the two of them in greater shock than during the service.

"His . . . *resignation*?" repeated Alasdair after several seconds.

"Aye," Mair said, nodding. "Like I said, I thocht ye kennt. The way Reddy spoke till us—"

"*Us*," interrupted Alasdair. "Who, exactly?"

"The elders o' the kirk."

"When was this?"

"He notified us o' a special meetin', the day afore yer weddin' it was, told us a' tae be at the kirk in twa days at six that evenin'. Wadna tak lang, he said. An' it didna—ten minutes, 'twas a'. He told us he had reached a lang an' prayerful decision, an' that was tae resign from Deskmill Parish, effective in a fortnight, after ane mair service. He had prepared a formal letter, he said, which he then handed till ilka ane o' us. He said it had already gane tae the session an' 'twas sealed an' dune."

By this time Alasdair was shaking his head, incredulous.

"Did he say why?" he asked.

"Nae that I cud make muckle o'," replied Mr. Mair, "only that he had been considerin' a change for a lang time an' 'twas for the good o' the parish an' its folks—"

When I heard those words I began to cry. In my heart, I *knew* why Iain had left. He had done it for us—for Alasdair and me.

"An' that arrangements for a supply minister had already been made," Mair went on, "a Reverend Gillihan fae Edinburgh—him ye heard this mornin'—wha was available for his replacement gien we liked him. He asked us tae say naethin' till he could tell folks him-sel', which he did the naist Sunday, which, as he said, was his last. That was a' there was tae it, Alasdair. Some folk cried an' a few secretly praised the Lord that they were rid o' the troublemaker wi' his radical notions. But whate'er folks thought, the naist Sunday came the Reverend Gillihan. Nane saw Reddy again, nor ken whan he gaed awa'. He left wi'oot a word. An' after twa weeks, the el-ders o' the kirk met again, an' there bein' no serious objections tae the new minister, for folks seemed pleased enough wi' his friendly manner an' his sermons an' the like...we voted t'accept him as permanent."

Alasdair still shook his head in disbelief.

"And where is he now?" asked Alasdair. "Has he accepted another church?"

"Reddy ye're meanin'?"

"Aye."

"Nae a soul kens," replied Mair. "He didna tell onybody his plans."

Finally Alasdair drew in a deep sigh. He and Mr. Mair exchanged a few more words I couldn't hear, then shook hands again before Alasdair walked slowly back to the car.

I drew in a quick couple of steadying breaths and hurriedly wiped my eyes. Though obviously we were both stunned, I couldn't let Alasdair see how deeply the news had hit me. I was surprised at my reaction myself.

Alasdair walked around to the driver's side. I kept looking out my open window as he climbed in, hoping I could avert his eyes for a moment or two.

"That's a shock," I said, trying to sound lighthearted.

"That is putting it mildly," rejoined Alasdair, starting the car. "I can't believe it...that he would leave without speaking to us."

We were both silent a few seconds.

"I'm sure he was thinking of us," I said after a moment as we pulled away from the parking lot.

"Maybe," sighed Alasdair. "Still, it seems to me a strange way to do it."

The next silence was longer. We were nearing the outlying houses of town when Alasdair spoke again.

"I will miss Reddy," he said. His voice was low, thoughtful, sad. "He was my best friend, and—"

He glanced away and again sighed deeply.

"I was looking forward to trying to be a friend to him again," he added in a voice that was softer yet and a little shaky. "After waiting so long, to have it so suddenly gone...I just wasn't ready for this, Marie. It is a blow."

I was glad for the open window and the gentle breeze against my hot eyes and cheeks as we drove. We were both pensive.

A huge chapter in our lives had suddenly been closed. The chapters titled "Iain Barclay" told very different parts of each of our life stories. Suddenly both had ended on the same day.

Instead of going back to the castle, Alasdair turned east on the A98 and we drove along the coast. It was a lovely day. The sea was a spectacular shade of blue. Neither of us spoke for a long while. Eventually we wound up in Banff, where we walked through the town, then had lunch at a small tearoom before returning to Port Scarnose about three.

Chapter Six

The Duchess and the Laird

Oh summer days and heather bells
Come blooming owre yon high, high hills.
There's yellow corn in a' the fields,
And autumn brings the shearin'.
—"The Band o' Shearers"

Having Iain gone simplified things, I suppose.

There had been no awkwardness leading up to the wedding. I am certain there wouldn't have been any had he still been in Port Scarnose. But in some ways it probably made it easier for us to begin anew as husband and wife, as duke and duchess.

Alasdair missed Iain more than I would have expected. Of course we spoke of Iain, wondering when we would hear from him, hoping he would come for a visit. There were times Alasdair actually pined for his friend. To have regained the treasured friendship after so many years, then to lose it—it was hard for him. At the same time, however, as crestfallen as he was at first—for a couple of days I saw hints of his former moody nature that I had not seen once since our engagement—I think Alasdair may have been liberated in some ways by Iain's departure as well. Without Iain's shadow hanging over his past, he was able to be his own man, as the saying goes.

When I had come to Scotland a year before, the rift between Alasdair Reidhaven and Iain Barclay—childhood friends, rivals in love as young men, and in the eyes of the community adversaries who had not spoken to each other ever since—was known by everyone for miles around. It had long since ceased to be a matter of

33

daily gossip, and though it was not put in such stark terms, most people more or less took one side or the other in the unspoken debate about who had caused what, who loved whom, and what were the real reasons behind the ill-fated first duchess Fiona Reidhaven's death. Doubts, therefore, had circulated for years about Iain as well as about Alasdair. Yet Iain's role as parish curate had slowly succeeded in raising him in the esteem of the community, while Alasdair's Howard Hughes imitation at the castle had diminished his. Because of his sister Olivia's subtle methods of swaying opinion, few recognized the true cause of Alasdair's self-imposed exile.

But most people are influenced more by example and practice than by persuasion. Olivia had been so successful in poisoning the general outlook of the community against Alasdair only in the absence of the counterbalancing influence of his own example. The moment Alasdair became visible again, first with me, then with Gwendolyn, then beginning to stand up against Olivia and in his reconciliation with Iain, and finally in his more active and benevolent relations with the community as a whole, nearly everyone was eager to give him the benefit of the doubt. While many people thrive on believing the worst about their fellows, and enjoy nothing more than spreading low gossip, I think there are an equal number who are eager to find the good and believe in it.

As we began being more a part of the community, he became all the more beloved by the people. He went to church occasionally, maybe once every month or two. I didn't mind going by myself, and he felt no stigma about not being regular. I think Reverend Gillihan wondered why I came alone. But for all the townspeople to see Alasdair even once a month was a blessing. He was so liberated, in fact, and so free in his newfound self-confidence, that to any potential criticism—such as his not going to church more often—he always replied with a laugh and, "Let them eat cake!"

When I went to church alone, I continued to sit up in the duke's box, or the *laird's loft*, instead of down in the regular pews. Actually, when Alasdair didn't accompany me I asked Alicia and our cook,

Jean Campbell, if they would like to go with me, which they often did. But then we split up when we entered the church, them to the pews, me up to the loft. I didn't like it at first, afraid it would appear that I felt entitled to a more exalted position. But since Alasdair and I sat there when he joined me, I thought it might reflect badly on him if I behaved differently when I was alone. I tried my best to accustom myself to it.

We had not once seen Alasdair's sister, Olivia, since our return, nor had she been in church. Everyone knew there was bad blood between them, so we didn't want to be too forward in making inquiries. Eventually we learned that she and her husband, Max, had bought a house in Aberdeen, ostensibly to make his work on the offshore oil rigs more convenient. It was a relief to know she wouldn't be in Port Scarnose spreading her subtle poison about Alasdair and me.

Alasdair had already begun some changes and renovations before the wedding; we now continued and expanded them. Together we set about personally visiting every tenant whose rent was directly payable to the estate to determine whether the rent was fair, and to learn whether there were hardships or grievances we should know about.

In many cases, rents were lowered. In some cases back payments were made to tenants to correct what Alasdair now considered excessive rent from past years. Alasdair also made available the purchase of property from the estate to those who might desire it, and set up favorable terms allowing them to do so.

Whatever grievances anyone might have had against him, or the estate, for any reason, Alasdair sought to learn the facts so as to remedy the matter justly. Though he still professed little overt religious belief, he reminded me of Zacchaeus, trying to make amends and restoration for his oversights and even sins of the past.

For all he was doing, whatever they might have once thought, the people revered him.

We also set about making improvements to the three villages that had once been in the feu of the former dukes of Buchan—Findectifeld, Port Scarnose, and Crannoch—refurbishing walking paths, dredging out and upgrading the three harbors, improving and making necessary repairs to churches and public buildings. Alasdair made money available to borrow at low interest to any who desired to make improvements to their own homes. Lanes and parks were spruced up, buildings cleaned, flowers and trees planted in public places.

We found more places to open the estate lands with gates and styles so that the villagers would be free to come and go in keeping with the right to roam and the public footpath system of Britain. The gate between the castle and the church was undertaken almost immediately. It was a "hands-on" project carried out by the men of the church and village, supervised by Alasdair and Leslie Mair, along with James Findlay and Alec Bruce, with Alicia Forbes and me supplying tea, ale, sandwiches, and scones throughout. Though Alasdair's valet, Norvill Campbell, Jean's husband, was a bit standoffish, Farquharson and Nicholls rolled up their sleeves with their boss and the men of the community and appeared to have a great time. Everyone had so much fun working together, and especially alongside the duke himself, whose hands were crusted with mortar and bruised by the occasional errant stone along with everyone else's, that Alasdair determined to find more such projects to bring the people of the community together.

We undertook an investigation of ancient public footpaths and had a map distributed so that everyone would know the routes of these former public byways. We encouraged all to make use of them again. Alasdair now viewed the estate property as a public trust, which, though legally it belonged to him, in a larger sense belonged to the entire community.

We also began a tradition of opening the castle for visitors on Sunday afternoons.

At first no one knew what to make of it. We posted a notice on the gate at the entrance to the grounds, and even asked Reverend

Gillihan to announce the Sunday opening of the castle in church. But apparently everyone merely assumed this meant they could walk on the *grounds*, which we had already been encouraging for some time. Some people came and wandered about, but no one ventured near the door.

On the following Sunday, therefore, I asked Reverend Gillihan if I could make the announcement myself from the laird's loft.

"Last week," I began when the time came, "it was announced that the castle would be open on Sunday afternoons. My husband and I were apparently not completely clear about our intent. You are invited to our home...*inside*...into the castle, for tea and a light buffet. The duke and I will be there, and we would like to visit with you personally. Please come. It will mean a great deal to Alasdair and...I mean, to the duke and me. Our doors will be open, we will both be on hand, and tea will be hot...anytime between three and six this afternoon. We look forward to seeing you."

I smiled and sat down as a general murmur of approval went round. And thus began a tradition every Sunday afternoon of what we would call an "open house" in Canada, which we held in either the Drawing Room, the library, or the Great Room. When the weather was particularly nice, we set tables and chairs about outside in the gardens.

Big crowds didn't come. Sometimes there were twenty or thirty, on other days only five or ten. But the mix of individuals was always different. It not only gave us the chance to visit with them, but acquaintances were made and renewed among the people of the neighborhood as well. It may be that this was the most important benefit of our Sunday gatherings.

After so long in isolation, Alasdair wanted personally to know everyone in the community, and he wanted each and every one to have free and unfettered access to him. As he gradually made this desire known and as people realized he was sincere, they began taking him at his word. The Sunday gatherings at the castle, therefore, were not the only change. Both Alasdair and I often walked through the village, together and alone. Gradually people became less shy about approaching us and talking to us.

That this desire of Alasdair's had been successfully conveyed was evidenced when we heard the door knocker echoing in our window from outside late one winter evening long after dark when we had been married about a year and a half. Neither Alicia nor Jean nor her husband—ostensibly our part-time "butler" and Alasdair's valet, but either too deaf or unwilling to be much good for that purpose at night—heard it. The knocking continued, and eventually Alasdair rose himself to investigate.

At the door stood a poor pig farmer from up over the other side of the Hill of Maud.

"Beggin' yer pardon, Duke," he said, "but after what ye said the ither week aboot us comin' till ye . . . I didna ken whaur else tae gae for help—"

"It is quite all right, Mr . . . . uh, Dingwall, isn't it?"

"Yes, sir."

"Go on, then—what can I do for you?"

"My wife's at her time, ye see, sir, but I canna find the new doctor an' old Dr. Mair, he's awa' the noo. The midwife's there, but . . . pardon the request, sir, but noo wi' Mrs. Urquhart gane, which dinna matter on account o' my wife canna bide the woman, meanin' nae disrespeck tae yer sister, sir. But as it was she wha helped wi' sich things, an' sae my Lettie wanted me see gien the duchess wud come till her. It would be a great comfort tae her, sir."

When word spread of Mr. Dingwall's visit to the castle, and my going to help his wife give birth, as it turned out, to twin sons, more and more people came to us for a variety of things.

I cannot say their requests were always convenient or pleasant to comply with. Having never been a mother, I did not fancy myself a midwife by any stretch of the imagination. But now many of the young women took it into their heads that their birthings, not to mention the lives of their children, would be blessed if I were present, a sentiment shared by their husbands in the respect of Alasdair and the offspring of their horses and cows.

Never had Alasdair and I been so busy attending births of man and beast!

Though fishing had once been the lifeblood of coastal Scotland, the region now tended to move more to the rhythms of the plantings and harvests of the farming life. The harvest was always an exciting time in the life of any agricultural community.

As the harvests of wheat and barley and oats got under way every August, followed by potatoes in September, Alasdair drove all about the area, standing at the side of one field or another and watching in fascination as great combines turned the stalks of huge fields of grain into chewed-up piles of straw in a single afternoon.

I was with him one day as one of the great machines lumbered toward us, then stopped to make the turn and begin the next row.

Alasdair waved to the man seated high on top, his face brown with dust. He turned off the engine and jumped down and walked over to greet us.

"How goes the harvest, Leith?" asked Alasdair.

"Weel enouch, Duke," replied the man. "Gien the sun hauds, we'll hae her all in afore the morn's morn."

"Do you have room for a passenger up there?" said Alasdair, pointing toward the combine. "I would dearly love to see how it works."

"There's aye room, but 'tis dirty wark for the likes o' yersel'."

"The likes of who—me?!" Alasdair laughed. "I can take the dust of the field as well as the next man!" he said, climbing up and leaping over the fence. "Come, Leith . . . give me a lesson in combine harvesting!"

Two minutes later, with Alasdair at his side, farmer Leith guided his combine into position to begin the next pass through the stalks of grain, then engaged the great paddle-wheel rollers and blades and away they went. What a sight—the rhythmic clatter and whirr of so many complex parts of the apparatus, the enormous paddles flattening and chewing grain beneath them like thousands of tiny impotent vanquished foes, dust spewing from beneath in all directions, straw pouring out behind in what appeared almost a liquid flow, speckles of silt and chaff floating up behind like a trailing cloud of tiny harvest angels.

The machine was alive!

When they slowly turned back toward me from the opposite side of the field some fifteen minutes later, they were moving jerkily and somewhat unevenly it appeared, even to my untrained eye. As they came closer I saw the reason why.

There was Alasdair at the controls!

Mr. Leith was giving him instructions as they went. Even from where I stood, I could see an expression of animation and pleasure on Alasdair's face that took my breath away.

It was wonderful to see him so happy, and tears filled my eyes.

They stopped at the end of the row. Alasdair jumped down and ran over to me. He was dirty...and radiant!

"If you want to go, Marie," he said, "go ahead and take the car. I am going to stay and help. Leith says that if I drive the John Deere over there with the wagons—"

He pointed across the field to a green tractor standing idle in front of two empty trailers.

"With a wagon moving beside him, he could make faster progress. His man isn't with him today—sick or something...Actually, I didn't quite understand it all! When Leith gets talking fast enough in his Doric, I can only follow about a fourth of it. And I grew up only four miles from where he did! In any event, he is shorthanded. Leith will bring me home later."

I did not see Alasdair for hours. When he finally appeared at the castle sometime after nine o'clock that evening, exhausted but radiant, his face was nearly black with remnants of the dust of Mr. Leith's field of barley.

The next day, midway through the morning, the telephone at the castle rang. Alicia came to the breakfast room where Alasdair and I sat with our tea.

"There is a Mr. Leith on the phone, Mr. Reidhaven," she said. "I could scarcely understand him, but he asked to speak to you."

Alasdair rose to answer it. He returned a few minutes later.

"Leith's man is still away," he said. "He fears rain tonight and cannot get the rest of his barley in alone. He asked if I might help him. He even offered to pay me!" he added, laughing.

"What are you going to do?" I asked.

"Go upstairs and change my clothes!" he replied. "I haven't had so much fun in years. Don't wait up for me. I know these farmers—if they have to, they'll work straight into the night! The harvest must get in."

The rain did come, but not before Mr. Leith's harvest of barley was safely stored in his barn.

Word of the new "hired hand" at the Leith farm, who refused pay for his work, quickly spread. By the time that season's harvests were all in and the fields plowed and planted with winter grasses, Alasdair had lent his assistance at another half-dozen farms between Fordyce, Berryhillock, and Drybridge.

Those were such happy times.

I could not imagine the people of a community loving their "laird" more than ours, and they truly took Alasdair into their hearts.

Chapter Seven

Six Harps for Castle Buchan

How sweet when dawn is around me gleaming beneath
the rock to recline, and hear
The joyous moor-hen so hoarsely screaming, and gallant
moor-cock soft croodling near!
The wren is bustling and briskly whistling, with mellow
music and ceaseless strain,
The thrush is singing, the redbreast ringing its cheery notes
in the glad refrain.
—Duncan Ban MacIntyre, "The Misty Dell"

When the crate with my things from Canada arrived, I was more concerned about my harps than anything. But they were well packed and arrived safely.

Now here they all were, with me in Scotland. I couldn't wait to play the *Queen* for Alasdair in the Music Room where he had first heard me play my traveling harp, *Journey*. Once she was set up, she looked so regal in her new surroundings. Now she was a queen indeed, with a whole castle for her domain.

I was itching to hear them being used again. I had no interest in having a mere collection of harps. I wanted to hear them being played and practiced on and making music.

Gwendolyn, of course, had been a unique case. But there were surely others in the community with talent and aptitude. What was I going to do with myself as a duchess—sit around all day, go for walks, poke about in the garden, make flower arrangements?

That sounded pretty boring!

I had a hard time getting used to having a cook and a housekeeper and maids and a butler and a chauffeur. It seemed that I ought to cook Alasdair's supper and make the beds and do the housework. That's what wives did. But neither did I want to upset the routine of life at the castle, and the order of things Alasdair was comfortable with and had been accustomed to for so long. I was the newcomer, after all. If there were adjustments to be made, it was up to *me* to make them, not try to change everyone else. But I have to admit that I spent a great deal of time with Jean in the kitchen and helping Alicia with the daily chores of the castle. I needed to have things to *do*.

Alasdair had his business affairs to attend to, and I couldn't be underfoot eight hours a day. I loved to read, and I could pass hours playing and practicing my harps. For a musician, the refining and expanding of one's available repertoire of music is a never-ending and delightful process.

But was it enough? I had to have more than my *own* interests to occupy my time and fill my days. And after all was said and done... I was a *teacher*. I loved to teach others to play the harp as much as I loved to play myself. Actually, I think I was better at teaching. I was an okay harpist. I could hold my own in a symphony or playing for a wedding. But as a teacher I was often able to get a higher level out of my students than I could hope to attain myself. Three of my students had far surpassed my own level of ability and had gone on to study the harp at university. Though I enjoyed making music, and could sit for hours at a time with the *Queen* or *Journey* resting on my shoulder, the achievements of my students gave me even more pride and satisfaction.

Resuming teaching, however, was more complicated now than merely hanging out my shingle and passing out business cards that read "Harp Lessons Given," or "Harp Music for Hire." I was married to the Duke of Buchan, for heaven's sake! I lived in a castle. To advertise myself—for either weddings or events, especially as an incomer to the region—would have been unseemly and presumptuous.

I spoke with Alasdair about it.

"What would you think about my giving harp lessons again?" I asked.

"I think it would be brilliant," he replied.

"How should I go about it? You must admit, the situation is much different than in Canada. I can't just anonymously set up a studio."

"Anonymity is something you will never know again, my dear!" Alasdair laughed.

"That's just it. Every move I make is scrutinized, and reflects on you besides. How do I go about it without seeming...I don't know, forward and presumptuous?"

"Everyone loves you!"

"Nevertheless, you do see the problem? I want to be accessible, but even more than that, I want to make harp music more known and available...What better way than beginning to give lessons again? Just think how wonderful it would be for children from around the community to come to the castle once a week for a harp lesson! That is, if you agree. It is your castle, not mine!"

Alasdair smiled. "Of course, my dear. Anything to make you happy. After so long living in virtual isolation, I welcome the commotion. I have to admit, the sights and sounds of children in the castle would probably remind me of Gwendolyn and make me sad. But it would be a good sadness. I think it would be wonderful for you to give lessons here. Why don't you just play during our Sunday open-house times and see what kind of interest it generates. Oh— I've an idea! You could play at the Deskmill Flower Show that's coming up—in a couple of weeks, I think it is?"

"I can't just show up and start playing!"

"Sure you can—why not?"

"It would be, you know...awkward. I'm not in charge of the thing. I know people have accepted me, but I am still a relative outsider. I can't just barge in. It would be like gate-crashing someone else's party."

"These things are community events. Anyone and everyone is welcome. But tell you what, I will talk to Judith Johnston. I think she's one of the organizers. Once she takes the thing in hand, it will be done."

True to his word, Alasdair spoke with his friend, and two evenings later she was on the telephone asking to speak with me.

"I would not want to presume on your kindness, Mrs. Reidhaven," said Mrs. Johnston, "but the duke told me you might be willing to bring your *clarsach* and play for our flower show. I had thought of you, but I didn't know if you would want to play for such an occasion. And I'm afraid we would not be able to pay you more than a few quid—"

"Mrs. Johnston," I said, "I would be delighted to play, and any thought of payment is out of the question. I wouldn't take so much as one quid. How much is a quid again?"

"A pound," she replied with a light laugh.

"In any case, if you would like me to, I would love to play. You must just tell me what time you want me there."

"That is very kind of you. I know everyone will look forward to it."

The people of Scotland are great for shows and festivals and all manner of community expositions. Just in our little corner of Moray, there were several craft fairs and numerous flower shows, for which the whole community turned out. The Portsoy Boat Festival drew visitors from everywhere throughout the north of Scotland.

As word spread that the duke's new Canadian wife was willing and able to play her harp for local events, invitations began to pour in through the summer months—more than I could accept. Before long I was being invited to play for every wedding between Elgin and Fraserburgh!

What had I opened myself up to?!

I did play for the Portsoy Boat Festival, though the bagpipe band from Shetland mostly drowned me out. I'm not sure the harp can compete with bagpipes, accordions, and drums, even under the best of conditions! But at a crowded harbor with several thousand people coming and going, with fifty booths selling their wares...those best of conditions did *not* prevail. But it was fun. Most people, I think, had no clue who I was. As they came closer and watched, their fascination with the harp and its music was always wonderful to see. Some children just stood and stared, and two or three times I overheard mothers whisper, "That's the duchess, dear."

A few sheepishly came up and spoke to me. If a child seemed particularly intrigued, I asked if they would like to try the harp, and some did, to the delight of the onlookers. I often say that it is impossible to make a harp sound bad. Even a child randomly plucking the strings creates tones that hint at the magic. And the greatest magic of all takes place within *them*.

Meanwhile, another telephone call came to the castle from an unexpected quarter, which had the result of starting my teaching again, though much differently than I had anticipated.

The call did not come directly to me, but to our housekeeper, Alicia Forbes. She found me and explained that she had been talking with Adela Cruickshank. Adela asked her, she said, to ask me if I would be willing to let her begin with the harp again.

"She was afraid, you now being the duchess," said Alicia, "that you would be too busy...or not want to because of how, she said, she had not been altogether gracious to you before, when Olivia began spreading tales about you and the duke."

"Did Olivia spread tales about me?" I asked. "I thought her only gossip was about Alasdair and what had happened years ago and not being a good father to Gwendolyn."

"That was always at root of it," Alicia said, nodding. "But yes, in stirring up the old suspicions about the duke, she made certain you were cast in none too positive a light."

Her words brought back all the trouble we'd had with Alasdair's sister over Gwendolyn.

"I never believed that part of Olivia's tales," said Alicia, "because I've been with the duke all these years. But a few did, especially among some of us who were friends years ago. But if I believed

what Olivia said, I would be crazy to live under the same roof with
the duke and serve his meals and make his bed. But he was always
kind to me, and I knew Olivia was just secretly angry that she wasn't
in the castle and duchess herself instead of him the duke."

"Was she really jealous of his title?"

"Not just the title, but everything—his power and influence, his
wealth. She hated him for it."

"How do you know all that? I had no idea you and Olivia were
close."

"We aren't . . . not anymore," replied Alicia, hesitating a little as an
uncertain expression crossed her features. "I used to know her well.
I think she thought that I was betraying her by working for Alasdair.
Those of us who were . . . Well, there were some of us to whom she
confided things. We were all young and knew no better. But some
of what she said was frightening."

"Like what?"

"It is no longer important," replied Alicia, shaking her head. She
obviously didn't want to "go there," as the saying is.

But I wanted to know more of what Alasdair had to deal with in
his family life. For good or ill, Olivia was his only living family, and
I doubted we had seen the last of her.

"But what if it is important?" I said. "If she actually made . . .
threats, I want to know. *What* was frightening?"

"I'm not talking about when you came, Marie . . . not recently, you
know, but when we were all girls. That's when I mean. She *wanted*
the castle; she *wanted* to be the duchess. It sometimes seemed she
was so determined that she would do anything to get them, even—"

Alicia glanced away, realizing she had said more than she intended.

"Go on, Alicia," I said. My voice held a firmer tone than I had
ever used with her. It wasn't my way to pull rank, but suddenly this
sounded serious.

It remained quiet for a moment. The air was tense.

"What did you mean, *anything*?" I asked.

"I don't know," said Alicia, speaking slowly, "*say* things, spread rumors...I have to admit the thought even crossed my mind that she might do something...something bad...try to hurt him. You know, the terrible kinds of things that go through your mind when you're young. I had visions of her trying to poison him or some such dreadful thing. She always said that he didn't deserve to live, that the world would be better without him, that we would all be better off if he was dead...'dead on his bed,' she said."

I glanced at Alicia, wondering if the sinister-sounding rhyme had been intentional. But she seemed oblivious to what had popped out of her mouth and continued.

"She said he didn't deserve to be duke. 'My brother as duke, it makes me puke,' she once said. Not very nice. But Olivia *wasn't* always nice. She said that no man deserved such a position."

"No *man*? Who else would deserve it?"

Alicia laughed a little nervously. "A woman, of course," she answered. "Olivia thought all men were fools."

"What about her own husband?"

Again Alicia laughed, a little scornfully I thought.

"Poor Max," she said almost wistfully. "He had no idea what he was getting into." She sighed. "Maybe I was wrong about him," she said with a sad smile. "Maybe he *was* a fool. I didn't think so. But anyone who would marry Olivia...Of course, she made all the rest of us believe her, too. She could make anyone believe whatever she wanted, so why should Max have been any different. He was once so strong and—"

Again the sad, wistful smile.

"And full of life and energy and fun...Now he is a shadow of the man he once was. I hate to say it, but he is weak. I don't know what he is like when he is on the oil rigs—maybe he is a man's man, for all I know. Maybe he lives a double life—the man and the mouse. But around Port Scarnose, he walks with stooped shoulders, like an old scarecrow who is afraid of his own shadow. It pains me every time I see him...which isn't often. I think he is afraid to show his face knowing what everyone thinks, that Olivia has completely dominated him into submission."

"Does he love her?"

"Who knows? I certainly have no idea."

"Does she love him?"

"*Love... Olivia...* I can't put the two words together in the same sentence. I can't even think how to answer you. Whether she is truly capable of love, I don't know. Doesn't love mean somehow putting others ahead of yourself? I can't imagine Olivia has ever done that in her life. I suppose that's a terrible thing to say—maybe I'm wrong. 'Keep man in check, hang threats from his neck... break him down, be his crown... he must be led, you are his head.'"

Again I did a double take at the strange use of words. But yet again Alicia hardly seemed aware of it.

"But what about Alasdair," I said. "She didn't actually threaten him?"

"I don't know. We were young. All I know is that she could make the rest of us tremble with the kinds of things she said. Alasdair—the duke, I mean, he never took her seriously. It enraged her when he laughed at her pranks and sayings. That's why through the years I've wondered..." Her voice trailed off.

"Wondered what?"

"Nothing, never mind... It's ridiculous. I'm sorry for bringing it up, Mrs. Reidhaven."

"Alicia, what?"

"Nothing. I was just going to say that I've wondered if his ailment, his condition... I don't really know anything about it, but if it might have been caused... But," she added, shaking her head, "it's something genetic, they say, isn't it? She couldn't have had anything to do with it."

"What did Olivia say about me, then, Alicia?"

"I would rather not go into it, Mrs. Reidhaven, if you don't mind," answered Alicia a little timidly. "That's all over now, with Olivia gone and you and the duke married. What came before doesn't matter anymore. 'Look behind, lose your mind.'"

Alicia was talking in such peculiar phrases!

"Then tell me about Adela," I said, steering the conversation away from this weird turn it had taken. "So she wants to take up the harp again?"

"Yes."

"Well, tell her I would be delighted," I said. "You arrange a time when she can come—tomorrow if she would like. Tell her I shall look forward to seeing her."

Chapter Eight

Ladies with Secrets

Still flourishin' the auld pear tree,
The bairnies liked to see;
And oh! how aften did they spier
When ripe they a' wad be.
The voices sweet, the wee bit feet,
Aye rinnin' here and there;
The merry shout—oh! whiles we greet
To think we'll hear nae mair!
—Lady Nairne, "The Auld Hoose"

Adela Cruickshank came to the castle the following day to resume her harp lessons. She was reserved, timid, a little awed to be in the castle for something as mundane as a music lesson. More than once as we made our way up to my studio and as she looked about, she made comments like, "'Tis jist as I remember it...Aye, there's the Drawing Room...Aye, an' the portrait o' the auld duke an' his green lady...Oh, aye—an' the tapestry o' the stag."

She was obviously well familiar with the place.

"You must have spent a great deal of time here in the past," I said.

"As a girl, my lady," Adela answered. "I was a frien' wi' Olivia, ye see."

"Oh...so you and Alicia must have been close, too."

"Aye...middlin'—but no' for some years noo. Not after she came tae the castle tae work. Olivia didna like her workin' for her brither the duke, ye ken."

"Well, maybe that will change with your coming regularly."

51

I needed only a small place to teach. The castle had dozens of rooms that would have sufficed perfectly. But Alasdair wanted to show off my harps and wanted them in the Music Room. So we set up the small end of it as my harp studio, where the dividers could be in place if I wanted the feel of a smaller room, or could be folded back to make the whole huge expanse into a magnificent concert hall.

And so began Adela Cruickshank's lessons. She was thrilled when I offered to let her borrow one of the harps so she could practice at home. I told her that Nicholls and I would be happy to bring either the *Aida* or the *Shamrock* to her house that afternoon, but the idea was too intimidating. However, she would be delighted, she said, to use either of the two lap harps. After an hour I sent her on her way with the *Limerick*, telling her she could come by the castle any time she liked to practice on something larger.

Obviously I didn't charge her for the lesson or the use of the little harp. In my former life, my teaching had provided a good portion of my income. Now I was married to one of Scotland's wealthiest men, if the stories were true. Good heavens, what was I going to do...charge twenty pounds (or *quid*) for an hour of my time?! I knew Alasdair's money wasn't technically mine. I had made sure of that fact with the prenup I'd insisted on, to prevent any unpleasant stories circulating about either of us. But Alasdair was so unbelievably generous with everything. In the same way I had insisted on a prenup, he now insisted on my having an account in Clydesdale Bank with £100,000 in it. It was twenty times—or more!—what I could possibly need, but he insisted and had followed through over my objections. Therefore, it was clear that henceforth my teaching would be more a hobby than an income, and that was just how I wanted it.

The next Sunday afternoon's open house on the castle grounds occurred on a lovely warm day, and I decided to take the *Queen* outside to play for a while as people came and went. Alicia was busy acting the part of hostess in my stead, with Alasdair entertaining the men and enjoying Stella with several local farmers. As word got around that Stella was nearly always on hand—chilled and with no limit, the bottles protruding from two great ice-filled half-casks from former distillery use sitting on the lawn beckoning thirsty palates—more and more of the local men turned up to visit with the duke. Alasdair loved it. The discussions were always animated, the topics of discussion ranging from cattle, pigs, and football to the price of barley, the weather, the good old days when fishing was king, the immigration problem, the nanny state, and the loss of jobs in Scotland.

As I played I saw a woman I recognized talking to Alicia, then noticed her staring at me. I didn't look toward her at first. As she moved imperceptibly closer, I could tell that she was mesmerized by the music and sound of the harp. Five minutes later she was standing nearly beside me, her eyes transfixed by the strings. I drew "MacPherson's Lament" to a close, then glanced toward her.

"Hello, Cora," I said. "It is nice to see you again. I haven't seen you since that evening at the Crannoch Bay Hotel. I didn't know you were interested in the harp."

"Oh, yes, my lady," replied my acquaintance from the co-op. "I've always loved the harpie, though yer's isna a wee harpie like the ballad makers use, but ane the likes o' the angels maun play."

That is often how it begins—the shy glances...the staring at the instrument with all its unique and historical and spiritual allure...the timid approach.

The next question I ask when I see the familiar pattern unfolding always catches people off guard, just as it did on this day.

"Would you like to try it?"

Before Cora knew what to think, I was on my feet and urging her to sit down in my chair and showing her where to put her fingers.

"I dinna ken...," she began as she flushed crimson.

Before she could finish her sentence, her fingers were touching the strings and she gently began to pluck at them.

The magic of the harp did the rest. Without either of us yet knowing it, I had just enlisted my second student.

"Would you like to learn to play a song?"

"I doobt I could, Yer Grace. I've ne'er been too smart at sich things. Adela says she's takin' lessons fae ye, but she was always mair o' a musical bent nor me."

"I think you could do it, too," I said. "Would you like to try?"

Cora nodded sheepishly.

"Then in an hour or two, after everyone leaves, why don't you come back? You and I will go inside and I will teach you a song."

"I'd be pleased, Yer Grace. But are ye sure ye dinna mind? I dinna want tae cause ye no bother."

"There is nothing that gives me greater pleasure than to see someone learning to play the harp. Come to the front door, and Alicia will bring you to me."

The next two women who asked me about learning to play the harp were also friends of both Cora MacKay and Alicia Forbes. At first it struck me as coincidental, until I remembered that in Port Scarnose everybody knew everybody. Their names were Tavia Maccallum and Fia Gordon. I had met Tavia at Isobel Gauld's B and B when I first came to Port Scarnose, and I had visited with her a few times when out walking. She worked for Mrs. Gauld part-time, and she also worked from home doing some kind of computer research. Fia now lived in Portsoy and worked at the bakery on the square and had seen me playing during the boat festival. The two of them had talked about me. Even before Fia had spoken with me about lessons, with Adela, Cora, and Tavia coming regularly to the castle once a week, I realized my supply of available practice harps was nearly exhausted. With the addition of two more students, I would no longer have enough to go around.

I began researching harpmakers in Scotland besides the one in Ballachulish, with an eye to purchasing more practice instruments as well as having information on availability for those who might want to buy their own. With the bank account Alasdair had given me, money wasn't a problem. But I was frugal by nature, and I wanted to find the best harps for the money, especially for those who would purchase their own. The nearest harpmaker, of course, was nearby in Fordyce, only five miles away, but his tended to be specialty harps not especially well suited for beginners.

My thoughts also turned to Ranald Bain. I might be able to borrow his harp on occasion—temporarily, of course . . . I would not want to deprive *him* of it for long! Or even send one or another of the ladies up the Bin, either to practice on Ranald's harp in his cottage or have a lesson with him. He had become accomplished enough in a short time to be able to help them work on the basics of technique and the same songs I would be teaching them.

I said nothing to the others about involving Ranald for the present, however. Until I actually needed another harp, it was best to keep the ladies practicing as much as possible every day in their own homes. I must admit my little studio looked suddenly bare with only the *Queen*, *Journey*, and *Ring*. But it gave me such a good feeling that the other three harps were out in the community being played upon.

After several weeks, I asked the ladies if they would like to come to the castle and bring their harps all at the same time and, along with their regular lessons, begin working together as an ensemble. I usually tried to involve my students in both avenues whenever possible. Being forced to play in rhythm and harmony with a group sharpened awareness and skills, and nearly always accelerated individual progress. All three women were enthusiastic, and so it was arranged. It was about that same time when Fia asked me one day in the bakery in Portsoy if I gave harp lessons. I suggested she come and have her first lesson just before I had arranged for the ensemble's first meeting. Then she could stay and meet the others.

I didn't realize beforehand that the four had known one another most of their lives. Nor until they arrived did the rest know that Fia had just had her first lesson. None of the other three had seen her in years. The unexpected reunion of their girlhood friendship was yet the more remarkable as our first ensemble lesson was breaking up and Alicia came in with tea. I had met Fia at the door earlier and until that moment, Alicia had not seen her.

"Fia!" she exclaimed. "I didn't...How do you come to be here?"

"I came for a harp lesson," replied Fia. "That's right...I had forgotten. So you are still the housekeeper here?"

"Still here," replied Alicia.

She set down the tea things. The two women embraced warmly. "And look who else is here!" said Fia. "Adela and Cora and Tavia. I couldn't believe it when I walked in—all together again at last."

"I knew they were coming," Alicia said with a nod. "I see them all regularly now, but you...It is so good to see you!"

"And you! You look so good—you're not a day older."

"And you're still as big a liar as ever!" rejoined Alicia. "But thank you. You look well, too."

"No' quite *ilka ane* is here," said Adela in a more somber tone as she walked over to join the other two.

A few glances went about that seemed to carry more significance than I was aware of.

"Has anyone seen Olivia recently?" asked Fia, obviously reminded of my sister-in-law by Adela's cryptic comment. "I heard she and Max moved to Aberdeen, but I haven't seen her in years."

"She is in Aberdeeen, 'tis true," said Adela. "But I wasna referrin' tae *her*."

A silence followed, with another few curious expressions that successfully put a damper on the conversation.

"I am so glad you all came," I said, trying to disperse the sudden cloud. "I thought you all did great. As soon as Fia has a few more lessons, we will be a regular fivesome ready to take our show out on the road!"

"Let me hear you play something while the tea is cooling," said Alicia, pouring out tea in six cups.

"You heard her, ladies," I said. "Back to your harps—how about 'The Shearin's No' for You'? Fia, right hand only. Oh, but wait just a minute...I'll run up and get *Journey* and join in. I was playing in my room before you came and left it there."

I hurried from the room, ran upstairs, and returned two or three minutes later. As I walked in, the five women were gathered together in a small circle, talking in hushed tones. The exuberance of their reunion had been replaced by secretive whispering. I managed to catch only snatches of a few phrases.

"...what aboot... dinna ye mind..."

"...the foreigner..."

"...married her brither... not anymore..."

"...what she said... aboot beware..."

"...jist mair o' her nonsense..."

"...wud she think... ken we were here..."

They clammed up and moved apart the moment I entered. We limped through "The Shearin's No' for You," then set aside the harps for tea, with Alicia joining us. However, the mood remained subdued for five or ten minutes.

It was a curious gathering. After the enthusiasm of their first greetings, I expected them to talk and laugh and babble like ladies do, catching up on their lives. Yet finding themselves all together so unexpectedly had just the opposite effect. The odd glances and peculiar bits of conversation continued. No matter how I tried to bring up subjects I thought would prompt more talk, and in spite of all the questions I asked about what it was like to grow up in Port Scarnose, they remained subdued. I felt more like an outsider than I had in a year. I couldn't help thinking the peculiar change in mood had something to do with Olivia.

"There is one other harper nearby," I said after a while. "When we have had a few more times together and you are all several months into your lessons and know more songs, I thought we could invite him to join us. He also plays the violin, so there would be all sorts of possibilities for music we could make together. Maybe some of you know him...He lives up toward Crannoch Bin—his name is Ranald Bain."

The words fell like a stone in our midst. The room went dead silent. I looked around at the others. Everyone sat with blank expressions, with wide eyes and white faces, hands holding cups arrested halfway to their mouths. I couldn't imagine what had caused such a reaction. Gradually they began to glance at one another, full of unspoken question. But no one uttered a peep.

My suggestion put an even greater damper on the rest of the afternoon. After tea and a little more awkward small talk, gradually the women left.

When they were gone, I found Alicia in the kitchen cleaning up the tea things.

"Alicia," I said, "do you mind if I ask you a question?"

"Of course not."

"When I came into the room after going upstairs to get my harp, you and the others were talking quietly. It's none of my business, I know, but I heard Adela saying the word *beware*—"

"Adela has too free a tongue for her own good," snapped Alicia with uncharacteristic bluntness. "She's too prone to tales."

"But what did she mean—beware? Beware of what?"

"It's nothing, Marie."

"Please, Alicia, tell me."

Alicia glanced away but still said nothing.

I waited. Finally, as she realized I wasn't going away, she drew in a breath of resignation.

"It's just one of those things Olivia spread after you came, when all the trouble about Gwendolyn and Alasdair was stirred up."

"What did she say?"

"She said that you were trying to keep her from what she deserved."

The reminder of Olivia's attempt to subvert Alasdair's reputation and keep Gwendolyn from her father made my blood boil.

"But beware of what, Alicia?"

"Of you, Marie."

"*Me?*"

Alicia nodded reluctantly.

"Why beware of me? What harm could I possibly have been to anyone?"

"She said that you were after Alasdair's money. I'm sorry."

"Ahhgh!" I exclaimed in disgust. "I can't believe it! I mean, I suppose I knew she was saying such things, but—"

I shook my head in disbelief.

"What did she say exactly?" I asked after a moment.

"There was a verse she whispered about town.—*Must* I tell you, Marie?"

"Yes, Alicia."

"All right," she sighed, then said:

"Of this stranger and idler beware.

Though her music seems soft and sweet,

and her words and smiles so fair,

in her heart lies only deceit."

"That's it?" I said.

Alicia nodded.

"It's mean-spirited," I said, actually relieved, "but it seems harmless enough. I thought it would be something really horrible."

"None of Olivia's verses are harmless," rejoined Alicia.

I asked her what she meant. But nothing I could say would induce her to say more on the subject, and at last I gave it up for the day.

Tavia's lesson was scheduled three days later, and Cora came on the same day right after Tavia. Whatever had been going on before seemed forgotten by then. As Alicia knew the other women, gradually it became our custom to have tea together between lessons, with Alicia joining us. She seemed to enjoy rekindling her former friendships after so long, despite the specter of Olivia that always seemed lurking not far away.

It occurred to me once or twice that Olivia might be preparing herself for the time when she would come back to Castle Buchan as a ghost. It almost seemed that she was *already* haunting the place, if only in the minds of the ladies who had coincidentally all been drawn back to the place they had known as children.

Being so far inside the castle, I hadn't heard Alasdair drive up as we were having our tea. I was surprised when he walked into the studio suddenly.

"Marie, I was thinking, if you were free this afternoon, we—" he began as he walked through the door.

He stopped abruptly as he saw Alicia, Tavia, and Cora sitting with me, teacups in hand.

"Oh . . . sorry—I didn't realize you had guests," he said, standing still with an expression on his face I didn't quite understand. He looked back and forth between the others for a moment. His mind was obviously revolving something.

"Hello, Tavia," he said at length. "I haven't seen you in some time . . . Cora," he added, then turned and left.

"Excuse me," I said. I set down my cup and ran to the door. Alasdair was disappearing along the corridor. I hurried after him, but he was walking quickly.

"Alasdair," I called behind him. I caught up with him and fell into step at his side. "I will be free in an hour," I said, "after my lesson with Cora, if you—"

"Forget it," he said, still walking rapidly and not looking at me.

"But if you—"

"Forget it," he said again. "It's all right. I can see you're busy."

"I only have the two lessons, and Tavia is just leaving. I didn't realize you knew her."

"Yes, well . . . life is full of surprises."

"Alasdair, what in the world is wrong?"

At last he stopped and turned toward me.

"What are those women doing here?" he asked almost angrily.

"I told you—just having harp lessons. I thought you—"

"But why are they here together . . . and with Alicia . . . Why are they *together*? What were you talking about?"

"I don't know . . . nothing. Harp stuff."

"Is that all?"

"Yes, of course. What else would you think it was?"

"I don't know, nothing . . . I just— Forget it. I just wondered if

Olivia's little clique of mischief was back in business and if you were getting drawn into the web."

"What web?"

"Olivia's web—they were all part of it."

"I know nothing about that. Please, Alasdair, I'm sure this is just a misunderstanding."

"There are things you don't know, Marie."

"Then tell me."

"It's best you don't know about them. Are you telling me that Olivia's name never came up . . . that you only talked about your harp lessons?"

"Yes . . . Well, she came up a time or two, but only in passing and then everyone clammed up and no one said anything about her. Actually, it was strange."

"So there was no talk of trying to initiate you into their little secretive club?"

"Secretive club? They haven't been together in years— Good heavens, no, there was nothing like that. If anything, just the opposite. I felt like the odd woman out."

"It would be Olivia's pattern—to worm her way between us anyway way she could to destroy the only time of happiness I have known in my life."

"Nothing will destroy it, Alasdair. Olivia is in Aberdeen. She's got nothing to do with any of this."

"She has *everything* to do with it when those ladies are together. She can manipulate and control even when she is nowhere around. Maybe it's telepathy, I don't know."

"I assure you, it's nothing at all like that."

"I hope you're right," said Alasdair, then he continued on down the hall, leaving me more perplexed than ever.

If this had been our first "fight," I suppose it was a mild one.

Still, I didn't like how it felt.

Chapter Nine

Crannoch Bin

Thickest night, o'erhang my dwelling!
Howling tempests, o'er me rave!
Turbid torrents, wintry swelling,
Still surround my lonely cave!

Crystal streamlets gently flowing,
Busy haunts of base mankind,
Western breezes softly blowing,
Suit not my distracted mind.
—Robert Burns, "Strathallan's Lament"

All this time we heard nothing from Iain Barclay. I cannot say I forgot about him—I could never do that—but memories of our times together gradually receded into the background of my life with Alasdair.

One day, however, my curiosity got the better of me. There was one man in the neighborhood who was sure to know what had become of the former minister of Deskmill Parish. If anyone knew, that man would be Iain's former spiritual mentor, Ranald Bain.

"How would you fancy a drive up the Bin to visit Ranald Bain?" I asked Alasdair at breakfast.

"I'm sorry, my love," he replied. "I have a meeting with the accountant of the Fochabers estate to review some of our contingent leases. We're having lunch together at Baxters. How about tomorrow?"

"Isn't a storm coming in from Shetland tonight?"

"Actually, I think you're right. Then go yourself and enjoy the sun while you can. And give Ranald my best."

Alicia came in to clear up the breakfast things a little while later.

"Alicia," I said, "how would you like to take a walk up the Bin with me later?"

She turned with the tray in her hands. "Today?" she said.

"Yes, in a few hours…when it warms up. I'm going to visit Ranald Bain—why don't you come with me?"

"You're going to the Bain croft," she said with a strange look on her face. *"Alone?"*

"Yes, of course!" I laughed. "What do you mean, alone?"

"I knew that you and the duke went to see him occasionally, but I…that is, I thought that was because the duke had business with him. I didn't dream you would go by yourself."

"What are you talking about?" I laughed again. "I've visited him a dozen times. He was one of my first friends here."

"But don't you know what they say?"

"What—you mean how the children are afraid of him? Of course I know about it. But that's all nonsense."

"It's not just children," said Alicia slowly. "And it's not all nonsense."

Her tone made me shiver. A weird sense of foreboding swept through me like a cloud had briefly passed overhead.

"What do you mean, Alicia? *You're* not afraid of him, are you?"

"I don't…No, not really, I mean…of course not," she answered. But her tone and fumbling were hardly convincing.

"Then come with me. We'll have a good time. If you don't want to visit Ranald, we'll just have a walk up the Bin."

She agreed, though reluctantly. We packed a light lunch and set off between eleven and noon. By then I had managed to coax Alicia mostly back out from under the spell that had come over her so suddenly. It was a fabulous day, warm and bright, fragrant and with just the lightest breeze to keep the air interesting and to prevent it from being sultry. We talked freely as we went, more than we had since she had helped me get ready for the wedding. I told her about Canada and my childhood and about my hippie parents, and even some about my first marriage, which I'd not spoken about to anyone locally except a mention or two to Alasdair and Iain and Ranald.

As we set out, since it had been my idea, I assumed I was leading the way. But as we went it gradually became obvious that I was following *her*. She left the path I always took to the Bain croft and struck through the woods, veering a little farther south than my usual route. A few minutes later I found that we were indeed on a trail, though I hadn't noticed when it had become one. Obviously, I realized, Alicia had grown up here and probably knew every path as well as she did her own backyard.

Most of the way took us through light woods blanketed with mossy undergrowth. At last we met the Bin trail coming from the south and began climbing the final steep slope, and I saw the trail of my usual path joining us.

We ate lunch at the summit. It was clear and beautiful as far as the eye could see. Alicia pointed out landmarks I hadn't known from previous visits.

Suddenly a low roar sounded in the distance.

"What is that?!" I asked. "I hear it all the time. At first I thought it was thunder, but there isn't a cloud in the sky."

"It's the RAF airfield at Lossiemouth...just there," said Alicia, pointing west along the coast. "It's probably a fighter jet taking off. Yes, look—there it is!"

About thirty miles away now, we saw a tiny speck banking almost straight up from the ground. Another roar sounded as a second jet took off. In seconds it had joined the first and was out of sight.

Peaceful silence again came to the top of the Bin. But not for long.

"Look, here they come," said Alicia, pointing again.

Out over the water straight ahead of us the two planes were visible again, and coming our way. They looked like birds in the distance, except they were moving too fast to be birds. Within seconds they were nearly overhead. Still we heard no sound. They zoomed over us frighteningly low with unbelievable speed.

"Plug your ears!" shouted Alicia, clasping her hands to her head.

The next instant a thunderous explosion followed. Even as the delayed sound hit, already the jets were nearly out of sight.

"I never get tired of watching them," said Alicia when stillness again reigned at the top of Crannoch Bin. "I have always been fascinated with airplanes. My father was in the RAF. Maybe that's why. That roar of a jet engine always sends a thrill through me. Can I tell you one of my secret dreams?" she added, looking at me with what was almost a girlishly timid smile.

"Yes, of course. Please do!"

"It's a little embarrassing, especially to tell *you*."

"What do you mean, *me*? Why shouldn't you tell me?"

"You're an important lady now, a duchess. Why should you care about me and my silly notions?"

"Alicia! How can you say that?"

"But you are."

"I'm still the same me I always was. I don't want to hear any more nonsense about me being an important lady. I would love for you to share it with me."

"All right—but you must promise not to laugh."

"I promise."

She glanced away. It seemed she was still staring after the two airplanes that had disappeared beyond the horizon.

"I would like to fly," she said at length. "Not with wings, not like an angel, I mean...you know, actually learn to fly an airplane."

"That *is* a big dream! Wouldn't you be scared?"

"I don't know—maybe a little. But I grew up hearing my father talk about flying as if it were no different than driving a car. Of course, I can't drive a car either!" She laughed. "But I would still like to learn to fly. Maybe some day," she added wistfully.

"I think it's an exciting thought," I said. "I would be frightened to death. But I was frightened when I first came to Scotland by myself, too. That was *my* dream, and look what happened!"

"Yes, but you're more adventurous than me."

"I never was. I've only had one adventure in my life ... and this was it!"

"They don't get much more exciting than marrying a duke and coming to live in a castle!" Alicia said with a light laugh.

"Does your father still fly?" I asked.

"He did. He was a pilot."

"Is he retired?"

"He's dead," replied Alicia with abrupt matter-of-factness.

"Oh, I'm sorry. Did he have an accident or something?"

"No. He retired, then died of a heart attack two years later."

"Oh." I nodded. "And your mother?"

"She's in a home in Elgin," replied Alicia. "She has Alzheimer's. I visit her twice a week, but she doesn't know who I am."

"That must be terribly hard," I said.

Alicia nodded and smiled sadly.

Ever since I'd known her I had been curious about Alicia's past, especially why she wasn't married. She was attractive enough, yet she seemed to have lived a lonely existence in the castle all these years. Of course, so had Alasdair. Maybe she *had* been married? Why hadn't she and Alasdair married? They were about the same age.

Now my thoughts were running away with themselves! None of it was any of my business.

Except that now *I* was Alasdair's wife. Technically Alicia worked for me now, too. I was interested. I wanted to *know* her. Besides, she was my friend. At least I hoped she could become my friend. Up till now we had been what you might call friendly acquaintances. I hoped our relationship would grow to become deeper than that.

"Have you ever been married?" I blurted out after several seconds. The words just came out, but I let them stand.

Alicia said nothing for a long time. Slowly another smile came to her lips. But this, like the last, was a sad smile.

"No," she said softly. Again it was silent. It was obvious she was reminiscing. I waited.

"I was engaged once," she said after three or four minutes.

Another smile followed that spoke of happy memories. "It didn't work out."

"What happened?" I asked. "I mean . . . I'm sorry—I don't mean to pry. I'm just interested. But you don't have to tell me if—"

"No, that's all right," said Alicia. "It's no big deal, really. He met someone else, that's all, and called off the engagement. I suppose it happens all the time."

"Not exactly *all* the time. It must have been awful."

Alicia shrugged. "I guess it was. But in a way I suppose I half expected it."

"What was his name?" I asked.

"It was Max . . . Max Urquhart."

I stared back at her with wide eyes, wondering if I'd heard her right.

"You don't mean *Olivia's* husband?" I said.

Alicia nodded.

"I had no idea. I didn't realize you were from around here. With your father in the RAF, I assumed you had moved around."

"We did when I was very young. My only memories are of living in Port Scarnose. I started school here and have been here ever since."

"So you knew Olivia . . . before?"

"All my life. We were close friends . . . well, as close as any of us could have been to Olivia. But of course after Max, that all changed. I hated her, but neither could I escape her."

"You weren't working for Alasdair at the time?"

"Oh, no—that came later. I worked part-time for his father and mother. Then after the duke's first marriage, when he went away, they asked me to come live at the castle to help keep things in order. When the duke returned, I just sort of went with the place. He kept me on, and here I am."

"Had you and Alasdair known one another well...before, I mean?"

"Well enough, I suppose. He was just Olivia's brother to me. Then he went away to university and I hardly saw him again."

"So there was never anything between the two of you?"

"Oh, no," replied Alicia, as if the idea were absurd. "How could there be? I was under the spell."

Her words took a few seconds to register. Before I could ask her what she meant, suddenly sounds from behind us interrupted the serenity of our picnic that had grown so serious. I turned to see a family of six hikers arrive, with four loud and energetic children and two rambunctious dogs that immediately began investigating our lunch. We scrambled to our feet and put our things away. We were through anyway and it was time to begin our descent, which I still hoped would result in a visit with Ranald Bain.

When we came to my usual path, I took it and Alicia followed. The easy slope down through the woods was much the same as the route we had taken before. But when we climbed the stone steps Ranald had placed into the wall bordering his meadow, Alicia became quiet, and she glanced several times in the direction where I knew the cottage lay. She clearly knew exactly where we were. I turned to cross the meadow in the direction of Ranald's house. Alicia hesitated.

"I told you, Marie," she said, "I am not going to that man's house. You do whatever you want, but I am going back down to the castle."

I stopped and turned around. "Do you know the way?" I asked.

She gave a little laugh. "I could find my way blindfolded," she answered. "We used to come up here all the time."

"Alicia, please," I said. "I would really like you to meet Mr. Bain. He is a delightful man. I know you'll find that he is—"

"Marie," she interrupted forcefully. "I will not set foot in that man's house." Her voice was strange, distant, impersonal, like nothing I had ever heard from her before.

"But why, Alicia? Tell me why. What are you afraid of?"

"It has a curse on it."

Without intending to, I broke out laughing for a moment. The look on Alicia's face stopped me cold.

"A curse?" I said. "How could that be? I've been there a dozen times. It's a wonderful place."

"You've not actually been . . . You didn't go *inside*?" said Alicia, her voice full of fear.

"Of course," I replied, laughing lightly again.

"Oh, Marie!" she wailed in a horrible and forlorn sound. "Don't you know what happens to people who tempt the curse? Don't you know about his wife and daughter? They're dead, Marie . . . *dead*. What have you done?!"

I couldn't imagine what had come over her. She was almost hysterical.

Shaking her head and wailing, Alicia turned to run away.

But as she spun around, her first step took her headlong straight into Ranald Bain, who had been walking noiselessly toward us. How much he had heard, I didn't know.

Alicia shrieked in terror and leaped back. I hurried to her and tried to calm her. She was trembling from head to foot.

"Hello, Marie," said Ranald calmly. Then in the most kindly voice imaginable, he added, "Hello, Alicia. I am happy to see you again. It has been many years."

Alicia only stared at him, her face pale, her body trembling. She was stiff and unmoving and made no attempt to leave my side.

Ranald stood where he was and moved no closer.

"Who put the curse on my house, Alicia?" he said. His voice, too, was unlike I had ever heard it—soft but commanding. He was staring straight into her eyes.

It was obvious he had heard the gist of our conversation.

"I . . . I don't . . . Why would I know?" she mumbled.

"Who, Alicia? Were you there? Did you hear it?"

Slowly Alicia nodded.

"*Who* put the curse on my house, Alicia?" Ranald persisted. The command in his tone was unmistakable.

Alicia seemed trying to speak. Her features were contorted, her eyes blinking, her mouth twitching strangely. Some terrible other-worldly battle was taking place, with Alicia in the middle of it.

At last her lips began to tremble. Finally she uttered a single word. It was but faintly audible.

"*Olivia*," she whispered. The moment the name passed her lips, her body collapsed and I grabbed for her.

I nearly fell backward from the sudden weight. Ranald hastened to my side. We eased Alicia to the ground, where I knelt to support her. Her eyes were closed.

I glanced up at Ranald with a bewildered look on my face.

"She will come to herself shortly," he said. "She will be spent. Get her home where she can rest, but do not speak of this unless Alicia brings it up herself. Otherwise, today's work is done. When she is ready, give her something to eat."

And with that, leaving me more perplexed than ever, Ranald Bain walked across the meadow toward his cottage. A minute after he was out of sight, Alicia's eyes began to flutter. She groaned, I helped her slowly to her feet, and, holding on to steady her, we began making our way home.

Chapter Ten

A Girl's Power

I am in love I cannot deny it
My heart lies troubled in my breast
It's not for me to let the world know it
A troubled heart can find no rest.
—"Peggy Gordon"

Alicia clung limply to my side all the way back to the castle. She was completely compliant, did not seem anxious about whether Ranald was around, and said nothing.

We reached the castle. I took her to her bedroom, then returned downstairs to the kitchen to fix her a light snack. She was able to eat but two or three bites of apple and oatcake. Within minutes she was sound asleep on top of her bed in the clothes she had worn for the walk.

I left her with much to reflect on. I had never seen such a dramatic change come over anyone as what I had witnessed in Alicia. I was glad Alasdair wasn't back from his meeting in Fochabers. Normally I would have gone straight to him and told him everything. But this wanted thinking out. I wasn't absolutely sure I should even tell Alasdair. As much as I loathed the idea of keeping something from him, I did not want to say or do anything that might in some way compromise his thoughts toward Alicia. She had been devoted to him for years.

When Alasdair returned about three-thirty, I fixed tea and took a tray with some oatcakes out to the rose garden and we sat down together. By then I was ready to talk. He told me about his meeting, then asked how I had passed the day. I told him that Alicia and I had walked to the Bin with a light picnic lunch.

"Two jets took off from Lossiemouth when we were at the summit," I said. "They screamed overhead so loud and close, it was terrifying. The ground shook!"

"I remember hearing them, too," Alasdair said, chuckling. "Growing up around here, you get used to it. Of course all the boys love it and dream of being pilots one day."

"Did you?"

"Sure. We all did."

"Alicia loves airplanes, too. She told me her father actually was an RAF pilot."

"Really—I didn't know that."

He thought a moment.

"Funny, isn't it," he mused, "how you don't know people as well as you think. We were around one another all the time as children, but I never knew anything about Alicia's parents."

"Oh?"

"She was in my sister's little clique of friends."

"So she knew the castle as a girl, then later became your housekeeper."

Alasdair became thoughtful again. I was afraid he would go back into that peculiar mood that had come over him at seeing me having tea with Alicia and the other women two weeks earlier. Luckily he didn't.

"Alicia was first hired by my father, as I recall," he said, "when I was down at Oxford if I'm not mistaken. Then I came back and had all my trouble. As she had never married, she stayed on. She maintained the place with a semblance of order during my absence, as well as after I returned. I don't know what I'd have done without her."

"Why did she not marry?" I asked. "She is attractive, bright, capable."

"There were several young men, as I recall," replied Alasdair. "I don't actually know, to tell you the truth. I was in England during those years. Now that I think of it, she was involved with Max for a time—Olivia's husband, you know. I didn't know the circumstances. I was much too sophisticated in my own eyes to pay much attention to my sister's love life. But now that I think of it, it seems Alicia and Max might even have been serious at one time. Suddenly it was off, and the next thing we knew it was Olivia walking down the aisle on our father's arm. I was still in England and only came north for the wedding and was then away again. When I next returned a year and a half later, our father was dead, I was the new duke, and my thoughts were too full of Fiona to think much about Olivia's childhood friends. I'm sorry for bringing her up, my dear," he added with an apologetic smile.

"Don't mention it," I said. "You may talk about Fiona as often as you like. She is part of your story and is Gwendolyn's mother, and therefore I am interested."

"But still, that is the past and I prefer to look ahead. In any event, our mother, too, was unwell. And faithful Alicia Forbes was by then her housekeeper and has been with me ever since."

"How much longer did your mother live?"

"Another two years. I was on the Continent at the time of her death."

Alasdair paused and shook his head. "I have much to repent of to both my parents, if such things are allowed in the next life," he said after a moment. "I'll leave the theology of that to Iain. But I do have many regrets that bite more deeply the older I grow. I was not with them for either of their last days on earth. I know they longed to see me, but I was too absorbed with my own self at the time."

He let out a long sigh. "Life is full of regrets," he added slowly. "At every age, it seems, we are stupider than we have any idea. It is only the future that reveals the truth about the past, and then continues to reveal it again and anew with every passing year. What would Iain say? Probably that if God forgives us, we have to learn to forgive ourselves . . . and then move on."

I could not help smiling to hear Alasdair speaking of God as if through Iain's thoughts. I nodded. "I think that is very much like what he would say."

"It is easier said than done," said Alasdair.

"Probably *all* forgiveness is easier said than done," I added.

We sipped at our tea and I took another oatcake.

"You know, it is a curious thing, now that I think of it," said Alasdair after several minutes. "Alicia isn't the only one of Olivia's friends who never married. I'd never thought of it before, but there is Adela, of course... and then Tavia and Cora—that is incredible now that I think of it."

"I didn't know whether Adela was married or not."

Alasdair shook his head, still thinking. "Oh, I'd forgotten about Fia," he said. "Didn't you say she was taking lessons from you, too?"

"Yes, she just started."

"And of course there's Winny Bain, who died before she was old enough to think about marriage. It's more remarkable than I realized. *None* of them ever married."

"An amazing coincidence."

"Or perhaps *more* than a coincidence," added Alasdair cryptically.

"What do you mean?"

"Oh, nothing... There couldn't possibly be anything to it. It's just that Olivia's group of friends was... I don't know, different. Separately the girls were all pleasant and perfectly normal, but when they were together, something changed. There was a bond between them that didn't seem entirely healthy. I don't know how else to describe it. When other children saw them together, roaming about on a Saturday or during the summer, they ran away. Even boys gave them wide berth. That's why seeing you with them the other day disturbed me. I am sorry—it just hit me hard."

"Think nothing more of it. But were people actually *frightened* of them?"

"Yes, I think they were. Especially the younger children. You remember what I told you before, about her rhyming curses.

"'Look on the path—a slithering snake...

Tonight Alasdair will tremble and quake.
Trolls, goblins, and monsters, kelpies, and witches . . .
will gnaw your insides like unscratchable itches.
Spiders, lizards, and black slimy leeches . . .
are Alasdair's friends and crawl up his breeches'—"

"Alasdair, stop, please . . . I don't want to hear any more of them."

"Sorry, but the fact is that Olivia's group of friends—Alicia and Adela and the others—were all drawn into that to such an extent that they didn't dare cross her."

"All I know is that it sounds weird!" I tried to laugh as I said it. But it wasn't funny. Obviously whatever Alicia had heard about Ranald and his house still held her in its grip. What I had seen on her face was no childish game but genuine fear. It was far more serious than being afraid of a snake.

"It was weird!" said Alasdair. "But even if half of it was imaginary, Olivia spread great evil around this community because people came to believe that she possessed the second sight and was in league with dark forces."

Chapter Eleven

Curse

The watercresses surround each fountain, with shaggy
eyebrows of darkest green;
And groves of sorrel ascend the mountain, where loose
white sand lies all soft and clean;
Thence bubbles boiling, yet coldly coiling the new-born
stream from the darksome deep;
Clear, blue, and curling, and swiftly swirling, it bends and
bounds in its headlong leap.
—Duncan Ban MacIntyre, "The Misty Dell"

I hoped *I* wasn't feeling the effects of Olivia's hexes!

Whatever the cause, I tossed and turned half the night thinking about spiders and snakes and wolves and monsters. It was awful.

The mind can play terrible tricks on you during the night. Mine certainly did. Over and over Olivia's silly chants played themselves in my brain until I thought they would drive me completely mad.

Never was I so glad to see morning come.

I can't say the sunrise brought any resolution other than the usual effect of the coming of light—that all the perplexities and doubts and fears and imaginary goblins that seemed creepy and terrifying in the middle of the night no longer appeared so sinister.

One resolution, however, did come with the morning. All this about Olivia and hexes and curses could not be ignored, hidden, swept under the carpet and not talked about. I knew what Iain would say—that the surest solution to any quandary is light.

Olivia's world was a world of hidden things . . . innuendo, suspicion, subtlety, doubt, fear, threat, secrecy. It was a world of darkness. It could not be allowed to infiltrate our lives again. Olivia's ways must not creep back and work new evil in Buchan Castle as they had for so many years in the past. Alasdair was at last free from all that. I wasn't about to let that evil come slinking back into our lives.

Light must prevail.

The reminder of Olivia's threatening ditties and Alasdair's being able to laugh about them himself, as much as they had swirled through my waking nightmares all night, had been a good thing— getting them out in the open where they could be exposed for the nonsense they were.

Obviously, however, they weren't nonsense in Alicia's mind.

Whatever Olivia had said about Ranald Bain still terrified her, even if her terror had been primarily for me. In Alicia's mind, the words still contained power. Because of that, as Alasdair said, they still exercised a control over her, though Olivia herself was miles away in Aberdeen.

I scarcely saw Alicia the rest of the day after our walk. She slept most of the afternoon, got up for an hour, had something to eat, then went to bed for the night.

The following morning she was quiet and subdued. Whether she was embarrassed over what had happened or a rift had come between us, I couldn't tell. She was distant, untalkative, and went about her day's duties saying hardly a word. Strange as it is to say, I felt Olivia's presence. I had spent enough time with Alasdair's sister to recognize subtle similar feelings now.

The predicted storm hadn't hit yet, though the wind had begun to whip up and clouds hung over the Firth that clearly meant business. But what I needed to do couldn't wait.

Midway through the morning I sought Alicia where she was cleaning in the pantry.

"Alicia," I said, "I am going up the Bin again. This time I am going specifically to visit Ranald Bain. I am going to have tea with him inside his house. I am going to play his harp. I would like you to come with me so you can see that there is nothing to any silly curse."

The progression of expressions that came over Alicia's face as I spoke were contorted and strange—first no expression at all, then a flash from her eyes of something very much like anger. For an instant I almost thought I was looking at *Olivia's* eyes, angry that I would dare go against her warnings about Ranald. That expression gave way quickly to one of horror and disbelief that I would actually challenge the curse, as if inviting it on my own head. But with my last words, suddenly she began shaking her head violently, with a return of the terror I had seen the day before.

"I won't do that," she said. "I am afraid for you, too, Marie. Don't do it, I beg you. No good can come of it. He is an evil man."

"Alicia, stop it," I said firmly. "He is *not* an evil man. I don't know what lies Olivia has told you, but he is as gentle and kind as any man I know."

"It's all a trick to lure you into his house . . . and then the curse will come upon you!"

"Alicia, there is no curse."

"There is, I tell you. I heard it."

Her words took me aback. Even after her exchange with Ranald, it wasn't what I had expected.

"*What* did you hear, Alicia?" I asked.

She looked away.

"Alicia."

Still she would not return my gaze.

I reached out and placed my hand on her shoulder.

"Alicia," I said, "look at me."

Slowly she turned her head, as if battling having to look at me. Her features were wincing and contorting visibly. I stared straight into her eyes.

"Alicia," I said, "I want you to tell me what you heard."

Her lips began to quiver, just as they had under the force of Ranald's stare. Then slowly, in a strange, almost gravelly voice, she spoke what she had heard from Olivia.

"The curse of madness will be the stain . . . of all who enter the house of Bain."

The moment the words were out of her mouth, her body wilted. As she collapsed in weakness, I eased her to a nearby chair. Shuddering from what I had heard, I turned and left her.

I wandered out of the castle in a flurry of emotions. If ever I needed Alasdair's arms around me to reassure me, it was at that moment. But he was not at home. And could Alasdair resolve my confusion? He was part of it—as were all who had been within Olivia's orbit.

Even now, Alicia was still under her influence. The force of Olivia's personality, the force of her powers of persuasion, were not so easily escaped.

I wandered through the rose garden, confused and bewildered.

I realized that there was no way I could force Alicia to visit Ranald Bain. The curse still held her in its grip. Until she *wanted* to, she would not be free from it.

But *I* had to talk to Ranald.

Five minutes later, after dashing off a quick note to Alasdair, I was setting out up the Bin.

Chapter Twelve

House of Bain

Loud the winds howl, loud the waves roar.
Thunderclaps rend the air,
Baffled, our foes stand by the shore,
Follow they will not dare.
—Harold Boulton, "Skye Boat Song"

As I made my way up the slopes of Crannoch Bin for the second day in a row, frightening and spooky thoughts assailed me. Even the trees blowing frenetically in the wind became menacing and sinister, as if they were conspiring to prevent my progress. I began to feel, as I had so many times since coming to Scotland, that I was part of a fairy tale. However, this time it was no Prince Charming story, but an evil tale with witches and goblins trying to lure me onto the mountain where they would kill me and my body would never be found.

Faster and faster I walked. The more I hurried, the more furiously the wind raged and the trees blew about me on every side. The worst of it was that the horrible, mesmerizing, chanting words of Olivia's curse rang over and over in my brain. Even the sound of her smooth, calm, seductive voice began to haunt my thoughts with her terrible words.

"Madness will be the stain . . . madness will be the stain . . . madness . . . madness . . . all who enter the house of Bain."

I hated it, but I couldn't stop it. The curse took on a life of its own.

Was I going mad?

I had lain awake half the night tormented by Olivia's words. Were her occultish powers getting inside me? Was I, too, falling under Olivia's control?

Had the madness begun the very first time Ranald had lured me into his cottage...lured me with his deceptive words...lured me with the spell of his music that sounded sweet but had seductive powers that had put my senses to sleep? That was how spells worked, turning everything upside down so you couldn't tell light from darkness, right from wrong, good from evil.

When had the madness begun? Had I slowly been going mad all along?

Alicia was the sane one, not me. I should have heeded her warnings. Now I was on my way to the very house of madness itself.

Doubts flew at me out of the wind and trees like invisible arrows. They bombarded me with evil thoughts about Ranald, about Alasdair, about everything that had happened since I first set foot in Scotland. Olivia's soft, soothing, mesmerizing words returned to me—

"You do not understand, Marie. You cannot understand. Things are not as they seem. But I will help you understand. I will help you see clearly. Only I can help you understand."

I forgot everything good. I forgot my harp. I forgot Gwendolyn. I forgot the music of the angels. I forgot God. I forgot to pray.

Suddenly, out of the wind and storm, words that Iain Barclay had once spoken returned to me like a still, small voice of calm.

"Character is the most reliable validation of truth. You have to discern individual character. It will lead you to truth."

When I'd had doubts about Alasdair—and those doubts, too, had been planted by Olivia—Iain's words about character had helped me see Alasdair for the man he truly was.

I couldn't let Olivia's lies and distortions twist my mind into terrible confusion again.

Character *mattered*. It mattered more than anything. And as I had discovered in Alasdair's case, Ranald's character was true. I knew it. I must hang on to that belief. Though I had no *proof* about her allegations, I knew Olivia's perceptions were lies. Alasdair's *character* spoke truth. So did Ranald's.

I pressed on. The wind continued to batter against me as if in angry retaliation against my resolve to defeat the force of Olivia's curse.

I reached the cottage under gloomy skies.

The place looked deserted, and unaccountably foreboding. I shivered and couldn't help Olivia's horrible chant running through my brain yet again. I hated myself for allowing it. But I couldn't help it. Once planted, the seeds of evil are hard to uproot.

I reached up and yanked on the rope that rang Ranald's bell, then rang it again even louder, as if the sound could banish the incantation from my mind.

In the distance I heard a dog bark. My heart almost leaped for joy at the familiar sound.

Several minutes later, the collie and two sheepdogs romped toward me, bounding and barking in a frenzy of canine greeting. Ranald himself was slower to arrive but at last came into view, well bundled against the approaching weather, his proud gray thatch shooting out in all directions from under a well-worn brown tartan wool cap, his familiar smile easily visible amid the gray-white beard blowing about in the wind.

"Marie, lass!" he greeted me warmly. "I had the feelin' I'd aye be seein' ye again afore lang after yesterday. Hoo's Alicia?"

"Not so well, I'm afraid," I answered. "I am so sorry about all that. I was mortified by what she said."

"Think nae mair aboot it. I've been used tae it these mony a lang year. Bein' at cross purposes wi' young Olivia Reidhaven made me ane wha had tae endure the slings an' arrows o' outrageous fortune mony a time afore yesterday. But come in oot o' the win'," he said as he led the way inside.

He put on water for tea, then added several chunks to his fireplace and jabbed the coals a few times with a poker.

"How do you know Alicia?" I asked as I sat down. "You seemed well acquainted."

"Aye, but I haena seen her for mony a lang year."

"You knew her when she was young, then?"

"Oh, aye. In a wee village the likes o' Port Scarnose, there are nae mony folk a man like me disna ken. Ilka body kens ilka body, as they say. Alicia an' oor Winny were frien's, wi' Olivia an' the rest o' her wee group o' lassies. I haena spoken wi' the lass for years as I say, an' hae only seen her fae a distance upon occasion, at yer weddin' an' the like. But I kennt there was ill-blud swirlin' aboot on account o' Olivia an' her mischief. I didn't ken 'twas still sae deep intil the puir lass's mind as we saw yesterday. I fear for her. When the seeds o' anither's evil get such a deep grip in a body's mind, naethin' but ill can come o't. The seeds o' Olivia's evil are still growin' aroun' us, I'm thinkin'."

"I was shocked at what she said," I said. "When I told her this morning that I was coming to see you, she became frightened all over again. She begged me not to come. She hasn't been herself since we were here yesterday. She slept most of the day. She looks different. Her voice is different."

Ranald sighed and shook his head. "'Tis deep spiritual mischief afoot," he said. His voice was grave. "Fit's lang lain dormant may be comin' back tae rear its head again. We maun be on oor guard, as the Lord says."

"What do you mean, *spiritual* mischief?" I asked.

Ranald had been standing near his hearth as we spoke. He now sat down opposite me and thought seriously for at least a minute before answering. As I waited, the cottage became so still and quiet inside that again I became aware of the wind blowing about outside, occasionally whistling or gusting down the chimney and agitating the fire.

"Hoo weel acquainted are ye, Marie," said Ranald at length, "wi' the forces o' spiritual darkness in the world?"

"I, uh...I don't know," I replied. "Are you talking about...you mean the devil and Satan and that kind of thing?"

"In a manner o' speakin'," said Ranald. "But no' wi' horns an' a tail an' dressed in red wi' flames dancin' up roun' his feet. There's all kin' o' ways o' thwartin' the ways o' God. In a superstitious land wi' a history steeped in paganism an' druids an' magic an' the like, e'en the natural spiritual nature o' the Scots people is all too curious aboot the dark side o' things. It gets a grip an' a hold on folk wi' genuine spiritual sensitivities mair nor it might ither folk. When an' hoo it took root in a lass like Olivia Reidhaven, I dinna ken. But the po'er o' darkness was aye alive in her the first time I laid een on the lass. I recognized the enemy o' God fae that first day, an' that gleam in her eyes ne'er left, though she's an elder in the kirk, her hert's set agin' the ways o' God. She discovered yoong that she had the po'er tae control ither lads an' lassies, that she cud make them de what she wanted, that she cud put fear intil them, that she cud make them afraid, that she cud put thoughts intil their heids. We saw it a', my Maggie an' me. We did oor best tae keep oor Winny fae her. We saw that naethin' but ill could come o' bein' too close tae sich a one. But in young nickums, evil is a terrible magnet. Evil attracts ither lads an' lassies. I dinna ken why 'tis so. Why doesna goodness an' purity an' humility an' honesty attract the young? 'Tis sin, not righteousness that attracts. 'Tis one o' the laws o' mankind that evil grows an' breeds an' bears readier fruit than goodness. Weeds o' the sinful nature grow wi'oot care, but roses o' righteousness take nurturin' an' love an' the work o' daily ministration, an' 'tis the same wi' the plant o' human character. 'Tis aye *hard* tae learn tae be good an' kind, but 'tis the easiest thing in the worl' tae be selfish an' cruel an' unkind."

Again Ranald sighed and appeared to sink once more into deep thought.

"Fan Olivia saw that she could bend ither lads an' lassies tae her will, she couldna resist usin' the po'er. Fan she saw she cud plant seeds o' fear wi' her words, already she was weel on her way toward the dark side o' God's worl'. 'Twas too intoxicatin' a drink tae the pride o' self for her no' tae keep drinkin' it, an' she nurtured that dark power by usin' it. An' the self grew, an' the po'er grew, an' the pride grew. The mair she used her powers, the greater they became, for evil always builds on its own success. By the time the lass was ten or twelve, the hale village was feart o' her for the strange things she said, for they'd all come to believe she had the po'er o' the de'il in her."

"*Did* she have special powers?" I asked.

"I dinna doubt she did," replied Ranald. "There's stories told o' a Highland gran'mither wi' the second sicht wha many say was a witch an' passed on her po'ers tae Olivia. 'Tis said the curses o' the duke's family came down fae the Highlands through the auld witch o' Skye, they called her."

"That's awful!" I said with a shudder, reminded of the horror I felt when Alasdair first told me about meeting his grandmother..

"No evil has mair po'er nor it's given. Evil has po'er o'er yersel', Marie, or o'er me or yer Alasdair ... *only* gien we gie it the po'er. But gien we *dinna*, it canna touch us. Evil has nae po'er o' its own. All the threats o' the devil's nae mair than a tiny puff agin' the mighty winds o' God's love. The devil has *naethin'* o' his own. Evil has only the po'er it's given ... nae mair than any man or woman gie it in themselves. When a body resists it, it canna weigh nae mair nor a feather agin' him."

"So what you are saying is that Olivia *did* give evil its power, because she gave into it and used it?"

"Aye. Then ithers gave Olivia po'er o'er them. Those she cud control wi' fear, she did control, but only because they let her. She learnt early tae hate me because I kennt her for what she was. The curse hae nae po'er o'er me because I gie it no po'er. One word o' God's trowth is enouch to send a thousand curses o' the de'il back tae hell where they belang. She couldna control me, so she tried tae destroy me. I hae nae doubt that's what's behind the nonsense wi' Alicia an' fit she was speikin' aboot."

"Have you ever heard the curse Olivia spoke against you?" I asked.

"I didna ken it till yesterday, though I suspected it. Wi' all the evil she's broucht agin' my family, I dinna doubt she had tae make up some curse or anither tae justify hersel'."

"Do you want to hear it?" I asked. I was having a hard time keeping my indignation from boiling over at how Ranald had been treated.

"Div ye ken it yersel'?"

I nodded. "I made Alicia tell me."

"Aye, then, I ought tae ken't. Gien we're gan tae brak the ill thing, we maun ken what we're battlin' agin'. Aye, tell me, Marie, lass."

"Now I don't *want* to. I feel foolish for allowing myself to listen. It's too horrible. I don't even want to say it."

"We maun bring it intil the licht," said Ranald. "Only licht can drive oot the darkness. Haena fear, lass—trowth's nae bothered by a few words o' the de'il's."

"All right, then," I said, "here it is—'*The curse of madness will be the stain, of all who enter the house of Bain.*'"

Ranald listened calmly, then sat several moments, whether in prayer or deep thought, I could not discern. Slowly the light of righteous anger flared in his eyes and he stood.

Even as he rose to his feet, a torrent of indignation poured forth from his mouth. The words were in a tongue I did not recognize, but it sounded earthy and ancient. I sensed myself in the presence of an Old Testament prophet calling down doom upon a city of sin.

"*A teanga a' diabhuil mhoir, tha thu ag dèanamh breug!*" Ranald cried in a deep voice of outraged power. "In the name o' the Father o' Jesus Christ, I break the curse spoken agin' this hoose where dwell the people o' God! I send the foul words back whence they came, tae be consumed in the fire o' hell wi' the de'il an' all wha consort wi' his evil ways."

His outburst was so commanding that I listened with wide eyes of awe. I had never in my life heard such a thundering outcry against evil or the devil. As quickly as it had come, it was over.

Silence again reigned.

Calm but spent, Ranald resumed his seat in the chair. He sat for some time breathing heavily and deeply.

Chapter Thirteen

Music in a Storm

Mirk and rainy is the night,
no' a star'n in a' the carry;
Lightnings gleam athwart the lift,
and winds drive wi' winter's fury.
—"O! Are Ye Sleeping, Maggie?"

Neither Ranald nor I said a word for many minutes.

Something had passed. A calm descended. The anxiety I had felt since yesterday gradually dissipated. A change had come. Without putting it in so many words, I realized that whatever effect may have lingered from Olivia's words had been broken.

Strange to say, perhaps they had been broken from their power to infect *me* more than Ranald. I had only just heard Olivia's curse. Yet overnight and on the walk up the Din, they had played enough tricks on my brain to make me begin believing them.

Gradually, as we sat, for the first time since Alicia and I had set out twenty-four hours earlier, I remembered why I had wanted to visit Ranald Bain in the first place.

At length Ranald rose and walked almost methodically to the stove and poured out water for tea.

"What can you tell me about Iain's leaving?" I asked, rising and following him.

The question didn't seem to surprise him.

"Ye'll be meanin' the *why* o' his leavin'?" he said.

"That, yes...and everything—how long he'd been planning it, where he's gone."

"I dinna doubt ye can guess the *why* well enouch."

"You mean, because of Alasdair and me...he was thinking of us more than himself?"

"Gien ye ken Iain Barclay as weel as I think ye do, ye'll ken there's nae a selfish bane in his body."

"Of course—I do know that. But that he said nothing...did not say good-bye to Alasdair and me, said nothing to us of his plans...It took us both completely by surprise. We were stunned when we went to church and found a stranger in the pulpit."

Ranald smiled as we both returned to our chairs with hot cups of tea.

"I canna say I was athegither taken by surprise at the turn o' the thing," Ranald said. "The lad paid me a number o' visits o'er the course o' several months leadin' up tae the weddin'. I had an idea he was thinkin' aboot some kin' o' change or anither."

"He didn't tell you?"

"Nae in sae many words."

"What about before he left?"

"He came for ane last visit. That's when he told me he had decided tae leave Port Scarnose, that a supply minister was bein' sent fae Edinburgh tae attend tae the affairs o' the kirk, an' that he'd contact me in time when he was settled."

"But where is he? Where did he go? Did he accept another church somewhere?"

"I dinna ken, lassie," replied Ranald. "He told me tae gie his best an' kindest regards tae ye an' the duke fan I saw ye. As for anither kirk...that I dinna ken, nor whaur he gaed."

"I can hardly believe he didn't tell *you.*"

"He thocht it was best."

I let out a sigh and sipped at my tea. I didn't like it, but I thought I probably did understand. The past being what it was, and with Alasdair having at one time thought I was in love with Iain, I was pretty sure I knew what Iain was thinking—that Alasdair and I needed to establish our new life together without any possible relational issues, past, present, or future.

The thought that I might actually never see him again was a blow. But I began to recognize in Iain's decision the loving sacrifice of one friend for another.

I had been paying no attention to the weather outside. But as it now fell silent again, I became aware that the storm had increased in intensity. The wind was blowing a fury. I heard no rain as yet, but a downpour seemed bound to erupt any second.

"I had better start for home," I said, rising from the chair. "Otherwise I am going to be trapped by what looks like a nasty rain."

"I dinna like tae see ye walkin' back doon in this," said Ranald. "But it luiks tae be a storm that, ance it breaks, it—"

He didn't finish his sentence. A burst of light flashed in the windows. It wasn't more than a second later when a mighty clap of thunder exploded. It seemed to rock the whole house on its foundation, though it may just have been my leaping out of my chair.

Instantly the skies emptied. Ranald's slate roof echoed with the downpour, which the wind confirmed by slashing it against the windowpanes as if God were outside heaving bucketfuls of water on the house.

"I dinna think ye'll be walkin' doon the Bin onytime soon." Ranald chuckled. "Wadna surprise me gien that blast hit up at the top o' the Bin. I jist hope naebody took it intil their heids tae hike it today."

I sat back in my chair and finished my cup of tea. No cozier place could have existed in the midst of such a violent storm than Ranald Bain's warm stone cottage on the slopes of Crannoch Bin. Though I hadn't planned to spend the whole day here.

"When ye're ready, lass," said Ranald, "I'll drive ye doon tae the castle. But first perhaps ye'd consent tae playin' a tune or twa."

"Only if you will join me." I smiled.

That was all the encouragement Ranald needed. He was into the next room in less than a minute, busily tightening his bow and tuning up his fiddle. I followed and sat down at his grandfather's old harp, which I had grown to love almost as much as my own. We had played so much together by now that the music flowed between us.

One of us would lead into a familiar tune, "Charlie Is My Darling" or "Lochnagar" or whatever it might be, and the other would simply follow. As one song ended, a few chords of the harp or a few runs up and down the neck of Ranald's fiddle would lead almost of its own accord into another, until without even planning it we were both playing again. No experience can compare with playing with another whose music you know almost as intimately as you do your own, on two instruments whose sounds intertwine so effortlessly they seem that they are being played by a single master hand.

After an hour or so, we took a break, had another cup of tea and some oatcakes, then got out Ranald's old book of Scottish tunes. I made him sit at the harp and play for me so that I could observe his progress on *my* chosen instrument. I had never attempted to give him "lessons," so to speak, only enough pointers on technique to enable him to progress on his own. He had *music* within him, which was the most important ingredient of all. He would never be able to make the harp live in the same way Gwendolyn had. But considering his late start and that it had been only about two years since I had restrung his harp and he had begun playing, he was doing exceptionally well. So well, in fact, that I had already begun to hatch a plan in my mind for us to put together a program of Scottish music, not only with my harp and his fiddle, but also with our two harps playing together along with the ladies. In the meantime, I had begun to arrange a few pieces for that purpose.

For today, however, after a short time on the harp, Ranald returned to his violin and we resumed as before.

The rain continued to pour down. By midafternoon I realized I needed to get back, letup in the weather or not. I didn't like Ranald having to drive me down the hill, but there was little other choice. It wasn't merely the thought of getting soaked if I tried to walk, but the fact that every possible route between Ranald's and the castle would by now be a stream rather than a path.

Music always seeks its own rhythms and cadences, especially melancholy Celtic music. The melodies and harmonies in Ranald's cottage began to ebb, then gave way to a prolonged diminuendo that slowly faded. Our fingers obeyed the invisible impulses that had been guiding them, and both instruments fell silent.

I drew in a deep sigh of contentment and sat listening to the rain pounding on the roof. God's music replaced mine and Ranald's as a fitting coda to the afternoon.

"Hae ye finished writin' oot the music tae the wee lass's sang?" asked Ranald at length.

"'Gwendolyn's Song'...not quite," I replied. "As often as I listen to the recordings, I cannot altogether succeed in replicating it on a page that captures the sound. A magic existed in those tiny fingers that may never be heard any other way than with Gwendolyn's own recordings."

"She was aye God's gift tae us a'."

"I cannot help wondering what might have been—for her and Alasdair—had she lived."

"Aye. But the Lord sent yersel' tae the duke in his time o' need. Wi'oot yer comin', the lass may ne'er hae kennt her daddy. An' noo ye're there tae gie him the love that she can only noo gie him in his memory."

"Why is life so sad, Ranald?" I asked.

"'Tis in sadness we turn till oor Maker."

"Why only then?"

"It isna *only* then. But the times o' sadness an' loss are particularly weel suited tae the buildin' o' the kin' o' character God's tryin' tae get intil us. Ye lost yer first man, I lost my Maggie an' my Winny, the puir laird lost his first wife an' noo his dochter. But we a' are growin' intil sons an' dochters o' the Father, an' that's aye the best o't."

"I hope you're right," I said thoughtfully. "And I hope Alasdair will recognize God's work in him and around him, too. I want him to be complete in every way."

"Gie the lad time, Marie. God's nae through wi' the makin' o' him yet, nor wi' me or yersel', for that matter. As lang as God's at wark, we can trust him wi' those we love. Oor eyes dinna see tae the end o't."

Again we sat listening to the rain. I fell into a reverie and began to doze.

Suddenly out of the silence came a pounding on Ranald's door. It was so unexpected and loud, it startled me awake and straight up in my chair. In the middle of weather like this, who could it possibly be?

Ranald leaped to his feet and hurried to the door.

There under the overhang of the porch, in his greatcoat and dripping oversized hat, stood my husband! Behind him next to Ranald's garage sat the BMW.

"Alasdair!" I exclaimed as I came toward him.

"Duke...welcome tae ye!" said Ranald. "Come in oot o' the doonpour—ye've come tae rescue yer lass, I'm thinkin'."

Alasdair took off his hat and coat and hung them on the peg outside the door.

"Rescuing my lass was only one of my errands," he said as he followed us inside, "though I am glad to see you safe and warm," he added to me. "I would have come up sooner or later anyway had the rain not let up. I know you love to walk in the rain, but this kind of weather is where I put my foot down!"

"I wasn't about to attempt it in this!" I laughed. "But what do you mean, 'anyway'?"

"Is Miss Forbes with you?" asked Alasdair.

"Alicia...no. Why?"

"She's been gone from the castle for hours, probably about as long as you. I made several calls; I even drove over to the market in town, but no one's seen her. I don't know why, but for some reason I became worried. Call it premonition. I decided to drive up here, hoping she was with you, and to rescue you from the rain at the same time."

"No, I haven't seen her since I left the castle," I said, concerned. "That was hours ago. What happened?"

"Nothing, maybe," replied Alasdair. "I don't know. I just had a funny feeling. I got home and saw your note and thought nothing more until lunchtime. Usually if you are gone, she asks me if I would like her to fix me something. One or the other of you is always pestering me about food. It's a wonder I don't weigh three hundred pounds, Ranald," he added with a laugh, "the way these women keep trying to shove food into me like stevedores loading a grain ship!"

"Just trying to keep you happy, my dear," I said. But when I glanced at Ranald, he wasn't smiling.

"I assumed she was with you, until Nicholls asked me if I'd seen her and said he *didn't* think you and she had gone together. The rain had just begun, and after an hour I became concerned. After two hours I went out to search for her . . . and here I am."

Before either Alasdair or I had time to conjecture further, Ranald was hurriedly brushing past us on his way to the door, throwing off his shoes as he went. As he opened it, a rainy blast flew in at us. He grabbed his rain boots and sat down on the bench just outside his door and tugged them onto his feet.

"Come, Duke . . . lass!" he called through the open door. "We must be awa'. We haena a moment tae lose!"

By the time Alasdair and I walked to the door and I had my coat on, Ranald was already bundled up and hurrying in the downpour toward the BMW.

"Ye'll hae tae drive, Duke!" he called back to us. "We haena time tae get the auld Maestro warm."

We ran after him. I jumped into the backseat. The two men sat in front, and we were soon creeping down the narrow gravel road back toward the main road as fast as the dreadful conditions would allow.

"Where are we going, Ranald?" I asked from behind. "Why are you so worried? Is it about Alicia?"

"Findlater, lass," Ranald replied "'Tis aye the lass I'm feared for. I only pray we are nae too late."

Chapter Fourteen

Fright at Findlater

Now welcome, ye dark stormy clouds that benight me,
Welcome ye ghosts of the good and the brave;
The pibroch's loud summons no more can delight me,
My song be the wild winds that sweep their lone grave.
—Alexander Maclagen, "Prince Charles's Farewell to Flora"

We reached the A98. Alasdair turned east onto the main road and quickly sped up. In three or four minutes we were through Crannoch and again racing along.

Three miles out of town Alasdair slowed, then turned off the road and wound his way along several single-track lanes through cultivated fields. We stopped at last where the road ended at what was called the Mains of Findlater. Immediately Ranald was out of the car and half running, half walking in the rain toward the muddy path through ripening barley, now under more than an inch of water, that led to the promontory overlooking Findlater Castle.

Alasdair glanced back at me with a look of question.

"I don't know what this is all about," I said, "but I'm going after him."

Alasdair opened the door and began to get out.

"Why don't you stay here and keep the car running and warm," I said. "You're not dressed for it. At least I've got on hiking boots."

"Be careful, then . . . both of you," said Alasdair as I got out. "That cliff is treacherous in the best of conditions!"

I nodded, then shut the door and hurried after Ranald. The wind

whipped my coat and hair into such a frenzy it was all I could do
to keep him in my sights. I hadn't even bothered with my hat. The
rain was slashing down at a forty-five-degree angle straight into my
face. I sloshed along, trying to run, but the footing was so difficult
in the mud it was all I could do to keep to my feet as I stumbled
forward.

It was probably two hundred yards from where we had parked to
the overlook. Ranald was halfway there by now. He had the footing
of a Highland goat!

I kept wiping my face, but my hair and nose and ears and finger-
tips were dripping as though I were standing in a shower. Ranald's
hat blew off his head and came flying toward me.

As I drew nearer the promontory ahead, I could faintly make out
through the frenzy of mist and rain a second figure standing overlooking the wild, turbulent sea. I recognized Alicia.

By the time I was close enough to see clearly, Ranald had stopped
and was standing about ten feet from the ledge. I hurried to his side.
I heard his voice faintly in spite of the wind. I knew he was praying.

The moment he saw me beside him, he began to inch forward
again. I followed his lead until we were both about five feet from
her back. He glanced toward me and gave a nod.

"Alicia," I said. "Alicia, it's Marie. I've come to take you home."

For a moment nothing happened. The rain and wind whipped
and lashed at us. For the first time I saw how dangerous the situation
truly was. Beneath our feet lay muck and mud. Alicia stood at the
very edge. The footing was treacherous. The sea below was a frenzied cauldron of gray and white. The wind howled and moaned
among the rocks and along the cliff face and through the ruins of
Findlater Castle down in front of us.

At last Alicia's head began to turn . . . slowly, almost mechanically,
as if she were being maneuvered by something outside herself. Her
face came into view, deathly white and drawn, her eyes wild, almost
vacant. The moment she saw Ranald, her features suddenly came to
life.

"What is *he* doing here?" she said in a low, almost growling voice.

"He has come to help you, Alicia," I said. "He came with me to take you home where you will be warm and safe."

"Help me . . . *help* me!" she spat with derision. "The old fool—he is the reason for the curse."

"We can talk about all that later, Alicia. Don't you want to go home and put on some warm clothes?"

"Not with *him*!" she snarled. "That's why I came, to get *away* from him, to get away from the madness that follows him. This is where I will be safe . . . safe from him . . . safe at Findlater's face."

I shuddered to hear her talk so.

"He was Winny's father," she went on in the strange voice. "He killed her, just like he wants to kill me if he can get his hands on me. It is his curse; he is mad. He is crazy. Get back . . . keep him away from me! *'His evil will betray, keep him away.'*"

"Please, Alicia," I said, "won't you come with me?"

I reached out a hand and took a step toward her.

"Get away. Get back I say!" she shrieked. "Olivia warned me about you. She warned me about everyone who is under the curse, that you would trick me, that you would lie to me, that I must get away . . . that I would only be safe here . . . with Olivia . . . safe where she could protect me."

"Alicia, please . . . wouldn't you like to come home and—"

Suddenly she cocked her head and looked at me with a strangely different expression.

"Who are you?!" she said, a wild look in her eye. "I don't know you. What do you have to do with *him*? Whoever you are, you ought to get away, too."

"Alicia," I began, taking another step forward.

"Stop!" she cried, stumbling back.

Her foot slipped in the mud. In a flash Ranald lunged past me with outstretched hand.

Alicia screamed as her feet gave way. Luckily the onshore gale blew her forward. Had Ranald's two hands not seized her flailing wrists in two viselike grips, she would have slid over and been gone. He flopped to his chest and held her arms for dear life.

"Marie!" cried Ranald. "Grab haud o' my ankles!"

I fell to my knees and clutched his trouser legs.

"Pull, Marie . . . Haud us frae slippin' o'er the edge!"

Ranald wriggled his way backward as I pulled with all my might. But in the mud, and clinging to the weight of Alicia's body half sprawled over the cliff face, all he could do was slip and slide about. Alicia was crying out in terror, yet somehow Ranald managed to keep hold of her wet wrists.

Between the two of us, we gradually inched her legs up and over, then pulled her a few inches away from the precipice. Feeling the ground beneath her legs again, Alicia stopped struggling. As she did, all the life seemed to drain out of her.

I helped Ranald to his feet. He stooped and lifted Alicia into his arms and we began making our way back to the car. Mud hanging from them both, Alicia drooped like a rag doll in Ranald's arms.

We reached the car. Alasdair jumped out and ran to us.

He and Ranald managed to get Alicia into the backseat. I scooted in next to her and wrapped my arms tightly around her. All three of us were soaked and muddy, but no one was thinking about the leather seats now. Alicia was a solid block of ice. Had I not heard her speak, I would have assumed her already dead for hours. Whether she was dead now, that I didn't know.

"Drive, Duke," said Ranald urgently. "The puir lassie's life is hangin' by a thread!"

Chapter Fifteen

Heather Song

I dream'd I lay where flow'rs were springing,
Gaily in the sunny beam;
List'ning to the wild birds singing,
By a falling crystal stream.
—Robert Burns, "I Dream'd I Lay Where Flow'rs Were Springing"

We arrived back at Castle Buchan in eight or ten minutes. Alicia had not moved a hair. Cold and soaking myself, there wasn't much I could do for her other than gently rub her arms and shoulders and try to stimulate a little circulation.

The rain was still coming down in a torrent as we pulled up. I jumped out and ran toward the door, Alasdair followed with Alicia in his arms and Ranald at his side. We hurried upstairs to her rooms, where Alasdair deposited Alicia on the floor of her bathroom then left me.

She was completely limp. It took me ten minutes to get the clinging muddy clothes off her and tossed into the tub. What she needed was a shower, but that would have to wait. I cleaned the mud from her hands and arms as best I could with a washcloth and towel, and dabbed at the splotches on her face, then got her mostly dry and somehow managed to get a robe around her. Then I opened the door to where Alasdair was waiting.

He came in and lifted Alicia and carried her to her bed. I wrapped a clean towel about her hair as he laid her down and we covered her with blankets.

"She's safe now," sighed Alasdair. "I hope she comes out of it."

"What do you think? Is she . . . will she recover?" I asked.

"I don't know," he answered. "Hypothermia wouldn't surprise me, though I don't actually think it's cold enough to kill her in that short a time. She has obviously fainted from more than mere exhaustion. Every inch of her is chilled. Hypothermia at some level would have overcome her soon."

"I wonder how long she had been out there."

"A long time, I imagine. If she walked from here, that's five or six miles in the rain. She could have been out in it as long as you were up the Bin."

"I'll sit by her until she warms up and seems to be sleeping. Right now she's just lying here unconscious."

"That's probably good—I'll bring some water bottles and heating pads to put in the bed with her."

Alasdair returned a few minutes later. We positioned the warm bottles and pads against Alicia's back and feet, then he left me alone with her.

I sat for twenty or thirty minutes. There was no change. Not a muscle moved. But as I held Alicia's hand in mine, I thought I imagined it becoming warmer. It may have only been the heat of my own hand, but I was hopeful.

I gently pulled my hand away and tiptoed from the room, then hurried down to my studio. I picked up *Journey* and carried it back to Alicia's room. Alasdair could have done it for me, but I assumed he was by now probably driving Ranald home. I managed to get the harp to Alicia's room and set it down at her bedside.

I brought over a chair from her writing table, drew in a deep breath, then closed my eyes. I knew of the harp's unique and wonderful capacity to soothe and bring healing. Many musicians use their gifts and instruments in hospitals and care homes with amazing results. I had seen enough to know that any music—and the mystical heavenly tones of the harp most of all—was capable of transcending the conscious mind and penetrating deep into the soul, there to vibrate with the most elemental rhythms of God's life, stirring and waking, giving hope to the hopeless, opening doors in the hardest of hearts, reviving memories, causing the despondent to smile, bringing courage in the face of death, uniting estranged hearts, even reversing disease itself. The power of the body to live, to revive, to hope, to heal, was deeper than medical research could often explain. It seemed there were times that the vibrations of a harp's strings acted invisibly as a musical electrical impulse to stimulate those deep, miraculous life-giving forces and powers within the body into renewed activity in ways no treatment of science could equal nor measurement of medicine account for. I had read cases of coma patients coming suddenly awake, of heart irregularities becoming regular, but more often of the music helping to calm people who were agitated . . . just as when David played for King Saul.

Now it was my own friend lying unconscious in front of me.

Oh, God, I breathed, *I am so small and weak and unknowing, but you know what is taking place in Alicia's mind and body. You made her. You are there with her at this moment. Your Spirit is the life within her. You know what she needs. Please, God, guide my fingers to make your music. Bring Alicia awake. Warm her body with your care and love. Heal her hurts and wounds of soul and whatever torments of mind drove her out there. Make her whole . . . and bring her peace.*

My prayers stopped. I set my fingers to the strings and, as softly as I was able, began to play.

Phrases from one song or another flowed randomly, here a line from a hymn, now a refrain from a Scottish ballad. Gradually I found "Gwendolyn's Song" filling the room with its mysterious melody that I never could seem to get exactly as I remembered it from the fingers of Alasdair's daughter.

Undefined sensations that something was at hand flowed through me as I played, as if I were playing with a great orchestra, playing in some majestic symphony with a thousand instruments and a thousand more voices raised in song. Yet I was able to hear only my own single part in what were enormously complex harmonies swirling about just beyond the range of my hearing. To me was given only my own sheet of music to play and to hear, not the entire score. That I could not hear the other voices and instruments, however, made my participation with them no less vital or real. Gradually as I played, almost as if I were following the guidance of an invisible master composer standing before a vast orchestra, the music from my harp began to change. A melody began to emerge from its strings that I had never heard before. It was majestic and happy, yet, like all Scottish music, set in melancholy tones. Its tune took me deep into the Highlands on a warm August afternoon. All around spread a blanket of luxuriant purple heather stretching in every direction, into the glens and along trickling streambeds and to the highest peaks. Everywhere was heather! It gave off a balm of light and warmth and healing. And over all spread the mysterious sounds of the music, from the tune that had no name.

I continued to play, and the melody went on and on, in new directions that I followed as they came. I knew even as I played that I would never hear them again in the same form. Something almost like Gwendolyn's own playing had come upon me. I played as one being moved by an invisible hand who knew the song and was guiding me through it, even though I did not.

How long I played, I cannot say. Time loses its temporal frame of reference when the music of the spheres takes you over.

However long it may have been, I became aware that my fingers were slowing. My harp was in the process of growing silent again.

At last, with reluctance, I admit, but knowing I must obey the inner impulse of the score even when an extended rest appeared on the page, I withdrew my fingers and the strings quivered away faintly into stillness.

I glanced toward the bed.

As the final harmonies of heavenly vibration evaporated into silence as if in response to the strings' dying sounds, I saw Alicia's eyelids twitch imperceptibly.

After a moment her eyes began to flutter. Slowly they opened.

She stared out for several seconds, seemingly unseeing, then gradually her vision came into focus. She appeared surprised to see me.

"Mrs. Reidhaven...," she said in the softest voice imaginable. It sounded odd for her to use such a formal expression, but I let it go. "What are you doing here... What am I doing in bed?"

"You were very cold," I said. "You were caught in the rain. We brought you back and put you to bed."

"I seem to remember going for a walk. That's right, it began to rain... Yes, it was very cold."

"How do you feel now?" I asked.

"I am still cold. But the bed is cozy, and..."

She paused and a strange light came into her eye.

"What is it, Alicia?" I said.

"I had the most wonderful dream," she said wistfully. "At least I think it was a dream. It must have been since I am lying in bed. But it seemed that I was somewhere else, that I had gone to another world. Wherever it was, it was like this one yet also very different. Would you like to hear the dream?"

"Yes, I would... very much."

"I was on a walk, just like I really was," Alicia began. "I don't know what made me go out. Something had frightened me, I think, but I cannot remember what. I was trying to get away, to get somewhere safe. Someone told me I would be safe if I got there, but I cannot remember where. It was a long way."

She spoke softly from the bed, almost as if she were still half asleep.

"Then it began to rain... very hard, but I kept going. It did not occur to me how foolish I was for going out without a coat or hat or umbrella when the sky was so blustery and black. But that's how dreams are. I was not thinking very well. It was a long way to where I was going, but I had to get there. It was the only place to be safe and escape the fear. But when I got there it wasn't safe. It was even more terrifying than what had frightened me. I was cold... very cold. I didn't know what to do. I was paralyzed between the two fears. I remember standing in the rain, the cold, cold rain . . . standing for what seemed hours and hours . . . so cold I could feel nothing at all.

"Then I heard voices—strange and confusing voices. I could not understand what they were telling me. I was too cold to think, too cold to understand. By then I was not walking anymore, only standing in the cold. I seem to remember falling, or maybe falling asleep for a time. Then the rain stopped, and slowly the confusing voices faded. I was walking again. But everything had changed. There was no more rain or wind or cold . . . I was walking with heather at my feet. I was happy, like a child in a snowfall. I was happy to be in the midst of so many tiny blossoms around me as far as I could see in every direction. The most wonderfully exquisite aroma filled the air. I know heather has little smell, but in my dream it gave off the most intoxicating perfume of roses and violets and carnations and gardenias.

"Then gradually as I walked I became aware that the perfume was coming from the faint sound of music in the distance. I know music has no more fragrance than heather. But in a dream all your senses mix together. And in mine as the music filled my head, so, too, did a fragrance of peace and healing and warmth. I was no longer cold . . . and the music made whatever I had been afraid of disappear. I kept walking, but instead of trying to escape the fear behind me, I was trying to get closer to the music. I was barefoot I think. I was walking through fields of heather. But instead of scratchy prickles, it was cushiony and soft, like fluffs of cotton beneath my feet. Maybe I was walking on *clouds* of heather and that's why it was so soft. Maybe I was dead and in heaven and having a vision—"

Alicia stopped and turned her head toward me.

"*Do* you think I was dead, Mrs. Reidhaven?" she asked in a child-like voice that contained no hint of anxiety. "I feel very strange, as if something that has been inside me for a very long time, for years and years, is gone. I feel different than I ever felt before."

"In what way?"

"I don't know...I cannot describe it. I think it feels good. But I cannot be quite sure—it is too new."

"I do not think you were dead, Alicia," I said. "I have been with you for some time, and you did not look dead. You were cold, but breathing."

"Well, no matter...Maybe I was half dead, if that is possible. Wherever I was, I kept walking on the fluffy heather clouds, and the music gradually became louder and louder. Then I came over the top of a hill and suddenly saw spread out in front of me beyond a little glen a huge orchestra on one side of the opposite slope. There were so many instruments that they extended up the slopes of a great hillside as far as it was possible to see. There must have been a thousand or more...maybe ten thousand. Never could such an orchestra be imagined! And opposite them was a vast choir, just as huge. They were all playing and singing together the most beautiful song that anyone has ever heard. It was like a song that could only have been composed in heaven. No one but the angels, or maybe God himself, could think up such a wonderful song. Maybe that's why I thought I was dead. And though there were so many instruments and people, the music was soft and resonant, full to overflowing with something different than loudness...It was full with quiet resonance. It was music that went into me through my heart, not my ears.

"At the very top of the hill stood the conductor of the vast throng, conducting softly, gently, with tiny movements. To the conductor's right sat the largest section of instruments of all—a hundred harps of every conceivable size and shape and color and kind of wood. There were harps as huge as buildings and tiny harps no larger than a violin. Some were tall and thin, some wide and stout...black, white, natural wood of all shades of brown and tan. There might have been two hundred...or a thousand harps; from where I stood I could not tell. And over the whole orchestra they spread their lovely tones of peace. Now that I remember it, I think the perfume of the music was coming from the harps, each of the harps a different flower in a vast, fragrant music-garden.

"I stopped and stood listening...just listening. No, it wasn't *listening*, exactly, because it would all have been no different even if I had been deaf. I would have heard the music just the same. I stood *absorbing* the music, with all my senses absorbing the sight and sound and magical perfume of the music. As I did, I felt life and strength welling up inside me. I felt strong and happy and free and full of peace.

"As I stood, I saw the conductor step down and walk down the hill between the orchestra to the right and the choir to the left. The music continued as she descended and gradually came toward me, and then I saw that the conductor was a woman. Or perhaps a girl...or an old lady...I could not tell which. Age meant no more there than music you could smell and heather that felt like clouds of cotton beneath the feet. *Everything* was different there.

"She came toward me. A peaceful, knowing smile was on her face as if she knew me and had gathered the orchestra and choir and composed this majestic symphony all around us just for me, because she had been expecting me. I seemed to recognize her faintly, though I cannot be sure.

"She approached with the most radiant expression, as if light itself were pouring forth out of her face.

"'The song is for you,' she said. 'I made it to send away your fears, so that you could be free from the past, and be whole.' She stooped down and plucked a sprig of heather from one of the plants at our feet.

"'You are loosed from fear of the past,' she said. 'If the voice that once enslaved you returns, remember the healing and strength-giving perfume. And say whenever fear assaults you: *"God's light is the fragrance of a musical throng, To banish evil on winds of the heather song."'*

"She handed me the heather, then turned and began walking back to her orchestra, then lifted her arms toward them. As she did, I noticed two protrusions on her back, just below the shoulder blades.

"'Wait,' I said after her. She paused and looked back.

"'What are those strange growths on your back?' I asked.

"She gave a musical little laugh. 'Those are my wings,' she said. 'They are not very big yet, but they will continue to grow the longer I am here. I am becoming an angel, you see . . . but it takes a long time.'

"'Will I remember the song?' I asked.

"'Some songs are like sunsets,' she replied. 'They are meant to get inside you just as they are, for what they are. They are meant to accomplish that for which God sent them, not to be saved except in the memory of quiet gratitude of God's peace. If the fragrant song of the heather fades like a dying sunset, give thanks that you have partaken of its wonder. Do not mourn its passing.'

"She turned and again walked away. Again she lifted her arms in a triumphant gesture. The music suddenly changed, and now for the first time increased greatly in volume and began a magnificent climax. Somehow I knew that it was because a battle had been waged and a victory won.

"Then I noticed that the conductor-lady had red hair. But I had no time to ponder it, for the next moment the great climax of the orchestra faded and all that was left was the sound of a single harp, and it began to wake me . . . and the music from the one harp was coming from somewhere else, faintly . . . very faintly, as a voice from afar. It was a voice I recognized, a kind voice, a voice of goodness, not the voice from before that had filled me with fear. And words came with the music of the one harp, and they were saying, *Whatever you find noble, lovely, kind, and pure, Think on these things, and fear and heartache cure.*

"The words made me happy and filled me with contentment. And something left me that had been inside me for a long time. It was fear, I think. And I was at peace.

"And my waking continued . . . and when I opened my eyes there you were beside my bed, with your own harp. Was it your music I heard all the time, Mrs. Reidhaven?"

"I don't know, Alicia," I replied in a husky voice, blinking hard. "Maybe some of mine, and . . . maybe someone else's mingled in with it. But don't you think I should be Marie to you again, without the *Mrs.*? We have been very good friends, remember."

Alicia smiled. "I am growing sleepy again," she said, with a look of happy contentment such as I think I had never seen.

"Would you like me to leave so you can have a little nap?" I asked, dabbing at my eyes.

"I think so, yes . . . Thank you, *Marie.*"

Chapter Sixteen

Music and the Word

Through many dangers, toils and snares,
We have already come.
'Twas grace that brought us safe thus far
And grace will lead us home.
—John Newton, "Amazing Grace"

As I left Alicia's room I had to stop in the corridor in a positive gush of tears. The heavenly vision, and even the part in it my own music had played, was so breathtakingly wonderful, I could do nothing but weep in wonder.

Five minutes later, as I recovered my emotions, I was surprised to find Alasdair and Ranald in the sitting room before a blazing fire, engaged in earnest conversation. Ranald's hair was still a little wet, but otherwise he appeared comfortable and dry in a shirt, pair of trousers, and slippers I assumed to be Nicholls's, since I had never seen them before.

"Hoo is the lassie?" Ranald asked, looking up as I walked in.

"She is warming up and sleeping comfortably," I replied, sitting down beside Alasdair. "She woke up and saw me and smiled and seems herself again. She has no memory of being at Findlater."

"The duke's been tellin' me mair aboot Olivia an' her incantations an' sich like as a lassie. The thing's mair serious nor I kennt gien it gangs back intil the generations. We maun be dealin' wi' mair entrenched strongholds than I kennt. 'Tis serious business, that, when it gets intil the generations."

"The *generations?*" I said slowly. "I'm not sure I understand what you mean."

"The root system o' a family's past. Nane o' us comes intil life as an athegither blank slate, ye ken. We are products o' the generations wha came afore us, wi' a' the traits an' quirks an' characteristics an' speeritual sensitivities that hae been bred intil oor family lines for baith guid an' ill. Tendencies, ye might call them. Proclivities tae do an' think an' act in certain ways. Scientists likely hae scientific ways o' explainin' parts o' it wi' genes an' the like. But I wud gie e'en mair credence tae the speeritual tendencies oor ancestors planted in the soil o' oor past. That doesna mean a body *will* follow those tendencies, because speeritually, in a manner o' speakin', we *are* a' blank slates wi' wills an' temperaments an' personalities o' oor ain that we make choices wi'. Nae ither man nor woman's responsible for those choices an' what we make o' that will an' personality than jist oorsel's. But there's forces at wark, too, urgin' noo this way, pushin' noo in that direction, goadin' us here an' there. Some o' those forces an' urgin's are inducin' and encouragin' us toward the licht; it may be fae some gran'mither or grit-gran'father wha spent his or her life on their knees prayin' for their posterity an' infusin' the line o' the generations wi' truth an' righteousness. The life o' sich a ones feeds the soil o' that family wi' ongoin' nutrients o' goodness that bears God's fruit for mony generations after them. But there's ither forces at wark as weel, unseen it may be, dark forces pushin' an' coaxin' toward the ill-one, whisperin' lies an' selfishnesses, inflamin' pride an' arrogance an' anger from anither grit-grit-gran'father or 'mither wha fed only the selfish side o' their nature, or may hae dabbled in the occult, or may hae been a conduit an' open door intil the generations for the warkin' o' some demon or anither—a demon o' gluttony or avarice or greed or revenge or po'er or envy or complaint or mammon. An' ilka ane o' these forces from those that hae come afore, a' mixed up an' warkin' t'gither, are what I call the generations."

"You're not saying we can't help what we do?"

"Nae, nae. We're gi'en oor ain wills an' lives an' circumstances an' temperaments an' the particular soil o' oor ain life's conditions tae make the best o' hoo we're made an' what life brings oor way, an' through it a' tae follow the promtin's toward righteousness, an' tae rebuke an' oppose an' resist wi' a' the strength o' oor higher natures whate'er may urge us agin' it, an' whate'er may whisper tae us tae follow the lower path whaur self is king. Doesna it gie ye a guid feelin' that some ancestor o' yers may hae prayed for ye an' asked the Speerit o' the Lord tae gie ye strength jist whan ye need it?"

"Do you really believe that a prayer prayed a hundred years ago, or even ten years ago, could be answered in my life...now...to-day?" I asked.

"Oh, aye! Wi' oot a doobt, lass," replied Ranald enthusiastically. "Wi' oot a doobt! The arrows o' prayer we launch upward intil the regions o' God's great hert are nae boond by time. Prayers that may hae gane intil God's ear a hundred years syne may be sent back tae earth as his answers in yer ain lifetime jist when ye maist sorely need them. My daddy's faithfulness an' his daddy's afore him, an' my dear mum, wha I can still see on her knees in my memory—I ken they prayed hours an' hours for *me*. Those prayers didna die oot an' become naethin' jist because *they're* noo gang tae be wi' him that made them. Those prayers are *still* in God's hert. An' I believe he's aye luikin' ilka day for chances tae answer them. An' I feel *strength* fae the generations that hae come afore me, an' no' a day gaes by that I'm no' filled wi' gratitude for them, an' that I dinna thank God for the life that's in me on account o' them."

"What does this all have to do with Alicia?" I asked.

"'Tis through the generations that strongholds form," answered Ranald. "Childish mischief may aye cause great ill. But it doesna be-come a stronghold o' evil till it's passed on fae ane generation till the naist. Then the danger is great o' the thing sendin' doon roots that are hard tae dislodge, an' becomin' perpetuated on an' on tae the third an' fourth generations like the Buik says, an' its evil spreadin' oot an' preventin' hundreds an' thousands frae gettin' a' the licht o' God's life inside them."

As I listened, my thoughts went back to my conversations with Ranald earlier in his cottage.

"When you spoke, or prayed . . . or whatever it was you did when you said you broke the curse against your house—what language was that?"

"The auld Gaelic, lass," replied Ranald.

"What was it you said?"

"'Twas an angry ootburst, I admit. I haup it didna frighten ye, lass. But the de'il angers me when he twists up folk tae believin' his lees. What I said was, *'Ye lying tongue o' the de'il.'*"

"And the rest, when you said, I think it was something like, 'I break the curse against my house and send it back to the fires of hell'—was that a prayer?"

"Nae in so many words. But when ye're conductin' the Almighty's business in sich realms, 'tisna always easy tae tell ane kin' o' speakin' till him fae anither. In a manner o' speikin', I was speikin' *for* the Lord, no' exactly prayin' *till* him, an' takin' his authority tae break the curse in its tracks. But though I may hae broken't for yersel' an' me, it didna break it in the lass Alicia's mind. 'Twas still haudin' her in its grip, an' I haena doobt that's what sent her oot intil the storm that way, for they say, ye ken, that the de'il's the prince o' the po'er o' the air, an' gien e'er he was makin' mischief wi' God's wind an' rain, 'twas today oot at Findlater. I was feared we wud lose the lass."

"But why didn't what you said help Alicia? It almost seemed to make it worse."

"It may hae dune jist that, lass," sighed Ranald. "Sometimes when ye stir up a sleepin' nest o' the de'il's handiwork, where he's had a free hand for a lang time, an' ye stir up his demons, they're like wasps an' they dinna like it, an' they fight back 'cause they ken their end is nigh. So wi' the brak'n came loosin's in the speeritual realm that we may no' hae anticipated. They were fightin' tae keep control o' what they kennt they were aboot tae lose. 'Tis a dangerous time

o' speeritual warfare when the forces o' evil are unleashed. An' the
puir lassie hersel' wasna yet ready tae join in the battle. She wasna
yet wantin' tae break the curse. Fear o't still held her in its grip. A
body's got tae *want* tae be rid o' the de'il's mischief in their life afore
they can come agin' him wi' po'er."

"You said the curse of *fear*?" I said.

"Aye. Wasna really a curse agin' me that Olivia had spoken, but a
curse o' fear in the hearts o' those wha believed it. A curse spoke as
Olivia spoke it, in God's realm, comes back onto the heids o' those
that spoke it, an' on them that believed it. Her words couldna harm
me. But luik at the misery they've brought Olivia hersel' an' the likes
o' Alicia, puir lass. The curse was the *fear* it put intil her, wasna ony-
thing aboot me."

"Just now, as I sat beside her bedside and played my harp, when
she woke up, something had changed. She was calm, at peace . . . as
gentle as a child. She said she felt fear leaving her."

"I'm aye happy tae hear it!" exclaimed Ranald.

"Why the change, do you think, Marie?" asked Alasdair.

I told them about Alicia's dream. By the end of it I was crying
again.

"That is absolutely remarkable," said Alasdair. He was also close
to tears.

"There's mony a way tae break the de'il's po'er," said Ranald.
"Sounds like in this case as gien yer music an' the words o' the Buik
must hae gotten intil her an' made her want tae break free hersel'."

"What words from the Book?" asked Alasdair.

"In her dream, she turned the words from Philippians 4:8 intil a
rhyme. It must hae been her min' bringin' Olivia's tactic o' rhymin'
intil the licht."

"Ah, right—the Bible, you mean." Alasdair nodded.

"'Tis a wunnerfu' thing what the min's capable o' when it's
pointed toward the licht. She turned the method o' Olivia's curses
on its heid jist like she was fightin' it wi' the po'er o' Scripture. Guid
for the lass! E'en in a dream, she was takin' up the fight!"

"What does the verse in question say?" Alasdair asked.

"'Tis one o' the most soarin' thoughts e'er tae flow frae the great Apostle's pen," replied Ranald, his eyes aglow. "Whate'er be true, whate'er be honorable, whate'er be just, whate'er be pure, whate'er be lovely, whate'er be gracious, gien there be ony excellence, gien there be onythin' at a' worthy o' praise, think aboot these things.'"

"What a lovely verse," I said. "But where would Alicia have gotten those words to come into her dream? I don't recall ever seeing her reading a Bible."

"Nae doobt frae Iain," replied Ranald. "'Twas ane o' his favorite passages. He quoted it mony a time fae the pulpit. She must hae heard it fae him, an' it must hae lodged in her subconscious tae lay there in readiness tae do its healin' wark fan the time was richt. The words o' the Buik's miraculous wi' their po'er tae heal. The music fae yer ain wee harpie, an' the words o' the Buik nae doobt fae Iain himself, bless the laddie, haunted her thoughts e'en in her sleep. Then God took them up as his weapons tae pull the dear lassie oot o' the dark!"

We all sat pondering the remarkable turnaround that had apparently taken place in Alicia.

Chapter Seventeen

Ancient Passing of Power

Braver field was never won,
Braver deeds were never done;
Braver blood was never shed,
Braver chieftain never led.
—Alexander Maclagen, "We'll Hae Nane but Highland
Bonnets Here"

I went down to the kitchen and prepared hot tea, toast, cheese, and a few meats and brought them back upstairs on a tray. By now dusk was settling in. The storm still raged. Alasdair had added several logs to the fire, which was blazing up cheerily, and had convinced Ranald to stay the night at the castle. His chief concern was for his dogs. But, he said, if they got hungry, there were rats to be had in the barn.

I brought in one tray, returned for the second, and we sat down to an enjoyable light tea.

Ranald remained animated and determined to get to the bottom of what had happened.

"There's still mair mischief afoot," he said as we chatted over our tea. "The roots o' the thing maun gang back deeper yet. Is there ony-thing mair ye can tell us, Duke, o' yer family? There's tales o' an auld gran'mither, as I recall, wha had the po'er o' the second sicht. I'm wunnerin' gien that's whaur some o' Olivia's nonsense came frae."

Alasdair became thoughtful. He related to Ranald the story about the visit he and Olivia had made to their grandmother on Skye that he had told me about before we were married.

I snuggled closer to Alasdair and put my hand through his arm as I heard the story again. It was just as spooky as the first time.

"I was frightened the instant I laid eyes on the old woman," Alasdair was saying. "I knew she was my grandmother, but that made no difference. She had things hung around her neck and bracelets around her thin wrists. From that day till this, witches and snakes have filled me with an unaccountable dread."

"No' athegither unacoontable, Duke," said Ranald. "Ye may hae had ilka reason an' right tae be unco feared oot o' yer young wits. Ye may hae had mair a discernin' speerit as a lad nor ye kennt."

"She was ancient beyond years," Alasdair went on, "wrinkled and white. We were five and six at the time. She took to Olivia immediately."

Ranald nodded occasionally as he listened, taking in Alasdair's story with obvious interest. His expression was serious.

"Was yer mither wi' ye at the time, Duke?" he asked after some time.

Alasdair nodded. "I don't recall her saying so much as a word, however. I think she was as intimidated by her mother-in-law as I was."

"I dinna athegither like the soun' o' the thing," said Ranald. "It may be as I suspected. The auld woman may hae been the purveyor o' the stronghold frae ane generation tae the ither. The thing begins tae bear some o' the marks o' a feminist speerit. 'Tis aye an ill one tae break on account o' the pride o' a woman's no' an easy thing tae contend wi'. 'Tis deep-rooted in the Scots blud all the way back tae the Picts wha chose their kings frae the line o' women, no' men. The warrior-lady Boadicea was fae the same speerit o' Salome an' her mither wha cost the good Baptist prophet his heid. Wasna athegither uncommon among ancient peoples—some o' the American Indians had the same matriarchal custom in connection wi' their kings. Sich a controllin' speerit's been the curse o' true womankind e'er since, an' the doonfall o' mair nor one people, no' tae mention Rome an' Pictland. Yet nae e'en Salome or Herodias was the start o' it, for we mauna forgit auld Jezebel hersel', wha was the curse o' Elijah. The thing gangs back as far as time itsel', which is why 'tis sich a ill curse tae break. The aulder the stronghold, the deeper its roots. But we maun ken mair afore we ken gien that's aye a' o' it. What happened wi' the auld woman, Duke?"

"Not much, actually," Alasdair replied. "Nothing so frightening as all the talk of witches and demons and goblins and wolves, as Olivia later used to terrify me."

"Did the lass keep the object ye speik o' that the woman gave her?" asked Ranald.

"I can't remember. I think she may have brought it home, now that you mention it. Seems I remember it in connection with some of her voodoo games."

"Div ye recall ony o' what the auld woman said, Duke? Think hard, gien ye can."

"Not when she was talking in the old tongue. It was completely unintelligible. But after a while she began talking to Olivia in rhyme, though I had the sense she wasn't really talking to Olivia, but almost... It seems strange to say it, but she seemed to almost be pronouncing a blessing or a benediction or some such thing over her."

"Aye... aye." Ranald nodded seriously. "I haena doobt she was passin' on a line o' po'er oot o' her druidic past, jist as it had come doon tae her. The speerit o' matriarchy's aye ane o' the maist difficult strongholds o' the generations tae break. It gits entrenched in the soil o' a family's line like a taproot o' control, an' it doesna want tae let loose o' that control, an' will fight like auld Jezebel hersel' tae keep haud o' it, an' woe tae ony man that dares stand agin' it, for then it'll unleash the hatred o' Salome an' Herodias an' do a' in its po'er tae destroy him. Puir auld John wasna the enemy o' King Herod. Nae, nae—the king wasna his problem, but the *women*. John set himself tae expose the speerit o' their control, an' paid for his courage wi' his heid. A strong man is the mortal enemy o' the feminist speerit. It canna bide sich a one. What did the auld woman say till the lassie, Duke?"

"I can hardly remember, it's been so many years. To tell you the truth, the whole thing was so unpleasant that I probably blocked it out of my mind."

"Try, Duke. 'Tis important."

"I seem to recall something about the younger ruling the older, though I may be thinking of Olivia. You remember, Marie," he said, turning to me, "how I told you that rhyme about the elder dancing on the younger's grave? I seem to remember Granny saying something like that. Isn't there somewhere in Scripture—a younger stealing his brother's birthright or some such thing?"

"Aye—Jacob an' Esau," replied Ranald, sitting forward in his chair with yet heightened interest, "the twin sons o' Isaac. The words say, *'The twa shall be divided, the ane strang an' the ither weak, an' the elder shall serve the yoonger.'*"

"That's it, Ranald!" exclaimed Alasdair. "That's it exactly. How did you know? That is just what the old woman said. I can hear it suddenly as plain as day. She muttered the words, then pulled out a rosary from around her neck and began to chant strange verse, exactly as Olivia does. Let me see, some of her words begin to come back..."

Alasdair thought a moment, then slowly began to speak.

"*'In our clan, woman rules man,'*" he said. "Yes, that was one of them. Let me see... *'By the power of the tongue, the old serves the young'*...and, *'Let curse be the tool, by which you rule.'*"

Alasdair's face lit up still more and he nodded.

"Yes... it's coming back. The words sound juvenile as I say them, but in her ancient terrifying voice, to the timid boy I was as I stood listening, I thought I was in the presence of a real live witch. The feeling of dread was indescribable. It was as if her words were coming down out of the sky like thunder."

"Or bubbling up from some lower place, in a' likelihood," rejoined Ranald.

"Suddenly I remember a whole string of them," Alasdair went on. "*'Havoc will wreak, from words you speak.'* It's all exactly what Olivia did . . . the same singsong kinds of phrases. I could not rid my brain of them. Look at how I remember them after, what has it been, forty years. And her words portended *exactly* what happened. Olivia wreaked havoc. Everyone was afraid of her. The whole thing is remarkable now that it comes back to me."

"Was Olivia making up verses and speaking hexes and curses before then?" I asked.

"No," replied Alasdair. "It was after the trip to Skye when it all began."

Ranald shook his head. "'Tis an ill thing," he said in mounting annoyance. "The auld demoness!" he added. I could see anger rising in his eyes. "God forgie her listenin' tae the lyin' de'il an' spreadin' the mischief o' her feminine pride tae an innocent lass that kennt nae mair hoo tae fight it than she wud ken hoo tae stop the sun fae risin'."

Suddenly the words of Gaelic I had heard in his cottage exploded from his lips again like a great invective denunciation against the evil powers of the universe.

"*A teanga a' diabhuil mhoir, tha thu ag dèanamh breug!*" Ranald cried. "By the po'er o' God Almighty, Creator o' the heavens an' the earth, may the roots o' the matriarchal speerit be broken o'er this hoose an' its family! Lord Jesus Christ, fill this hoose an' a' wha enter it wi' the licht o' yer life an' po'er, an' may the Father o' Lichts rule wi' his goodness an' truth an' love."

At least I had witnessed the like before and was halfway prepared for it. But Alasdair sat staring at Ranald with eyes as round as plates. He had never seen or heard anything like this in his life.

We sat in silence for a minute or two. The atmosphere calmed and conversation resumed. It was Alasdair who spoke first.

"Poor Gwendolyn had to live with that darkness all her life," he said. "I cannot thank you enough for what you did, Marie . . . for rescuing her." He let out a long sigh. "But why, Ranald, if all you say is true," he went on, turning to Ranald, "was I not permanently scarred by all that devilish business, in the same way Alicia must have been if it nearly drove her to take her own life?"

"The answer may surprise ye, Duke," replied Ranald. "It may be because ye learned tae lauch at it. Ye didna let it *intil* ye—all the way inside yer soul. Olivia's frien's did. They alloo'd it tae take root. The de'il's got nae mair po'er nor we gie him. Ye didna let Olivia's words gie him po'er o'er ye. E'en my ain Winny was guilty o't, an' it cost the puir lassie her life. I dinna doobt there's mair areas o' yer life whaur ye didna hae sae good a time o' it, as is true wi' us a'. But agin' yer auld Granny's mischief, ye battled agin' the speerit wi'oot kennin' what ye were doin', sendin' the words o' Olivia's curses awa' fae ye rather than takin' them intil ye. Ye may had been frightened for a season when ye was yoong, but as ye grew ye learned that she couldna control ye. Learnin' that, ye learned tae lauch fan Olivia's frien's an' many o' the folk in the village were feared o' her. Their fear was their ain doonfall. By fearin' what she said, they embraced her words an' opened the door intil their ain herts for the curse tae enter. Her words took root in them, an' she controlled them. Ye were a speeritual warrior, Duke, e'en as a lad, wi'oot kennin' it. It may hae protected ye from great harm."

"It is difficult to absorb what you say, Ranald." Alasdair laughed. "My reputation has never been as a spiritual giant! Just ask anyone. Ask Reddy Barclay!"

"Gie yersel' time, Duke," Ranald said and smiled. "The Speerit o' God's on a unique timetable o' revelation wi' us a'. Ye may surprise yersel' yet. I ken ye had some difficult years, but it may hae been that the Lord was protectin' ye through those years mair nor ye kennt, an' it may be that lauchin' at yer sister's wiles gae ye a speeritual strength ye didna ken was there, an' that may stand ye in guid stead afore ye're dune."

"I'll have to take your word for that, Ranald."

Ranald cast me a glance and a smile, as if to say, *The man's a' right, lass, an' he'll be wi' us hert an' soul afore lang.*

Chapter Eighteen

Breaking the Spell

For thou hast delivered my soul from death,
mine eyes from tears,
and my feet from falling.
I will walk before the LORD in the land of the living.
—Psalm 116:8–9

Alicia was herself in a day or two.

Actually, she was *more* than herself. She was newly liberated from an oppression she had not even realized had hovered over her all her adult life. It could not be helped that things began to change with the other ladies as well.

As the Thursday of the next ensemble meeting of my little group of harp ladies drew closer, I sensed that something was weighing on Alicia's mind. It was she who finally brought it up.

"Do you mind if I ask you a question, Marie?" she said.

"No, certainly not... Go ahead."

"Do you think I ought to tell the others... you know, about everything that happened, that you now know about Olivia and her strange ways, and the curses and hexes... about my dream and everything? It's been plaguing me. I don't know what they might think. Adela especially is still devoted to Olivia. She would do anything Olivia told her."

"I had no idea they were still so close."

"I don't know if *close* is exactly the word I would use. But if I told them everything, it would not surprise me if she was on the Bluebird the next morning into Aberdeen to give Olivia a full report."

"What would Olivia do?"

"I don't know, maybe contact the others and resume her tales about you and the duke, and now include me and try to discredit me as well. Ever since I went to work here at the castle, I have been on the outs with her anyway. This would give her the excuse she needs to attack me. It would be subtle, of course. That's Olivia's way—she is a master of subtlety and innuendo. Nothing so obvious as her childhood hexes as she passed a house of someone she didn't like. Her methods have become much more skilled through the years, and even more devious."

"Does the thought of it frighten you?" I asked.

"A little, I suppose. She is a formidable person. But I am tired of living under the cloud of fear of her."

"Good for you—I am glad to hear it, Alicia. That was the whole point of the dream, wasn't it, that you felt yourself free from fear?"

Alicia smiled and nodded. "But Olivia's hold on my thoughts is so powerful. It's been there so long, it is hard to break free from it."

"But you are breaking free. And you are glad, aren't you?"

"Yes, I really am. But it doesn't go away all at once. So do you think I should tell the others?"

"That will have to be your decision, Alicia," I replied. "All I can say is that light and truth are always the way forward. Do you want to live in light, where things are exposed and out in the open and seen for what they are, or in darkness, where things remain hidden—as you called it, under a cloud?"

"I think you've helped me answer my own question." Alicia smiled. "You're right—Olivia's way was secrets, threats, shadows, uncertainties, fears, insinuations. No, I don't want to live in that murky world where you never know which way is up."

I hoped it wasn't duplicitous, or, if it was, it was justifiably so, to bring Alasdair in on what Alicia planned to do. Because of his initial doubts about the ladies coming to see me, and after our little dustup in the corridor, I wanted him fully aware of what was going on in Alicia's attempt to break the bonds of Olivia's influence. I mentioned to him the possibility, if he thought it appropriate, that he might listen in—very quietly!—on our ensemble music from the other side of the room divider, from where he had first heard my harp. Sort of a command performance in reverse! I would have preferred to invite him to participate openly. He was as much a part of the whole thing as any of the rest. But with him present, I was afraid the others would only clam up.

When Thursday came, Alicia was agitated but eager, nervous about what would be the response, but still convinced it was the right thing to do. It was the next step forward, we both agreed, in the healing of the scars of the past.

We had our harp ensemble practice, then Alicia came into the studio with tea and cakes. I looked toward her. Our eyes met with a smile.

"Alicia has something she would like to share with the rest of you," I said, "something she believes represents an exciting change in her life, but which may be the last thing you expect."

From my buildup, I think they thought she was about to announce that she was engaged or something!

Alicia poured tea for everyone, then sat down. The others waited expectantly.

"It is hard to know where to start," Alicia began at length. "Marie and I went for a walk two or three weeks ago, up Crannoch Bin. It was the day before the big storm. A lot of things happened. I don't know how else to say it but that I became confused and went out in the rain. I know it sounds bizarre, but I really believe I lost my mind for a few hours. I became so possessed by fear—fear of Olivia and her words and her threats and all those awful verses and rhymes she always said. I hadn't realized what a hold they still had on me and how controlled I had been by them. It was a dreadful day. I nearly wound up taking my own life."

A few shocked expressions went around the room.

"I have Marie to thank," Alicia went on, "and someone else—they literally saved my life. *Literally* . . . I mean it. Since that day Marie has helped me begin to put all that behind me, to break free of the fear of the past. It feels like the sun is coming out in my life for the first time. And though I don't want to speak ill of anyone, much of it has been because I have at last come to see Olivia as she truly is—as a controller and manipulator of us all, as one who is completely self-motivated. She never really cared about us at all. She had to have power over people, and we helped give it to her. We were not true friends to her or even to one another. We were enablers. We were weak and powerless, and she held us in her grip with all her threats. Even her hexes toward everyone else—people who had never spoken a cross word to her in her life—were directed as much at us as at them, to keep us so afraid of her we would do her bidding and would never question her. She was mean and cruel. We all knew it. But none of us spoke up. We went along because we were afraid not to. Maybe I was afraid of the rest of you, too, I don't know. But now as I look back, I am ashamed that I had so little backbone. I can't help thinking about Winny, too, and . . . if I'd had more courage, she might—"

Alicia choked momentarily and was blinking hard. She sniffed and wiped at her eyes, struggling to continue.

"I don't know about any of the rest of you," she said. "Maybe you all broke free from it years ago, but I am only now realizing for the first time the bondage I have been under to Olivia's control. And now I am breaking free from it, and I have to tell you that it feels good. I am so sorry for my own part in it all that may have made it harder for the rest of you."

She stopped and took a deep breath. The stunned silence that filled the room was almost deafening.

I hoped Alasdair didn't cough or rustle on the other side of the divider!

It was quiet a good long while. At last Alicia gave way to her tears. She cried without shame and blew her nose several times. Cora was the first to speak.

"I haena told a soul aboot it," she said timidly, "but I had what may hae been a similar kin' o' experience mony a year syne. I went oot walkin' an' then I fell into a trance like, almost like I was sleep-walkin', though I dinna ken aboot that. An' when I came tae mysel', I was at the veery edge o' the cliff o' Findlater wi' Olivia's words ringin' in my lug, div ye mind hoo she said, *'Welcome, O deith, thy warm embrace, on the cliff at Findlater's face.'"*

At the words, this time it was Alicia who gasped. I glanced over. Her face was white as a sheet.

"I had forgotten those words!" she said. "But they were in my mind that day, too—urging and goading me on, almost as if Olivia herself was beside me whispering them into my ear, telling me the only way I would know peace was to go to Findlater's cliffs."

That was all it took. Within minutes the four women were talking and sharing furiously, as if the floodgates of twenty years had been opened. Doubts and fears they had each kept to themselves and borne in silence were suddenly exposed to the light of day. All except for Adela. She contributed nothing to the discussion. Tavia, Fia, and Cora, it turned out, all had had remarkably parallel experiences and were no less eager than Alicia to be free of the bondages from the past. No one brought up the fact that none of them had ever married, nor questioned whether Olivia's influence and tendencies of feminist power and control—to use Ranald's description—might be at the root of their own distant and confusing relationships with men.

The instant rapport of free, tearful, heart-gushing and liberating sharing was wonderful to behold. I knew old wounds and scars and doubts and guilts were being healed before my very eyes. Before they left, the five agreed to meet the following day at the Puddle-duck in Crannoch for lunch. They were kind to invite me, but I declined. It was best they help one another sort out their feelings without me.

When the ladies were gone, I crept around the tapestry divider into the other side of the sitting area. The room was empty.

I went in search of Alasdair. I found him in his study. He was sitting at his desk staring out the window, obviously lost in thought. I walked in and sat down. He turned to me, and the expression on his face told me that he had been there at least part of the time.

"How much did you hear?" I asked.

"The music." He smiled. "It was positively lovely. You've done a masterful job with them in such a short time. You really are a gifted teacher. Listening to the way you talk to them, encourage them, and are able to draw their gifts out of them—listening to you *teach* is as wonderful as the music itself. It was truly amazing. It really is a gift, isn't it?"

"I hope so," I said, returning his smile. "Thank you, Alasdair. That's one of the nicest things anyone has ever said to me."

"It's true—I mean every word. And the music, too, was beautiful. Not *quite* so lovely as that I heard the first time a harp was played in this room, back in my 'Eleanor Rigby' days. But you are right—more than one harp together, even in the hands of relative beginners, is magical."

"It is wonderful to see the music of the harp expanding," I said. "That is my dream—for more and more people to learn to play. That is what I hope will be my contribution to the harp world— expanding awareness and teaching as many as possible to take the music out with them into their worlds, where it will continue expanding and influencing lives, like a pebble thrown into a pond rippling outward in its ever-widening effect . . . touching the lives and working to heal the hearts of people I will never know. Did you hear anything *else?*" I asked.

"A little," replied Alasdair. "After how Alicia shared—after that, I can no longer think of her as *Miss Forbes*—and then the others began . . . I realized I should not be there. They were speaking from such depths that I had no right to listen in. So I crept out."

"I didn't hear you leave."

"I was very careful. Picture an elephant on tiptoes! But even the little I heard was healing for me, too—to realize that I wasn't alone. Those poor ladies, I feel bad for them. And by the way, I am sorry, my dear, for overreacting the other day when they were here. I was wrong to jump to the conclusion I did. I completely misread the situation. Please, forgive me."

"Oh, Alasdair—of course!" I said. I walked to him and put my arms around him where he still sat and leaned my head on his shoulder. "I understood... At least, the more I am learning about what you all went through, I am *beginning* to understand. Hopefully all that will now be behind them, and you."

The ladies got together almost every day for the next week, though Adela was not always with them, rekindling on a new footing their long-dormant friendships. Whether Adela did in fact take the bus into Aberdeen, neither Alicia nor I ever knew.

Our ensemble "lessons" for several weeks hardly produced a note of music. There was so much the ladies had to talk about and learn and see in a new light, the sessions turned out to be more of therapy than music.

"Marie, you should hang up a sign in your studio," said Tavia one day after several tearful confessions and hugs and tissues scattered all over the floor, "'Harp Lessons, Counseling Services, and Inner Healing Sessions.'"

Everyone laughed.

But she wasn't far wrong.

Chapter Nineteen

The Bin...Again

Away in the Hielands
There stands a wee hoose
And it stands on the breast of the brae.
Where we played as laddies
Sae long long ago,
And it seems it was just yesterday.
—M. MacFarlane, "Granny's Hielan' Hame"

I knew Alicia would not be completely over what had happened when she and I went out the day before the storm, and with what had transpired on the cliffs of Findlater, until she was able to meet Ranald Bain face-to-face and could be comfortable in his cottage. To truly be broken, Olivia's phantom curse had to be broken within *her.*

After several weeks, after two more summer storms had blown through and another dry spell had set in and the ground had mostly dried out, I suggested another walk up the Bin.

She nodded. "Do you think I am ready?" she said.

"I do. But it's your call."

She drew in a deep breath of resolve. "I would like to," she said. "I need to find out if I am at last master of my own fate. If I am still afraid, then Olivia has still got her hooks in me. I have to find out, so let's go."

It was mostly quiet as we retraced our steps from the earlier walk. It was truly a pilgrimage of sorts for Alicia, maybe a little like coming to Scotland the first time had been for me. When we came out of the woods, rather than taking the same route to the summit that

127

we had before, Alicia headed straight into the meadow where I had first encountered Ranald. A few sheep were grazing, and the barking of dogs as we climbed over the dyke told us that Ranald himself was not far away. In another minute we saw him walking toward us, sheep and dogs surrounding him, the dogs bounding about playfully.

"Guid day tae ye, lassies!" he shouted while still some distance away.

I waved and we continued toward him. He approached and we slowed.

"Hello, Marie," said Ranald, "an' greetings tae ye, Alicia, lass. I'm aye glad tae see ye again. 'Tis been mony a lang year."

"Hello, Mr. Bain," replied Alicia, then held out her hand. "Thank you for saving my life."

I could tell it was a hard thing for her to do, far more than a mere gesture. She did not want to shy away from what she knew she must do. Ranald took her hand, clasped it a moment, then shook it twice softly and gently.

Alicia looked up into Ranald's face and sheepishly smiled.

"I am sorry about before, Mr. Bain," she said. "I was confused and afraid. I said terrible things. I am truly sorry."

"Think nae mair aboot it, lass," Ranald replied. "'Tis o'er an' past, jist like the sin o' the worl' will vanish in the licht o' God's eternal Sun. We're a' pilgrims on the road, an' we a' stumble fae time tae time. But gien God doesna luik back, nae mair should we. I'm haupin' ye ladies hae time tae bide a wee an' come ben the hoosie for a drap o' tea wi' an auld shepherd."

"We would be delighted," I said.

Ranald turned and led us toward his cottage, chatting with me as we went so that Alicia could watch and listen and grow comfortable in his presence.

"An' hoo's the duke, Marie, lass?" asked Ranald.

"Just fine, thank you," I replied. "Busier than ever and to all appearances loving every minute of it. He visits with most of the farmers in the community regularly and even lends them a hand whenever they let him. He has never enjoyed hard honest work so much."

"An' yer harpie ladies?"

"They are doing well. I am anxious for you to hear them."

"A' in guid time, lass."

As we walked into the cottage, I saw Alicia hesitate momentarily, glancing above her at the roof and ceiling, almost as if she were entering a den of danger. I knew Olivia's words were going through her head. She kept on bravely, resisting them, and, in the very act of walking through the door, sending away their power to hurt her again. The moment we were inside, she brightened. A fire burned on Ranald's cookstove almost as if he had been expecting us, a thin wisp of steam rising from the spout of the kettle sitting on top of it.

"A drap o' tea an' then hoo de ye fancy a wee bit o' music? 'Tis been awhile since the auld wife an' the harpie made melody thegither."

"What's an auld wife?" asked Alicia.

"That's what Ranald calls his violin." I laughed.

"I didn't think you could be talking about your wife, Mr. Bain."

"Nae, nae . . . she'll always be my Maggie."

Alicia glanced down and a serious expression came over her face. "I am sorry about your wife, Mr. Bain," she said after a moment. "And Winny, of course. I don't think I ever told you what a good friend she was. I still miss her, but I'm sure not nearly as much as you. It must be very hard."

"There be times, I winna deny't, fan the tears come upo' me unbidden. But I ken they're thegither an' happy, an' I'll join them soon by-an'-by. Sae I dinna greet lang. God is guid, an' that's aye the end o' a' things. His guidness swallows my sorrows, an' I rest content. After a', this wee cottage, nor this whole worl', isna my hame . . . I'm jist bidin' here a wee while."

We visited with Ranald for two hours, had tea and oatcakes and made music, and Alicia thoroughly enjoyed herself. By the end of that time she was clapping along to our music and laughing and even singing now and then to a familiar tune. She had the most lovely deep, throaty alto voice I had ever heard.

Suddenly Ranald set down his violin and ran into the adjacent room. He returned a moment later with two swords. He laid them on the floor perpendicularly across each other. The next instant the violin was back on his neck and a rousing jig exploded from it. He looked at Alicia with a grin.

"Oh, Mr. Bain, it's been years!"

"As I recall, ye won mair nor one ribbon at mair nor one Hieland games wi' yer twa wee feet atween the swords."

"That was thirty years ago, even more!"

"Nae Scots lassie forgits the fling. Yer feet'll de the rememberin'. Show oor Canadian frien' the duchess hoo Scots lassies learn tae skip lightly through the heather."

He began the music again. Reluctant but beaming, Alicia took her place at one of the four sword-corners and then, on cue from Ranald, began to leap on her toes in the familiar dance of the Highland fling. Whatever she might have lost from the years certainly escaped me. I was speechless to see how high she jumped, how effortless the movements ... the pointed toes perfectly skimming her calves in rhythm ... like a ballerina at a barn dance! I began to clap in time and Ranald whooped and hollered, and by the time Alicia made her way around all four squares of the swords, she was panting and laughing like I had never seen her.

She crumpled into a heap on the couch, laughing with delight and exhaustion, while Ranald and I applauded and praised her blue-ribbon effort.

"Wud ye ladies like a ride doon the hill?" asked Ranald as we prepared to leave some time later.

"I think I would like to walk," I said. "What about you, Alicia?"

"I'm fine with that."

"Then I'll gie ye what's better," said Ranald, "a Scots conveyance."

Alicia burst out laughing. "I haven't heard that expression in years!"

"What's that," I asked, "a special kind of ride?"

"'Tis a walk hame in the company o' yer host," replied Ranald, walking across the room and taking his cap from a peg on the wall. "Or at least—halfway hame."

When we said our good-byes to him awhile later on the lower slopes of his own meadows and then continued our way back toward the castle, it was obvious that a friendship had begun and that one more root of Olivia's influence was broken.

Alicia told the other ladies about our afternoon at the "house of Bain." I suggested that one or another of them might like to accompany us sometime. The idea met with mixed reviews. I did not push the matter. I did, however, continue to drop periodic hints that I intended to invite Ranald to join us one day with his harp. I wanted them slowly to become accustomed to the idea without pressing it before they were ready.

Meanwhile, summer at last gave way to autumn. Leaves fell, the wind grew chillier. A faint hint of coming snow in the air could occasionally be detected. The songs of the birds subtly changed. The translucent Mediterranean blue of the coastline gave way more frequently to menacing grays and deep cold, sinister greens. The sudden dousings of rain for which Scotland is infamous were occasionally laced with a few peltings of hail.

The advent of the cold weather turned my thoughts toward an advent of another kind—the Christmas season. The ladies were doing well enough on the harps by now that I pulled out my holiday music and began teaching them four or five Christmas pieces. Alicia and I had driven to visit a harpmaker near Glencoe, another in Aberdeen, and a third in Edinburgh. As a result of our investigations and my trying out a number of different instruments, I ordered two more floor-size lever harps, which I hoped would arrive sometime in the middle of November. My plan was to organize a community Christmas concert, with all four of the ladies and myself on large harps, but also to invite other local musicians and groups, such as the renowned Duncan Wood Quartet from Milton, to join us. I had privately already given Ranald the same Christmas music we were working on so that he could participate with us.

At last, in early November, I made plans to drive up the hill—in my own new car this time—to pick up Ranald and his harp and bring him to the castle to join us for the Thursday ensemble as we prepared for the Christmas program. His appearance was met a little skeptically at first. But the warmth with which Alicia embraced him in front of the others went a long way toward breaking the ice.

As well as did the Christmas music itself. Who can listen to Christmas music and not be happy?!

As we worked our way through "The First Noel," with Ranald fingering the high notes of the counter melody I had taught him, most lingering reservations about him vanished. Music is healing by its very nature. What could be more healing than music about the Lord's coming to earth to heal humanity from its sin?

I asked Ranald if he would like to host the rest of us at his cottage the following Thursday. He consented eagerly. And so it was that our two cars made their way up the winding road, loaded down with our harps—alas, the *Queen* had to stay behind!—and music stands and benches. It took a little longer in Fia's case to break free of her reservations. She wasn't at all certain she liked the idea of going to Ranald's house. But as Alicia had discovered, Ranald was a delightful and entertaining host whose engaging warmth no one, not even Olivia's former friends, could resist.

Most of them, that is.

With Ranald's participation at the castle still fresh, the day after I announced that the ensemble would meet at his cottage, Adela telephoned to say that she would be discontinuing her lessons and that either I or Nicholls could come round to collect the harp at our convenience.

It was a sad turn of events, though now Fia was able to graduate from the *Ring* to the *Shamrock* while I awaited the delivery of the two new harps. The next day Alicia asked, since the *Ring* was now available, if she could begin learning on it. Naturally I was delighted.

The others were concerned about Adela. But none wanted to turn back from their own newly energized pilgrimages of growth and wholeness. In some cases, sad to say, spiritual growth requires leaving friends behind. But all growth in life must be forward. To remain still is in fact stagnation and regression. I had been in that danger myself several years before. Adela was making a conscious *choice* not to move forward with what life had to offer. Her friends and I could only hope and pray that a time would come when she would make the choice to leave her past behind.

One of the wonderfully unexpected consequences of Ranald's increasing involvement in the lives of the ladies, and his weekly visits to the castle with his two instruments, was a deepening friendship between Ranald and Alasdair. They had obviously known each other all Alasdair's life, and had enjoyed a relationship of camaraderie and increasing mutual respect during the years of our marriage. But now something deeper began to blossom. It is possible, I suppose, that on both sides the departure of Iain Barclay created a void that the other was able to fill. Yet there was more to it than that. It would have been different, perhaps, had Iain still been in the area, but I think it would have happened regardless. For reasons I was never quite able to identify, Alasdair recognized in Ranald a wisdom he could learn from, even at such a mature stage in his life. But he did not merely recognize wisdom, he wanted to *partake* of it—a unique quality in the world of self-sufficiency in which men often dwell. The hunger to grow and change and learn and *become* more than they are is not usually part of the masculine makeup. It is not always part of the feminine constitution either, as evidenced in the case of Adela. The relationship I observed between the two men I can describe only as between a mentor and a protégé, between an aging man of wisdom and a younger man in his prime, hungry and eager to glean all he could from him.

This realization on Alasdair's part had a subtle spiritual component, as *any* relationship with Ranald must develop eventually. Ranald's entire existence was bound up in a thoroughgoing awareness of *spirit* life. But their new friendship was at first not *primarily* spiritual. Alasdair was not what I would call a spiritual seeker. At the same time, obviously connected with my own spiritual rebirth and growth of recent years, Alasdair was interested in my spiritual development and *open* to spiritual influences. Looking past the externals of his humble garb and unimposing station in the world, I think he came to recognize in Ranald a man of years and stature whom he could respect on many levels. It was not that he was reluctant to glean spiritual food, so to speak, from me because I was a woman and his wife. Not at all. He was wonderfully accepting of my faith and my own maturity as a person. He often asked questions about things that came up, even decisions concerning the estate. He gave weight and respect to my responses. If ever a man treated a wife as an equal, even ahead of himself, as *more* than an equal when it came to spiritual things, that man was Alasdair Reidhaven. He was truly a *humble* man.

At the same time, in the same way that women need other women to talk to and share with and pray with and with whom they can explore what their womanhood means, men also need other *men* with whom to explore and develop their manhood together. In that process—perhaps more than do women, though being a woman I'm not *sure* of this—men need other men whom they can look up to with respect, whom they can learn from and whom they know are looking out for them and praying for them, men to energize and stimulate them in the right directions toward truth and wholeness, men who will help them see things in the right light, men who have been through the same manly struggles and understand the same manly thoughts and emotions and hardships, men to laugh with and cry with and question with and work with and be silent with . . . and with whom they can discover life's meaning.

Mentors . . . friends . . . comrades.

All this Alasdair began to discover with Ranald Bain. At first they simply talked and visited when Ranald came to the castle. Gradually those conversations lengthened and became more substantive. Before long Alasdair was driving up the hill to visit Ranald on his own. Those visits became more involved. Alasdair helped Ranald with his next sheepshearing and had as much fun, he said, as he had helping the farmer Leith harvest his fields of grain. Afterward, with the oil from the wool mixed with the occasional stain of sheep's blood on their hands and arms and messy clothes, they had laughed and talked until dusk. From Alasdair's mood when he returned well after dark, I knew that he'd had one or two too many Stellas. I was glad he made it down the hill in one piece!

Despite twenty-five years or more difference in their ages, Ranald truly became Alasdair's best friend. Ranald filled the vacuum that had been left by Iain's move. Yet it was more than that. Being of the same age and with a lifetime of a mixed and occasionally turbulent relationship—involving not one, but *two* women!—I wonder whether it would have been possible for Alasdair to receive the full measure of spiritual mentoring from Iain that he was now deriving from Ranald. The question was moot anyway. Iain was gone.

More and more as time went on, I knew that Ranald and Alasdair were talking about serious things, life things, eternal things, God things. Ranald was being for Alasdair what I could never be. I was delighted for him.

The relationship went both ways. I could tell that Ranald was equally stimulated to have a man-friend in these years of aloneness since the loss of his wife, a man to romp the meadows below Crannoch Bin with, to chop wood with, to look for a lost sheep with, to enjoy a lager with, to reflect on hard questions with and share doubts and frustrations with, to be serious with when the time came for that as well. I was as pleased for Ranald as I was for Alasdair. When I saw them together, and saw the occasional look of manly affection that passed between them, my heart glowed.

Alasdair became the son Ranald had never had. Even more than a son of childhood, he was a son of strong and vibrant manhood with whom Ranald could share not mere sonship . . . but *friendship*.

Chapter Twenty

Happy Christmas in a Minor Key

The auld dial, the auld dial,
It tauld how time did pass;
The wintry winds ha'e dang it down,
Now hid 'mang weeds and grass.
—Lady Nairne, "The Auld Hoose"

After my acceptance of his proposal of marriage, Alasdair had taken me on a long drive to discuss many things. It was then he revealed that Gwendolyn's illness was congenital and that in all likelihood she had inherited it from him.

He explained that it hit hardest in the early teen years, as was the case with Gwendolyn. However, he went on, if one thus afflicted arrived in reasonable health to the age of twenty, at that point the chances became good that he or she had escaped the worst, and would live a long and healthy life. He wanted me to know, however, that in some cases symptoms resurfaced at forty-five or fifty. He had himself shown few symptoms as a child and had been but nominally affected during his late teens while at Oxford. His personal health history and Gwendolyn's could not have been more different. Nevertheless, he wanted me to know the state of affairs. I must not marry him, he insisted, without full knowledge of the potential implications.

As is often the case, love tends to blindly ignore such cautions. So did I. I told Alasdair that even if he had but a year to live, I would marry him just the same.

He was obviously happy, adding that he had every intention of living to a ripe old age and growing gray with me.

As it turned out, however, my words rather than his were those that carried the ominously prophetic note.

The first signs I noticed of things not being quite right came that third winter we were together as I was preparing my harp group for our first Christmas program, and coping with their variable responses to Ranald Bain as the newest member of our ensemble group. I couldn't call them harp "ladies" now that we were integrated!

As the cold of that winter set in, Alasdair often became chilled. Nothing could get him out of it. He wore layer upon layer of underclothing and sweaters and jackets, but still shivered most of the time. His headaches, always something of a problem, increased, both in duration and severity. The doctor prescribed migraine medication. That helped somewhat but did not eliminate them. He simply wasn't himself.

The Christmas party at the castle, however, was a wonderful diversion from my concern over his condition.

I don't know whether it was that he sensed perhaps he did not have many more Christmases left, or whether it was a continuation of his desire to be fully available and accessible and a part of every aspect of community life, viewing Castle Buchan as the possession and heritage of *everyone* in the community. Whatever the case, Alasdair was determined to invite—literally!—everyone in the twin villages of Port Scarnose and Crannoch to a lavish Christmas celebration at the castle. I had no more than mentioned my Christmas harp program in October and he immediately began making plans for five hundred or more guests.

"Where will we put them all?" I laughed. "The castle won't even hold five hundred people!"

"Don't be too sure of that, my dear," Alasdair rejoined confidently. "The place is huge. We will stuff them in every nook and cranny! Let them fill the castle and grounds to overflowing. Hey, I've an idea!" he exclaimed suddenly. "Oh, this will be brilliant! We'll use the church—with Curate Gillihan's permission, of course. Then we'll open the old tunnel that goes underground from the castle to the church!" he teased.

"I thought all that about the tunnel was just a legend."

"Perhaps it is a *true* legend...dark and cobwebby and full of dead men's bones!"

"Ugh, Alasdair! I'm not sure I like the sound of that. Bones... yuck! Whose bones would they be...I mean, *if* the legend were true?"

"I don't know—old monks who died, Catholics killed by the Covenanters...Covenanters killed by the Catholics. All I know is, as a boy I was terrified that I might stumble upon a human skull in the darkness of the castle somewhere, and trip and find myself lying on the floor with two vacant eyeholes staring at me from six inches away. Then Olivia would run away with the lantern and leave me not knowing the way out."

"Do you think a tunnel really does go under the basement of the church?" I asked.

"It is certainly part of Castle Buchan lore. The legend says an old burial crypt lies beneath the church—but who knows if it is true. The floor of the church has been sealed over for centuries with great slabs of stone, with enough former lairds and dukes buried beneath it that no one has ever seriously proposed excavating it. The disruption and controversy would be enormous. You'd never get permission from the authorities anyway. The whole notion of an underground crypt may be a legend that emerged out of the fact that there were people buried beneath the present floor. On the other hand, the present church is probably the third structure built on the same site since the first chapel was founded in the twelfth or thirteenth century. Who is to say one of those earlier buildings didn't have a crypt that was covered over when the present church was built in the early 1500s? As for the tunnel, it is well known that originally Castle Buchan had a monastery attached to it. All I know is that Olivia frightened me to death with her grisly ditties. I asked my father about the tales once. He just said that the tunnel between castle and chapel had been blocked up centuries ago, then scolded me for wanting to tamper with the ghosts of the past. The monks who had once occupied the castle, he said, and used the passage to go back and forth to the church, deserved to rest in peace. He said he knew nothing about it and advised me to adopt the same policy. But Olivia couldn't resist all that ghostly kind of thing. It was in her blood ever after we made the visit to Skye. She positively thrived on stuff about crypts and burial vaults and bones and dungeons. All right, I've succeeded in convincing myself . . . It's a stupid idea to try to find the tunnel for the Christmas party!" He laughed again. "But we'll still invite everyone."

And we did! By word of mouth and by great posters placed in the town squares of Port Scarnose and Crannoch. Throughout all the month of December, the party was all people talked about. Alasdair also sent out invitations to many from the aristocracy throughout Moray and Aberdeenshire whom he hadn't seen in years.

The great Castle Buchan Christmas Celebration was scheduled for December 23. It snowed on the twenty-first, then a massive high-pressure cold front moved in off the Atlantic, bright, fair, windless . . . and freezing! More than freezing! The brilliantly clear skies, with temperatures in the teens at night and low twenties through the five to six daylight hours, ensured that four inches of snow still lay on the ground as the morning of the twenty-third dawned. It sounded even colder to track the weather in Celsius—from minus eight to minus four! It never even came close to the zero mark!

We might not have room to fit everyone comfortably, but fit them we would—somehow . . . somewhere. The years of distance between himself and the people were over. Some of Alasdair's closest friends were now the local farmers and shopkeepers and what few fishermen were left, as well as sheepherders from the slopes of the Bin. By midafternoon he was already having the time of his life, getting himself ready for the evening's festivities in his full Highland regalia and kilt.

The guests began arriving between four-thirty and five. Normally

by then it would have long since been pitch black. But the clear
skies kept the dying reds of the sunset twenty or thirty minutes
longer than usual, and the sky, full of emerging stars and a half
moon overhead, contributed enough light for most to walk to the
castle. By six the castle was bulging to overflowing. It could not have
suited Alasdair better. He was the perfect host, enthusiastically welcoming every guest at the door with handshakes and backslaps and
a jovial word of personal greeting. It continually amazed me that he
knew everyone's name.

An extensive buffet and tea was set out in the ground-floor
Great Room as well as the formal dining room. It started off with
Cullen skink, cock-a-leekie soup, and Scotch broth, followed with
big bowls of haggis, platters of goose and pheasant, steak and kid-
ney pies, and mounds of Scotch eggs and kippers. Then came the
desserts—or "puddings," as they called them. The buffet tables were
cleared and refilled with Christmas and plum puddings, trifle, clootie
dumpling and sponge cakes. Pitchers of double cream sat beside
every dessert. The rooms became so crowded and loud that it felt
like a church potluck and community social and carnival rolled into
one. Many attempted to venture outside with their cups of tea and
loaded plates, but the cold kept the flow as sort of a revolving door
in and out, and many gathered in the entry hall or sat on the steps
of the grand staircase with their tea and plates. No one minded the
tight quarters or bumping elbows, or the occasional tea splash onto
trousers or dress. The boisterous close press of happy humanity was
part of the evening's charm. I don't know what some of Alasdair's
highbrow titled friends thought about mixing so close with common-
ers, but Alasdair obviously thought it was great.

As strains of music began filtering down the grand staircase
shortly before seven-thirty, a gradual drift upward to investigate en-
sued. That relieved the pressure of the crowd around the long buffet
tables. While some remained behind to enjoy another round or two
from the lavish spread, dozens, then a hundred, then two hundred
began to swarm upstairs toward the Grand Ballroom, where the

Duncan Wood Quartet was already in fine fettle and threatening to steal the show from my small orchestra of harps.

Ranald joined in on his violin for several numbers. Before I knew what was happening, furniture was being scooted aside, and suddenly the ballroom was alive with a hundred men and women dancing Scottish jigs and reels and strathspeys to the most rousing music imaginable—from Corn Rigs to Petronella to Strip the Willow and the Dashing White Sergeant and so many other dances that everyone knew as well as their multiplication tables. I had never seen anything like it—a gorgeous display. Everyone was singing along. Those who weren't dancing swayed and clapped with the music. If anyone forgot the words to any of the songs, all they had to do was stand next to Danny Cook and they would soon come back to memory.

As the dancers swept gracefully about the hard-oak floor, the quartet was joined in turn by Alexander Legge and John Simpson on their pennywhistles, Tom Johnston and Brian Slorach on their accordions, James George Addison and Alan McPherson crooning ballads in tenor duets, and Alex Hay and Leslie Mair drowning everyone out with their dueling bagpipes.

Meanwhile, I scurried my ladies away to the Music Room—sans dividers—of my expanded studio. We set up our harps and music at the far end where we practiced on Thursdays, then brought in all available chairs to the sitting area. When we were ready, I returned to the ballroom. When Duncan finished the dance in progress, I went to the front and held up my hands. Gradually something resembling a quieting took place.

"I would like to announce that in the Music Room at the eastern end of the north wing, several ladies and I—and Ranald Bain, if we can urge him to join us—will be playing an assortment of Christmas music on our harps. You are of course free to remain here enjoying Duncan's entertainment as well. 'Something for Everyone' is our motto!"

I turned back to Duncan and gestured for him to continue. Before

I was even out of the room and on my way back, another dance was in progress.

For the next hour or two, both concerts continued simultaneously. Luckily the Music Room and the Grand Ballroom were almost completely kitty-corner from each other in the castle. While the atmosphere in the Music Room, with people gradually coming and going, was not exactly quiet enough to hear a pin drop, it was sufficiently conducive to the peaceful music of the harps. The ladies and Ranald performed wonderfully and surprised even themselves. Nearly everyone in the community had known Duncan Wood and his talents for years. But the harp ensemble was something new. Most went away suitably impressed and, I hoped, touched by the music.

So it was that the three separate venues—the buffet in the Great Room, the quartet and dancing in the Grand Ballroom, and an evening of carols with harps in the Music Room—absorbed what was probably a greater crowd by double or triple than had ever been witnessed within the stone walls of Castle Buchan.

By ten the crowd began to thin. Hot cider, more tea, makings for hot toddies, and enormous bowls of eggnog were announced, resulting in a general exodus back downstairs to the Great Room. The quartet packed up their instruments, having put in a rigorous evening's work. Another half hour or forty minutes of harp music followed to a standing-room-only audience. Now that the dancing feet were stilled, most sang peacefully along to our music. By eleven, weary and happy, a more general exodus toward the front doorway on the ground floor began.

Alasdair could not resist the opportunity to address his departing guests. Bundled in scarf, hat, gloves, and as many layers as would fit under his greatcoat, he crunched out onto the snow-covered lawn and turned toward five or six hundred faces clustered in the castle entryway and drive.

"I cannot thank you all enough for coming tonight," he began. "You have made this a joyous Christmas for Marie and myself, and probably the most memorable Christmas of my life. You are all our family, and we consider this your home as well as our own. We hope you consider it such as well. I want to thank Duncan Wood and his quartet—"

Cheers and applause burst out for the local musicians.

"And my dear wife and her group of harpists—"

More cheers and clapping.

"And all those men and ladies from the parish church who helped tonight with food and drink. And now . . . it is cold, and we are all freezing our ears and noses off, so I shall detain you no longer. Only long enough to say that we love you all, and to each and every one of you a joyous and merry Christmas, and may the New Year bring you happiness, prosperity, and good health. Good night, everyone."

A great round of applause went up again. Alasdair was swarmed by handshakers and well-wishers.

From somewhere a voice began to sing "Angels We Have Heard on High." Instantly the entire throng joined in. It was followed by "The First Noel," "O Come, All Ye Faithful," and "God Rest Ye Merry, Gentlemen." What had been a move to depart for home changed to an additional twenty minutes of caroling in the cold and dark. The crisp air made the women's high harmonies clean, precise, perfect, and exquisite, and the deep base of the men's resonant, clear, and strong. No man-made acoustics can compare with the acoustics of God's air on a cold Christmassy night.

Gradually, as "Joy to the World" came to an end, a few began making their way along the two roads, the one leading to Crannoch, the other to Port Scarnose. Most of the crowd now followed, gradually flipping on their battery-torches, as Alicia—for she was the mysterious voice leading into each new carol—began "In the Bleak Midwinter." The two streams of walkers slowly diverged through the trees to the departing words of the haunting Christmas lullaby.

As the song drew to a close, for a few moments silence reigned. Then softly, someone among the Crannoch walkers softly began to hum, a week early it is true, "Auld Lang Syne."

The rest from both groups gradually joined in. The great Scots anthem continued over and over all the way, long after the walkers and their gently bobbing flashlights were out of our sight. Standing in the open door of the castle, we could still hear the sounds thirty minutes later from the revelers, apparently in no hurry to reach their homes, in stereo under brilliantly clear skies. The haunting strains seemed to rise into the night air from the two communities separated by a mile in those closing minutes before the midnight hour when Christmas Eve Day would officially begin.

When at last we closed the door for the night and climbed the stairs to our apartment a few minutes after midnight, Alasdair nearly collapsed from fatigue and exertion. He slept fourteen hours—through half of Christmas Eve Day!—in happy exhaustion. He talked about nothing else for weeks, but he was in bed for most of a week himself.

What a memorable night, and memorable happy Christmas that followed. We didn't make it to the Christmas Eve service at church, but we heard the singing from across the wall, and especially enjoyed listening to the children's recorder songs.

It was not long afterward when Alasdair gradually began to lose weight, which could be accounted for by no change in his eating habits. Ordinarily this would have been a good thing. He was too heavy and knew it. But that it was taking place involuntarily caused Dr. Mair and his new young assistant concern. Gwendolyn, too, was a little stout when I first met her, but she had thinned noticeably toward the end.

As the warm weather returned the following spring, Alasdair did not improve.

At Dr. Mair's request, we flew to London for a battery of tests. The only result was confirmation of what we feared—that the lymphomatic condition that had taken Gwendolyn's life had emerged from its long dormancy in her father, and that, unless it reversed itself naturally, the prognosis was not optimistic. Nothing could be done but wait. The disease went in waves, we were told. If Alasdair could make it through this newly active phase, it might again lapse into dormancy for another ten or twenty years. They suggested a sort of chemo treatment as an experiment, but really offered little hope.

Alasdair was calm, even cheery in the face of the news. He insisted that he was feeling better every day. He handled it far better than I did, I'm afraid. His main concern was for me, not for himself.

We returned from London to Scotland and made great plans for the many things we wanted to undertake through the summer—more footpaths through the precincts of the estate, a renovation of a nineteenth-century summerhouse between the castle and the shore, along with its underground tunnel to the beach. Originally called "the temple," the circular domed structure was now overgrown and virtually inaccessible from the woods.

Chapter Twenty-one

A Fright

Sing on, sing mair o' thae auld sangs,
For ilka ane can tell
O' joy or sorrow i' the past
Where mem'ry lo'es to dwell;
Tho' hair grows gray and limbs grow auld,
Until the day I dee,
I'll bless the Scottish tongue that sings
The auld Scotch sangs to me.
I'll bless the Scottish tongue that sings
The auld Scotch sangs to me.
—"The Auld Scotch Sangs"

Summer came on. Alasdair and I celebrated our third anniversary. We got the temple project and several of the memorials under way. Workers were busily engaged everywhere, and the people of both villages were in high spirits. This one corner of Scotland at least enjoyed full employment. Any local man or woman capable of wielding a shovel, ax, hammer, saw, masonry trowel, or wheelbarrow had no shortage of work that summer. Ranald was at the castle nearly every day, helping both as laborer and as a sort of unspoken clan chieftain and bard over the work.

It was a warmer year than usual. This helped lessen the chills from winter. Alasdair said he felt fine. The worst of the illness had passed, he insisted. He remembered a brief bout when he was at Oxford. He recognized the signs of improvement. The worst was over. He could tell.

I feared he was being unrealistically optimistic for my benefit. I still read fatigue in his pale face. Some of this could obviously be accounted for by the work on the castle grounds, which he tried to supervise along with the normal duties of the estate. But it seemed to have deeper causes as well.

By late July, Alasdair was getting out to visit the various work sites less and less. His weight did not come back. His appetite languished. In spite of favorable weather, our outside walks grew shorter. All the while Alasdair continued to insist that full recovery was just around the corner.

The work in the villages and around the grounds progressed nicely. But Alasdair left much of the day-to-day inspections to Ranald and me. He often said he was a little tired and would rather the two of us drove out and had a look ourselves. When the workmen and builders and stonemasons had specific questions, he told me to bring them to the castle to confer with him there.

Most of the work was completed by mid-September. I regretted that Alasdair was not able to help as much as he had hoped. When the renovation of the summerhouse was completed and a glass roof installed and a wide new path to it cleared and graveled and packed, it was all Alasdair could do to summon the energy to ride out to see it in a horse-drawn carriage. I packed a picnic lunch to enjoy in the newly refurbished temple. But when we arrived, Alasdair said he was too tired to get out and walk up the hill the final few yards. We could hear the workers busy in the tunnel that would again connect the temple with the beach, which we wanted to make passable again as it had been in bygone generations. We would come back tomorrow for a closer inspection, Alasdair said.

But we never did.

Then came a day in October I will never forget. I heard a loud thud from what sounded like the library above me. I raced upstairs, terrified that a bookcase had toppled over.

I ran in. Alasdair lay on the library floor unconscious. I shouted for Alicia, then ran for wet washcloths and hurried back and knelt down to try to revive him. Alicia was already on the telephone. Dr. Mair arrived ten minutes later. By then I had managed to get Alasdair awake and alert enough and, with the help of Alasdair's valet Campbell, up and to a bed in a guest room on the same floor.

He lay mostly unconscious the rest of the day. He ate nothing. Dr. Mair wanted to attach an IV to keep his fluids up. I said I would rather wait till morning. I didn't want Alasdair waking up and finding needles in his arm and tubes attached to him. Indeed, by the next day he had come back to himself enough to drink. I began pouring water and tea and juice and broth into him by the gallon, as much as he could tolerate.

Now at last I think Alasdair recognized the severity of his condition. His first words this time were not about getting out of bed, and pronouncements about everything soon being back to normal. He smiled wanly and accepted my ministrations with gratitude.

I realized how seriously he was now taking the situation when the next day he asked me to send for Mr. Crathie, his solicitor from Buckie. The request itself, in Alasdair's weak voice, made me gulp and go a little pale. When Mr. Crathie came, he and Alasdair spent an hour together.

Mr. Crathie left, went back to his office, returned later in the afternoon with a briefcase full of papers, and again disappeared into Alasdair's room.

All I could think of, as I tried to be brave and keep the proverbial British stiff upper lip, were the words of Dr. Mair from months earlier: *"If he can only weather this onslaught of the disease and hold off its worst effects until the wave passes, he should be robust for many more years to come. But there is little we can do now besides wait to see how strong his immune system is to fight it."*

Several more days went by. A little color came back to Alasdair's face. He tried to begin eating again. He managed to get up and into his favorite chair for a few hours one day. But even that tired him out. He spent most of the two days following that again in bed.

Chapter Twenty-two

Closing the Everlasting Life Circle

Mary, dearest maid, I leave thee;
Hame an' frien's, an' country dear;
Oh! ne'er let our partin' grieve thee,
Happier days may soon be here.
See yon bark sae proudly bounding,
Soon shall bear me o'er the sea;
Hark! the trumpet loudly sounding,
Calls me far frae love an' thee.
—Alexander Hume, "The Partin'"

Alasdair's request several days later did not surprise me. I wondered if he was requesting to see a friend or a spiritual sage.

"Would you ask Ranald Bain to come?" Alasdair said to me.

"Of course, dear," I said. "When . . . now?"

"As soon as he is able."

The two men had spent much time together over the course of the past three years. But something in Alasdair's voice made it clear that his request on this day was different, like his request to see Mr. Crathie—as if, having seen to his temporal affairs with his solicitor, he now sought some resolution to the loose ends of his eternal affairs with his spiritual mentor. But it was not the priesthood of clerical officialdom he sought in the person of Reverend Gillihan, as much as we both had come to respect and appreciate Iain's replacement. Rather, it was his own personal wise man whom he needed close to him at this time.

Knowing how unassuming Ranald had been, just like Iain, in the

149

matter of my own faith as it had developed, I doubted he had been
any different with Alasdair. What might he say, however, with eternity staring his younger friend in the face? Would he feel a greater
urgency than before?

How concerned was Ranald for Alasdair's soul? Would he press
him toward a salvation prayer? I had no idea. Perhaps as his wife
I should have been more concerned for his soul than I was. I
knew that Alasdair believed in God, and that under Ranald's quiet
and unobtrusive influence that belief had been slowly deepening.
But Alasdair was completely honest about the fact that belief was
not as personal for him as it had become for me and obviously
was for Iain and Ranald. Yet the God I had come to know since
coming to Scotland was so entirely a good and trustworthy Father
who cared for his children, I could not be anxious. He obviously
loved Alasdair, too, more than I did or Iain did or Ranald did, or
all the people of the community did who had so taken their laird
into their hearts. Whatever happened, he would be a good Father
to Alasdair no less than to me or anyone else. I know that some
people get anxious about salvation as death approaches. But I
couldn't be fearful. Whenever I thought of God and Alasdair together, I saw God with a smile on his face waiting to welcome
one of his dear ones home. I was *sad* as the weight of it was
borne more steadily upon me. But not *afraid*. Ranald had said
concerning his own loss, "God is guid, an' that's aye the end o'
a' things." I had never forgotten his words. It was now my turn
to apply them in what appeared to be the inevitable approach of
coming sorrow in my life.

Ranald came to the castle the moment the request came. I led him
upstairs to the room where Alasdair lay.

"Aye, Ranald, my frien'," said Alasdair, reaching up a hand, which
Ranald took lovingly. "It doesna luik sae guid, ye ken."

Ranald sat down beside the bed. "Are ye in ony pain, Ally?" he
asked.

"Nae till speik o'—only pain o' the hert, ye ken—things fae my past comin' back tae haunt me noo that 'tis too late tae set them tae the richt."

"'Tis ne'er too late for that, Ally. Ye've already set a guid mony things richt."

"Ye maun aye ken fit I mean—too late tae gang tae a' those my tongue was sharp wi' an' spier their forgieness."

"Gien yer hert's ane wi' God, ye shall see the licht on yer friens' faces soon enouch. Ye'll aye be able then tae set richt onythin' left ower frae this worl'."

"Ye mean . . . afterward . . . in heaven, ye mean?"

"I am nae so particular aboot what ye ca' it. I only ken that a' wull be made richt in God's family wi' his sons an' dochters."

Alasdair did not reply. He was thinking hard about Ranald's words.

"Ye hae been the best frien' a man cud hae, Ranald," he said after a minute. "I'm sorry I wasna a better frien' till ye mysel' durin' a' those years whan I hid mysel' awa' ahind these walls, afore my Marie cam tae help open my een."

I was astonished as I continued to listen to the conversation. I had never heard Alasdair speak in Doric before. I understood it well enough by now. But to hear the local dialect from Alasdair's lips was a surprise.

"But at least I kin spier o' ye tae spier Reddy tae forgie me for some o' the dreadful things I said tae *him* when we were yoong . . . whan ye see him agin', that is. My mind's sair grieved aboot it. He's ane I wish I cud see noo mair nor a'."

"I ken his hert lies open till ye, Ally, an' the forgieness is jis' spillin' oot wi'oot him hearin' ye spier for't."

"'Tis good o' ye tae say, Ranald. I haup ye're in the richt. I hae jis' ane mair favor tae spier o' ye. Tak' care o' Marie. She's been like an angel come tae open my hert these last years o' my life."

Ranald looked at me and smiled at the word *angel*.

"I wull, Ally," he said.

I stared down at my lap where I sat on the opposite side of the bed. It was awkward listening to two men talk about me. I didn't dare glance up. When I did chance a peep at Ranald a minute later, he was not looking at me but was still gazing intently into Alasdair's face.

"An' noo, Ranald," Alasdair went on, "ye been a guid frien' till me these last years, an' 'tis time for ye tae see what ye kin de for this tired auld soul noo that my body's aboot till gang the way o' the earth. I hae been a prood man, too prood for my ain good. But I'm ready for ye tae pray an' spier God gien he might hae me at the last."

"I'm afraid I canna de that, Ally," said Ranald. "God doesna open his gates for ain man jist because anither man spiers him."

"But ye could try, cudna ye, Ranald, for a frien'? Ye wadna hae me left outside the gates?"

"I wud gie my verra life tae open them for ye, Ally. I wud hae ye go inside in my place, an' bide oot in the darkness mysel' gien I cud. I'd gang tae hell itsel' for ye gien it meant ye'd be saved yersel'."

"Ye'd do that for me, ye'd let me gang in yer ain place?"

"Aye, wud I, Ally. Gien I cud. But I canna."

"Why for no'?"

"God doesna open his gates like that. His hert's aye open, jis' like his arms are waitin' for ilka prodigal wha's ready tae admit what he is an' come hame. But he's no' luikin' for folk fa comes bein' dragged in. A body canna git intil heaven bein' pulled by his feet."

"I'm no' spierin' ye tae drag me, Ranald, jis' gie me a helpin' han'."

"'Tis anither, no' me, wha's hand's oot tae lead ye, Ally. He's taken yer place ootside the gates, taken yer place in the verra darkness o' hell itsel', so ye can come tae the licht as he leads ye till his Father."

"Ah, I ken wha ye mean."

It was silent a moment. Then Alasdair looked over at me.

"Do you remember, Marie," he said, "that first day I heard the sound of your harp over the wall, coming from the churchyard, how I followed the sound of it and listened to it on the other side of the wall?"

I smiled and nodded.

"I told you that it was your music that began to wake something inside me."

Now he looked toward Ranald. "Isna there somethin' in the Bible, Ranald, aboot God drawing men till him?"

"Aye, Ally. Jesus said that no one comes till him wi'oot his Father drawin' him."

"I was just thinking," Alasdair went on, looking at me again, "that maybe it was *God* drawing me, way back then—drawing me through your music, Marie. I suppose I was more than a little stubborn about it at first. I didn't want to get drawn all the way. So I stood on the other side of the wall. Then when you came to the castle I kept on the other side of the partitions, afraid to show myself. Maybe all that time I was afraid to get too close to God. Kind of cowardly, now that I think of it. Maybe I've always been that way—keeping up the partitions, staying on the other side of the wall, keeping myself isolated."

"You've not been that way with me," I said, struggling to keep my voice under control, "or with the farmers and villagers or Ranald. You've opened yourself like no laird I know of ever has. Isn't that right, Ranald?"

"Aye, ye speik trowth, lass."

Alasdair smiled and nodded. "Maybe," he said. "It has been rather wonderful for me, too. But I still haven't quite taken down all the partitions with God, have I? I've still got the barrier up blocking the way to my *innermost* soul—exactly like I hid from you and kept you from seeing me in my private sanctuary that first day you played for me."

I did not reply. These were questions only Alasdair could answer.

He paused and closed his eyes briefly, then took in a deep breath. "Maybe I'm finally ready. Tell me what to do, Ranald."

"Ye maun gang in wi' him through the door in the wall o' yer ain free wull," said Ranald. "'Tis jist like the door ye had broken through atween the castle an' the kirk—ye maun open a door jist like that atween yer ain hert an' God's. 'Tis yer ain free wull, wi' Jesus leadin' ye, that's the pathway through those gates intil God's hert."

"Div ye think I'm a prodigal, then, Ranald?"

"Aye, ye are, Ally. Jis' like me. We're a' prodigals. 'Tis why we maun gang till oor Father. 'Tis why Jesus put the words intil the mouth o' the prodigal, 'I wull arise an' gang till him.' 'Tis what we a' got tae do. Ye're nae mair worse a prodigal nor me."

"What's a man like me tae do, then, wha's waited sae lang?"

"Jis' take the Lord's han', an' pray yersel'. Ilka man an' woman's got tae pray it for themsel's. We're a' prodigals, Ally. We got tae say, 'I wull arise an' gang tae my Father,' an' then go tae Jesus an' say, 'Tak me tae yer Father,' an' then say till God, 'I'm ready for ye tae make a son o' me.'"

"But there's nae time for him tae do the makin'... nae time left for me."

"He's already been doin' the wark, Ally. Ye're a changed man. But there's mair tae do, an' there's all eternity left tae make ye his son. He's jis' spierin' yer leave tae du a' he can noo so that ye're on the richt road whan ye meet him—the road o' sonship. He canna du it wi'oot yer leave, no' until ye're ready yersel'. 'Tis a beginnin' ye're wantin' tae make, but no' exactly a beginnin', but a closin' up o' the everlastin' life circle he began when he first made ye mony lang years syne."

Alasdair looked over at me. "It's just what you told me on the deck of the *Gwendolyn*," he said, "that he's waiting for us to be ready. I am sorry, Marie," he added, "that I wasn't ready sooner. I've been stubborn as well as proud. But I think I am ready now."

Again he turned to Ranald. "Tell me what to pray, Ranald," he said, in the same tongue he had used in speaking to me.

"Pray till him yersel', Ally, fae yer ain hert," replied Ranald.

"I wouldn't know what to say."

"Ye dinna need me tae put words intil yer mouth. Pray *live, livin'* words, Alasdair, my son... my dear frien'—*yer ain* words."

"You don't make it easy."

"'Tis the simplest thing a man can du—talk tae his Father. He's closer than ye ken. Tell him ye're ready tae be completely his son—

no' jist dabblin' at the thing fae a distance for Marie's sake, but gaein' a' the way wi' him 'cause 'tis fit ye want tae du *yersel'*. Tell him ye're sorry it took ye sae lang. Tell him ye're ready tae follow his Son, Jesus, in learnin' hoo tae be a son. Then spier o' Jesus tae teach ye."

Alasdair glanced over at me and reached out his hand. I took it in both of mine. He closed his eyes.

The prayer he prayed was so simple yet profound, a humble acknowledgment of spiritual childness, with a willingness to see things in new ways, an eagerness to set right what lay in his power, and such an innocent trust in God to see to those things that didn't, I could not help weeping. I had never heard such a prayer from the lips of a man in my life. I imagined that God was smiling and weeping even more than me. I had known Alasdair only four years. God, the Father who made him and loved him, had known him all his life, and had been drawing him and waiting for this moment all that time.

When he was through, Ranald looked toward me with a loving smile. "If ye dinna mind, lass," he said, "I would like tae talk tae yer man alone."

I nodded and left the room, still wiping my eyes. I waited in the sitting room next to the bedroom, my mind and heart so full I could not possibly have put all I was feeling into words. After the beautiful exchange I had just witnessed, I tried to convince myself all over again that Alasdair would surely recover—that God would not take him just when he had finally taken the last step toward intimacy with him.

The two men were together thirty or forty minutes. When the door opened and Ranald came out his eyes were red and wet. He was folding several sheets of blue paper and putting them inside the pocket of his coat. He sat down beside me.

"I am sae sorry, Marie," he said.

"Is he . . . ," I began.

"He is sleepin' comfortably. I think the dear man is content."

He paused, then looked at me with a sad but tender smile. "I ken hoo hard this maun be for ye, lass."

"I don't understand why this is happening, Ranald," I said. "I am happy for him, of course—what a beautiful prayer! I am glad he is at peace with God. But why do such things happen? Why now, after poor Alasdair has changed so much and is trying to do good, and *be* good. It doesn't seem fair that this would come upon him now."

"Sich things are part o' life, part o' man's condition. Maybe this is what it took tae awaken him all the way tae his need o' his Father. He's aye been comin' awake a lang time. Wakin' up's whiles a slow process o' the hert. Doesna come in a flash, whate'er some o' the auld preachers like tae say at their altars. The altar may make a beginnin', but 'tis only life that can bring the full wakin'. An' I think noo at last Ally's a' the way awake."

"But it is so hard to understand."

Ranald nodded thoughtfully. "But 'tis no' hard tae understand why God brought ye till us here in this little oot-o'-the-way village in Scotland. Ye an' yer wee harpie brought life an' healing an' reconciliation tae this whole community."

He paused, thinking. "Div ye mind my tellin' ye aboot Iain speakin' o' the prayer o' Christlikeness?" he said after a moment.

"No, please do."

"He always says that prayin' tae be made like Jesus isna a guarantee o' a life o' ease. Jist the opposite. We are sma', an' sometimes oor prayers are sma'. There are times when God canna du as we want in the matter o' sma' prayers, 'cause he's waitin' for us tae pray big prayers. Big prayers swallow sma' worries an' lift them tae higher places. The prayer o' Christlikeness is the biggest o' the big prayers. Whan we pray tae be like oor Lord, we gie up oor rights tae pray for things that might suit oor ain convenience, e'en oor ain happiness, or tae be spared life's pain. When things dinna turn oot as we might like, 'tis those circumstances that God uses tae answer that big prayer in oor lives.

"God's desire for Alasdair, as for us a', is that he be a son—a hum-

ble son o' his heavenly Father. 'Tis the biggest, maist important thing
in life. Gien a mortal illness is what it takes for God tae achieve that
end, though pain an' grief come wi' it, then God willna spare't. He
doesna mind the pain, even pain tae himsel' when it leads tae the
sonship o' Christlikeness. Think hoo Jesus suffered. Yet in his sufferin' his sonship was perfected. Hoo can we complain whan God
takes us upo' the same road o' sufferin'?"

I continued to cry softly. After a minute Ranald rose, took me in
his arms, and held me.

"Be strong, lass," he whispered. "I'll bide a wee doonstairs gien ye
need me again," he said as he left the room.

I went back in to sit at Alasdair's side. I remained with him about
forty minutes. He was dozing. After a while he became alert once
more and asked if Ranald was still at the castle.

"He is downstairs with Alicia," I said.

He asked to see him again.

When Ranald appeared, Alasdair held out his hand toward him.
Ranald approached, took it with a tender smile of fatherliness, held
it a moment, then sat down.

"I need to tell you something, Ranald my friend," said Alasdair in
a weak voice, "something that happened a long time ago."

"If it's aboot the Dove's Cove ye're thinking, Ally," said Ranald,
"Iain telt me aboot it mony years ago, fan ye were in England tae
the university."

An astonished look came over Alasdair's face.

"Ye *ken*?" he said.

Ranald nodded.

Alasdair continued to stare at him from the bed. "But ye teld naebody?" he said at length.

"I think my Maggie kennt," answered Ranald. "An' it ate at her
through the years. But there was naethin' tae be deen. No one wud
hae believed *us*. Tales full o' innuendo had already begun tae circulate that wud hae thwarted anythin' we might hae deen. The maitter
was best left tae God's hand."

Alasdair laid his head back on the pillow and closed his eyes. I had no idea what they were talking about. "But there is still the matter of my own conscience to be dealt with," he said at length.

He looked over at me. "I'm sorry, Marie," he said, "but I need to ask you to step out again. There is something we need to discuss alone."

The two men were alone together for an hour. When Ranald left this time, Alasdair was exhausted and immediately fell asleep.

Chapter Twenty-three

Surprise Letter

The settin' sun, the settin' sun,
How glorious it gaed doun;
The cloudy splendour raised our hearts
To cloudless skies aboon.
—Lady Nairne, "The Auld Hoose"

Life's troubles so often come in waves.

In the midst of my grief to see Alasdair weakening and trying to keep my spirits up for his benefit, a letter arrived one day from the last quarter I had expected.

The familiar handwriting immediately sent me back to my college years and receiving the perfunctory twice-yearly letter.

Dear Angel Dawn,

You have now been married, what is it, two or three years. I hope and trust you are happy. I am sorry my schedule has not been such as to have permitted me to visit you and meet your new husband. A real duke! Just imagine, my little girl married to British royalty!

I am afraid I have some regrettable news. I would rather not have to tell you, but realize you must know and I want to tell you before it is too late. Last month I was diagnosed with cancer. I have been to a round of specialists and have begun chemo treatments. But it is more a prolonging than a cure. It is the same old story—too busy to take the time for regular colonoscopies, and then when finally forced into it by my doctor after complaining of bowel irritation . . . by then it was too late. They think the colon cancer has begun to spread to my liver.

The long and the short of it is that I probably have less than two years. Even two years is optimistic. I hope I will be able to see you before then. I have some things I need to discuss with you. Unfortunately it does not look like a trip to Scotland is in the cards for me, so it will be up to you if you can find time to get over to Portland.

Sincerely,
Your father,
Richard Buchan

The single sheet dropped from my hand and I began to cry. They were tears containing many mixed and confusing emotions. *What a horrible time for this*, was all I could think. How could he do this to me now? I had my hands full with Alasdair. How could I possibly leave for a trip to America?

I suppose it revealed a lot about me that my first thoughts were of *myself*, not my poor father. How selfish we can be, even unknowingly at times when other people need us the most. I'm not proud of that reaction. But I can't pretend I'm something I'm not. My reaction was selfish, pure and simple—feeling sorry for myself.

Now it might be *me* needing the counseling services of my harping friends. Still crying, I went to find Alicia. The look on my face said most of what there was to say.

"Oh, Marie," she said in alarm, "what *is* it? . . . Is Alasdair—"

I shook my head and handed her the letter.

She read it, then opened her arms and held me tight. I broke down and wept harder than I had in years—maybe ever. I wasn't even weeping for my father, or because he was suddenly dying. I wept for the years of a relationship that had never been right, never been complete, never been whole. I don't even know how to describe what had been wrong with it, or whose fault it was. Maybe it was my fault—though I'd spent my whole life blaming my father and never considering my own half of the relational equation. But when you get to the age I was, things begin to look different. You don't see all your own past motives in such an idealistic light. My initial self-centered reaction was compounded as suddenly a lifetime of doubts came rushing over me like a flood. Inexplicably, one of the emotions I felt was *guilt*. I'd been in the habit of blaming *him*, not myself. Why did I suddenly feel guilty?

Alicia led me to a chair. I sat down and she pulled another chair over and sat down opposite me.

"Alicia," I said, "you've got to promise me to say nothing about this. We have to keep it between ourselves, at least for now. Alasdair must not know. It would only make him anxious and sorry for me. I can't do that to him, not now. He is my first priority. I'm sorry he's got cancer, but . . . it's probably a terrible thing to say, but my father just doesn't matter to me as much right now as Alasdair."

Alicia nodded. "What are you going to do?" she asked.

"I don't know!" I moaned. "I'll write him I suppose, though what will I say—'Gee, Dad . . . sorry you're dying, but I'm busy now. See ya'? We haven't had the kind of relationship that fostered much honesty or reality. All those years he was too busy for me . . . How ironic that now I'm too busy taking care of a dying husband for him. Life is so cruel sometimes. I really wish I could care more deeply, but the honest truth is, my feelings are . . . just sort of a numbness. I don't know that I *do* care. What a terrible thing to say. He doesn't know me. I don't know him."

"Will you tell your father about Alasdair?"

"I don't know. I'll have to think about it. I'll have to give *some* reason for not dropping everything and rushing over to see him. But I don't want to unburden myself to him either. He's got enough to worry about without me dumping on him with my problems that he's never cared about before now. How did you deal with it?"

"I didn't have to," replied Alicia. "My dad died suddenly. There was no warning or preparation. But we had a good relationship, so

I had no regrets. With my mom it's different. With her Alzheimer's she doesn't even know who I am."

"But you go see her twice a week."

"Out of duty, not because of anything I really believe she is getting out of it—or me either, for that matter. Frankly, it's depressing."

"But you do it."

Alicia nodded a little sadly. "You do what you have to do. And usually, I think, most people try to do the right thing. I've never made any pretense of being a saint. But I try to do the right thing. So will you. I hope that matters to God when my time comes. So, tell me about your father," she said.

The directness of the question caught me off guard. Suddenly our roles were reversed. I suppose it's that way in most friendships—no one person is *always* the strong one. The roles of strong and weak in a friendship of honesty and transparency are fluid and changing as two people grow together. Marriages are like that, too; husbands and wives lean on each other in different ways and at different times.

There had been a time when Alicia had leaned on me for strength. Now it was my turn to lean on her.

I drew in a long breath and slowly let it out. My relationship with my father had always been troubled. Even the recent years of spiritual renewal in my life had done little to resolve the deep conflicts in my mind whenever I thought about my parents. It was one of those areas in my life I compartmentalized and stuck off in a corner where I wouldn't have to look at it. I had never opened that box to God's scrutiny either, never asked if there was anything he wanted me to do with it. As personal as you think your faith is, maybe there are always areas you close off like that, both to yourself and to God. I wasn't feeling like a very dynamic or mature Christian right about then. What did my last few years of growth matter if there were areas left I refused to look at, and refused to let God into?

"I don't even know how to answer you," I said at length. "My father and I . . . we were never close. He is a lawyer. He was always busy . . . gone, involved with other people whose needs, as I saw it, he put ahead of his family...ahead of me. It's the same story you always hear—career man neglects children...children resent it...estrangement results. I didn't think he loved me. I know that's not true, but when you're young you think those kinds of things. Then my mom died, and at a time when I really could have used a father and maybe we might have repaired the damage and grown close, he buried himself even more in his work and his clients and his causes. Though he mostly mainstreamed, he was always sort of a Greenpeace, Save the Whale, Free Tibet type. But even then he still had no time for me. I suppose I never forgave him for that. Basically, I suppose I gave up trying to have a relationship after that. Who's to say it wasn't as much my fault? I blamed him for not making room in his life for me, never coming to visit. But then how many times did I go visit him?...How much room did I make for him in my heart?

"It gets confusing, you know. You can be completely sane and rational and mature in every other area of your life, but with your parents, all the emotions and confusions and longings and dis-appointments get twisted into a mess, and you're nothing but a confused hurting child again. Maturity...what's that? In any event, whatever there was between us degenerated into a Christmas-letter relationship. I never thought he liked my husband—my first hus-band. I don't know if it's true. Who can tell with such things? But in all the wedding pictures my dad had a scowl on his face. It's like he didn't care about developing a relationship with me, but he resented my husband taking his little girl, his little angel, away from him. But like I say, my impressions of the thing might be completely cock-eyed from what was really going on. I guess I was more confused than ever. By the time you get to be an adult—or when you *think* you are—your relationship with your parents is based more on false expectations and misunderstandings and disappointments and guilts than actual facts. If there'd been grandchildren, maybe it would have been different, I don't know. But there weren't."

"Do you regret not having children?"

"Sure...I suppose. But life isn't always what you expect. Do you?"

"No, not anymore. You adjust. Sure, there's an unfulfilled part of life you won't experience. The way it's going," she added with a light laugh, "I'll never know what it's like to be intimate with a man either. But the older you get, the more you realize there are more important things in life. I'm dealing with it. I've got no major regrets."

"But minor ones?"

"Sure," she said, smiling, "who hasn't?"

Chapter Twenty-four

Home at Last

We'll meet nae mair at sunset, when the weary day is done;
Nor wander hame thegither by the lee licht o' the moon.
I'll hear your step nae longer among the dewy corn,
For we'll meet nae mair, my dearest, at eve or early morn.
—Lady Jane Scott, "Durisdeer"

The hours went by. The days lengthened into a week. Alasdair's physical condition did not dramatically worsen, but his *spirits* were noticeably altered. He was at peace. But as sure as I now was that he would, neither did he improve.

He got out of bed when he could, but did not seem concerned when he could not. Ranald came to the castle almost every day. They spoke of many things. A number of letters from Alasdair resulted, which he asked me to post. All were addressed to people I had never heard of. When I asked about them, Alasdair only replied with a faraway look and words to the effect, "Just unfinished business from long ago."

I knew he was trying to set right relationships that had gone wrong. But he remained stymied in that regard with his sister. He sent several messages to Olivia requesting a visit. But she did not come.

When he was through with the letters, a calm came over him. He asked me for my Bible. A wedding gift from Professor McHardy's sister Moira, who lived in Crannoch, the Bible was becoming well-worn from my use. Alasdair read for hours a day in the Gospels, and when he was unable to he asked me to read to him. He wanted to

165

hear all the words that Jesus had to say about his Father. Sometimes we would talk about what we were reading, sometimes not. Most of what we read was not unfamiliar, yet was altogether new. Alasdair was reading with deep personal interest for the first time. Every story, every parable, every teaching was newly alive with meaning. It became newly real to me all over again as I listened to the words of Jesus through Alasdair's ears.

One afternoon Alasdair set down the Bible and laid his head back on his pillow and closed his eyes.

"Would you play me the tape of Gwendolyn's singing?" he said softly. "I would like to hear her little song."

I brought the CD that included Gwendolyn singing with her harp music. When I again heard the little song she had called "Daddy's Song," the sound of her pure high voice was so poignant I could hardly stand it. But Alasdair listened calmly, his eyes dry, a sad but content and happy smile on his face.

> A baby came to Mummy and Daddy.
> I do not remember—I had just begun to be.
> Mummy and Daddy loved baby.
> That baby was me.

"Imagine, Marie," he said, "it will not be long before I will see her again."

My eyes stung. I glanced away, trying to hold myself together for his sake. I still could not make myself believe it. I was so *sure* he would recover.

"And her mother," he added. "There is much I need to make right with her. I hope Ranald is right, that I shall be able to do so face-to-face. By now Gwendolyn is with her. She will have told her about me . . . and about you. You and Fiona will like each other. I hope she will already have forgiven me for doubting her, for thinking ill of her and Iain. But I will talk to her about it myself. That is the important thing, that everything be brought into the light, that everything be made clean...that *I* be made clean and pure. Maybe I will see your first husband, too."

For the next two days he listened again and again to the CDs I had made of Gwendolyn. He did not speak of her again. After that day, he did not say much. He tried to read, but often simply lay back with his eyes closed, holding the Bible and listening to the music.

One morning I came into the room after being away for about an hour. Alasdair was holding several blue sheets of what looked like a letter. Quickly he stuffed them beneath the blanket. I was puzzled, but he obviously didn't want me seeing it. The only thing I could conclude was that it was a private communication between him and Ranald, the same one I had seen Ranald with before.

I walked over to turn on the CD player. He motioned for me to come. I walked to the bedside and bent down to kiss him.

"*You* play for me," he said weakly. "You play me...play the angels' music."

Journey was set up in the room. I began playing mostly what I had myself learned of Gwendolyn's music, though try as I might, I could not succeed in achieving her same magical sound.

But Alasdair also wanted to hear my own music. He wanted to hear everything—every song I knew, every song he had ever heard me play. He wanted to hear them all over again, as if I were reprising my first two private concerts for him—in the churchyard and in the Music Room where he had listened without my being able to see him—and then every other time he had ever heard me play. He even wanted to hear "Eleanor Rigby." He listened to it with the most delightful smile on his face.

He hardly said a word now. His body was weak. His large frame had thinned steadily over the months. Now at last his face grew gaunt as well, his eyes and cheekbones accentuated as never before.

It was all I could do not to burst into sobs every moment. I recognized everything exactly as it had been with Gwendolyn, the same progression, even some of the same facial expressions, the same smile of weak contentment and anticipation, the same gradual letting go of earthly attachments.

Gradually I sensed the end was near. I don't know how. I just knew. He was *not* going to recover.

One day in the middle of my playing, I glanced over at him. A smile of such radiance shone on his thin features. I stopped and went to him and bent down to his face. I could see that he wanted to speak.

"I think," he whispered, though I could just barely make out his words, "that this has been the happiest day of my life."

"Oh, Alasdair!" I said, blinking hard and kissing his forehead and cheeks, then his lips.

"You have made these," he went on, "the happiest years...the happiest days imaginable. Marie...I love you...I will never...will not forget you. Thank you...love you...I love you."

He closed his eyes and lay back again, smiling and content. I sat up weeping, but remained on the bedside, one of his hands in mine.

Those were his last words to me.

By morning he was with Gwendolyn again, with Fiona, with the angels, and with the Father of them all.

Chapter Twenty-five

Aftermath of a Farewell

There is sorrow, deep sorrow, heavy sorrow down-weighs me;
Sorrow long, dark, forlorn, from which nothing can raise me.
Yea, my heart's filled with sorrow, deep sorrow undying
For MacGregor of Ro-ro, whose home is Glen Lyon.
—"MacGregor o' Ruara"

For the second time in my life, I was a widow. I no longer cared about being a duchess. I no longer cared about living in a castle. I was more glad than ever that I had anticipated exactly those feelings—not dreaming anything would actually come of it—before my marriage to Alasdair.

I had wanted only to be a *wife*. Twice I had been. Now twice that privilege was gone.

Alasdair's funeral was nearly identical to Gwendolyn's. Only myself and Olivia—who, notified of her brother's passing, returned to Port Scarnose at last—walked behind the horse-drawn hearse bearing Alasdair's casket from the castle through the village and to the churchyard, where he would be laid to rest next to Gwendolyn and Fiona. The tears and outpourings of grief from the entire region were more heartfelt and genuine than they could possibly have been a few years before. Alasdair had so endeared himself to the community, and was so greatly beloved, that there was scarcely a dry eye in the streets. Earls and dukes and baronets, a number of MPs, and various dignitaries from Aberdeen and Edinburgh and Glasgow and as far away as London all came to pay their respects. Every man, woman, and child of the village stood silent and solemn as we passed, and then joined the procession. He was, of course, the *laird*. But the outpouring of grief was so real that it was almost as if he had been chief of an ancient Highland clan. Women I did not even know wept with abandon.

Reverend Gillihan awaited the funeral procession at the church. I wondered what Olivia was thinking, to have to walk beside me behind Alasdair's casket. I knew what she thought of me. We had hardly spoken since Gwendolyn's death. Not a word passed between us that day. Not so much as a sign of recognition passed her lips when she looked at me.

I had asked Alicia, Jean, Tavia, and Cora to arrange an informal gathering at the town hall after the brief graveside ceremony. The community needed some means to express its grief as a whole. I was not up to playing the role of hostess to a thousand people at the castle. Not only did I have my own grief to contend with, but without Alasdair's covering protection I suddenly felt exposed and vulnerable to the stares and gossip and talk to which an incomer in such a community is always subjected.

All the past anxieties from my first months in Scotland returned. For the past several years I had felt completely loved and accepted and had made so many new friends. But I had been loved as *Alasdair's wife*. Would that same acceptance continue now that I was alone, especially with Olivia free again to begin planting the seeds of her subtle persuasions? Would people again give me strange looks, as if I were a gold digger from Canada . . . and had been all along?

I knew well enough how it often went—the woman from outside, knowing of a man's mortal illness, worms her way into his affections, persuades him to marry her, and within a year inherits a vast fortune. Hopefully the prenup had put all that to rest. But I was still nervous. Much of my anxiety, of course, was because of Olivia. She was such a *presence* that her influence could not be ignored. And I was probably not thinking straight. Trauma and personal tragedy do not produce clear thinking. As loving as were

Ranald and Alicia and my other dear friends, they could not help me make the decisions that suddenly loomed on my horizon. They always say it is not wise to make major decisions within a year or two of major life crises and changes. But I didn't have two years. I would be afforded as much time as I needed, I knew that. But I still had to look forward.

What would I do now?

The letter from my father weighed on me. I still had not sent him a reply. I had delayed doing so in hopes that events would make my way clear. Suddenly, with Alasdair gone, everything changed. The thought of going back to America could not but figure prominently among my options.

I could think of only one thing to do in the *immediate* days ahead that even halfway appealed to me. I hoped it would not raise too much untoward speculation. After the events of the funeral settled down, I would set out aboard the *Gwendolyn*. I had to think . . . and pray. How desperately I would have liked to take along my two dearest friends—Ranald Bain and Alicia Forbes—for comfort and fellowship and counsel. But somehow I knew this was something I needed to do alone.

Where would I go? I had no idea.

Just out . . . away . . . where I could be alone . . . to think and cry out to God, and hopefully come to terms with yet one more sudden change that had come to my life. There, on the sea, I could commune with God and Alasdair's memory together.

I notified Captain Travis to assemble Alasdair's small crew, which was only a local boy or two, depending on the length of trip, and to lay in stores and be ready to sail.

I sailed three days after Alasdair's funeral. We did not announce the fact, and managed to depart the Port Scarnose harbor with a minimum of fanfare.

I sent a letter to Reverend Gillihan, asking him, if he felt it appropriate, to read it in church, or, if not, post it in town, or both if he thought best. In it I wrote:

Dear friends of Port Scarnose,

I want to thank you from the bottom of my heart for the outpouring of sympathy, affection, and kindness you have shown me since the duke's death, and for your kind and gracious words of love toward my dear Alasdair. I know you loved him as I did. We will all miss him sorely.

I will be gone for several days, a week, maybe even two, on the Gwendolyn, thinking and praying and grieving on the solitude of the sea, which my Alasdair and your duke loved. Be assured that my thoughts and prayers will be with you, and I hope you will remember me in yours as well.

Affectionately,
Marie Buchan
Reidhaven

Chapter Twenty-six

At Sea

With the Loorgeen o hee, with the Loorgeen o ho,
In the gray dusk of eve, o'er the waves let us go.
On the ocean, o hee, waves in motion, o ho,
Naught but clouds could we see, o'er the blue sea below.
—*"A Boat Song"*

The open sea revived my spirits.

Ever since I had come to Scotland, the sea had had that effect on me. Out on the blue expanse, I was free to think about Alasdair and Gwendolyn, to cry but also to rejoice that I had been able to know them both while there was still time.

Again the sea became my refuge and consolation. I was reminded of my revelation of earlier when watching the tide rise and fall over rocks and the shoreline, that the sea was like the great love of God, sweeping in and out and through the lives of mankind as a great tide, giving life to the whole world and everything in it. I now felt that I had been left all alone in the world except for God. I was floating on that sea of his love, upheld by love, sustained by love. All earthly loves might be taken away. But the great sea of the universal love of God would never cease giving its life to man, and to me.

God's life and love had entered me and changed me. I had left Port Scarnose *feeling* alone. I knew that God was with me and that I was never *really* alone. But now I could not but wonder if the time had come—sooner than I had anticipated—when I would spend the rest of my life alone.

Tears flooded my eyes. I walked toward the bow of the yacht, and

173

there stood, face into the wind, unable to stop the flow of tears as they streamed down my cheeks.

Tears are usually good—the cleansing agents of God's healing processes. Those tears that day, though they stung my heart, I knew were *good* tears.

The *Gwendolyn* sailed north to Shetland, which I had not visited before. We sailed about its islands and inlets for two days, then set a southwesterly course, laying over at several of the small islands of the Inner and Outer Hebrides, then Skye, then Iona, and from there to Ireland. I was not feeling touristy. I simply wanted to travel, to move, to see new sights and stay away long enough to let Alasdair's death settle. So many decisions were facing me. I wanted to have some idea of their resolution prior to my return, and with only Captain Travis and one boy aboard keeping to themselves, most of my time was spent in perfect solitude.

On the fourth day out I began the long-overdue letter to my father.

From Ireland we sailed around the south of England and northward up through the Channel, finally past the Forth, the Tay, the Dee, the Don, and finally home. I had been gone eleven days.

I was not anxious for a high-profile return. I told Captain Travis to gauge our speed such that we would enter the harbor on an incoming tide about eleven o'clock that night, at a time when most of Port Scarnose would be in their beds. He radioed ahead and Nicholls was there to meet us with the BMW. Alicia was waiting for me when I walked into Castle Buchan, which seemed colder and quieter and drearier than ever, half an hour before midnight. She and I embraced and wept like the friends of the heart we had become.

I awoke the next morning surprisingly early. My first thought, seeing sun through my window, was to jump up and go for a walk along the Scar Nose and headland. Then I remembered that I was no longer renting Mrs. Mair's self-catering cottage. I was in a castle that, until a short while ago, had been half my own.

Suddenly I felt very lonely and very sad. I wished I *were* back in

Mrs. Mair's cottage and that Gwendolyn and Alasdair were still alive and that I was free to go on walks beside the sea as an anonymous visitor to Port Scarnose.

I got out of bed and glanced over at my harp where it sat across the room. I had not played since I had taken it to Alasdair's bedside for our final hours together.

I slipped on my robe and walked over to it and sat down. Gently my fingers touched the strings, but something prevented me from continuing.

The last sounds to come from *Journey* had been Gwendolyn's music, welcoming her father to his new home with their mutual Father. Whatever came next from this instrument, I would have to think about carefully. I did not want to sit down and start playing randomly. This harp had taken on a mystical import all its own. From the first moment Gwendolyn had set her little fingers to it, an invisible transformation had taken place. Music from another world had come from these strings, music that touched the senses on a deeper level than could be explained by the rational. Two people—a father and a daughter—had come together because of the music of this harp. Both had entered the next life to the sounds of its strings. In my eyes, this instrument had taken on an aura of holiness. Its music had transcended the bonds of earth and reached in some small way beyond the veil into eternity.

Perhaps its strings, for fleeting moments as Gwendolyn and Alasdair had hovered between life and death, had been invisibly plucked by the fingers of heavenly beings reaching down to welcome them home. Never again would I think of it as *my* harp.

It was a harp that belonged to God and his angels.

I dressed and went downstairs. Alicia would have brought me tea, as she often had for Alasdair and me. But I didn't like the feeling of being waited on. So I went to the kitchen to fix my own. The place was deserted. After our late-night arrival, I assumed she was still asleep.

After a cup of tea, I went out into the grounds. I walked for a long while, thoughtfully and prayerfully. The rest of my life began today. What would my future hold?

I also wanted to make music again today. I needed to touch the music of the angels. But the time and the circumstances had to be right.

Chapter Twenty-seven

Remembering the Past, Facing the Future

Be Thou my Vision, O Lord of my heart;
Naught be all else to me, save that Thou art,—
Thou my best thought, by day or by night,
Waking or sleeping, Thy presence my light.
—Eleanor Hull, "Be Thou My Vision,"
to Irish Traditional Melody

By eleven o'clock the sun was high and the morning warm. I had decided to play my harp again where Alasdair and I had first connected, though we did not see each other on that day, nor yet even know of the other's existence.

I tuned *Journey* and packed it in its case, then picked it up and left the castle. I walked slowly across the drive and grassy lawn, then through the new gate in the stone wall and into the churchyard.

I paused and glanced around at the familiar building and the irregular gravestones surrounding it. All was so still and quiet. Everything I had been thinking and feeling that first day returned to me now four years later. How could I have imagined how dramatically my life would change because of that day, and what effect the music from this magical instrument would have on one whom I had not even known was listening.

Yet the greatest impact of that day had taken place within me. That had been the day I had begun to discover the Fatherhood of God, and what it meant to be his daughter.

177

A calm and peace slowly stole into my heart, a deeper peace than I had felt since Alasdair's death.

God was good. I needn't worry about my future. He had something wonderful planned that I could not yet see. But I could trust him. Love and goodness were eternally trustworthy.

I sat down on the same gravestone I had sat on that day four years ago. Slowly I unpacked my harp, put on its legs, and set my fingers to its strings.

I drew in a deep breath, then slowly and gently began to play the majestic but simple hymn that had become the most meaningful expression of my life with God. Softly the music came at first, then gradually louder. Tears filled my eyes as the words became yet again my prayer of yielding my life, my future, my whole being into the Father's tender and loving hands.

> Be Thou my Vision, O Lord of my heart;
> Naught be all else to me, save that Thou art,—
> Thou my best thought, by day or by night,
> Waking or sleeping, Thy presence my light.
>
> Be Thou my Wisdom, Thou my true Word;
> I ever with Thee, Thou with me, Lord;
> Thou my great Father, I Thy true son;
> Thou in me dwelling, and I with Thee one.
>
> Riches I heed not, nor man's empty praise,
> Thou my inheritance, now and always;
> Thou and Thou only, first in my heart,
> High King of heaven, my treasure Thou art.
>
> High King of heaven, after victory won,
> May I reach heaven's joys, O bright heaven's Sun!
> Heart of my own heart, whatever befall,
> Still be my Vision, O Ruler of all.

I remained in the churchyard and played for an hour. I was so conscious of Alasdair's words about the angels making music on my harp, and of my own thought that God and the angels had been listening that day four years before.

I was aware on this day of playing for God again…and for the angels…and for Gwendolyn…and for Alasdair…and for Edward, my first husband, and my mother. They were all in my heart. I was sure they were all together listening.

How could I be sad with an audience like that!

The thought of Alasdair and Gwendolyn and Fiona all together finally did it—my fingers stilled and I broke into weeping.

Happy weeping! God bless them all!

I was so full as I walked back from the churchyard some time later, I was certainly in no frame of mind for what I found awaiting me. I had vaguely heard a car drive into the castle grounds awhile before. It had scarcely registered in my subconscious.

Alicia had known where I was and was waiting to intercept me.

"I'm sorry, Marie," she said, "I couldn't get rid of him. There is a man waiting to see you."

"Who is he?" I asked.

"A reporter, I'm afraid. I told him you were in mourning, but he wouldn't take no for an answer. If you want to slip upstairs, he'll get tired of waiting and leave eventually."

"No, that wouldn't be right," I sighed. "I'd just as soon nip whatever it is in the bud and be done with it. I'll get rid of him myself. Where is he?"

"In the Drawing Room."

"Would you take my harp up to the studio?" I said, handing it to her. "Well, here I go…Wish me luck."

I walked into the Drawing Room. The man was walking slowly about, looking at the bookcases and portraits on the walls.

"Hello," I said, "I am Marie Reidhaven."

"And I am Giles McDermott," he said, turning and approaching with a smile and outstretched hand. "Thank you for seeing me. Let me say first that I am sorry for your loss."

"Thank you. I understand you are a reporter."

"That's right. I am from the *Inverness Courier*. Our paper would like to do a feature article on Moray's 'First Lady,' as you are now being called. I know your husband's death is less than three weeks old, but there is major interest in your story—Canadian tourist falls in love with local duke and now finds herself not only a duchess in her own right but heir to one of Scotland's largest estates and presumably one of Britain's wealthiest women. Scotland's Grace Kelly, you know. There is talk in the wind of a major television special on your life and assumption to the title, and the *Courier* is hopeful that—"

"Excuse me, Mr. McDermott," I interrupted.

He stopped abruptly and looked at me with a puzzled expression.

"In the first place," I said, "even if it were all true, I would have no interest in allowing myself to become a public figure or an object of media examination or gossip—especially so soon after my husband's death. But in the second place, you must have gotten your signals crossed somewhere, or been given incorrect information, because what you say is *not* true. I am not the duchess, nor one of the wealthiest women in Scotland at all."

"I don't under— I mean...What are you saying? The duke is dead, long live the duchess, isn't that how it works?"

"Not in our case."

"I'm sorry, but I am confused!"

"'Duchess' was an honorary title, or a temporary title, if you will. Have you heard nothing about the prenuptial agreement made between the duke and myself?"

"I recall some vague reference to such a thing at the time of your marriage. I assumed it applied only in the case of divorce."

"Not at all. I made certain that it extended also to my husband's possible death. We made sure the terms were made public locally. I merely assumed that everyone knew the details."

"What were the terms of this prenup?"

I hesitated before answering.

"Mr. McDermott," I said at length. "I have explained that I am neither the Duchess of Buchan nor the heir to the Buchan estate, and that I have no interest in a story being either written or televised about me. That is all I have to say of an official nature. Anything else we discuss, because it will obviously be more personal, will have to be strictly off the record."

Obviously disappointed, the man thought a moment, then sighed and nodded.

"Fair enough," he said. "I cannot claim to like it, but I will agree, so long as you promise me the story ... if and when you change your mind and decide to go on the record."

"I'm sorry, I will make no such promise."

Again, his disappointment was evident.

"You are a tough cookie!" he said. "But all right, you win. Off the record and no promises. So what can you tell me about your prenup?"

"Let's sit down, shall we," I said, motioning to the couches and chairs.

When we were seated, I began.

"It is not so complicated, really," I said. "I did not want either Alasdair—the duke, I mean—or the community thinking I was marrying him for his money or his position or title, or for any other reason than that I loved him—simply as a *man*. Therefore, over Alasdair's objections, I insisted on a prenuptial agreement by which I would be considered the duchess only so long as the duke was alive, and by which I would inherit nothing of his fortune or property. My concern was not in anticipation of Alasdair's not living a long and healthy life, but that everyone knew I loved him for the man he was. Alasdair, of course, argued strenuously against it. But finally, when he saw that I would not marry him otherwise, he consented."

I paused, drew in a breath and let it out, and smiled. "So you see, Mr. McDermott," I added, "sitting before you is no one other than

Marie Reidhaven, widow. No duchess, no fortune, no property, no castle, no Grace Kelly . . . and no story."

"Surely your husband did not leave you destitute?" asked the journalist.

I smiled again. "No, I am hardly that!" I replied. "I have a bank account which will supply me with all my needs for a good long while. In Alasdair's eyes it was a trivial amount. But for me it is more than sufficient. *And* I have a relatively new Volvo that Alasdair bought for me."

"Still, none of that is a great deal for one who shared a fortune a month ago."

"It is enough for me. It was not *my* fortune. I have enough to buy a modest house if I want to. I also still own a home in Canada which we had not yet sold. So you see, I am more than amply provided for. The bank account, like the prenup, was part of our prewedding negotiations. I insisted on the prenup. Alasdair insisted on leaving me an account in my name. I agreed on a modest amount. So it was finally settled on."

McDermott laughed. "Not your normal negotiation—each one trying to give *more* to the other, and receive *less* himself!"

"That was our arrangement." I smiled. "It was how we tried to do things. Of course, I am free to stay on at the castle and use the grounds for as long as I like until I am settled elsewhere."

"What will become of it all—the castle, the management of the estate, the duke's fortune?"

"Actually, I don't know very many details," I replied. "I didn't need to know; therefore I left all that to Alasdair and his solicitors. The only matter he and I discussed at length was about the future of Castle Buchan, which we felt would be best preserved as the historic castle it is in the hands of the National Trust for Scotland. Alasdair had, I believe, begun talks with the National Trust through his solicitors. Of course, as you know, large endowments are also necessary to enable the National Trust to adequately maintain its properties. I assume a large financial component will be included in the arrangement. I know it may sound as if I am not interested, but I assure you such is not the case. I simply had to keep a distance from those aspects of Alasdair's affairs for *his* sake, so that it could never be said that I had influenced matters connected with his estate."

"Does the duke have other living relatives?"

"Only a sister. They were not close, though I assume she will be handsomely provided for by Alasdair's will. As for management of the estate and distribution of its other assets, Alasdair was a shrewd enough businessman to have made arrangements that will be best for all concerned, for the community, and for Scotland. I believe some property will be sold to local farmers. The estate will of course continue to operate as it has, but as to Alasdair's desire for the distribution of its profits beyond, as I say, what will I assume be a generous endowment to the National Trust for permanent upkeep of the castle . . . that I know nothing about. I am sure the thing is very complex with tax considerations as well."

"The duke has a daughter, I believe?"

"*Had.* She died four years ago."

"Oh, I see. Well, this is a remarkable turn of events. So, what will you do, uh . . . Mrs. Reidhaven?"

"I don't know yet. My life, my friends, are here. But my father is dying of cancer back in the States. I have that to think of, too."

"I am sorry. You seem to have had a great deal thrown at you all at once."

"One manages to survive. I have no complaints. I have lived a dream."

"You must be a strong woman."

"I don't feel strong. But to use a cliché—you do what you have to do."

McDermott sighed, then rose. "I thank you for your time, and for being as open with me as you have. You are a remarkable woman, and you have my esteem and admiration. Be assured that I will treat what you have told me with confidentiality. I wish you the best, Mrs. Reidhaven."

Chapter Twenty-eight

A Decision and a Dream

Summer flow'rs shall cease to blossom,
Streams run backward frae the sea;
Cauld in death maun be this bosom,
Ere it cease to throb for thee.
Fare thee weel—may ev'ry blessin'
Shed by Heav'n around thee fa';
As last time thy lov'd form pressin'—
Think o' me when far awa'.
—Alexander Hume, "The Partin'"

The interview with the reporter McDermott, off the record though it had been, helped me coalesce and focus my thoughts. That process was helped further by the arrival the following day—I cannot believe coincidentally—of a second letter from my father. It was impossible to miss the note of urgency this time.

Dear Angel,

I had hoped to hear from you by now, but realize you are probably busy with your own life. But as I try to sort out my affairs and plan for my suddenly shortened future, I confess that I have no one else to turn to. I do hope that you will be able to arrange a short visit in the near future so that you and I can go over a few things in person. I have not accumulated much in this life, which I hope is as it should be. But I have a few business matters of concern, some charitable interests which I desire to continue, and my house, which will be yours when I am gone, or perhaps we will judge it best to sell it before then. As my affairs will inevitably concern you later, I hope we can resolve as many of them beforehand as possible.

Thank you for considering my request.

It was simply signed *Dad*.

Even before I had finished reading it, I realized that my decision was made. I would return to America. I *had* to. Alicia was doing her duty to a mother with Alzheimer's who didn't even know her. I also had a duty to my father, whether he deserved my affection or not— maybe I should say whether I *thought* he deserved it or not. Alicia said that most people tried to do the right thing. It was my turn to see what I was really made of.

Did I have any depth of character? It's easy to fall in love, to go sailing on a yacht, to play pretty music on a warm day overlooking a gorgeous blue sea. It takes no character to fall in love. Shallow, selfish, stupid people fall in love every day.

But it takes *character* to show compassion, to put another's needs ahead of your own, to care for a dying parent as Alicia was doing.

What was I made of? How deeply had Christlikeness penetrated the fiber of my character?

It was time I found out.

Alicia and I cried and cried when I told her I was making plans to fly to Oregon to see my father.

"Your own example has been important to me," I said. "I can't say I want to do this. I would rather stay here. I love it here. But it's my duty. It's the right thing. You have helped me see that."

"I will miss you."

"And I you!"

"But you will be back?"

"I'm sure . . . of course, sometime. I will have to see how it goes, what my father's situation is. I honestly can't look too far ahead until Alasdair's estate is sorted out and the National Trust and the castle and everything is resolved. But I think my leaving will be best—a clean break. Then I will think about whether to return to Scotland and in what capacity."

A terrific unseasonable storm came suddenly off the sea that same night. The wind whipped up into a cauldron, the trees everywhere lashed back and forth like blades of grass.

As we shut the doors of the castle that night, Alicia and Nicholls and I had the feeling that we were boarding ourselves in against a siege. Nicholls acted stoic and brave, as if it were nothing out of the ordinary, and went to his room. Alicia and I weren't anxious to go alone to our beds and instead had tea together. We talked late into the evening, almost like a final slumber party before the end of summer between two schoolgirls who would soon be parted. Of all the silly things, we found ourselves telling scary stories to each other, and laughing at the absurdity of them. I think we did so to keep from thinking about real ghosts on a night like this.

Sometime about ten o'clock the rain came. Rather than bringing a calm to the wind as often happens when the clouds finally release, the rain brought with it an increased ferocity in the storm. The rain slashed down in a torrent and blew against the windows with such force I wondered if the glass would hold. Still Alicia and I sat up talking together, doing our best to ignore it. By midnight we were so sleepy we had no choice but to finally say our good nights and depart to our beds.

Still the wind howled on and the rain pelted at the windows as if both were determined to tear the whole place to bits.

Usually rain is a comforting sound at night. But with Alasdair gone, and knowing that I was temporarily mistress of the place, with the wildness of the night, I didn't like it. Gradually I fell into an uneasy sleep.

A noise, as of a door banging, woke me sometime later. It was pitch black.

I lay for a moment wondering if I should turn on the lights and go to investigate. That's what Alasdair would do. If a shutter was banging, or if maybe a window had broken, it ought to be attended to.

But as I lay snug in my bed, I could not summon the courage to get up. Nicholls would see whatever it was in the morning. The wind was still frightful, but I heard no more of banging doors or shutters, and slowly drifted to sleep again.

By now my mind was full of storms and intruders and old monks and long-disused passageways and the chanting of medieval dirges, all woven together in a dreamy tapestry on the warp of the rain and the woof of the wind that my brain, even in sleep, could not completely shut out. Weird grotesque images came and went, one after another, like the fantasy of a horror movie...a girl laughing hideously, holding a human skull in her hands. Slowly the features of the skull began to move, its horrible mouth trying to speak but no words would come, then the hollow sockets of its eyes began to drip with tears...tears that were red...tears of blood. I tried to scream in my sleep, but my voice was as mute as the lifeless skull! The vision faded, the skull disappeared, the face of the girl changed to that of a woman...She held a stick of wood in one hand, and in the other a rag that had been dipped in blood held around a palm-sized rock. With the stick she beat the rag, but noiselessly...though as she chanted I could hear the words as they fell from her mouth: *"I beat this rag upon this stane, to raise the wind in the devil's name. It shall not fall till I please again."* The words sent a frozen shudder into my bones. Even as I dreamed I was conscious again of the wind howling terribly outside the castle and somehow I knew that the storm had been caused by the witch's incantation. Then suddenly it was as if I woke and sat up in my bed. A face was staring close upon me.

The ghost of my dream was Olivia Urquhart!

I tried to cry out but still was mute. Again she spoke the curse and beat the rag upon the stone, then slowly faded into the blackness.

Just before the dream ended, I seemed to see the hand that held the stick throw something. There was no light because the night was completely black, but I thought I saw specks of grass flickering as if in moonlight. Then my consciousness faded and sleep again overtook me.

When I woke, sunlight was streaming in my window and there was not so much as a breath of wind. I was so relieved that the storm and the night had passed that I got up in high spirits and tried to put the memory of the frightening dream behind me. Nicholls checked every door and window of the castle and found no damage, nor any door ajar.

The only thing that still puzzled me were a few fragments of what looked like straw on my bed, as if they had blown in from the storm. But they were not wet. And all the windows of my room had been tightly shut all night.

Chapter Twenty-nine

Home but Not Home

Ben of peaks the clouds that sever, oft thy steeps have wearied me;
Must I leave thy shade for ever? Then farewell, farewell to thee!
Every corrie, crag, and hollow, heath'ry brae and flowery dell,
Now awaken pangs of sorrow; but my thoughts I dare not tell.
—"Farewell"

The next day I went to see Alasdair's local solicitor and friend Nigel Crathie in Elgin. He was a man about my own age, early to midforties, I guessed, with a thick crop of light brown hair, personable and warm and sensitive to both the difficulties and the delicacies of my situation. He was very thin, which I noticed immediately, then remembered Alasdair telling me that he was an avid cyclist. It was obvious that he had cared a great deal for Alasdair, which in its own way was an added consolation. He was expecting me and had a thick sheaf of papers spread out on his desk. I hated to disappoint him. He was probably looking forward to an extensive lawyerly outline of all the intricate details of Alasdair's estate.

"I am not actually desirous of a detailed report right now, Mr. Crathie," I began. "Perhaps in time, after everything is sorted out and the disposition of the estate and its assets is complete. Of course I want to be helpful in any way possible to ensure that Alasdair's desires are thoroughly carried out. However, Alasdair always expressed his supreme confidence in you. I strongly want to avoid the appearance of exerting influence on decisions that are being made. I hope you understand my reluctance to be more deeply involved. My purpose today is simply to inform you of my immediate plans. My

189

father, who is living in the United States, is very ill. I will be flying to America next week to see him. Of course at that time I will be assessing my own future plans."

"I understand, Mrs. Reidhaven." Mr. Crathie nodded. "I am sorry about your father, of course. But with all due respect, I would urge you to delay the trip, if possible, for a month or two, until things are more clear in the matter of your husband's affairs. There are several other solicitors involved in Edinburgh. The complications will take some time to—"

"I'm sorry, Mr. Crathie," I said. "But my decision is made. Surely none of Alasdair's business interests will involve me. Our agreement ensures that I have no legal standing in my husband's affairs at this point, which is how I wanted it. Insofar as what details involve me, as specified in our prenuptial agreement, I simply want to be very clear so that there are no misunderstandings. As I understand it, the bank account my husband set up in my name will remain mine—"

"Yes, Mrs. Reidhaven—£100,000 . . . that is correct."

"And the car and the right to use the castle as long as I need."

The lawyer nodded.

"As I will be returning soon to Canada and the States, obviously I will not require accommodation after that. I would simply ask that ample provision be given Mr. Nicholls and Miss Forbes and the Campbells, and that they be afforded ample time to make other plans. I am sure Alasdair considered that as well, perhaps even made arrangements for them to stay on to see to the upkeep of the castle after it passes to the National Trust."

"Yes, those things are being looked into, as I say. The duke was very aware of their security."

"Good. I knew he would be. It would be a great help to me, Mr. Crathie, if you could arrange for the ownership of the Volvo to be transferred to Miss Forbes, and if you could see to my bank account in my absence—I plan to transfer £10,000 to my account in Canada. But the balance I would rather have you look after until my plans are more firm. When the time comes, I may ask you to wire it to me there, or if my plans bring me back to Scotland, we can discuss it in person."

"Are you . . . that is, might you *not* return, Mrs. Reidhaven?" asked Mr. Crathie.

"I honestly don't know. My life has been here for four years; my friends are here. I think there is every possibility that I will return and perhaps buy a small house in Port Scarnose or Crannoch. But I also have a lifetime of roots in Canada. I still own a home there, and I have to consider the possibility that my future is back there also. I have to consider my options for employment and for supporting myself. And of course there is my father's situation to think of. I have much to consider, and I simply cannot make any permanent decisions at this time."

"I understand."

"What few of my own belongings I am unable to take with me or ship I assume may be left at the castle until its future with the National Trust is settled?"

"Yes, of course, that should be no problem."

"I am thinking of my harps primarily, and two or three pieces of my own furniture. They can be shipped to me later if need be, or put in storage in some out-of-the-way place in the castle until I return."

"Certainly. I anticipate no difficulty in that regard. My experience with the National Trust is that they prefer to maintain everything as it is, including staff when possible, so that their properties are kept just as they have been. They are generally more than gracious and adaptable, seeking smooth and harmonious transitions and ongoing relationships. It is not even unusual for a portion of a castle or great house, even an entire wing, to be set aside for the use of the former owners. That is something I will look into. An Edinburgh solicitor by the name of Murdoch is actually handling negotiations with the National Trust on your husband's behalf, so I am not entirely conversant in all the specific details. It would not surprise me, knowing your husband, that he would have made arrangements for you to continue using an apartment in the castle."

"That would be nice, of course . . . as long as my presence interferes in no way with the management of the castle or estate. I would rather such an arrangement be made for Miss Forbes than for myself."

"I can assure you that you need have no concerns regarding the domestic staff. The National Trust is very sensitive in such matters."

"Thank you. That sets my mind at ease."

I gave Mr. Crathie my Canadian address and bank account information, signed a power of attorney for him to act on my behalf, then drove back to Port Scarnose feeling satisfied in my mind that I had left no problematic loose ends.

I had never been a showy person and therefore did not make a fanfare of my leaving. Now that I was no longer the Duchess of Buchan, and without the cover of Alasdair's position, suddenly I felt almost like the last four years had never happened, or had been a dream.

Suddenly I was back to my old self again. I felt like Lucy or Susan at the end of *The Lion, the Witch and the Wardrobe*, after being queens of Narnia for years and riding through the woods in all their royal regalia, suddenly to find themselves stumbling through the wardrobe again—back to everything as before, no time passed, no more crowns and robes and signet rings of gold . . . just their old selves . . . unchanged.

That was me.

I was again a visitor to Scotland getting ready to fly back to Canada . . . back through the wardrobe of my duchess dream . . . back to the reality of my former life.

There was no going-away party, no hoopla as I left. I made no announcements. I didn't even go to church on my last Sunday in Port Scarnose. I wanted to just slip out quietly.

There were of course many hugs and tearful good-byes. Ranald Bain wept when he took me in his arms.

"I shallna forgit ye, lass," he said with wet eyes and cheeks. "Ye've aye brought grit joy tae this auld hert."

And so it was with Tavia and Cora and Fia and Mrs. Gauld. Even stoic Harvey Nicholls seemed a little choked up as he offered me his hand.

The good-byes all said, and Alicia waiting for me in the Volvo at the garage, I took one last brief walk through the castle alone, saying good-bye. I passed slowly through the library, meandering through its high shelves of books, so solemn and regal. The whole place reminded me of Alasdair. I could not help shedding a new bucket of tears. Then I went across the hall to the Great Room and my studio, the first place I had played my harp for Alasdair. This room contained so many memories! I cried a little more, and smiled sadly and contentedly, allowing my eyes to linger on every piece of furniture, every tapestry, every sideboard and secretary . . . and the *Queen* and that portion of her court that was staying behind. I had told the ladies that they could continue using those harps until my future was more settled. Of course I took *Journey* with me.

From there I walked down the main central staircase. At last, drawing in a deep breath of melancholy finality, I opened the great oak door and walked outside. I closed the door slowly, gently, and laid my hand upon it.

"Good-bye, dear Castle Buchan," I whispered. "I have loved you. I hope I shall see you again. But if not, you will always be dear to my heart."

Then I turned, wiping my eyes one last time, and walked to the waiting car.

Alicia drove me to the airport in Aberdeen. We both cried a lot, with many promises to write and call . . . and then I was gone.

My Scotland adventure and dream were over.

The house of my former life in Calgary did not seem so sad and lonely and dreary as I had expected. I arrived in late September and it was still warm. I had always intended to sell the house, but some-how we had never gotten around to it. Now I was glad. Most of my furniture was still there. When Alasdair had arranged to pack the things I wanted and closed up the house before, we had shipped only a few things. The only harp I had on the plane was *Journey*. I would begin shopping for a new harp or two immediately so as to be available for lessons if I needed them when I saw what would become of my new life back on this side of the wardrobe.

After a week in Alberta getting my house livable again, I flew to Oregon for that part of my future I was least looking forward to.

I had written ahead for my father to expect me.

Chapter Thirty

Deep-Rooted Healing

I'll come back and see ye, again, again,
Since ye gi'ed me yer promise to be mine ain;
Nae langer I'll tarry alane, alane,
But haste to be happiest man among men.
—John Campbell, "I'll Come Back and See Ye"

I had never been to his house in Portland. I had not seen my father in eight years.

When I arrived by rented car at about five-thirty he wasn't home from his office yet . . . still carrying on his workload as always. Some of my old feelings crept back. Taking second fiddle to his work. I suppose as old as you get, some things never change. Childhood impressions are hard to get rid of.

I sat in the car and waited, taking in the neighborhood. Actually, as I looked around, the surroundings weren't all that classy. It was strictly middle-class, even slightly submedian. The house was an ordinary tract house. Nothing special.

An oldish Ford drove into the driveway about 6:15. I knew it was him from the shape of his head as I saw him from behind. I got out and walked over to greet my father as he stepped out.

I was shocked at what a visible change had taken place in him. Even though he was only sixty-six, he looked seventy-five. I would not have recognized him walking down the street—thinning hair of pure white, slightly stooped, not nearly as tall as I remembered him, and fifteen or twenty pounds lighter.

A pang of compassion stabbed my heart. Instantly I regretted all the thoughts I had harbored and my hesitations about coming. I now regretted that I had waited so long.

The recognition that a parent is getting *old* has to be one of the most poignant moments in the life of any son or daughter. The mere sight of him—I can't say it changed everything, but it *began* to change my heart toward him immediately. Blame, regret, misunderstanding... These all began to recede into the background as a wave of compassion swept through me.

I approached and smiled.

"Hello, Daddy," I said. "I'm here."

"Indeed you are, Angel—you look great!" he boomed. At least his voice was strong and unchanged. "I can't tell you how much I appreciate this."

I stepped forward and hugged him. It was a little stiff, made more awkward by the briefcase he still held in one hand. But it was a beginning. And often the first step, especially in relationships, is the most important of all.

"I ordered pizza," said my father as we walked toward the house. "It should be here in half an hour. You do still like pizza?"

"Of course."

"Half pepperoni, half Hawaiian, thin crust?"

"You remembered—that's exactly what I always ordered! I haven't had pizza in four years. It's not one of Scotland's specialties."

"Good—you will like this. I get it from a little place on twenty-third—best pizza in Portland. Come on in!"

The first evening went okay. You never know what to expect in such situations. We ate the pizza—my dad was right, it was one of the best I'd ever had!—and chatted and caught up...superficially in a way, but it was necessary to get past the opening pourparlers of trying to reengage together.

He showed me my room, and I must say it was more than I expected. The bedroom was spacious, with an easy chair, full cable TV with TiVo and all the trimmings. I wasn't a big TV addict. I hadn't watched as much as two hours of TV in four years, but I could tell that my father was trying to make me comfortable. The room had its own bathroom with separate shower *and* bath, a full-sized desk, and a lovely queen bed. There was even a little counter along one wall with a water boiler, hot plate, wet bar and sink, and minimal kitchen service in a cabinet above. I could be as independent as suited me. It was not just a guest room but a studio apartment. Much of the interior and furnishings were clearly new. My father had obviously gone to great lengths and expense to make my stay enjoyable and to put me at ease so that I could feel independent. His consideration touched me, though I felt bad that he had gone to so much trouble for a short stay.

I went to bed that evening emotionally worn out. I felt a sense of relief to be past the first evening, yet was filled with an array of mixed feelings. I didn't know where to put them all. My long-comfortable psyche was shifting wildly about on its emotional axis.

I had been dreading coming here as an ordeal to be faced. Yet as I laid my head down on the pillow and tried to pray and say my good nights to God, all I could think to say was, *Thank you, Lord...Maybe this isn't going to be so bad.*

Maybe seeing another's weakness and vulnerability opens your heart to them in different ways. Especially toward one's parents. You harbor so many images from childhood and your teens, and even from your twenties when you flatter yourself that you're finally an adult and are capable of seeing life and the world with such maturity and perspective...Then you reach your forties—and probably your fifties, too, though I wasn't there yet—and you begin to realize how little of life you really saw accurately. What is called the hubris of youth isn't really a hubris limited to youth at all, it is the hubris of *life*—we think we know more than we *really* know at *every* age.

I wonder if it's only on your deathbed that you begin to see with anything resembling true perspective. I couldn't know that yet. But I did know that suddenly everything about my father seemed different. He was no longer strong, indestructible, tall, handsome, powerful, intimidating, fearless...no longer a man I both feared and longed for, loved but resented, wanted to be close to yet wanted to avoid ... a man whose praise meant everything yet whom I had ignored for twenty years.

No wonder this was confusing.

Whatever annoyances and resentments and uncertainties sons and daughters heap in their imaginations upon their mothers and fathers, surely most of the relational schizophrenia between the generations lies on the child's side, even the *adult* child's side.

My father was just a *person*, an ordinary man—and suddenly vulnerable, weak, uncertain. I even detected fear in his eyes—fear of the future, the unknown, fear of death ... even fear of what I might think of him. What a realization for a child—humbling, awesome, frightful. He was still enough of a man that he tried to put on a macho front. But I could see all these uncertainties in the occasional dart of his eyes.

Such realizations plunged into my heart with emotions I had never felt, like I was being zapped by a spiritual defibrillator. It was shocking first one and then another region of my emotional and *human* sensitivities awake to changing realities in this most foundational of all human relationships to which I had been blind for over forty years—the relationship of a child to his or her own father.

My dad was up early the morning after my arrival. As I walked into the kitchen I found him preparing a lavish breakfast. It was ten times what I was accustomed to, but he was playing the part of parent and host, obviously enjoying himself, and I couldn't deny him that.

"Good morning, Angel!" he said. "Coffee ... or are you a thorough Brit now?"

"I'm afraid so, Dad—*do* you have tea?"

"Of course! I bought every kind I could find, hoping that one would suit your aristocratic tastes."

"I'm no aristocrat!" I laughed. "I just happened to marry one. But all that is over now. I'm just plain old me again."

"Hardly plain—you're a beautiful woman. I had forgotten how stunning you are."

His words silenced anything I might have been about to say. He had never said anything like that to me in my life!

"By the way, Angel," he went on, "how *did* you become a duchess? It sounds like it must have been a real fairy tale."

I smiled. "I suppose it was," I said. "Actually, it all has to do with a certain little redheaded girl—the duke's daughter. I guess you could say I stood up for her, maybe a little like you and your hard-luck cases, Dad."

"That reminds me," my father said. "I am sorry, again, about your husband, the duke. It must have been terrible to lose a second husband."

"Thank you. It wasn't easy."

"When you're up to it, I want to hear everything about him and your days as a duchess and the castle—every detail. And while we're on the subject of apologies, I am sorry, too, that I wasn't more supportive when Edward died. I don't suppose I was a very good father in those days—I'm sorry. Edward was, or at least he seemed, so self-sufficient, I didn't want to push myself on him. We just never seemed to click. I should have done more, I see that now. But I didn't and I deeply regret it. Can't make up for it now, though. The years went so fast. I always dreamed of you and I getting together more, of taking a trip together, maybe a cruise down the Danube or on the Med or something. But I never pursued it. Again ... I am sorry for not being more attentive as your father. That's why I feel like a heel asking you to come now. I hardly deserve it. But I had no one else to turn to. It means the world to me that you came."

"I'm glad you asked me, Dad." I felt totally disarmed with his being so open and appreciative.

"I know you've got your own life to live, and I'm not expecting you to stay long. Just to know I can call you is a great relief to me. All I want is for you to be familiar with my affairs—but I won't burden you beyond that. I've named you executor of my estate. I hope you don't mind. If you do, I'll get one of my partners to do it, but I'd rather it was you."

"I guess that's okay." I nodded. "You said it's not complicated. I don't know that I'm much of a businessperson."

"You won't have to be. No, it's not complicated. I have enough money set aside—not a fortune, but two or three hundred thousand, plus the house, which should be enough to get me into a decent care facility when the time comes. There are plenty of good ones in the Portland area. I won't be able to afford the luxury ones with the insane buy-ins that rip off wealthy elderly people and make lots of money for their owners. Don't get me started! All lawyers have a little Don Quixote in them, you know. I'd love to take those guys on, but I've already got more windmills than I can handle, and time is running out. Anyway, I will be able to afford a reasonable place that cares for people more than profits."

He paused and drew in a breath. "So when my time comes," he went on, "and this nuisance of a cancer finally gets me, all my needs should be taken care of. I've also made, you know, my final arrangements with a funeral home, so that's another thing you won't have to worry about. Cremation . . . that seems best . . . buried with your mom. I don't want anything to be a burden for you."

I could hardly stand to hear him talk so bluntly. But he was obviously trying to be straightforward and not dance around it—which was probably good.

"I have to go into the office this morning, but I'll be home by one or two. That will give us a chance to spend some more time together. Thank you again, sweetheart, for coming. I can't tell you what it means to me."

"Are you . . . How long are you going to keep working?" I asked.

"As long as I can. What am I going to do, sit around and wait to die . . . walk the dog, feed the pigeons? I don't have a dog, and I don't like pigeons. That's always the hope, isn't it—stay active. There is still a lot of good I can do, so I will keep trying to do what I can."

"But surely...other people, the rest of your law firm...they will take your cases."

He smiled. "There's really no one else that does what I do," he said cryptically. "I don't mean that boastfully, it's just a fact. I have what you might call a unique niche in the legal profession. I like to think it is a ministry. It always has been to me. My own personal windmills. Jones helps me—he's my right-hand man, so to speak. Most of my other colleagues think I'm nuts. But how much of it will continue is a serious concern of mine. That's why I am devoting my last efforts to trying to ensure its continuation."

I had no idea what he was talking about. But if I needed to know, I would surely find out in time.

True to his word, my father arrived home about one-thirty that afternoon. I'd slept half the morning and hadn't really done much of anything. He took me out and we drove through part of Portland and walked awhile along twenty-first and twenty-third streets. He took me by his office and introduced me to his three partners. After we were back at his house he pulled out his will and asked if I wanted to see it.

"Do you want me to?" I asked.

"I just want you to be familiar enough with things so that it's easy on you when the time comes. I know we won't have a lot of time together and that you have to get back home."

I looked through his will, but most of it was in legalese I didn't understand. He pointed out the sections that specified what he had already told me.

"And then...I don't know if you'd mind," he went on, "but would you maybe want to drive around with me tomorrow and look at a few of the care places I've narrowed it down to and tell me what you think? I'd like you to help me with the decision. I don't want to presume on your time and your kindness for coming, but it would be a big help to me."

"Uh, yeah, sure," I replied. "I guess that would be fine."

Driving around the following day with my father was sad and gloomy.

We visited four care facilities. Though they had rooms and apartments and whole buildings for self-sufficient retired people called "independent living," my father was focused on the "continuing-care" and "assisted-living" facilities. His situation was obviously different from that of someone moving into such a place with ten or twenty years left to live. My father's final diagnosis was already in—he was on a predictable timetable that would lead to his death, and he knew it. He would not even move into one of these places until he could no longer take care of himself. So he would go straight to assisted living when that time came.

We spent our time touring apartments and rooms and medical facilities that looked more like hospital wards than care *homes*. It was genuinely depressing—people in wheelchairs and on IVs, sitting staring blankly ahead, some walking up and down hallways pushing walkers and talking gibberish to themselves, many lying in beds motionless with mouths open, looking like they were already dead. An atmosphere of gloom and impending death pervaded everywhere...the smell of antiseptic and oldness, unpleasant bodily odors and medicines and alcohol...and occasionally the faint whiff of stale urine in the air...and worse.

Was this how we were all destined to end up? But my dad was cheerful and upbeat, visiting with nurses and all the residents, asking questions. He had obviously come to terms with his future better than I had.

We made no decisions, but my father seemed pleased with the day, and from his comments succeeded in narrowing his choices down to two of the four places we visited. That's how we left it when I returned to Calgary two days later.

Chapter Thirty-one

Decision of Privilege

I wish, I wish, I wish in vain;
I wish I were a maid again.
But a maid again I'll never be,
Till an apple grows on an orange tree.
—"Will Ye Gang Love?"

I tried to convince myself that I still had plenty of time to accustom myself to this new role in my dad's life that had come upon me so suddenly. I told myself that nothing would change immediately, that I had time to adjust.

But it weighed on me. I knew more and bigger change was coming.

However, I was not prepared for how quickly it came.

A month later I received a call from one of my father's partners. My dad had collapsed in court and been taken to the hospital in an ambulance.

I gulped and braced myself for what might be coming next.

"Is it . . . I mean, is he—"

"He will recover," said Mr. Jones, a man in his mid-fifties whom I had met and who was obviously devoted to my father. I would later learn that my father had been his mentor in the legal profession and had financed most of his years in law school. "Actually, it's not the cancer," Jones went on. "He also has congestive heart failure and they think he may have suffered a mini heart attack. They want to keep him for another few days, but it is doubtful he will be able to keep working much longer. Nor live alone, for that matter. I know you and he have talked about arrangements—it might be time for some decisions."

"I see. Well, I appreciate the call," I said. "I will be there as soon as I can get a flight."

When I walked into the hospital room two days later, my dad was sitting up in bed and looking fine, joking with a couple of nurses who were reading various monitors attached to him.

"Angel!" he exclaimed. "Look, ladies, here is my gorgeous daughter I told you about. You're just in time, Angel . . . They're getting ready to release me from this prison!" he added with a wink to one of the nurses.

"Please, Mr. Buchan," she said, laughing. "We have to work here!"

The hospital discharge coordinator was blunt when we met with her two hours later.

"You do realize, Mr. Buchan," she said, "that you will not be able to remain alone indefinitely. Both of your conditions are progressing. As your body weakens, you will need care."

"We know—yes, it's all taken care of," said my father. "We're looking at a couple of places where an old worn-out attorney can live out his last days, aren't we, Angel?"

I nodded, but it was still hard hearing him talk so.

"And what is your situation, Mrs. Reidhaven?" the lady asked me.

"I live in Calgary," I replied. "I just flew in."

"Oh . . . right, I see. Well, just make sure you don't delay a decision beyond the point where the change becomes unnecessarily difficult."

I had rented a car again. As I drove my father back to his house, he continued to sound the optimistic note. But there had obviously been a change. The fall . . . an ambulance . . . a hospital stay. These were serious developments. The inevitable was approaching.

I was thinking hard as we drove.

When I had him comfortable in his own bed at home, I sat down on the edge of it beside him. "Do you *want* to live in a care home, Daddy?" I asked.

"Nobody *wants* to. But you have to go someplace. After your mother was gone I figured that's how it would end up for me, and so I made plans accordingly."

"What if you could stay here?" I asked.

"You mean in the house?"

I nodded.

"Sure, who wouldn't want to stay home? Believe me, I'll stay as long as I can. But with terminal cancer, and this ticker of mine giving way, like the lady said, it's about time when I will need help. It won't be a pretty picture. By then it will be impossible for me to be alone."

"But what if you *could* stay here...even then?"

"I've thought of the in-home-care scenario. But do you know what round-the-clock nursing care costs? Probably five or eight, maybe even ten grand a month. It's outrageous."

"You could afford it."

"For a while, but not for long. And there'd be nothing left at the end. What if I got lucky and held on longer than they think I will and ran out of money? That's the thing...timing it so you have enough for whatever care you will need. That's why I dismissed the home-nurse thing—I can get into a facility for a third or fourth of what nursing would cost."

"But what if it *was* possible?"

"Well, of course, that's the dream, isn't it, to die in your own home in your own bed? But not everyone has that luxury."

When it was that I realized I would stay in Portland to be with my father—to be his caregiver until he died—I can't say. I think the possibility began to play around the corners of my subconscious that first day of my previous trip. I had come to Portland having never considered the possibility. The moment I saw my father, my whole outlook and attitude began to change—about my own life as much as my father's.

Probably the final decision was made on the airplane that same morning as I thought of him lying in the hospital, then thought of the various places we had visited. I didn't know it, but I think the die was cast by the time I landed at the Portland airport.

Who can say which one of us had done the most changing?

I realized that I *wanted* to stay with him and be with him. I *loved* him. I was finally ready to be a true daughter. I wanted to make the last weeks, months, or years of his life, however long it was, peaceful and happy. I suppose my decision and the reason for it answered my own question . . . The greatest change had taken place within *me*. It was not my father's attitude toward me that had needed remaking all those years, it was mine toward him.

That I had waited so long would probably bring tears to my eyes for the rest of my life. I wished I could go back and get it right far sooner in life than now. But life doesn't go back. It unfolds in only one direction. And to get it right *sometime* is the main thing. I was so grateful that the change in my heart had come before it was completely too late to be a daughter again.

"I'll stay with you, Daddy," I said, taking his hand in mine. "I'll be here as long as you need me."

"I couldn't ask you to do that, Angel, not after all the years I—"

"Don't say it, Daddy. Those years have passed. Neither of us did as much as we might have. Whatever distance and misunderstandings may have existed were as much my fault as anyone's. All that's behind us now. I have regrets, you have regrets. But we have *this* time now to be together. I want to spend it with you. It's the one last thing I can do for you— Make it possible for you to—"

I paused and swallowed. "Well, you know, to die in your own bed. It would be my privilege to do that for you."

Tears rose in his eyes. He was actually crying. I swallowed hard again. I had never seen my father cry in my life.

And so it was that I moved into my father's house and nursed him for eight months. I consider it one of the most meaningful times of my life, a privilege that few have, and even fewer take advantage of. My spiritual life probably deepened more in those eight months than in all the previous four years.

Strangely, it was thus the approach, after losing several people I loved, of yet *another* death that enabled me to cope with having lost a second husband.

Chapter Thirty-two

Cultivating Eyes of Devotion and Honor

Though I dare not call thee mine, bonnie lassie, O,
As the smile of fortune's thine, bonnie lassie, O;
Yet with fortune on my side,
I could stay thy father's pride,
And win thee for my bride, bonnie lassie, O.
—Thomas Lyle, "Kelvin Grove"

What accounts for learning to see with eternal eyes?

Maybe it is the approach of eternity itself.

Almost immediately after my decision to move in and be my father's final caregiver, and committing to do all I could to make his last days ones of contentment, new awarenesses came over me of things I had never seen before.

I began to get glimpses that I realized were tiny windows into my father's deepest self.

Little observations snuck into my mind, seemingly insignificant details that few would think twice about. But now they worked on me. For so many years I had been too busy reacting only by considering the effect my father had on *me*. It was a *self*-concentric worldview of everything about him. But was that the best way to see him accurately? Obviously not. I hadn't seen the real him. What I now began to notice had probably been in front of my nose all my life. But I had never seen what those glimpses of reality said about the real Richard Buchan.

Why did he drive an old Ford when he could have afforded a more expensive car?

Why did he live in a modest house in a neighborhood that was on the wane instead of somewhere more upscale?

Why was his furniture so unpretentious?

Why was half the carpet in his house threadbare?

The guest room he had fixed up for me was the nicest room in the house. Everything for *him* was plain and ordinary, his clothes off the rack, whereas his colleagues all wore thousand-dollar suits.

He had been a lawyer for forty years. Lawyers make big money. Why didn't he have a five-million-dollar investment portfolio? Where had the money gone? Here he was, at the end of his life, with only enough put away to afford a mediocre care facility that smelled like a public bathroom. How many lawyers in a large city would think of retiring on less than a million dollars?

I looked around the house. The conclusion was obvious: My dad lived simply. He had simple tastes, he put on no airs. I noticed the tools in his shop in the garage—everything neat, tidy, orderly; every tool sharp, oiled, clean, polished, and well-maintained.

He *loved* his tools. Yet he was willing to lend to anyone in an instant without thought for what might be the tool's condition when returned. His tools were just like money to him—not possessions to be guarded or hoarded, but to be used for the good of whomever they could benefit.

One of his neighbors came over to borrow his lawn mower, a Mexican man obviously new to the US and relatively poor. But there was my dad in the same neighborhood, not only lending him the lawn mower, but going over to help him with his lawn...when he was dying of cancer! He spent the whole afternoon with the man and returned aglow from the opportunity to help someone. *Helping* people was his meat and drink. Okay, maybe he hadn't been the perfect father to me, as I saw it. But was *my* perspective all that accurate? Had I been a perfect daughter?

He was kind, caring, and unassuming. What had I expected him to be all those years if not that?

My dad was a good, selfless, others-focused, *humble* man. His faith *meant* something. He had not lived for himself.

What a legacy for a man to leave behind!

As this process developed in me, I saw that eyes capable of seeing devotion and honor weren't automatically handed out—you had to *cultivate* them. You had to train yourself to see through eyes of love. You had to *work* at it. You had to learn to see and interpret life differently than you did when you were young and you viewed your parents through the eyes of self. You had to *choose* a different orientation.

Wasn't having a father of *character*, who was faithful to one woman all his life, who worked hard and invested his life in people—a true role model—wasn't that more important than anything else? During my years in Calgary I had known lots of harp families with Disneyland dads who did all sorts of fun things with their kids and spent time with them, but who had been married two or three times, who couldn't hold a job, and whose lives revolved around themselves.

I had a father of *character*. Why hadn't I been able to see it?

It was with a real sense of grief and pain that I realized I had fallen into the same error with my father that I had briefly with Alasdair before I met him. I had misjudged him and taken the child's "side," so to speak, in that case Gwendolyn's, before knowing the whole story. I had been doing that all my life with my father. I had taken the side of *my* perspectives, without really knowing my father at all—even though I was his own daughter.

Over the next several months, my father slowly weakened. He rarely went to his office. Eventually we mutually decided that he should stop driving. It was hard for him, but he accepted it practically and stoically. When he needed to run errands after that, I drove him. He gradually slept more and continued to lose weight. His movements about the house slowed to puttering rather than the kind of work he had so long been accustomed to. He kept trying to rake the leaves on the lawn, and even talked about getting up on a ladder to clean out the gutters. But I was increasingly worried about him falling, and kept a careful watch on that ladder!

I tried to take him out as often as we could—drives into the country, stopping by the office to see his friends; even going to the market for fried chicken was a highlight.

Then came the time when he began using a walker, another difficult transition for such a robust man. More and more of his time was spent in front of the television. His life became reduced to moving back and forth between bedroom and bathroom and living room.

As the months progressed there were occasional stumbles and periodic falls. It killed me to see him in his weakness. Though it took us both a good deal of getting used to, I had to start helping with bathroom cleanliness, and helping him take showers. It's part of life. Such was the price of being able to keep him at home. Nothing worthwhile comes without sacrifice.

Hospital visits...chemo...endless blood tests...occasional blood transfusions...the spread of the cancer to his liver...everything moved according to the progression my father's oncologist had prepared me to expect.

In his final two months it became necessary for my father to wear adult diapers—"senior shorts," he jokingly called them—one more indignity he had to get used to. Yet more and more I considered these months one of the great privileges of my life.

I played my harp for hours at his bedside. Whenever I found myself playing one of Gwendolyn's songs, he perked up and asked, "What's that?...It's so far away—it reminds me of heaven."

If he only knew! I thought.

"I'm afraid of dying, Angel," he surprised me by saying one day.

"Let me tell you about a girl I met in Scotland," I said, "who faced death more bravely than anyone I could imagine. She wasn't afraid because she wanted to play a harp with the angels."

He nodded but said nothing as he listened.

"She's the girl I told you about, the duke's daughter who is the reason I became a duchess."

"You said you stood up for her?"

"In a manner of speaking," I answered. "She was living with her aunt at the time and her father had not been allowed to see her for years."

I briefly told him the story, then recounted my visit with Iain to confront Olivia Urquhart. His eyes filled with light as he listened.

"That's my girl!" he exclaimed. "Everyone else was afraid of her, but you took her on! Good for you. You never could sit still for injustice."

"Just like you, Daddy."

He chuckled. "I suppose you're right. Anyway, what you did took courage, and look how lives were changed as a result."

I was amazed as I listened. Maybe my father had been more proud of me than I had realized.

"Remember Betsy and Clarissa in high school...and the prom, and how I told Clarissa off?" I asked.

"Of course," he answered. "I always kind of regretted that I was a little hard on you at the time."

"No you weren't, Dad."

"I said you overreacted."

"You were right."

"Perhaps. But it wasn't what you wanted to hear. Do you want me to let you in on a secret? Down inside I was proud of what you did, for standing up for a friend. Your overreaction wasn't nearly so important as that. I felt I needed to speak a cautionary word—but I knew that it took character and courage to stand up for a friend. Seeing that character inside you warmed my heart. That's when I said to myself, 'This girl of mine is going to be all right—she's got her priorities straight.'"

I didn't know what to say. I think if I'd tried to say anything I'd have gotten all choked up. I had no idea my father had such thoughts about me. I was glad for the silence that followed.

"Will you be afraid to die, Angel?" asked my father after a minute or two.

"I don't think so, Daddy," I said softly. "I hope not. But how can I know until I am facing it. But I want to play my harp with the angels, too, and see little Gwendolyn and play with her again—though she will be older than me then. And I believe God is a good and loving Father—a little like you, Daddy, but even more, I hope you don't mind me saying. He is so good that he won't let anything bad happen to any of his children. I trust him."

"All those years when I was sold out for Jesus, as we street Christians called it, they seem so far away now."

"But God is the same."

"I hope you're right. Death brings doubt, though. You want so badly to see beyond. But you can't."

Gradually he became quieter, more withdrawn, interested less and less in what was going on around him. I could tell he was letting go of the final remnants of this life. The doctor said it was time for hospice to be brought in.

The failing continued until Dr. Stokes basically said that he was probably in his last two or three weeks.

I began sleeping on the couch outside his room. Getting him to and from the bathroom became an enormous chore. His legs were so thin and weak he could hardly stand. I became *so* tired from being up and down and half asleep all night listening for any sound that might require my attention. Sleep deprivation became one of the most difficult aspects of all.

There were several more falls. Gradually more silence, increasing withdrawal. I wondered if he was aware of my presence at all. Occasional mumbling...He seemed to be talking to people he had known. Once or twice I was sure he was talking to my mother. More and more hours he spent in bed, until a day came when he remained in bed all day, eating and drinking nothing, saying nothing, just staring blankly up at the ceiling. I sat at his side and tried to spoon water between his parched lips. It was obvious he was drifting away. The tide was ebbing out of the harbor.

Two nights later I heard nothing all night. When morning came I was shocked to find that I'd slept seven hours straight through.

I went into my dad's room. His face was ghostly white with a gray pallor. I touched his right hand where it hung out from beneath the covers. It was icy cold.

My father was gone. He had died in the middle of the night.

I sat at his bedside and cried awhile. Then I set about making the necessary calls and arrangements.

The long vigil was over. I felt empty, numb, but clean in a strange way... whole, like I had completed something important, even touched the edges of eternity leaking down into my own life in this temporal world.

Mr. Jones came to the house midmorning. He told me that a large memorial service was already being arranged by my father's partners.

"Do you really think it's necessary?" I said. "Wouldn't a small ceremony just with your office people and me be enough?"

Mr. Jones smiled. "Yes, there definitely has to be a memorial service," he said.

"But why?"

"The community needs it. You will see. You will be amazed."

He was right. I had been so sure that the church where the service was to be held was far too big. But it was crowded to overflowing. There must have been a thousand people. I was stunned at the outpouring of love and gratitude for my father. Once he opened the service to testimonials, the minister could not stop what he had begun.

"Mr. Buchan helped me and my wife qualify to buy our house when no one else believed in us..."

"Richard cosigned the loan for the first car I ever bought. Now I have a car dealership of my own..."

"Richard agreed to represent me in court when I had no one else..."

"Richard helped me remodel my kitchen, never a word, not a thought of payment for all the evenings he came over and worked with me..."

"Richard was always willing...no, *eager* to lend a helping hand. There was nothing he loved so much as helping someone in need..."

"I first met Richard Buchan at a time when I was doing very badly. Within a week he had led me to the Lord, taught me how to pray, and was instrumental in getting me involved in church. Now, believe it or not, I am an assistant pastor..."

"When my husband was in jail, Mr. Buchan prayed with me. He prayed that I would trust God, then he prayed for himself, that he would be given wisdom to know how best to defend him. His prayers were answered and my husband was released..."

"Richard lent me a thousand dollars one time when I was really in dire straits. When I finally got together enough to pay him back— and this was after four years, and during all that time he never so much as mentioned the money—and I asked him how much the interest would be, he just laughed and brushed my question away with a wave of the hand. 'I don't believe in interest,' he said..."

And so it went for at least forty-five minutes!

After a while my mind was unable to absorb the specifics of story after story about my father. I just sat shaking my head in amazement as yet one more person stood with some altogether different tale of how my father's life had touched him deeply and personally. Afterward, literally dozens of men and women I did not know came up to me. Nearly all said some variation of the same thing—*"How fortunate you must feel to have had such a man for a father."* I could only smile and nod, quietly grateful that at last I understood...and I was indeed grateful for him.

Mr. Jones walked me to my car after the service.

"Even after all this time with him, I just had no idea," I said, still amazed at what had taken place.

"Your father was one of the shrewdest lawyers in Portland,"

Mr. Jones said. "He didn't take on hard-luck cases because he was a patsy, but because he believed in truth, in trying to right wrongs, in justice. He believed in *people*. He was also one of the most respected lawyers in Portland. He would have made a great judge and probably could easily have been elected. I tried to talk him into running many times. But he wanted to invest work at the grassroots level where people's needs were. That's where he felt he could do the most good. His life was devoted to others. When I say he believed in people, I am the living example of it. I wouldn't be an attorney today if it weren't for your father. I hope I can be worthy to try to carry on his work with a tenth of his effectiveness."

"Did he ever date again, or anything like that?" I asked, surprised by my own question.

"He was too devoted to your mother for that. He wasn't interested. He was a one-woman man. He never stopped loving her. *And* you. He talked about you all the time. I am so glad we have had the chance to get to know one another, and I hope that you will keep in touch. If there is anything you ever need, please contact me. Your father was my best friend. I owe him everything."

"Thank you, Mr. Jones," I said with a smile. "I will keep in touch, I promise."

He gave me a hug and we parted. I drove back to my father's house, mine now . . . or soon would be when the legalities of my father's affairs were concluded.

I walked into the house, so silent, so empty, so devoid of the life that had been here such a short time ago . . . now departed.

Ichabod. I was truly alone now.

I walked all through the house, then into the garage, with my father's workshop to one side. He had loved this area more than any other place in the house. Woodworking had been such a passion for him. His radio sat on the workbench. Beside it sat a bookstand with a Bible opened to 2 Thessalonians.

Absently I moved closer and gazed at the page. At the end of the last verse, in his familiar hand, were penciled several dates—Feb 1979, Nov 1987, June 1999, Aug 2007.

Hmm, I thought to myself, *what could those mean?*

I flipped to the next book, 1 Timothy. It had similar markings after its final verse. I continued to page forward and back, randomly checking other books—every book of the Bible had four dates, and all in rough sequence through the years 1976, 1987, 1999, and 2008. It gradually dawned on me that I had stumbled upon my father's schedule of Bible readings. He had been through this Bible four times!

Even after his death, still more windows into the man were opening to my consciousness.

I began looking around his workshop. Little handwritten notes— Scriptures, reminders, prayers—were taped or stuck on nails all around me—my father's reminders to himself to stay spiritually focused. I saw a prayer list full of names I had never heard of—all except one . . . *Angel Dawn Marie.*

Tears came to my eyes. My father had been praying for me! I wondered how long this prayer list had been here.

I continued to gaze about his workbench. A small bookcase stood at the back to one end of the worktable against the wall, partially obscured by a circular saw and belt sander, with a T square, level, and several long clamps leaning against it. I removed them all and set them aside so I could examine the contents.

It was a shelf full of Bibles! There was a New English, and a New American Standard, a King James, a Concordant Literal New Testament, something called an Emphasized Bible. Then my eyes fell on a Revised English Bible similar to the one Moira in Crannoch had given Alasdair and me. There were several Revised Standard Versions, two editions of the New International, even something called a Greek-English Interlinear New Testament.

I had no idea my father studied the Bible in Greek!

As I pulled out one, now another, every one was thumb-worn, and all with the same dates listed at the ends of the Bible's books noting the month and year when my father had completed reading them. Most had a Gideons Bible reading schedule stuffed somewhere between the pages. He must have read through the Bible in a different translation every year or two. As I began to tally it up in my head, a remarkable fact dawned on me: *My dad must have read the Bible through at least twenty times!*

From being a man I had been dreading to come to Portland to see, he had become a man I was proud and honored to call my father. How thankful I was to God for this year I'd had with him, and that my eyes had been opened at last to the true measure of his eternal manhood.

Chapter Thirty-three

Aftermath of Another Parting

The homes of my kinsmen are blazing to Heaven,
The bright sun of morning has blushed at the view;
The moon has stood still on the verge of the even,
To wipe from her pale cheek the tint of the dew.
—"Callum O'Glen"

Compared with Alasdair's estate, my father's affairs were simplicity itself. As I had already realized, for a lawyer, he didn't have much stashed away. The outpouring of testimonials at his service no doubt explained where much of his income over the years had gone, as did his penchant for hopeless but worthy cases where some principle he believed in was at stake. His partner Mr. Jones told me that fully half his cases never saw a dollar of income, which frustrated his associates but only added to the esteem in which Richard Buchan was held in many circles. Wherever I went, it seemed, once people learned that I was Richard Buchan's daughter, their faces lit up with the memory of some story.

In spite of his generosity, my father had managed to put away some $240,000 in investments, which had been the nest egg he had intended to spend in full-time care as his cancer had advanced. Whatever might be left was stipulated in his will to be split equally between me and the Portland Area Foundation, which was taking over the administration of two smaller foundations my father had started and had been funding—one for Portland-area orphans of veterans, the other for financial and medical assistance for widows of vets. Given his semihippie and, I assumed, antiwar background of

218

the '60s and '70s, it was an interesting cause for my father to have devoted himself to—probably another of those aspects of his life with a story behind it I did not know. As it turned out, the whole $240,000 still remained. Both I and the two foundations were the recipients of more than might otherwise have been the case. Mr. Jones sat on the boards of both foundations and was committed to the advancement of my father's vision. My father had hoped I might also want to be involved in the ongoing work of the foundations but did not want to impose it upon me. Now I *wanted* to keep abreast of their activities to whatever extent I was able.

The house he left to me also, which was paid for, and a modest $50,000 life insurance policy. The two men in my life—Alasdair and my father, both now gone—had made sure that I would not have to go to work for a good long while, possibly indefinitely. I felt wealthy beyond my wildest dreams, and I even began to think about what I ought to do to begin getting *rid* of some of the money they had left me. Until then, I needed to wisely invest the cash and proceeds from the house so as to make the best use of what they had entrusted to me.

I put the house in Portland up for sale, left everything in the hands of Mr. Jones, and returned to Calgary with a full heart of thankful sadness.

Flying back on the plane with the box of his ashes, strange to say, I don't think I had ever felt closer to my father in my life. All the realizations of the previous year culminated in a level of knowing and love that I never could have imagined feeling toward him.

I took the small box to the memorial garden where it was laid to rest beside my mother. It put me through many emotions to see their two bronze plaques together there side by side.

I was alone in the world. Suddenly again, my future loomed large.

As for life after my father's death, I knew I had to establish some new directions. Obviously I thought about returning eventually to Scotland. But I needed to let more time pass. And my father's work tugged at me. Was my future meant to include carrying on that work in some way?

I suppose most people in similar circumstances, without pressing financial worries, would simply have asked themselves, "What do I *want* to do? What would make me *happy*?" and then followed the course that presented itself.

But things were different for me now. I had been tutored in matters of faith by two men who did not order their lives by what they might *want*, or even by what they might consider best *for them*, but by the question "What does my Master want me to do?"

Along with Ranald Bain and Iain Barclay, who first taught me to see things through different eyes, I also now had the example of my own father—long overlooked—to guide me. It was an example of service, selflessness, and tireless work on behalf of others less fortunate than himself. All around me were examples of giving and sacrifice and dedication to the will of God.

How could I follow any other course? How could I even think to ask what *I* wanted?

Therefore, the question I now asked myself, and the prayer that went with it, was, "God, what do *you* want me to do?"

It seemed entirely possible that the answer *might* be a return to Scotland. But I was not yet sure of that.

Were the new directions that must necessarily come to my life to be found in Scotland . . . in Calgary . . . or in Portland helping to further my father's charitable work? A child is largely unaware of the many lives touched and influenced by his or her parents. My father had devoted his life as a Christian to changing lives. I had been too self-motivated for most of my life to recognize the widespread impact of his efforts. Maybe I was supposed to be an ongoing part of that vision now that he was gone.

Yet Scotland was in my blood.

I now had two Scottish names. Even though I was back on this side of the magical wardrobe, I could never forget the part of me that would always remain linked to my own real-life Narnia, which happened to be called Port Scarnose, Morayshire, Scotland.

I was concerned about Alicia; I had not heard from her in a long time—almost nine months, in fact. I had been so caught up with my father's last days and the increasingly twenty-four-hour nature of his illness and decline, that time had flown by. I had written to her several times but had received no replies. When I tried to telephone, I found that the number at the castle had been changed. I kept telling myself I needed to set aside time to investigate and try information or call Mrs. Gauld, and somehow to get Alicia's number. But I never did. I wrote another two letters after arriving back in Calgary, but still received no reply.

My life didn't settle into its old routine because too much time had passed for that. But I began to establish some new routines while awaiting leading or guidance concerning whether my future lay in Calgary, Scotland, or Portland. I found a church I liked. I gradually made new friends. I played on my harp, though I desperately missed the *Queen* and lamented her plight, which amounted to being kept in storage back at the castle, wrote a few songs, traveled some, took on two or three new students, and ordered two new harps.

Chapter Thirty-four

A Shocking Tale

Give me the land where torrents flash,
Where loud tha angry cat'racts roar,
As wildly on their course they dash,
Then here's a health to Scotia's shore.
Give me the land of mountains steep,
Where wild and free the eagles soar,
The dizzy crags where tempests sweep,
Then here's a health to Scotia's shore.
—James Little, "Here's a Health to Scotia's Shore"

I had been back in Calgary nearly three months when the doorbell rang one afternoon about three o'clock.

I glanced out the window as I got up and walked across the room to answer it. There sat a taxicab in front of my house.

I opened the door and my jaw dropped three inches.

"Alicia!" I cried and ran forward and buried her in a hug that nearly knocked her over on my porch.

"Oh, Marie . . . I can't believe I'm finally here!" She sighed wearily and went limp in my arms.

"But what *are* you doing here?" I said, stepping back.

"It is a long story . . . a very long story."

"All I can say is that this is wonderful! I am so happy to see you. Come in!"

"Let me first go pay the taxi—I wasn't sure I had the right house. I have my suitcase and everything. I came straight from the airport . . . You'll be able to help me find a place to stay?"

"Alicia, what are you talking about?! You're staying with me."

Still standing where she was, she began to cry. I ran back inside, got my purse, and hurried out to pay the cab. The driver carried Alicia's suitcase and a smaller bag up and set them on the porch. I got Alicia inside and to the couch, where she collapsed in relief and utter exhaustion.

"Oh, Marie," she sighed as I put water on to boil for tea, "you can't imagine what I've been through. I didn't think I would *ever* get here. The flight is so long. And I wasn't sure if you wanted me to come."

"Why wouldn't I? It's wonderful. I am so excited to see you!"

"It's just that when I didn't hear from you—"

"I just wrote you two weeks ago . . . and a week before that."

"I didn't receive any letters."

"The mail can't be *that* slow."

"There's been nothing in four months."

"How could that be?"

"I haven't heard from you since you wrote just after your father died. That's why I wasn't sure you would be here."

"I haven't heard from you either," I said. "It's been . . . Let me see, I think it was about nine months ago . . . Well, before my father began to fail badly."

"But I must have written a dozen times."

"Alicia, I have had no letters in all that time."

"You didn't even know I was coming?"

"Not until I saw you standing on the porch."

"It's all such a bad dream! Now it begins to make sense. I was despondent to hear nothing from you. I thought you had decided to cut your ties to Scotland. I didn't think you wanted to keep in touch with me."

"Nothing could be further from what I was thinking."

"Oh!" she wailed. "It's even worse than I thought!"

"What is, Alicia? What is going on? You are worrying me. You're making it sound like some disaster has taken place!"

"Maybe that's not so far wrong either—it is a disaster in a way."

"What is ... what's going on?"

"Oh, I'm so tired, I don't know if I can go through it all," she said, sighing again.

"Do you want to take a short nap first? Or have some tea? A brief nap will perk you up and help you get through the day. But no more than thirty minutes, otherwise the jet lag will be dreadful."

"Maybe just a cat nap, then. You can wake me when you think it's been long enough."

"In the meantime, I'll have tea and a snack ready. Come—I'll show you your room."

I pulled Alicia up and we walked arm in arm to my bedroom. I had no other bed in the house, but my hide-a-bed love seat would suit me fine. She plopped onto the mattress facedown without even taking her shoes off, and was asleep in three minutes.

Promptly thirty minutes later I nudged her awake. Groggily she begged me for a few minutes more, but I knew from experience that to give in would be deadly. I dragged her into the kitchen and placed a steaming strong cup of Nambarrie beneath her nose. Gradually the aroma of the nectar acted like timed-release smelling salts to her brain. She slowly began to come to herself. By the time we were enjoying a second cup, she had revived and was beginning the astonishing tale that had sent her four thousand miles over the polar ice cap in search of me. It was indeed an incredible story. I listened with eyes wide, mouth hanging open, alternating between disbelief and fury.

"She wasted no time. It was just after you left, three days exactly," Alicia began, "when Olivia presented herself at the castle. I don't know where Max was—he wasn't with her. She did not sound the knocker or ring the bell or anything but simply walked in like she owned the place, which she assumed she did. Everyone knew about your prenuptial arrangement with the duke ... Alasdair, God bless him, he won't mind me calling him that now. It was the talk of the whole place after you left. No one liked it because everyone was fond of you and the duke and no one wanted to see the castle in anyone else's hands. They pestered me with questions about you, why you left, when you were coming back. I said nothing more than that your father had cancer and that you had to see to him before making any decisions, but that you had said the castle and estate weren't yours anyway and that everything was in the hands of the solicitors now, just like you told me to say. But people were worried. No one knew what would happen. I think Olivia was on people's minds even before she marched in and took over. Olivia naturally assumed everything would go to her as next of kin. She apparently knew nothing about the National Trust, and no one else knew anything different . . . except me, and I couldn't say anything. But it was no accident that she waited until the minute you were gone before marching up to the place and moving in and taking over and—"

"She moved into the castle!" I exclaimed.

"Right in front of my eyes. I heard footsteps and I went to see who it was who had come walking in. The door wasn't locked anyway, but she had keys. I don't know where she got them, or if they were from years before, but she had keys to every room in the place. Two minutes later a lorry drove up and three men got out and began unloading her things."

"I can't believe it. She had the effrontery to just move in without permission, without papers, without *anything*!" I said.

"She never said a word to me—just stared through me like I wasn't there. And she's been there ever since, assuming herself the duchess now that her brother is dead, and acting like it, too."

"How . . . What is she doing? She surely wouldn't have access to bank accounts or any official standing with the affairs of the estate."

"I don't know about the money or any of that," replied Alicia. "Mostly she went around giving orders—telling Harvey and me what to do."

"What about Mr. Crathie, what about the National Trust, what about Alasdair's will? She can't just ignore all the legalities involved."

"At first Mr. Crathie knew nothing about it. She'd been living in the castle a month before he even got wind of it. After he found out he said he couldn't forcibly oust her—or at least he didn't want to, preferring to allow things to proceed in an orderly manner, he called it. He tried to hurry the proceedings along and arranged for a reading of Alasdair's will even though, he said, there remained aspects to be sorted out by Alasdair's Edinburgh solicitors. He came to the castle and asked Harvey and myself and Olivia to be present."

She paused and pulled out a sheet of paper from her purse.

"Mr. Crathie gave me this summary," she said. "I brought it with me so I could tell it to you exactly right. The duke left £50,000 each to myself and Harvey Nicholls, with kind words about our years of loyal service, and £75,000 to Jean and Norvill Campbell. A perpetual stipend of £30,000 annually is to be given to the Deskmill Parish Church from the income of the estate, as well as equal yearly stipends to the burghs of Port Scarnose and Crannoch for whatever purposes the town leaders feel will benefit their communities. Alasdair's sister, Olivia Urquhart, is awarded £400,000, half, if applicable taxes permit, in cash, the remainder to be paid in £50,000 installments over the following four years."

Even before Alicia finished reading me Mr. Crathie's summary, I was crying. It was like hearing Alasdair's own voice again.

"Mr. Crathie hoped Alasdair's generosity toward Olivia would mollify her," said Alicia, glancing up from the paper, "and result in a harmonious resolution to her 'takeover' of the castle, was what he called it. He came to talk to her several times prior to the reading of the will, trying to be reasonable, trying to explain that she had no legal rights insofar as the castle was concerned. That's when he and I first met. That's when he told Olivia about the castle being turned over to the National Trust, trying to persuade her to remove herself so there would be no unpleasantness later. But it was all to no avail, and she, of course, hearing that, was furious at Alasdair. The reading of the will only made matters worse. She sat silent and obviously fuming over the paltry sum, as she called it, that she had been left. I could see it immediately. I recognized the look. I knew what she was thinking. In her eyes she had not been given her rightful due. She immediately enlisted her own solicitors to contest the will."

"Can she do that?"

"She *is* doing it," replied Alicia. "Mr. Crathie said that his hands were tied as long as the thing was working its way through the court system. Once she filed legal papers, it had to be seen through. She has successfully blocked the final resolution of all Alasdair's affairs. He said she could tie up a resolution to the estate for years. Any show of force, he said, would only make her position stronger in the end. The fact that she *is* next of kin is a persuasive factor. And of course the National Trust, he says, will never touch a property that is entangled in a lawsuit. So they have backed off for the present as well."

"Where does it stand now?" I asked.

"Basically unchanged," replied Alicia. "Only the most preliminary petitions of Olivia's lawsuit have been filed. Meanwhile, Olivia is still at the castle, daring anyone to challenge her. She has closed down all access to the castle grounds, changed all the locks and phones, and has erected imposing iron gates and threatening signs warning against trespassing. Where Alasdair tried to win the goodwill of the community, she is doing everything she can to alienate everyone within twenty miles. She has fenced up all the public access routes and public footpaths that you and Alasdair opened. She had the gate into the churchyard bricked up. She put your harps and all your things in the worst possible place, off in one of the coldest and most remote storerooms that get no heat. It can't possibly be good for them. I know she did it out of spite. Then finally she began raising rents all through Port Scarnose and Crannoch."

I sat shaking my head in disbelief.

"That was when I began writing you frantic letters—months ago. I guess we know what happened to them, as well as yours to me."

"Could Olivia actually intercept our mail?" I said. "That would be a crime."

"I don't think Olivia views legalities in the way most people do.

She justifies in her mind anything that suits her ends. She has allies, too. She can convince anyone that everything is so reasonable. It's almost hypnotic, until you cross her and see the flash in her eyes. I've seen it. Once I began standing up to her, everything changed. I saw things I had been blind to for thirty years."

"But *how* is she intercepting our mail?"

"Adela—she works at the post office."

"Of course! I had forgotten. But you make it sound like Olivia has other allies?"

"No one wants to alienate her. If she *does* win in court and succeeds in convincing some judge to award her the castle and control of the estate, they know that she will never forget those who opposed her. People are walking very carefully."

"Everyone?"

"No, thankfully. Others are mad. Everything is in an uproar. Everyone wants you back, Marie. Well, not everyone. The community is split. People are afraid to speak openly. Everyone is careful for fear of a careless word getting back to Olivia. It's like living in an occupied country with spies everywhere. The whole atmosphere has changed. Those who are on our side came to me in secret asking if I've heard from you yet. I wrote and wrote, but when we didn't hear from you—"

I was furious at how Olivia had changed everything and was interfering with the village and the people's lives. Maybe I was more my father's daughter than I realized!

"I'm sorry, Alicia," I said, reaching over and placing a hand on her arm. "She must have...Oh, it really makes me furious! I don't even know what to say!"

"It's not just Adela's being at the post office. She's at the castle now, too—as Olivia's constant eyes and ears."

"Surely you don't mean she's *living* there?"

"Yes." Alicia nodded. "She's Olivia's new housekeeper."

"What about you?"

"Two months ago Olivia fired me. She gave me a week to be out."

I drew in a sharp breath of outrage.

"Please come back, Marie," said Alicia. "Everyone is depending on you. That's why we decided that one of us had to come…to beg you if we had to—"

"You keep saying we. We who? Who else is in this with you?"

"Nigel and me…Mr. Crathie, I mean."

"But what can I do?" I said. "It is out of my hands. I have less legal standing than Olivia now that Alasdair is gone. Mr. Crathie knows that better than anyone. He drew up the document that ended my legal standing with the Buchan estate immediately upon Alasdair's death."

"That may not be altogether correct, Marie. It is true that that is how things appeared to stand until recently. Nigel…that is, Mr. Crathie, came to see me privately two weeks ago. I've been staying with Tavia. He and I have, uh, seen a good deal of one another this year," she said, hesitating briefly. I thought I detected the slightest of blushes but said nothing. "He knows that you and I are close and that I was trying to contact you. He had something momentous to tell me, he said, something he had just learned himself. Actually, he was a little annoyed at being, he felt, used by Alasdair. Yet at the same time I know he was pleased. That's when we made arrangements for me to come see you secretly."

"Secretly?"

"Before Olivia herself learned of it, or it was made public."

"Before *what* was made public? Alicia, you are being very mysterious."

"Three weeks ago Mr. Crathie was contacted by Alasdair's solicitor in Edinburgh, a Mr. Murdoch. Apparently it took so long because, aware of the lawsuit pending that Olivia set in motion, he had taken the thing through probate court in private, consulting barristers and judges to make absolutely certain *nothing* could rear its head later. And the way Alasdair did it, signing conflicting documents so close to one another, involved legal complications that he had to make completely sure of before making it known."

"The way he did *what*?...Alicia, please!"

"The prenuptial agreement...Alasdair voided the agreement you and he drew up."

"What!"

"He signed a later document in Edinburgh. Don't you remember, just before the wedding when you and I were working on the plans and your dress and everything, you told me he had gone to Edinburgh to see his solicitors. *That's* what he was doing in Edinburgh. He was taking steps to ensure the continuity of the estate."

"I can't believe it could be true. There has to be some mistake."

"Nigel reviewed it backward and forward and was on the phone for two days with people all over Scotland."

I sat listening as one in a dream.

"There is no prenup in effect, Marie," Alicia said. "Alasdair left everything to you after all...the castle, the management and administration of the entire estate, everything. You are *still* the Duchess of Buchan."

The smile on her face was too precious.

"There *must* be some mistake," I repeated.

"Maybe Alasdair foresaw what would happen," said Alicia. "I don't know, but Nigel has already been to Edinburgh to meet with Alasdair's other solicitors personally. He says it is legal and binding. The prenup is null and void. That's when he asked me—Nigel, I mean—he asked if I would come tell you in person, and implore you to return—for the good of the estate, the community, everyone."

I sat stunned.

"Just when I thought my life was beginning to simplify...I never wanted to be anything but Alasdair's wife."

"That's what he wanted you to be, too," said Alicia. "And in *every* way, with *all* that entailed."

"What do you mean?" I asked.

"Maybe Alasdair recognized what your being his *wife* actually meant more fully than you did."

Alicia's words sobered me. It was something I had never considered. Perhaps I had never recognized the full implications of what *wife* meant. Maybe it was Alasdair who had seen more deeply into the larger scope of what our marriage signified than I had.

"Marie, you are the Duchess of Buchan, whether you like it or not," said Alicia.

We sat silent a long time.

"And Olivia?" I said at length.

"As yet, Olivia knows nothing of it."

Chapter Thirty-five

Nine-Tenths of the Law

I mourn for the Highlands, now drear and forsaken,
The land of my fathers, the gallant and brave;
To make room for the sportsman their lands were all taken,
And they had to seek out new homes o'er the wave.
Oh shame on the tyrants who brought desolation,
Who banished the brave, and put sheep in their place.
Where once smiled the garden, rank weeds have their station,
And deer are preferr'd to a leal-hearted race.
—Henry Whyte, "I Mourn for the Highlands"

Needless to say, Alicia's surprise visit and stunning news threw me into a tailspin of renewed uncertainty.

She slept twelve hours that night. I slept about two! My mind was racing. I still did not believe it could *really* be true. But I had no choice other than to return to Port Scarnose until the thing was resolved. True or not, I was at the center of it. Many people, the whole community, the future of Alasdair's estate...much depended on a resolution. I had to do my part to help in that process. I still cared nothing for the title or the property. But I cared very much for Alasdair's legacy, and that his desires for the good of the community were carried out. I might not fight on my own behalf, but I would fight for Alasdair.

The uncertainty of my immediate future had been decided for me. As is often the case, God used circumstances to point the way.

I notified Mr. Jones of the developments. I told him I would be in touch with him from Scotland if matters came up in connection with the sale of my father's house or whatever else might require my signature. Where I would be in Scotland was anyone's guess, but I told him I would let him know. I warned him not to contact me by regular mail. He wished me luck.

Alicia and I flew into Aberdeen a week later. She had just managed to get over her jet lag from the one flight before returning over the Atlantic again. This time, however, she was keyed up and excited, and the flight went by quickly. In her mind the mere fact that I was on my way back would take care of everything.

In my own mind, I wasn't so sure. I had agreed to return because it seemed the right thing to do. But the next step *after* that remained cloudy in my mind.

It was during the plane flight back to Aberdeen that my resolve clarified about what I was to do. My heart and mind were so full of my father. He had become completely changed in my thoughts, though it was really *I* who had done the changing. Everything was different now. I was a *daughter* in a way I had never been before. I was the *proud* daughter of Richard Buchan, a good and honored man of integrity and principle and courage. For the first time in my life, I wanted to make my father proud. And I had come to realize how much like my father I really was. I had inherited more of that old sixties' fire from him than I ever knew. I *had* to fight for truth, for justice, for right . . . because that's what he would have done.

All the way back to Scotland, though I suppose I should have been asking myself what God wanted me to do, what I was actually asking myself was, "What would Alasdair and my father want me to do?" Yet sometimes such questions help toward discovering what God wants, too.

What finally sealed my decision, strangely enough, was an article in one of the airline magazines about Sidney Poitier. In speaking of his devotion to his father, I saw a powerful truth, and I realized that I felt exactly as he did. "My father was a certain kind of man," he said. "I saw how he treated my mother and his family and how he treated strangers. And I vowed I would never make a film that would not reflect dignity and honor on my father's character and name."

What an incredible thing for a successful man to say. In spite of all he had accomplished, his father's character was ever before him as a guiding principle for his own conduct. Even as I read his words, I made the same vow to myself, and to God. From that point on in my life, as far as I was aware of and to the best of my ability, I would try to do and say nothing but what would reflect dignity and honor on the character and name of *both* my fathers—Richard Buchan, my *earthly* father; and the Creator and God of the universe, the Father of Jesus Christ, my *heavenly* Father.

In keeping with that, I would fight for truth on behalf of the villagers of Port Scarnose and Crannoch, and for the legacy of Alasdair Reidhaven, Duke of Buchan.

We had been in touch with Mr. Crathie by phone. He was at the airport to meet us.

He and I shook hands. The look that passed between him and Alicia as they met confirmed my suspicions. Something was definitely brewing between them!

"I think it best, Mrs. Reidhaven," said Mr. Crathie as he turned his car out of the precincts of the airport and started along the A96, "that you do not stay in Port Scarnose or Crannoch at first. For you to be seen would tip our hand. I have taken the liberty of booking you into a very nice bed-and-breakfast in Elgin."

"I am still bewildered by everything," I said. "Surely there must be some logical explanation to all this other than . . ."

My voice trailed away. I still had a difficult time putting into words everything Alicia had told me.

"I'm afraid the only explanation," the lawyer replied, "is that the duke feared what his sister might do and wanted you to inherit in spite of your objections. I admit that it is difficult to understand in light of what almost appears his deception to both of us in signing what he knew to be, or knew would soon become, a spurious document—one that would be certain to cast clouds of debate and doubt over his affairs. It is this aspect of the thing that has troubled me from the moment I learned of the Edinburgh affidavit, and which is sure to be analyzed up, down, and sideways in court if Mrs. Urquhart's suit goes forward. Your late husband's mental state will almost surely be called into question, and that likelihood, I must confess, troubles me. However, I can only assume that the duke felt his actions with the two documents would lead to a greater good, and that he was thus justified in signing what amounted to a false prenuptial agreement. But so that everything will be clarified in your mind—as you are obviously now the key player in all this—I have arranged for Mr. Murdoch to meet with us in three days, at my office in Elgin. He will explain everything to you. At that time we will attempt to decide upon a strategy for proceeding in the most efficacious manner to meet the legal complications that the duke's sister has thrown at us all."

"What will you do, Alicia?" I asked.

"Return to Tavia's and pretend nothing is going on," she answered.

"That may be a little problematic," interjected Mr. Crathie. "You gave her my number, I take it?"

"With my being gone, I thought she should be able to contact you . . . just in case?" replied Alicia.

"And she did," rejoined Mr. Crathie. "She telephoned me three days ago. Apparently Mrs. Urquhart has been asking about you. Her suspicions have been raised. The other lady—what's her name?"

"Adela . . . Adela Cruickshank?"

"Right—Cruickshank . . . She has been questioning everyone in town about your whereabouts, asking if anyone has seen you or knows where you have gone. Rumors have apparently begun to fly. We have to think through our movements very carefully."

"What do you mean, Mr. Crathie?" I asked.

"We have to get you into the castle before she gets wind of it and is able to secure a restraining order against you. That's why I don't want to arouse her suspicions."

"But how? Alicia said she has locked the castle up tight—with new locks and gates and everything."

"She has done precisely that. Whether she is on firm legal footing is debatable, but the fact is, she has made the castle and grounds almost impregnable. You cannot simply show up at the front gate. She would deny you entry and be on the phone to her solicitors the next minute, with an injunction against you drawn up within the hour. It might not prove legal in the long run, but she could continue, in a sense, to hold the entirety of the duke's estate hostage for the duration of a court battle, and remain in possession of the castle all that time. I would not be surprised to see her use every tactic she can to delay things and keep everything tied up as long as possible."

"I simply can't understand how she could get away with it."

"She has a legal case that can be made. In the hands of the right barrister, I fear that case could be made quite persuasively. It would be argued that you were a continent away having publicly disavowed any interest in or claim to your husband's property. She is the legal next of kin. She simply acted on what facts she possessed, assuming herself now the duchess, and, acting in good faith, moved back to her childhood home and the seat of the Buchan estate. That will be her claim."

"How would, as you say, getting me into the castle, help with all that?" I asked.

"Once you were both, as it were, on the premises and tacitly in *possession* of the castle, a final resolution would necessarily rest with the courts. As long as it could be demonstrated that you, too, were acting on good faith and with legal grounds—which obviously you now have in the form of the Edinburgh affidavit and my having informed you that you *are* in fact the duchess and heir—no move would be made to forcibly have you removed. She could *prevent* your entry. But once you are both there, with equally justified legal claims, it would remain as a stalemate until a resolution comes in court."

"I think I understand, but it sounds rather obscure and uncertain."

"That is not an incorrect assessment. Without putting too fine a point on it, what it boils down to is the old adage about possession being nine-tenths of the law. Of course in the final analysis that will mean nothing. But for the present, it may be significant. We are, I'm afraid, in a rather tenuous position. But we will talk everything over with Mr. Murdoch."

"What should I do, Nigel?" asked Alicia.

Mr. Crathie was silent a moment.

"Didn't you say you had a sister somewhere in the south?"

"Yes, in Glasgow."

"Why don't we drive into Elgin and we'll put you up there, too, for the night so that you have a good night's rest. Tonight we will have you telephone someone in Port Scarnose. We'll use my mobile. We'll have you call someone who will be certain to spread it about. You'll say that you have been unable to reach—what's the lady's name you're staying with?"

"Tavia Maccallum."

"Right . . . You've been unable to get through, but would they mind popping over to her place to tell her that you'll be home from your sister's tomorrow."

"You could call Mrs. Gauld," I suggested. "Whose side is she on?"

"You know her," replied Alicia. "She always tries to play both sides. She's still friendly to me, but I know she listens to every morsel of gossip she can pick up, and passes most of it on to Adela and Olivia."

"Whoever you notify," said Mr. Crathie, "be vague and just tell them that you're coming in on the Bluebird. Then simply take the bus into Port Scarnose as if nothing was out of the ordinary."

"Adela and Olivia will be suspicious that Tavia said nothing about it before."

"Let them stew all they want. You will be back. There will be nothing for them to conclude other than that you were gone for a week. Mrs. Reidhaven will never enter into the thing. Then go about your life as usual."

Chapter Thirty-six

The Edinburgh Affidavit

To the raid and the onslaught our chieftains have gone,
Like the course of the fire-slaught their clansmen pass'd on;
With the lance and the shield 'gainst the foe they have bound them,
And have ta'en to the field, with their vassals around them.
—G. Allan, "Is Your War-Pipe Asleep, M'Crimman!"

It was torment almost beyond belief to be stuck in Elgin and cooped up in a B and B for two days.

There was so much I wanted to do, people I was dying to see. I had no ocean, no seagulls, no trails, no headlands to walk along, no Crannoch Bin—only city streets and big-box stores and bustle and traffic and noise.

For the first time in my life, I was thankful for jet lag. What better way to pass the time than sleeping the day away.

Finally Thursday came and the meeting with Alasdair's Edinburgh solicitor. Mr. Murdoch was utterly gracious and respectful. He treated me like a duchess whether I really was one or not. After Mr. Crathie told him of my doubts and reservations, he went to great lengths to establish the veracity of the claim and to explain why it had taken so long to make the content of Alasdair's affidavit public.

"We had to get it all the way through the network of probate court," he concluded, "and all the complex legal channels involved, with everything documented and recorded, before any potential challenge could be mounted."

I nodded. "I appreciate how thorough you have been with everything, Mr. Murdoch," I said. "But you do understand my own mixed feelings and reactions."

"Of course. They are understandable given the circumstances. We are all very sympathetic. But you see, Mrs. Reidhaven," he went on, "it is already beyond the point where you have to do anything, or even whether you have to take my word for it. The matter is concluded. You will be listed in the forthcoming edition of Debrett's *Peerage* as Lady Angel Dawn Marie Buchan Reidhaven, Duchess of Buchan."

I shook my head again in disbelief. Hearing him say it like that, especially with the *Lady* in front of my name, was like hearing it all again for the first time.

"I didn't realize you knew my full name." I smiled.

"Indeed, Mrs. Reidhaven, I probably know more about you than you have any idea. The legalities involved have required the most exhaustive research into your background."

"In any event, I am honored," I said, "and I will do my duty to Alasdair's memory. But it is still very difficult for me to fathom why he did it in this way."

"I understand," rejoined Mr. Murdoch. "He anticipated exactly this contingency, even this moment when you would raise these very questions. He attempted, he said, to convince you against the prenuptial agreement, but did not want to pressure you unduly. He hoped your precautions, and this whole matter of his subsequent precautions as well, would turn out to be moot anyway. But to make certain nothing untoward should eventuate, he then undertook, as he said when he first broached the subject to me, 'Plan B.' He asked me to convey to you his sincere apologies for the subterfuge. But he could not help fearing what his sister might do. While respecting your selfless desire to marry him without anticipation of future benefit to yourself, the fact of the matter is that he *trusted* you to deal with his affairs more than he trusted anyone else. It was for the good of the estate and the community that he did what he did. He prayed you would understand and forgive the temporary deception.

Even if you couldn't forgive him, he said, he would still rather *you*, not Mrs.Urquhart, not even the National Trust, were in a position to make decisions on his behalf. After all was said and done, if you still chose to relinquish the title and all claim to the estate, that would be your decision to make after you saw, as he put it, the direction the winds of future change were blowing."

Even before he was through, I was weeping. It was Alasdair again—thinking of me, thinking of everyone, trying to cover every contingency. How could I blame him—he was trying to do what he thought best. None of it would even have come up had I not insisted on the prenup. In a way, I had only myself to blame for making it all as complicated as it was.

"He wanted me to tell you above all, Mrs. Reidhaven," added Mr. Murdoch, "how much and how deeply he loved you."

I nodded and smiled, wiping my eyes. But I could say nothing. It was quiet a minute or two.

"What am I supposed to do now?" I asked at length.

"As I see it," replied Mr. Murdoch after a moment, "we must do two things—get you into the castle and in control of the estate, and get Mrs. Urquhart out. The legalities of the thing are established. You *are* the owner of Castle Buchan and the legal administrator of the Buchan estate. Mr. Crathie and I have been, as your husband's solicitors, acting on his, and your, behalf for the past year. With a few signatures, we will put everything at your disposal that will enable you to assume your position and take over the estate's affairs and begin acting accordingly. However, your sister-in-law's legal action in contestation of your husband's will remains problematic. We must proceed carefully so that she is not able to block us in the establishment of your position. As I believe Mr. Crathie has explained to you, we have to get you physically into the castle. Once there, you may, under our supervision and with our help, begin your administrative duties on behalf of the estate until the courts play out her lawsuit and her claims are denied. Hopefully we will then be able to ease Mrs. Urquhart out with as little difficulty as possible. Therefore, we

want you in the castle and in possession of the property before going public with all this. You might want to wait until a time when
she is away on errands or at her solicitors. I will leave the logistics of
your next moves to you and Mr. Crathie. Unfortunately, I have some
pressing matters and must be back in Edinburgh this evening."

When Mr. Crathie and I were left alone, he outlined his plan.

"I want you to be able to contact me easily at any time, day or
night." He handed me a mobile phone and charger. "Keep this with
you at all times. My number and Alicia's . . . Miss Forbes's—both are
programmed into it. She has an identical phone. The three of us may
need to be in close contact and able to act quickly. I have booked a
room at the Crannoch Bay Hotel. It is in my name. All they know is
that it will be occupied by an out-of-town client. Tonight I will drive
you there. We will slip in late in the evening through the back door.
I have reserved their largest room on the seaward side. I hope you
will be comfortable. I know it may not be pleasant, but at least you
will have a view of the bay and harbor and Florimel's Rock and Bow
Fiddle Rock."

"What do I do then?" I asked.

"I'm afraid you wait. Either Alicia or I will contact you when the
time is right."

"The time for what?"

"Actually, I am uncertain," replied Mr. Crathie. "It is my hope to
find an opportunity when Mrs. Urquhart is gone for a few hours, as
Mr. Murdoch suggested, and one of the gates to one of the three en-
tries to the castle is open. If such a time presents itself and Alicia is
able to get word to me, I will collect you and simply drive you into
the grounds."

"But with the castle locked and the locks changed?"

"There remain contingencies to be worked out. We will have to
see. Alicia tells me that she is aware of Mr. Nicholls's movements and
occasional errands in the village. She hopes to intercept him. She
believes he will be sympathetic and may provide us with a key to
the castle, possibly even the remote-control code to one of the outer

gates, though she is uncertain whether even he knows it. *Everything*, she says, has become secretive about the place. She also fears the Cruickshank woman. Her exact words were, 'Adela is a bloodhound. We won't be able to do anything that escapes her notice.' But the first step is to have you nearby so as to be ready to move quickly."

Chapter Thirty-seven

Midnight Summons

Then raise your wild slogan cry! on to the foray!
Sons of the heather hill, pinewood, and glen!
Shout for M'Pherson, M'Leod, and the Moray,
Till the Lomonds re-echo the challenge again.
—G. Allan, "Is Your War-Pipe Asleep, M'Crimman!"

I crept through the rear entrance to the Crannoch Bay Hotel that evening about ten-thirty. Mr. Crathie had gone in some forty-five seconds earlier to make sure the coast was clear and now signaled me to follow.

We snuck up the stairway, with the old wooden steps squeaking so loudly under our feet in spite of the carpet it seemed sure everyone in the place would be roused. Within a minute I was down the corridor and safely in the room with the door shut behind me.

Whew! I sighed in relief.

"So far so good," said Mr. Crathie. "I'll be right back with your bags and your harp."

He disappeared again to his car and returned two or three minutes later with my things. Once more he left, and when he returned for the last time it was with several bags of groceries.

"I told the hotel manager that my client was a recluse," he said. "He was not completely pleased, but I said I would pay for the extra services and he reluctantly obliged me. So call down if you want anything brought up. They will bring you a tray with breakfast at 8:30—I hope that will be all right."

"Just fine, thank you."

"The imperative thing is that you are not seen and recognized. Mrs. Urquhart would know of it within minutes. We *must* not allow her to file an injunction. Once you are inside the castle, it will be too late. Wresting possession *away* from you would be very difficult for her, especially with the papers you will have in documentation of your rights. Actually, that reminds me—"

He removed a thick envelope from inside his coat.

"This may not be enough in itself," he said, handing it to me. "It is a legal documentation, with all appropriate seals and signatures from Edinburgh, attesting to your position as Duchess of Buchan and your rightful ownership of Castle Buchan. Mrs. Urquhart may still be able to cause us difficulties, but if you get into the castle and she should try any strong-arm tactics with the local authorities, this document should slow them down long enough for me to get there. Call me instantly at the sign of any trouble."

"I will, believe me. I have no desire to tangle with Olivia. What shall I do in the meantime?"

"Wait, I'm afraid. Alicia will look for an opportunity to intercept the fellow Nicholls, and then hopefully an opportunity will arise when Mrs. Urquhart is away. Until then...I hope you have all you need—water boiler, tea, tele. If there is anything else, don't hesitate to call."

He left me and I sat down on the bed and sighed. At least my immediate way was clear. It was time for bed.

What a glorious awakening the morning brought. I threw back the curtains. Spread out before me like a spectacular wide-screen movie was Crannoch Bay stretching from Bow Fiddle Rock all the way around to Crannoch Harbor.

How I had missed the sea!

I was home!

I made tea and sat down in front of the window and remained staring out at the lovely expanse with the gentle sound of the tide making the most pleasant background music imaginable. If the whole world had the peaceful sounds of the sea at their disposal, there would be no need for harps. Then a thought occurred to me that had never crossed my mind before that moment: *Are there oceans in heaven?*

I sat gazing at the sea through two cups of tea, until my reverie was broken by a knock on the door.

"Breakfast," announced a man's voice.

I rose and walked across the floor.

"Just leave it outside, thank you," I said through the door, trying to fake a British accent.

I heard footsteps retreating. I opened the door a moment later and retrieved the tray from the floor. A full cooked breakfast with another pot of steaming tea. With provision like this, I would hardly need Mr. Crathie's groceries!

In spite of the best view I had ever enjoyed from any window of any room or house or hotel, by afternoon I must confess the hours began to drag by slowly. I played my harp softly, I read, I slept, I sat in front of the window—but a hotel room offers you only so much to entertain yourself until boredom sets in. By the second day I was getting antsy, by the third going stir-crazy.

I had just settled into bed shortly after ten that night when I was startled by a light knock on the door.

I crept from bed and hesitated. It came again. I rose and went to it.

"Yes?" I said softly through the door.

"It's Alicia," came the answer.

I fumbled with the lock, opened the door, and pulled her inside.

"Alicia!" I said in a loud whisper. "What are you doing here? You look like you're off for a cross-country hike!"

"Not so far wrong," she said. "What I'm doing is sneaking around hoping no one will see me. Get dressed. It's time."

Hurriedly I prepared to change out of my nightgown.

"We're not in that big a hurry," she said. "I wanted to get here before the hotel locked its doors."

"Is Mr. Crathie coming?" I said.

"No, just us. Put on trousers and walking shoes. We're walking, not driving. You won't need anything but a jacket and your mobile."

"Walking...where? You mean to the castle? Is Olivia gone?"

"No, she's there. We're going to sneak in right under her nose."

"How?"

"Harvey is meeting us at the entry to the tunnel you and Alasdair renovated."

"You're right!" I exclaimed. "Why didn't I think of that?!"

"It's the one entrance to the grounds Olivia didn't secure. At least Harvey doesn't think so."

"I wonder if she even knows about it. She was in Aberdeen that whole time we were carrying out the renovations. What a fantastic idea!"

"It's not entirely foolproof," said Alicia. "Alasdair's old grounds-keeper, you remember Farquharson—he's one of Olivia's lackeys now. He prowls around at all hours with his rifle trying to keep the foxes away from his pheasants. Harvey says he is drunk with what he supposes is his new power, lording it over everyone and giving the villagers orders as if he's Olivia's little puppet colonel."

We waited two hours—the longest two hours of my life. When we finally put on our jackets and turned out the lights, it was about thirty minutes after midnight.

My heart was racing and my anticipation high as we crept down the stairs a minute later and out the back door of the hotel. Every sound echoed through the darkened hallways. I knew if we weren't out and gone quickly, someone would be up to investigate. It did no good to tiptoe, the stairs creaked just the same. So we hurried along, didn't worry about the noise, let the outside door bang shut, and ran across the parking lot toward the main road. Crossing the road, we made our way down the steep incline to the golf links bordering the wide sands of Crannoch Bay. It was a dusky night, not quite black but misting heavily and without a moon. Alicia had a hand-torch. She flipped it on and we made our way along the base of the hill beneath the road until we arrived at a door into the hillside, framed by a bricked-in arch. Behind it stretched the long-disused tunnel connecting the beach and the temple.

We reached it and knocked on the green door. I had painted it myself just two years ago.

A fumbling sound came from the other side. A moment later the door swung back. There stood Harvey Nicholls with the blackness of the tunnel behind him.

"Nicholls!" I exclaimed.

"Evening to you, Duchess," he said with a slight bow. "'Tis a pleasure to welcome you home, and an honor to be in your service again."

"Thank you, Nicholls."

"And welcome back to you, Alicia," he added. "It's been a gloomy place without you. That Cruickshank woman's a bit of raw work, with her nose snooping into other people's affairs. Campbell keeps to himself saying nothing to nobody, and Farquharson's letting his supposed power go to his head like he's the woman's bloomin' bodyguard! 'Tis good to have you both back."

He reached past us as we stepped inside and pulled the door closed, flipping on his own torch at the same time.

"Now come, ladies," he said, "follow me."

He turned and led the way through the darkened tunnel with the beam of his light bobbing in front of us. When Alasdair and I had set about to have the place cleaned up of debris, strengthened, reexcavated, and secured with new doors and locks on both ends, we had envisioned walking this way to the shore on bright warm summer days as they had in the early twentieth century. It never occurred to us that one of us would be using it with an invasion army of two in order to infiltrate the ranks of an enemy who had taken control of the castle. But here the three of us were, sneaking through occupied lines in the dead of night!

We reached the temple at the other end of the tunnel and again felt the night air on our faces.

It was deathly still and quiet. Even the crows were asleep. The way was easy enough going now, thanks to the wide path we had smoothed and laid with crushed gravel two summers before.

Suddenly a deafening shot exploded in the night only fifty feet in front of us.

"Stop, whate'er or whoe'er ye be!" shouted a voice in the darkness, "or the naist ane willna be jist a warnin'!"

Nicholls spun around as the crows in the trees above erupted in a frenzy.

"Quickly, both of you into the brush!" he whispered. "Get down and don't move until I get him away from here. South wing...old servants' entrance. I'll wait there."

He turned away from us again. "Put yer rifle doon, Farquharson!" he called, marching hurriedly in the direction of the gunfire. "'Tis jist me."

"Nicholls, ye auld fool! What are ye doin' here?" said the gameskeeper as we crouched down in the bracken and trees a few feet off the path. "I could hae shot ye deid!"

"Then ye'd hae had murder on yer heid!" retorted Nicholls, borrowing one of Olivia's tactics. We watched anxiously as the outline of our only ally disappeared from sight. "What are *ye* doin' oot prowlin' aboot wi' a gun?" he added, continuing to walk forward to meet the man.

"'Tis my ain business, Nicholls."

"An' maybe what I'm aboot is mine. But gie ye maun ken...Alexander Legge called an' said ane o' his dogs had gane missin' an' spiered o' me tae keep an eye oot for it."

"At one in the bloomin' mornin'!"

"'Tis a night dog."

"I dinna ken whether tae believe a word ye say, Nicholls. Come on, then, back tae the castle wi' ye. I'll hae tae report this tae the mistress in the mornin'."

"Wha made ye my watchdog, Farquharson?"

"Maybe the mistress hersel'. Maybe she doesna trust yer loyalties."

"Tell her whate'er ye like, Farquharson. My loyalties are my ain affair an' I'm nae bothered by her ony mair than I am yer threats. What can she de tae me?"

"She can aye fire ye."

"I dinna think the duchess will be firin' me onytime soon," replied Nicholls as the two men walked off, leaving us alone in the night.

Neither of us dared make a move for several minutes.

"I think they're gone," I whispered at length. "But maybe another minute or two. I don't want Farquharson emptying his rifle in our direction."

"What is he doing shooting at night?" Alicia asked.

"I don't know. I would rather not wait to find out."

As we waited, the crows finally settled down, silence returned, and the loneliness of the night descended upon us. It didn't take long before we were both ready to take our chances with Farquharson rather than whatever creatures might be roaming the night. I rose and led the way out of the brush onto the path.

"I think we had better feel our way without the light," I said. "I don't trust him not to start shooting."

We made our way along as quickly as we could manage in the dark as the path led along the course of Crannoch Burn where it trickled its way down from the Bin to Seatown. In the distance we heard the thud of a door closing.

"They must be back inside," said Alicia.

"*Both* of them, I hope. I do not want to encounter Farquharson again!"

As we approached the castle, my heart began to pound. It was like coming home, though not exactly under the circumstances I might have envisioned. Hardly the triumphant return of a conquering hero! Even in the dark, the silhouette of the imposing edifice loomed ahead with the shadowy outlines of the trees against the faint night sky. A light shone in an upper-floor window. I knew it as the bedroom Alasdair and I had occupied so happily together.

"I take it that would be Olivia's room now?" I said.

"I'm sorry, Marie," replied Alicia. "She moved all your and Alasdair's things out immediately. She has been there ever since."

We climbed the steep hill out of the valley of the burn, walking up the path of the old laundry. There was Castle Buchan before us.

We turned toward the west wing and crept along past the kitchen. As slowly as we went, I was still afraid of our steps sounding on the gravel.

Suddenly a light came on in a ground-floor window only thirty feet away. Almost the same moment we heard the latch.

Quickly we turned and ran to the edge of the gravel, across the thin border of close-mown grass, ducking behind the trunk of a great beech the moment the bolt clanked back and the door of the kitchen opened behind us.

Very slowly I poked one eye around the edge of the trunk.

"*Adela!*" I breathed as I saw the outline in the light pouring through the open door. "What is *she* doing up at this hour?!"

"She has positively preternatural senses," whispered Alicia in a voice barely audible. "I'm beginning to think she has second sight, too."

"No wonder she and Olivia are birds of a feather!"

Neither of us dared utter another peep. Adela pulled out a small hand-torch and sent its beam from the entryway 180 degrees to the north, all the way around to the end of the west wing. Something had obviously aroused her attention and I doubted it was only Farquharson's gun. I ducked behind the tree and we both held our breath. She was less than a hundred feet away. We only hoped she didn't get it into her mind to conduct a thorough search. The beam from her flashlight flitted back and forth across the gravel and grass, coming right next to us and passing by, broken by the shadow of the tree, then back two or three times in both directions.

A minute or two later, the door closed again and the bolt slid into place inside.

I ventured another peep from our hiding place just in time to see the light of the kitchen window go black again.

"It's clear," I said softly. "Let's go."

We darted out and ran on the grass as far as the southern limit of the lawn. We slowed and tiptoed across the gravel drive. As careful as we tried to be, the silence was so deep at one in the morning that the faint crunch of our steps across the gravel was still audible. Reaching the wall, we crept alongside the end of the west wing, then hurried across the opening into the central courtyard to the western wall of the little-used south wing. Its high, windowless wall protected us from the entire rest of the castle, and we crept along in darkness until we reached the southeast corner. Rounding it, we arrived at last at the old door to the nineteenth-century servants' quarters. I knocked as lightly as possible.

No reply came.

Another knock . . . nothing.

I thought to try the latch. I was astonished to find that it gave way easily under my touch, without so much as a hint of rust or scraping. I pushed gently. The door swung back noiselessly on its hinges.

We stepped inside. I closed the door as gently as I could, easing it back into place against its casing without so much as a sound, then s-l-o-w-l-y released the latch, keeping my hand carefully on it until I was sure no inadvertent clunk or clank would betray us.

Now we truly found ourselves in pitch blackness.

"Where should we go?" asked Alicia.

"What are you asking me for?" I said. "I've been gone a year. I thought *you* were leading this expedition."

"Me—you own the place!"

"I feel like a burglar, not a duchess. Actually," I added, "I'm not sure I even know where we are."

We didn't have long to wait. A beam of light came bobbing down the stairs directly in front of us. To our great relief, at last Nicholls appeared.

"I am sorry about the wait," he said. "That Farquharson was a bit of a bother. This way, ladies, I will escort you to your quarters."

We followed our unlikely squire up the narrow staircase, and soon found ourselves in a small but serviceable room. I had myself been in this portion of the castle only two or three times. The rooms hadn't been used in three-quarters of a century. A musty aroma of age and mildew clung to the walls. Yet belying what our nostrils told us, there sat two beds made up with fresh linens, pillows, and duvets. Folded towels were supplied on the top of each, and a small table held a lamp, a pitcher of water, glasses, cups, a water-cooker, a bowl of fruit and biscuits, and all the necessary supplies for tea.

"Nicholls, my goodness!" I exclaimed. "This is lovely. Accommodations fit for the queen herself."

"'Tis hardly worthy of your homecoming, Your Grace, but perhaps for a temporary government in exile, I hope you will be able to manage."

"We will manage, but how did *you* manage it?"

"By stealth, my lady," he replied. "When Miss Forbes brought me into her confidence two days ago outside Slorach's Hardware, I began laying in stores—now a pillow, now a blanket, an electric heater. I got Campbell to help me lug the two mattresses and heater from storage and we were fortunate not to be seen. Then last night after the castle was asleep, I managed to creep in and clean the room and make the beds and lubricate the door and hinges to make certain we would not be heard."

"I am touched and deeply appreciative of your efforts," I said. "Did you tell Campbell what it was about?"

"I hope I judged the man right, my lady . . . I did indeed. You will hardly believe the light that flashed in his eye. He was a boy again, taking up his claymore to march with the bonnie prince! He's one of your men, Duchess!"

"Bless the dear man!" I said.

"But I made him promise not to tell his wife," added Nicholls. "You can never be too sure of the talk that goes around a kitchen. Mrs. Urquhart has a powerful hold over women."

"I must say, these beds appear laid out by a professional!"

"My mum made sure her sons as well as her daughters could keep house," Nicholls said, smiling. I had almost forgotten his killer smile.

"Then we owe her our gratitude as well."

"I do wish the accommodations might have been better, my lady," added Nicholls, "but as things stand at the far end, I fear we have little choice. The distance is enough that you will not be heard. Being an interior room the light will not be seen. It is spartan, but I hope you will not be here long. You have supplies for tea, some fruit and cheese and biscuits. The loo and tub down the corridor are in working order and I hope clean enough even for two ladies until the castle is yours again."

"Thank you, Nicholls, again...for everything. We could not do this without you."

"I will come to you as soon as I am able in the morning for whatever may be your instructions. Again, my lady, let me say welcome home, and that I am pleased to be back in your service."

"Thank you, Nicholls, very much."

The good man departed, leaving Alicia and me alone, feeling a little like housebreakers. At the same time we were revived and energized by the successful completion of our clandestine siege.

"This is exciting!" I said, sitting down on one of the beds. "I wish I had a harp—I would play a victory ballad! When was the last time you spoke with Mr. Crathie?"

"Earlier today. I told him what we were going to try to do."

"Did he have any other instructions?"

"Only to call him day or night with any news."

"Then I will," I said.

I took out the mobile phone he had given me and auto-rang the number.

"Mr. Crathie," I said. "I'm sorry it's so late...it's Marie—everything went fine. We're in!"

"Undetected?" he asked groggily.

"We believe so. Nicholls was spotted, but not Alicia or me. We're in a little-used wing where Nicholls set up sleeping quarters for us."

"Good, excellent. Get some sleep. I shall be in touch tomorrow, or possibly the next day. The worst of it is behind us. I must say I am greatly relieved. If Mrs. Urquhart sees you now, there's nothing she can do. Good work! Don't worry about your things at the hotel, I will bring them. But don't leave the castle. We must keep you there until your position is secure."

Chapter Thirty-eight

In Castle Buchan

Hark when the night is falling
Hear! The pipes are calling,
Loudly and proudly calling,
Down thro' the glen.
There where the hills are sleeping,
Now feel the blood a-leaping.
Nigh as the spirits of the old Highland men.
—"Scotland the Brave"

I don't know what time we finally got to sleep, probably not until after 3:00 a.m. Alicia and I were so keyed up at first that sleep was the farthest thing from our minds. In the intoxication of our success, and knowing we were out of earshot, we began to get silly—two schoolgirls again, only this time at the *beginning* of summer after a long absence. I can't even remember what we talked about, but after the tension and ordeal of the last week, following so closely on the heels of my father's long decline and eventual death, it felt *so* good to laugh again with a friend.

When I began to come to myself after a sound sleep, the room was still pitch black, as how could it not be with no windows. I fumbled for my watch, then heard a voice.

"Are you awake?" whispered Alicia.

"I am," I said. "So if we both are, let's get a light on. What time is it?"

"A little after ten," replied Alicia. "I woke up a few minutes ago."

It took some feeling about in the dark, but we soon had the lamp and electric heater on and water boiling and tea brewing and plans being made for who would take the first bath.

"What is the state of my studio and the Music Room?" I asked.

"They're about the same," answered Alicia. "At least when I was here, she hadn't made any changes, except getting rid of your harps. She rarely uses that room. What are you thinking?"

"I am thinking that if we don't hear anything from Mr. Crathie by midafternoon, what do we have to be afraid of? I would like to reclaim my right to that room at the very least. If this is an infiltration campaign, that will be our beachhead. You are probably still more familiar with the passageways and stairways than I am— Can you get us there from here without detection?"

"I am pretty sure that we can go from here up to the third floor, then across through the storage loft through the east wing, then down the supply staircase to the first floor using the library stairs—the back staircase, I mean, not the main one—and through the library and across to the Music Room and your studio. As long as no one is using the laundry or library."

"I doubt Olivia, Adela, Farquharson, or Campbell spend much time in the library," I said. "What about my harps? You mentioned they're in a storeroom?"

"Down in the basement below the east wing."

"That might be more difficult, then . . . unless we can get Nicholls to help. He can still come and go."

"If she saw him carrying or wheeling a harp about, Olivia would be down on him in a flash. I only hope your harps are still there. I've been worried she might sell them or even give them away."

"She wouldn't dare!"

"Don't be too sure."

"Then that decides it," I said. "At least *one* of my harps comes back to the studio, and today!"

After baths and the most exquisite breakfast of tea and cheese and oatcakes, I was ready to take the next step in this campaign.

Nicholls came to us sometime after eleven. I told him that I wanted to retrieve one or both of my midsized harps from the storage room and have them brought to my studio. Could he manage it somehow?

"I believe so, my lady. I chanced to get wind that Mrs. Urquhart is going to Crannoch early in the afternoon."

"Will she want you to drive her?"

"'Tis doubtful, my lady. She mostly drives herself. I've become 'persona non grata,' as I believe they say. I could bring the harp up then. I'd have to take it outside, around the corner, and to the service elevator. I might be seen. Cruickshank watches my every move."

"We will take that chance. If she sees you, what will it hurt?"

"How will I know which harp to bring, my lady?"

"There should be one very large harp, two very small ones that you could pick up with one hand, and two in-between-sized ones—Is that right, Alicia? . . . *Journey* is at the hotel; I had the two new ones sent to Canada . . . Yes, there should be five still here in all. So bring either one of the midsized harps. There may be a small wheel-cart with them, if she had that removed with the harps as well. Otherwise, I think you will be able to manage carrying it."

"I'm sure I shall, my lady. I will be very careful."

"We will be in the Music Room at two. If Adela sees you, invite her to join you. I have nothing to hide from her. If she asks what you are doing, say you are under orders from the duchess and leave it at that. If she doesn't like it, as I say, invite her along!"

Feeling fresh in spite of having to wear our walking clothes from the night before, excited, and reasonably rested, Alicia and I set out through the castle about one. Getting to the Music Room proved easy enough. The castle was so big that, if you kept your wits about you and listened for footsteps, it wasn't so very difficult to keep out of sight and not be heard. Going slow, with many stops and only two or three false turns from having to take the most circuitous route, we arrived at our destination in less than fifteen minutes. The Music Room as well as my studio end of it looked exactly the same.

My heart swelled just to stand inside the wonderful room again. It contained so many memories. For the first time I felt like I was really back in Castle Buchan.

A little less than an hour later, Nicholls appeared right on schedule. When my eyes fell on the *Aida*, it was like seeing a long-lost old friend rescued from a kidnapper. It looked no worse for wear other than two broken strings.

"Thank you, Nicholls," I said excitedly. "Did you see Adela?"

"Thankfully no, my lady. Is there anything more I can do for you?"

"Just don't be too far away in case we need you. Leave the door ajar when you go—I'm not going to hide."

I checked the drawer in the sideboard and found my string supply still intact. I put on the new strings, and quietly set about retuning them all.

"Shall we have a little fun with Olivia?" I said sometime around three when I assumed she was back.

"What did you have in mind?" asked Alicia.

"Oh, I don't know . . . something like this!"

I set the levers, then played out an F7 glissando up and down the strings several times as loud as I could.

Alicia's eyes popped out. "She'll hear you!"

"You think so?" I said, then repeated the brief slide up the strings even louder. Already I detected a slight stretching in the two new strings, and retuned them. Then I began to play: "Will Ye No' Come Back Again" . . . "Charlie Is My Darling" . . . "The Black Isle" . . . "Wild Mountain Thyme" . . . "MacPherson's Lament" . . . "Highland Cathedral" . . . even a triumphant verse or two of "Scotland the Brave," and others as they flowed effortlessly from one to another.

It felt so good to make music in this room again! Not since I had returned to Canada had my fingers and heart felt truly *one*. Today they did. Gradually the music of Scotland gave way to the music of the angels, with reminders of Alicia's "Heather Song," and at length I found myself playing Gwendolyn's music.

Fittingly, it was those haunting melodies that eventually brought

Gwendolyn's aunt to investigate what could be causing this musical disturbance at the heart of her domain. We heard footsteps in the corridor, then Olivia came through the door and stopped, gazing in shock at the sight before her.

I glanced toward her as if nothing were out of the ordinary, but kept playing. Gradually my hands stilled and Gwendolyn's music, as it often did, drifted peacefully away into silence. I turned toward Alasdair's sister.

"Hello, Olivia," I said.

I must give Olivia Urquhart credit, when the situation demanded it, she could maintain remarkable poise. I detected the fire in her eyes and the smoke coming out of her ears as she came into the room and saw Alicia and me sitting there. Now, only a few seconds later, she forced a smile and advanced toward me.

"Marie," she said softly, "this *is* a surprise. How nice to see you again."

I rose and went forward to meet her. She offered her hand. I took it and we shook hands...limply, lifelessly on both our parts. We both knew we were playing a game. But we went along with the pretended cordiality.

"You should have let me know you were coming," she said, moving into her dreamy, beguiling, mesmerizing voice. "I could have prepared a *guest* room for you."

I doubted that her phrasing and choice of word were accidental.

"Where *are* you staying, Marie dear?" she added.

"I was at the Crannoch Bay for a couple of nights," I replied.

"But wanted to see your former home—I understand, for old times' sake. How did you, ah..."

"How did I manage to get in when you had the locks changed and gates installed?" I said bluntly.

Olivia smiled as if humoring a child. "It seemed best under the circumstances," she said. "New ownership is always so awkward and difficult for people to accustom themselves to. As I did not intend to continue the unpleasant come-and-go policies of my brother, I thought gates the simplest solution. I'm sure you would have done the same in my position."

"I would not have done the same at all. I think what you have done is a travesty."

"Ah, well, that is, of course, your opinion. But as you are no longer in a position to interfere in my affairs, it really doesn't matter, does it? Did you, ah, speak with Adela? Was it she who allowed you access?"

"I have not seen Adela," I said, "though I am aware that you replaced Alicia with her."

"Yes." Olivia nodded. "Again, I thought it best. Miss Forbes and I were no longer seeing eye-to-eye about many things."

"Such as mail delivery?" I asked.

"I'm afraid I do not understand you, Marie dear. Even as the new duchess, there are certain things that remain outside my control. So, were the gates not locked?" she went on. "I saw no car outside—Did you come by taxi?"

"No, we walked in," I replied. "Actually, I have no idea whether the gates were opened or closed."

Puzzled and clearly unnerved by this breach in her security, Olivia nevertheless did not pursue it.

"And you will continue on at the Crannoch Bay for your visit, or will you perhaps be staying with friends?" she asked, casting a brief glance in Alicia's direction.

"My immediate plans are, shall we say, in flux," I replied. "Like you, I am facing changes in my life that will require adjustments by many people. You may be one of them, Olivia."

"I see, though I fail to grasp how anything in your life could possibly concern me. As I say, had I known, we might have made some possible arrangement to accommodate you, out of courtesy to my brother's memory. However, under the circumstances, with you coming in apparently without permission—in what would in all likelihood be viewed by the authorities as trespassing—I do not see how I could entertain as a guest one who—"

Alicia was not about to let the subtle condescension continue. She was no longer intimidated by Olivia, and had finally had enough.

"Marie is not here as a *guest*, Olivia!" she blurted out. "She is not staying at the Crannoch Bay. She will not be staying with friends. She is staying *here*! She has returned to take possession of Castle Buchan."

"And *you*!" Olivia spat as she spun around to face her. "What do *you* have to do with it other than sneaking about where you have no right to be?"

"I have nothing to do with it," replied Alicia. "But Marie has everything to do with it. She is not trespassing, but exerting her legal rights. It is *you* who are trespassing, Olivia."

At last Olivia's eyes flashed visibly with fire.

"You deceitful little hussy!" she cried. "How did you get in—climb the fence, bribe one of the maids? I told you I did not want to see your face on my property again, and this time I will make you pay for your insolence. If you do not leave, the police will be here within thirty minutes, and believe me, I *will* bring charges."

Alicia sat unmoving. Olivia turned again toward me. Her face was red, but she tried to regain a portion of her composure.

"I don't know what lies she has told you, Marie," she said. "But I am certain they are just that—lies. I do not want to see you hurt. I have nothing against you personally, even though I believe you hastened the death of my poor niece. But you must understand that I cannot sit idly by and listen to absurdities and accusations. I am sorry, but you will need to leave . . . immediately, I'm afraid. Perhaps if you can talk some sense into Alicia, and with an apology, I might be persuaded to be lenient. Then perhaps you can come back for a visit, through proper channels rather than this sneaking about. But if you do not leave my property, I cannot be responsible for the consequences to either of you."

She turned and left the room.

Alicia and I looked at each other with expressions that silently shouted, *Whoa!*

"What now?" Alicia asked. "Are we going to leave?"

"Of course not," I replied. "We are not going to kowtow to threats."

"She *will* call the police," said Alicia. "If I know her, she will tell them that there has been a break-in at the castle and that she has the trespassers in custody. She won't tell them who we are, so they will come expecting hoodlums."

"Making it sound like an emergency and robbery attempt. A clever way to get the police here in a hurry, planning to make an arrest."

"What shall we do?"

"You are going to call Mr. Crathie immediately to tell him I blew it and confronted Olivia and that he had better come rescue us. That's what *you* are going to do. As for me, I am going to keep playing my harp."

Chapter Thirty-nine

Duchess vs. Impostor

Lay the proud usurpers low!
Tyrants fall in every foe.
Liberty's in every blow.
Let us do, or dee!
—Robert Burns, "Scots, Wha Hae"

I continued playing from my Scottish repertoire. Alicia went to the far end of the room to telephone Nigel Crathie. She returned five minutes later.

"Was he upset with us?" I asked.

"A little I think," replied Alicia. "But he said he understood. There had to be a confrontation eventually, he said, so we might as well have it over with. I know he would rather we had let him do it. But he said he would be here in forty minutes."

"I just hope we're not being hauled off in the paddy wagon by then!" I laughed. "In the meantime, I intend to enjoy myself. Besides, surely the policemen will recognize me and give us the benefit of the doubt."

About twenty minutes later we heard sirens in the distance. They grew louder until they screamed into the grounds and eventually stopped outside the front of the castle. Two minutes later, many feet in the corridor came running toward us. The door burst open and two uniformed policemen rushed in, followed by Olivia. Alicia was seated calmly on a couch, and I was at my harp playing "Scotland the Brave."

The men stopped and looked around in confusion.

"There they are," demanded Olivia. "Arrest them."

"These are your intruders?" said one of the policemen, turning toward her with a puzzled expression. "They're just a couple of women. I thought you said you had a burglary in progress."

They obviously had no idea who I was. Were they flunkies of Olivia's, too? Where had they come from?

"I said I had caught two trespassers who had broken into the grounds and also broken into the castle and that I had no idea what they might do."

"This hardly appears to be quite such a dangerous situation as all that, my lady."

"Nevertheless, they are trespassers. They broke into my property. I intend to file charges, and I want them arrested."

The man sighed, then looked back and forth between Alicia and me.

"Either of you care to tell me what's going on?" he said. "Are you here without permission?"

"What she has told you is partially true," I replied. "We are here without Mrs. Urquhart's permission. However, we did *not* break in. Any charge of breaking and entering would be false. There are witnesses who can testify to that fact. I do not think it would go well for those who tried to arrest us on such a basis."

"That is patently absurd...as big a lie as I've ever heard," said Olivia heatedly, lapsing, whether intentionally or not, into the rhyming habit of her childhood.

"How did you get in, then?" asked the man.

"We were let in," I replied.

"By whom?"

"I would rather not say."

"I'm afraid you will have to say, ma'am."

"I am sorry, but I have no intention of divulging that information."

The man stared back at me, surprised at the brazenness of my refusal.

"And you?" he said, turning to Alicia.

"I have nothing to say," she replied.

Obviously irritated, our stubbornness to cooperate at last swayed him to take action.

"All right, then," he said. "You leave me no choice but to take you in. You'll both have to come with me." He stood and waited for us to get up and follow. Neither of us moved.

"I'm sorry," I said. "We cannot comply with your request. We are under orders to remain in the castle."

"Under *whose* orders?"

"I cannot tell you that."

"Look, lady, I don't know what your game is," he retorted angrily. "But I've had enough of it. Now get your bum off that chair and come with us."

Suddenly behind him footsteps again came along the corridor and a suited man hurried into the room. He glanced first at Olivia, then surveyed the situation.

"I am Marshall Warmington," he said, turning to the uniformed officer. "I am Mrs. Urquhart's solicitor. She informs me there has been a break-in."

"It is contained and under control, Mr. Warmington," said the policeman. "I was just in the process of arresting these two ladies."

During the brief exchange, the solicitor had thrown two or three quick glances in my direction. I did not know him, but he seemed to recognize me, and the wheels of his brain were obviously turning rapidly.

The policeman in charge now turned to his assistant, who had not spoken a word. "Cuff her," he said, nodding his head in Alicia's direction. He then strode toward me, reached down, grabbed my wrist, and yanked me to my feet. I let out a little cry. I was more astonished than anything, though his grip did hurt. I thought British bobbies were supposed to be gentle!

"Stop it, stop it!" now cried Alicia. "Don't you know who that is?!"

"A trespasser is all I know," the policeman shot back. "Come on, lady!" he said and pulled me, still holding tight to my wrist, toward the door. "I'll cuff you myself when we get outside. Sorry for the disturbance, Duchess," he said, nodding to Olivia as we passed. The smirk of satisfaction on Olivia's face was worth a thousand words.

"Are you blind? Don't you realize what you're doing?" insisted Alicia as the younger man clipped a handcuff around one of her wrists and pulled her to her feet. "*That* is the duchess you're dragging from the room!"

Whatever he may have thought, her words stopped the man in his tracks.

"Are you crazy, lady?" he said.

"I am as sane as you, and I am telling you that you are about to arrest the Duchess of Buchan."

"And who are you, then, Mickey Mouse?" he retorted.

"She is nothing but a disgruntled former employee," put in Olivia. "I had to fire her two months ago. Now she is determined to get back at me however she can."

Out of the corner of my eye I had seen a knowing look dawn on the face of Olivia's solicitor the moment Alicia spoke up.

"Just a moment, Officer," he said, stepping forward. "You might ask the lady her name."

"You heard the man," said the policeman to me. "Out with it."

"My name is Marie Reidhaven," I said.

"Reidhaven?" he repeated.

"I am the widow of the late Alasdair Reidhaven, Duke of Buchan." Instantly the man's grip on my wrist relaxed.

"Show them the papers, Marie," said Alicia desperately. "They can't treat you like this—show them the papers."

"I insist that you arrest them at once!" demanded Olivia.

The policeman, however, suddenly hesitant, saw that he had stumbled into a more complicated situation than he had bargained for. Slowly he released me and stepped back, glancing helplessly back and forth between the solicitor and his client.

"Arrest them!" repeated Olivia. "Marshall, I demand that these intruders be arrested. You know as well as I do that the fact that this woman was married to my brother gives her no right to trespass and break into what is now my property and my home. She *has* broken in and I intend to file charges. Now, Officer," she said, turning again to the policeman, "if you value your job, arrest these women and remove them from my property at once."

Still the man hesitated. At last the solicitor spoke.

"What papers is she referring to?" he asked me.

I walked across the room to where I had laid my coat over the back of one of the couches. From its pocket I withdrew the envelope Mr. Crathie had given me at the hotel. I returned to the scene of the standoff and handed it to him. Everyone waited in silence as he took out the documents and quickly scanned their contents. The raised eyebrows and low whistle that followed evidenced his astonishment clearly enough. Finally he let out a long breath as he turned to me.

"You are no doubt aware," he said, "that your late husband's will and the disposition of his assets and property are being contested by the duke's sister and will be adjudicated by the courts."

"I am," I said.

"Depending on the resolution of the suit, this may be nothing more than a meaningless piece of paper," he said, indicating the document in his hand.

"Unless I am mistaken," I replied, "I think you will find that it is a legally binding document upon which the lawsuit will have no bearing whatever."

"What is it, Marshall?" asked Olivia, walking toward him.

"It alleges that your brother's prenuptial agreement with Mrs. Reidhaven is null and void, that it was superseded by another document, and claims that, er . . . that Mrs. Reidhaven is the Duchess of Buchan."

"That can't be! It's a forgery. Let me see it. You will pay for this, Marie! Who have you bribed to tell your lies? Marshall, are you just going to stand there and do nothing? I want her arrested, I tell you—for trespassing, for these, these false claims! This is absurd. Arrest her!"

The two policemen were by now inclined to do nothing but get out of there. And though he was the solicitor handling Olivia's affairs, Mr. Warmington was sufficiently sobered by what he had seen to weigh his moves carefully before doing something he might later regret.

How far the standoff might have gone, or what might have been the final result, we would never know. Just then the man Farquharson appeared at the door, cap in hand, obviously intimidated as he saw the tense gathering. He begged Olivia's pardon for interrupting, but had come to tell her that a man in a car was at the Port Scarnose gate being very insistent on the intercom and demanding to be let in immediately.

"Who is he, Mr. Farquharson?" she asked.

"A Mr. Crathie, m'leddy."

"Bah! He was my brother's rascal. He'll do us no good. I've got all the solicitors I need. Send him away—I have no interest in seeing him."

"He didna spier tae see yersel', m'leddy."

"Who, then?"

"Mrs. Reidhaven, m'leddy. I didna ken she was here, but he telt me tae gang an' spier o' ye."

"You had better let him in, Olivia," I said. "I am certain you do not want to be in a position of refusing my solicitor access to me. Mr. Crathie is my solicitor," I said to Mr. Warmington. "He is handling my affairs and is the one who gave me those documents I just showed you. He is also one of the solicitors in charge of my late husband's estate."

"I see." He nodded. "Yes, Mrs. Urquhart...let him in. I need to hear what he has to say."

Still fuming, Olivia nodded to Farquharson, who disappeared. Warmington took the papers back from her. Luckily she had not ripped them to shreds. He then walked toward the two policemen. "I don't think there will be any arrests today," he said. "You had better get that cuff off her," he said, nodding toward Alicia. "Then I think we can handle it from here, gentlemen."

Only too glad to be dismissed, the two policemen were gone a moment later. Two or three minutes elapsed, then Adela appeared with Nigel Crathie at her side. She did a double take when she saw Alicia and me.

He walked in confidently with a briefcase in one hand and Adela left, though it wouldn't surprise me if she stopped somewhere within earshot to listen. The two solicitors obviously knew each other and shook hands.

"What's this all about, Crathie?" said Warmington.

"Only that the duchess"—he indicated me with a slight nod of his head—"upon learning that she still is the rightful Duchess of Buchan and the heir to the late duke's estate, has returned from Canada to take possession of her property and assume her position."

"Lies! Nothing but lies!" shrieked Olivia. "She's an impostor! It's all lies. Warmington, you fool—get rid of them!"

"I am afraid, Mrs. Urquhart," he said, trying to calm her, "that we have little alternative but to take this up in court."

"Mr. Crathie," I said, "the way things stand, with our not exactly being welcomed here by my sister-in-law, Miss Forbes and I find ourselves in an awkward position. We will, of course, be staying at the castle, and thus we need to be able to come and go freely."

"I understand, and I hope we can alleviate your awkwardness, Your Grace," he said.

He turned to his fellow solicitor.

"It goes without saying that we will require keys to the castle," he said, "*all* keys—as well as all access codes, so that my client and anyone associated with her is free to come and go."

"After the matter is decided in court," began Mr. Warmington. "At that time we will of course be willing—"

"You don't understand, Warmington," interrupted Mr. Crathie. "I mean *now*...today. I mean this minute—*all* keys and access codes."

Mr. Crathie laid his briefcase down on one of the coffee tables, flipped the snaps open, and pulled out more papers. "I have already filed in Elgin," he said, "a writ to this effect based on Mrs. Reidhaven's right to regain and hold full possession of the property that is legally hers. You have seen the documentation, I believe."

"I have seen what *purports* to be documentation to that effect. Its legitimacy, of course, will be subjected to the closest legal scrutiny."

"By all means. But until then, we want full access, as I say, immediately. Any attempt not to comply or to inhibit or prohibit her full access would, I need hardly remind you, not be taken kindly when and if this case does come to court. I would suggest that you and your client consider your moves very carefully so that *you* are not found to be complicit in your client's attempted illegal seizure of Castle Buchan and these crude tactics against my client."

"How dare you!" spat Olivia.

"Caw canny, Mrs. Urquhart," said Mr. Crathie, spinning to face her. "You cannot intimidate me, and I would suggest you do not try. Don't forget how close your brother and I were. I am very familiar with your ways, Mrs. Urquhart. It may be that I know things you would prefer not became public. You would not do well to anger me."

Alicia was watching all this unfold with eyes aglow with awe and admiration toward Nigel Crathie.

"You will be free to come and go as you please, Duchess," said Mr. Crathie to me. "If there is the slightest attempt to prevent you in any way, you may contact either myself or Mr. Warmington, whom I am certain will be able to assist you. I know he will not want his client to be found in violation of this court order. I must ask you further," he added, "if you want me to take steps to have Mrs. Urquhart removed from the premises. I can recall the police officers and—"

"No, Mr. Crathie, she may stay," I said. "As both you and Mr. Warmington have indicated, final resolution of this will rest with the courts, and I would not want to prevent my sister-in-law access to the castle any more than I know she will not want to prevent mine."

In a speechless white wrath, Olivia left the room. Warmington followed. When he returned ten minutes later, it was to present Mr. Crathie with a full set of keys and a paper indicating all the access codes to the three entrances to the grounds where Olivia had installed security gates.

Chapter Forty

Community Welcome

How pleasant 'twas in the sweet May morning,
The rising sun thy gay fields adorning;
The feathered songsters their lays were singing,
While rocks and woods were with echoes ringing.
—Dugald MacPhail, "The Isle of Mull"

Neither Alicia nor I nor Harvey Nicholls, as far as I knew, left the grounds the rest of that day. It was obvious none of Olivia's minions had any intention of broadcasting news about what had taken place in the castle between myself and Mr. Crathie and Olivia and Mr. Warmington. Though she was sworn to absolute secrecy, obviously Tavia knew about Alicia's mission to Canada. However, Alicia had told her nothing of what had happened since or even what we had planned. Yet by the next day everyone in Port Scarnose and Crannoch seemed to know that I was back and how things stood.

We saw neither Olivia nor Adela for the rest of the day and did not press our presence in the castle upon them. Having won the first skirmish with Olivia's solicitor, Mr. Crathie advised us to move slowly, not attempt too much too soon, and not to unnecessarily anger Olivia further. We must allow her, he said, to get used to my presence by degrees.

It was obviously good advice. We kept to ourselves. We made no attempt to set about trying to move back in to the whole front of the castle. We spent our second night back in our little spartan room in the old servants' wing. I was already fond of the place.

Mr. Crathie returned with my things, including *Journey*. We also

271

asked him to bring us some food so we would not have to go down to the kitchen. He complied, bringing the unused groceries from the Crannoch Bay Hotel and more besides, topped off by a lavish take-out order of fish-and-chips and onion rings from Linda and Eddie's Chip Shop in Crannoch. We were in heaven! We invited Harvey Nicholls in for the feast. He loosened up and began to laugh and joke and occasionally lapse into the same Scots he spoke with the locals.

The following day we got down to the business of trying to put some kind of life back together. Though it wasn't my nature to be authoritative, I knew I had to stand up for my right not merely to *be* there, but to be *in charge* of the castle. It would be a level of control that Olivia would not easily relinquish. According to those who had known her far longer than I, *control* was the chief demon that possessed her. Alasdair had threatened her power to control him early in life, and she had done everything possible to ruin him almost until the day he died.

Now here was Alasdair reaching out from the grave and threatening to upset her apple cart just when she thought she had finally gained the control she had so long sought. She could do nothing more to *him*, but I had no doubt she would do everything in her power to destroy *me*. How far it would go, I had no idea. But I had to assert myself. If I did not, she would eventually grind me under her heel. There were no in-between options.

I knew what Alasdair would want me to do. It would be awkward for a while. But I had to take steps to assume my position with dignity and authority, for Alasdair's sake. He had made his will clear. I had to be faithful to his wishes. I had not desired this. But if *he* desired it, I would try to carry out my destiny as his widow faithfully.

Accordingly, the following morning we began as quietly and courteously as possible to make plans to unobtrusively take up residence again in the front of the castle.

We had no intention of dislocating Olivia, but Adela was another matter. She had taken up residence in Alicia's apartment on the second floor of the west wing. That occupation I did not intend to allow longer than necessary. I went to find her midway through the morning. I was glad she was alone.

"Hello, Adela," I said.

She stared daggers through me.

"I wanted to let you know," I went on, "that Alicia will be staying on as my housekeeper. As such, she will require her apartment again. I will appreciate you having your belongings removed by this afternoon. You are of course free to remain in any of the unused rooms of the castle as long as Olivia is here. I don't know what arrangement you and she have, but it is only fair that I tell you that she will have no access to any estate funds and I, of course, will be unable to employ or pay you for your services. Perhaps she is paying you from her own inheritance, which I understand Alasdair left her. That is between you and her. As I say, you are free to remain with her, rent-free, for as long as she needs you. If either you or your mistress have questions, you may find me either in my studio in the Music Room, or in the south wing."

All the while I was speaking, her expression revealed nothing. When I finished, a light glowed from her eyes so fierce that I could have been looking at Olivia herself.

In spite of Mr. Crathie's cautions to Olivia not to hinder our movements, I thought it best that I remain in the castle. But about noon I sent Alicia into town with Nicholls to fetch her things and the Volvo. She was free, I said, to apprise Tavia of the recent developments. If they had any trouble getting back in, I said, they could ring me on my mobile and I would see to it. But they had the access codes to the gates and everything went smoothly.

By that afternoon we again had an automobile at our disposal. With Nicholls's help, Alicia began to move her things from Tavia's back into her former rooms. By evening she was again in possession of her apartment. I moved my things into a guest room across the hall. Campbell was friendlier to me than he had ever been during the years of my marriage to Alasdair, and came to me several times a day to ask if there was anything I needed. His wife, Jean, and young Sarah Duff were more cautious, still more than a little confused about everything.

I couldn't wait to get back into the countryside—to walk my favorite loop down along the coastline to the Salmon Bothy, and to visit Ranald Bain! Alicia came and went freely for a few days without incident. Eventually I ventured out of the castle myself. I walked from the castle through Port Scarnose and to the promontory and my favorite bench where I had first met both Gwendolyn and Iain and where my Scottish adventure had begun. Everywhere people came up to me joyfully and enthusiastically, greeting me warmly with hugs and such exuberance that it brought tears to my eyes.

It is humbling to be loved. I was awestruck.

When I went into the co-op for the first time, the moment they saw me, several of the clerks, then all the customers in the store, began clapping and cheering. I was simply unprepared for the outpouring of affection from the community. If I thought about returning to my days of anonymity when I took walks along the sea and nobody knew who I was, I had another think coming. I would never be anonymous again.

Olivia caused us no trouble. The thought began to occur to me that perhaps I had misjudged her, that despite her outbursts she had now accepted the inevitable, and that everything would work out fine. Alicia, however, was privy to gossip that was not spoken around me. According to reports that came to her, Olivia was angrier than a wet hen to see how the community instantly opened its arms to receive me again as its duchess.

My first visit up the hill to see Ranald Bain was tearful and joyful. He of course had heard the general gist of what was known of my recent saga, though being out of the daily loop of village gossip he wanted to hear it from my own mouth, every juicy detail. When I had told my story, he shook his head and wept for joy. I think he was more proud of Alasdair than he was happy for me. And of course we made music together on his harp and violin—happy, gay, frivolous, fast...jigs and dances and wonderful Highland melodies. No laments or dirges or sad ballads on that day!

"An' are ye plannin' tae tak up the teachin' again, lass?" he asked. "Ye'll be the duchess noo, wi' mair responsibilities nor afore—wi' the affairs o' the estate, an' people comin' tae yersel' no' yer husband. Ye'll be a busy lady noo. But I'll sair miss the harpin' wi' the ither lassies."

"You won't have to," I said. "What good would all this be if I couldn't do what I enjoy doing most in all the world—teaching people to play the harp? Resuming my teaching is one of the *first* things I intend to do, when the time is right. It is still awkward in the castle and will be until, you know, things are decided. But I look forward to the day when children are coming and going all day long for lessons. Our little harp ensemble will meet again soon as well."

And so the first week of my return to Castle Buchan progressed without difficulties or ticklish situations. Life settled into something of a routine. We lived in what might be called a dual occupation of the castle by the Reidhaven camp, with myself and my allies; and the Urquhart camp, with Olivia and hers. But there were no hostilities. Olivia and Adela and one or two of the maids whom Olivia had brought in kept to themselves, as did Alicia and I. Though he wasn't technically on my staff, Mr. Farquharson softened toward me, tipped his hat and spoke kindly whenever we met. I think he and Nicholls began to warm a little toward each other, too. That was good. Because once everything was resolved, I would have to decide what to do with everyone, whom to keep and whom to let go. I wasn't about to have dissension within the ranks of the castle staff.

I telephoned Mr. Jones in Portland and we had a long talk. He seemed delighted for me, but was also anxious to fill me in on the work of my father's foundations, as well as bring me up to date on a few details pertaining to my father's estate. I asked him if he could arrange for shipment to me of the two harps as well as a few other things I had in Calgary. How many times would I ship harps back and forth between Scotland and Canada? But as I told him, it now appeared that I would in all likelihood be here for a long while.

Mr. Crathie issued a brief statement to the press. Remembering the reporter McDermott from Inverness, Mr. Crathie now encouraged me to speak with him again, openly this time, and allow him to print a major story if he liked. The idea of being so obviously in the public spotlight was a difficult one for me, but I saw Mr. Crathie's point. I couldn't avoid it—I *was* a public figure now, like it or not. He felt the publicity was a good means by which to solidify my position in the public mind when and if Olivia's contestation of Alasdair's will came to court. We had to deepen the perception, he said, that everything was proceeding exactly as the duke had wished it, and that I was merely assuming the rightful role dictated by his final instructions.

In that light, I contacted Mr. McDermott and met with him again, this time *on* the record. Avoiding the fact of having crept through the tunnel in the dead of night, and not mentioning the tense scene with Olivia and her solicitor, I told him about Alasdair's Edinburgh affidavit and Alicia's trip to Canada to inform me of it, about my return and all the adjustments I was having to make now since my future looked so very different than I had anticipated.

As I had promised, I invited Ranald, along with Tavia and Cora and Fia, to the castle for tea and harping.

Making preparations for the ensemble's meeting precipitated my second tense encounter with Olivia. I had of course been shown by Alicia and Nicholls to the out-of-the-way corner of the castle basement where Olivia had taken the few belongings I had not taken with me to Canada, as well as much of Alasdair's bedroom and office furniture. Every time my thoughts toward my sister-in-law began to soften, something like this would remind me to be wary. *Why*, I asked myself, with the entire castle at her disposal, would she intentionally put our things in the *worst* possible place for dampness and mildew? It made absolutely no sense, other than intentional retaliation. When I recovered them, half the clothes were mildewed and moth-eaten. Though they were clothes I did not care that much about, the *why* of it was a puzzle. Many of Alasdair's prized books had been boxed up and carted to the basement as well. I was dreadfully worried about their condition. The harps were in better shape. Being primarily wood, they could not be badly damaged in so short a time from dampness and cold. Several years in such conditions, however, would be different. There were some signs of mildew that I had to treat with extreme delicacy, being careful not to mar the finish, but otherwise they were okay. A little-known fact to most people is that mildew contributes its own share to the tone of all stringed instruments, harps included.

Added to the peculiarity of what she had done was the fact that my belongings had not been taken to just one place but were spread out through several rooms of the basement. All these doors still had very old locks that had not been recently changed. During the years of my marriage, I had never even been in most of those lower rooms. I had no idea where the keys were kept. Nicholls took charge of the search, but reported to me that the keys were not in their customary place, and what keys he was able to locate were not complete. Olivia proved singularly unhelpful, professing ignorance where the rest of the keys might be. She offered no hint as to why Alasdair's and my things had been so spread out in so many places . . . when *she* was obviously the one responsible!

After a week, Nicholls managed to find most of the keys scattered in out-of-the-way places, and he was able to unlock most of the rooms. Nearly all the clothes and books and furniture were soon removed to safer, warmer, dryer conditions.

But one mystery remained. The *Queen* had still not been found.

The *Ring*, the *Shamrock*, and *Limerick* had all joined the *Aida* and *Journey* back upstairs in my studio. The broken strings had been replaced and all were back in tune. Within a month or two I hoped they would be joined by their newer cousins being shipped from Canada, the two new Merlins, *Cairn* and the *Bard*.

But where was the empress who towered above them all?

I began to grow genuinely worried. I told Nicholls to turn the basement upside down. There remained three or four rooms he had not been able to open, he said, though the rust on the locks showed no signs of having been disturbed in a century. He very much doubted Olivia had stored anything behind them. Nevertheless, I told him, the *Queen* had to be found, even if it meant breaking locks apart and tearing doors off their hinges to locate her.

"What's that big brass key there on your ring?" I asked Nicholls as he was detailing his search efforts to me. "It is unusual and very pretty."

"That it is, my lady," he said. "But I doubt it's of any use. Never opened a lock I knew of, though it's been part of the basement key ring ever since I can remember. Probably just a decorative key someone had made."

I had laid eyes on Olivia only two or three times during the week and a half since my return to the castle, and then only from a distance. We had not once spoken since the incident involving the two lawyers. Finally my anxiety over the whereabouts of my cherished pedal harp outweighed all other considerations. For the first time since leaving for Canada, I climbed the stairs and walked along the familiar corridor toward the apartments Alasdair and I had shared together for three happy years. This had once been my home, my place of refuge, my inner sanctum of happiness with a man I loved. Now it had become, if Mr. Crathie's reports were to be believed, the GHQ of one who, if she prevailed, would strip me of everything I held dear, and if Alicia's perspectives were accurate, of one who would destroy me if that was what it took.

I drew in a deep breath and knocked on the door.

For several long seconds I heard nothing. Then footsteps approached and the door opened.

There stood Olivia. She looked straight into my face without the slightest movement of muscle, eyebrow, or lips—utterly dispassionate, as if she had known it was me before opening the door. Her silent nonexpression was neither inviting nor repelling, encouraged nothing, repulsed nothing. It was just *empty*, devoid of feeling.

She stood staring straight into me like a corpse, and waited.

"I am sorry to disturb you," I said, trying to keep my voice from quivering, "but I need to know where you took my pedal harp. Nicholls has located the others, but has been unable to find the large one."

"I am afraid I have no idea," Olivia replied at length. Her voice contained no more feeling than her expression. It was not the answer I expected.

"I, uh . . . then, who would know?" I said. "You did have my things moved?"

"As you were no longer here, I saw no reason to clutter up my home with things I had no interest in."

"Then where did you take my big harp?"

"I really cannot say. I assumed it was with the others."

"It was not."

"Then I do not see how I can help you. It is apparently no longer with us."

"What do you mean? You're the one who had them moved."

"I hired a man from the village to see to it."

"What instructions did you give him?"

"To take everything to the basement."

I let out a sigh of frustration. She was not being terribly cooperative.

"Then what is the man's name?" I asked. "I will talk to him."

"I am afraid I don't remember. He may have been an itinerant."

"Are you saying he is no longer in the area?"

"I really have no idea."

"And that is it, then? You refuse to help me locate my harp?"

She stared daggers back at me, then slowly closed the door in my face. It had been a stupid thing to say. I had unnecessarily alienated her, just as Mr. Crathie had warned me not to.

I sighed again and slunk away, irritated at both myself and Olivia.

Even without the presence of their reigning monarch, however, the ensemble harps still made lovely sounds when Ranald and the ladies arrived on Thursday of that week. What a time we had! I could only imagine Olivia's fury if word reached her about Ranald's visit. But I hardly thought about her. It was wonderful to hear laughter and music again from my studio. All four were anxious for me to put them to work with new pieces to learn, and begged to resume their weekly lessons.

Those were two requests I would never refuse.

But I remained nervous about the *Queen*.

Chapter Forty-one

Accusations

It was by a woman' treacherous hand,
That I was condemned tae dee.
Upon a ledge at a window she stood,
And a blanket she threw ower me.
—Robert Burns, "MacPherson's Lament"

Whether coincidentally or not, two days after the brief encounter in the doorway of my former apartment, Olivia suddenly walked into my studio. I was alone. It was Thursday, a little after noon. I was preparing for the ensemble get-together later in the day.

"Hello, Marie dear," she said, not exactly smiling, but in a soft and friendly tone. "I thought you should know that I will be away for a few days, so obviously the castle will be in your hands."

I was so stunned by her appearance and unexpected tone that I sat not knowing what to say.

"I feel bad about your missing harp," she went on. "I have asked Adela to jog her memory. I am certain it will turn up. It is no doubt in one of the rooms that we have not been able to find the keys to."

"Thank you," I said. "It is kind of you to help."

The next day Olivia left Port Scarnose for London.

Her recent puzzling changed tone sent me into a new round of conflicting thoughts and feelings about everything. I wondered if I had misjudged her, even misread the conversation at her door, wondered further if perhaps she and I *could* both remain in the castle and live and work together in harmony. Ever since she and Gwendolyn had come walking along the headland path and I had seen them for the first time, Olivia Urquhart had been a woman of mysterious dimensions whom I could not for the life of me understand. *Nothing* with her was straightforward.

When I mentioned these thoughts to Alicia, she came as close to being angry with me as I had ever seen.

"Marie," she said, "you cannot let her weave her spell over you. You have to see through it. Remember, I was under it for thirty years, and it nearly cost me my life. She never turns on the charm without some ulterior motive. That soft mesmerizing voice is a facade to lull you to sleep. Don't succumb, Marie."

I must say that Olivia's absence was a relief. I took to walking every day. I hadn't realized how much I had missed it, nor what a silent, invisible burden Olivia's presence in the castle had become. With her gone, I realized that without knowing it, and in spite of the affection shown by so many, I had yet been a little reluctant to venture out as much as I might have wanted to, afraid that Olivia's all-seeing eye knew my every move.

Now the village drew me again, as it had when I first came. I walked everywhere—through its streets and along its promontories and beaches. I resumed all my favorite walks, from up toward the Bin to Ranald's croft to the Salmon Bothy to the Crannoch viaduct loop. I greeted people with a newfound openness and walked with a renewed lightness in my step. I determined to get out every day, to be out among the people, Alasdair's people, and now *my* people. I walked along the coastline all the way from Findectifeld to Findlater.

Meanwhile, in Olivia's absence, we widened our search for the *Queen* to include every room in the castle. But still we were unable to turn up so much as a trace.

Early in the week following Olivia's departure, a big storm blew in, dumped half an inch of rain, roused the sea into a cauldron, and then left as quickly as it had come. Storms were always blowing in and out of northern Scotland. Ask a local what is Scotland's weather and he will say that whatever you've got in the afternoon will be different from what you had that same morning. Within thirty-six hours

the sun was back out, shining gloriously, and inviting me to my favorite place—the sea.

I laced up my hiking boots and grabbed my jacket and went to
ask Alicia if she would like to join me.

"I can't. Mrs. Gauld invited me for lunch. I was actually a little
surprised, but glad, too. Where are you going?" she asked.

"To the coast. I think I'll go to Seatown and along the shoreline to
the Salmon Bothy."

"Oh, Marie, I wish you wouldn't go that way," she said, "not today,
not after a storm."

"Why not?"

"The rocks may be slippery and the swell still big. Especially if it's
a high tide. People get swept off along there, or slip on the moss
and algae."

"I'll be careful."

"Be *very* careful, Marie. The North Sea is far from tame."

"Not a tame lion?" I suggested with a smile.

"Not at all tame. They think that's where poor Winny may have
been when she was lost."

"Ranald's daughter?"

Alicia nodded. "They think she may have been out walking along
the coastline there east of Crannoch and slipped on the rocks. She
was never found. They think the tide washed her body out to sea,
probably between Logie Head and Findlater."

"She must have been alone, then. How does anyone know where
she was?"

Olivia said she saw her in the distance the morning she went
missing—walking that way."

"Logie Head is a long way from town. How would Olivia possibly
have seen her?"

"I don't know."

"What about her mother—Ranald's wife . . . How did she die?"

"She fell from the cliffs. She apparently slipped, just like I almost
did. Though it hadn't rained for days when her body was found

down at the bottom west of Findlater. It's always been a mystery why she fell. But that is the irony, both mother and daughter were claimed by the rocky coastline."

After hearing that, I promised to be doubly careful. "Poor Ranald," I said, "to lose *both* a wife and a daughter. I cannot imagine the grief. How he can be so optimistic and enthusiastic about life after all that. He is a remarkable man."

"I wish I had seen him for what he truly is sooner," sighed Alicia. "I am thankful you helped open my eyes when you did."

I set out from the castle on the Crannoch road, reached the village, made my way along Grant Street to Seafield Street, turned and descended to the harbor, and thence made my way past the pet cemetery and eastward along the narrow path that hugged the shore. The tide was about halfway out and did not appear dangerous. But, mindful of my promise to Alicia, I kept a watchful eye out for sleepers. As I went, I grew reflective.

Since returning to Scotland and with everything my return entailed, I had obviously been thinking almost continually about my future. With my father gone now, too, and with this latest development brought about by Alasdair's affidavit and the invalidation of our prenuptial agreement, my fortunes were radically altered. The previous two weeks had reconciled me to the fact that everything in my life was changed, that I could never again be who I was before.

I was fine with that. If Alasdair wanted me to be the duchess, then I would be faithful to that. I would embrace it and enjoy it. But I could not envision myself living forever secluded away in the castle. I would rather live in town and open a harp studio in my home. I also had to make an attempt to heal the rift with Olivia, even bring her into the affairs of the estate if possible. In time, why *not* give her half of it? She was Alasdair's sister, after all. She had more right to it by blood than I did. If she wanted to play the aristocratic role, why not let her share in Alasdair's estate?

My thoughts and plans, however, were abruptly altered when Mr. Crathie called at the castle about two weeks after Olivia's departure. The expression on his face was grim. His bombshell certainly brought an abrupt end to my idealistic hope that Olivia and I might work harmoniously together in the future.

"Your sister-in-law has been busy," he said.

"What do you mean?" I said. "She's gone."

"Yes, and now we know why. I received these papers today from one of the most prestigious barristers in London. It is a formal affidavit to be added in support of her suit contesting the duke's will. Copies were sent by overnight courier to both myself and Mr. Murdoch in Edinburgh."

"Is there any major change?" I asked.

"Not in what she is asking for, only in the allegations she is bringing forth in support of her claim. She is still contesting your right to everything."

"So what new information is in this affidavit?"

"It is not a pretty picture, Mrs. Reidhaven," he replied. "Are you sure you want to know? Would you not rather I simply seek to handle it through legal avenues?"

"No, I want to know. Please tell me everything, Mr. Crathie."

He hesitated a moment. "Extortion is the primary focus of the charge," he said at length.

"Extortion!" I exclaimed. "Now I am really confused."

"The basis of the claim is that your marriage to Alasdair was premeditated and therefore invalid, and that therefore you have no right to inherit. There are pages and pages of documents, some going back as far as twenty years, allegations about your past in Canada, the charge that you came here knowing of Alasdair's illness for the express purpose of extorting money from him. Your UK citizenship is being investigated. They are even digging into your parents' pasts to see what can be discovered. Kidnapping also comes into it."

"Kidnapping . . . of whom?!"

"Gwendolyn—the charge that you took Gwendolyn against both her own will and Olivia's, who was her legal guardian at the time, and kept her from Olivia, as it turned out, for the rest of her life. She alleges that you used the kidnapping of Gwendolyn as a means of blackmail against Alasdair to get what you wanted, which was control of the Buchan estate. She alleges that you have been planning this for years, ever since your discovery of your Buchan ancestral roots. She even implies that you accelerated the effects of the illnesses of both father and daughter, in Alasdair's case with drugs—an even more sinister claim with *very* dark legal implications. If she can prove collusion, she will have a strong case. She has documentation to show that you were investigating your family connections to Scotland as long as fifteen years ago."

"That was an innocent computer search. It was just a lark. Nothing came of it."

"Nevertheless, along with everything else . . ."

By then I was in tears. I groped my way to a chair.

"You don't mean to tell me that there is *more?*"

"I am sorry, Mrs. Reidhaven, I am afraid so."

"What else could there possibly be?"

"She also says that you were . . . intimately involved—"

The lawyer paused a moment.

"—with the curate during your marriage to Alasdair."

I groaned with sickening despair, and shook my head. Mr. Crathie waited patiently.

"How could she possibly have gotten all this together in a short two weeks?"

"She didn't," rejoined Mr. Crathie. "Some of these drafts are over a year old. She has been working on this, in my opinion, since before your marriage to Alasdair. Even if she is not successful in overturning Alasdair's will, I fear she will be able to seriously damage, if not completely ruin, your reputation throughout Scotland. It appears now that the original filing of her initial suit several months ago was merely the beginning. Whether she intended to use these latest allegations, or has only now decided to make them public because of your return, and our challenge to her right of control in the castle, that we may never know."

I sat shaking my head.

"As I attempt to look at this whole thing with some perspective," Mr. Crathie mused, "I cannot but be struck by the fact that revenge against you seems to be as strong a driving motivation as any hope that she will actually gain control of the estate. Tell me, is there any history that you know of that might point to mental imbalance? If so, that might be something we could use against her."

"I would never stoop to such tactics," I answered. "Not even if it meant losing everything. That's out of the question."

"But might there be something to it? This is so far over the top. She seems intent on destroying you completely in the eyes of everyone who knows you. It's not normal, not sane. I read this affidavit in complete disbelief. She cannot possibly believe even half of it herself. *Could* she actually be mad?"

"I think Olivia convinces herself that her lies are true, then actually comes to believe them."

"If she cannot tell fact from fiction, reality from unreality, then she *is* insane."

We both quietly contemplated his conclusion.

"What happens next?" I said finally.

"I will begin preparing our own case. We will have to answer and refute each of her allegations."

"I'm not sure I want to do that, Mr. Crathie," I said. "My goodness—extortion, kidnapping, adultery, not to mention attempted murder. To answer a lie only gives it credibility. Perhaps silence would be best."

"That would be risky, in my opinion. To leave the matter up to the court, and say nothing in your own defense, would give her a decided upper hand."

"Then why don't we simply draw up papers and give her the estate?" I said in reply, letting out a long sigh. "Let her have it. I'm not sure I have it in me to fight it."

"Is that what Alasdair would want?" asked Mr. Crathie.

His question put an end to the discussion. It was the simplest of statements, yet also the most compelling. I knew the answer well enough. Alasdair would be outraged—not on his own behalf, but for me.

"If only Iain—that is, Mr. Barclay, were here," I said. "He would be able to resolve at least some of these charges. Do you suppose there is any way to learn where he is? I don't even know if he is aware of Alasdair's death."

"I will make some discreet inquiries, Mrs. Reidhaven. But as far as I understand it, no one knows anything of his whereabouts."

Chapter Forty-two

Silence or Defense?

Lord, as to Thy dear cross we flee, and plead to be forgiven,
So let Thy life our pattern be, and form our souls for heaven.
Should friends misjudge, or foes defame, or brethren faithless prove,
Then, like Thine own, be all our aim to conquer them by love.
Kept peaceful in the midst of strife, forgiving and forgiven,
O may we lead the pilgrim life, and follow Thee to heaven.
—John Hampden Gurney, "Lord, as to Thy Dear Cross We Flee"

Immediately after Mr. Crathie left, Alicia got the full story, and the full flow of my tears. Whereas I was heartbroken, bewildered, and frustrated, Alicia was furious. Her loyalty to both Alasdair and me spilled out with story after story about Olivia through the years, some so unbelievable I hardly *could* believe them. I thought I had already heard everything.

Alicia's stories kept Mr. Crathie's question about Olivia's sanity fresh in my mind. It was a bizarre thing to wonder. Yet Olivia's irrational lust to control and exact revenge and, in Alasdair's case, simply to hurt, almost did seem deranged. I did not know if I would ever be able to forgive her for keeping Gwendolyn from her father all those years. Ranald spoke to me about the promise that God will restore the years the locusts have eaten. But I did not see how those years Alasdair had missed with his daughter could ever be restored. Thoughts of them together in heaven didn't alleviate in my mind the unconscionable travesty of what Olivia had done.

"You *have* to fight this, Marie," said Alicia, hot and red-faced.

"Somebody must finally stand up to that woman and expose her for what she is."

"I just don't know if that someone is me," I said, feeling very weak.

"There is no one else, Marie. Alasdair is gone. If you don't, she will take everything. It is up to you. Her lies nearly destroyed Alasdair years ago. Never have I seen a man suffer like she made him suffer. Can you imagine—taking a man's child from him, denying him even the right to name his own baby, and then refusing him contact forever after? Had it not been for you, Marie, Alasdair would literally never have seen his daughter again. She would have died without knowing him. Who but a mean-spirited woman would do such a thing? I remained neutral too long. Even though I was in his house, I was still under her control. I don't know what I could have done, but I should have spoken up—should have done *something*. I regret my long silence now. She will take everything from you, too, Marie, if you allow it. You cannot let that happen . . . for Alasdair's sake, for Gwendolyn's sake, if not for your own."

As long as she had brought it up, I decided to ask her something I had wanted to know for a long time.

"Alicia," I said, "what do you think happened when Gwendolyn was born? Everyone tells such a different story. It is confusing."

"I wasn't in the room," she replied. "For years all I heard was Olivia's side of it, which made Alasdair out to be a monster."

"But you kept working for him."

"I couldn't believe everything she said. I really didn't know what to believe. I tried not to think about it."

"But you were in the castle at the time? You were working for Alasdair's parents by then, didn't you say?"

"Yes, I was here. I knew Fiona's time had come. I heard things— comings and goings . . . Dr. Mair, Iain Barclay, of course . . . doors banging, occasional yelling, the shrieks of a woman's voice. Listening from a distance, I had no idea what was going on. Everything sounded terrible, but I didn't know. Then later, of course, Alasdair left and was gone a long time. I had been Olivia's friend for so long, I suppose it was natural to accept her portrayal of events. I didn't stop to analyze it. I didn't realize what a master of manipulation Olivia was, and how she subtly twisted everything she wanted people to think and believe. With someone like that you don't even recognize the mind control, because she is working it on your *own* mind. I am embarrassed; no, I am horrified now to realize how easily I was duped all those years. How many people go all their lives never breaking free from the coersive mind games of some of those who are closest to them."

She exhaled a great sigh.

"I have you to thank, Marie," Alicia went on, "you and Ranald, for fighting for me, for engaging in a battle I did not even know was going on around me— You fought for me when I couldn't fight for myself. I didn't even know I was in a battle for control of my very soul. You fought, you helped wake me up, helped me open my eyes, helped me wake into my own *true* self. I am more appreciative than I can tell you."

I smiled and nodded in acknowledgment.

"And now," she went on, "I am gradually coming to see two effects of that waking—one, Olivia now hates me with the same venom she directed toward poor Alasdair all those years. It is like she hates those who break free from her even more than those who were never under her influence."

"I think it is having stood up to her that produces the hatred," I said. "Alasdair once said something like that—that it was his confronting her and laughing at her that made her so determined to get even, whatever it took."

Alicia nodded thoughtfully.

"What's the second change you mentioned?" I asked.

"I am also seeing much of the past differently," Alicia replied. "My eyes are opening to the realization that my perceptions about many things may not have been accurate. For years my perceptions were colored and dominated and shaped by Olivia's subtle persuasions and invisible influences. Someone like that influences the way people think in ways they are never aware of. I know from personal experience. I would not say I was a mindless clone. It's more subtle than that. It's an undercurrent. Your whole way of looking at things is altered by little comments and sighs and gestures and facial expressions and knowing glances. There are a thousand ways a manipulative woman exerts her influence. An unsuspecting victim never sees it.

"Breaking free from all that, suddenly new light is shining in on the past from different angles," said Alicia. "Of course I always disliked Iain Barclay. I never knew why. I never recognized that I was a victim of Olivia's subtle persuasions about him. I was merely reflecting her perspectives. I have not seen Reverend Barclay since he left. I know nothing more about him. I have not heard him speak another word. I know nothing about his life now—whether he is still in the pulpit, whether he is married . . . nothing. Yet he has become a very different man in my thoughts now as I reflect back—almost a saint. I wish I could see him again and apologize for misjudging him. I recall things I heard him say. I realize that he could have been speaking to me, if I'd only had ears to hear. Yet maybe it is not entirely too late. I hope growth can take place through the memory as well as the present. And I think it can, I believe it can."

"I'm sure you are right."

"It's not only with Reverend Barclay," Alicia continued. "I now see Alasdair differently, too. Of course during these last years since you came, I had already begun to understand him differently, even love him, I hope I can say, just as a good and kind man. But now things are coming back to me from the distant past that appear much different than I thought at the time. I wonder if everything that happened that night might be *completely* different than Olivia allowed everyone to believe. To answer your question . . . I don't know what happened. But at this point, I have begun to doubt the stories Olivia allowed to circulate. Look what she is now telling about you, which you know to be pure lies. So why would it not be the same back then?"

"But you can't absolutely know that I didn't come here with designs on Alasdair," I said. "You can't *know* that I didn't have an affair with Iain. Not absolutely, because you weren't there."

"Yes I can, Marie. I know *you*. I know who you are; I know what you are made of. I know your character. I also know your accuser, and what she is made of."

I smiled and took Alicia's hand and gave it a squeeze.

"I am so thankful to have a friend like you, Alicia," I said. "I don't know if I could get through all this without you."

While we were still talking Tavia, Fia, and Mrs. Gauld appeared at the front door of the castle. I had completely forgotten that we had invited them to join us for tea. Now here they were with a basket of fresh home-bakes.

The moment Olivia had departed for London, I gave orders that all the gates to the castle property were to be kept open twenty-four hours a day while she was gone. I also told Nicholls to disconnect the electrical power to the gates so that they would *remain* open, hopefully until I had complete control of the estate again. What Olivia would do upon her return was anyone's guess. But at least it was a beginning to the reestablishment of the right of the community to full and unfettered access to the roads, and to me. Thus, the women had been able to walk straight in from the village all the way to the castle. I wanted to remove her new "Keep Out" signs, too, but remembered Mr. Crathie's advice about taking one thing at a time.

We invited our guests in. The five of us went to the kitchen to put on water and see what they had brought. We sliced some apples and strawberries to go with the oatcakes, rock cakes, scones, and shortbread.

"Should we invite Adela to join us?" suggested Fia as we sat down. "Maybe with Olivia gone, I don't know—do you think she would?"

"After what I have just heard, I am not sure I could—" began Alicia, her anger resurfacing over what I had told her about Olivia's latest charges.

Suddenly she got up and hurried from the room.

"Alicia does not seem herself today," said Mrs. Gauld.

"We have just had a bit of a shock," I said. "She will join us again in a few minutes."

"I hope nothing is the matter, dear," said Mrs. Gauld. She still called me *Dear*, even after all the changes that had taken place.

"No, nothing . . . only—"

I glanced away, feeling the tears returning to my eyes.

"What is it, dear?" asked Mrs. Gauld, placing a gentle hand on my arm.

"Only a few new developments in Olivia's lawsuit about the will," I said. I didn't want to divulge too much. I knew that's why Alicia had left suddenly. Though we were trying to win her over, Mrs. Gauld was still straddling the fence in her loyalties. I knew there was a chance that anything I said could get back to Olivia. While I wouldn't exactly call her and Olivia bosom buddies, they were yet friends. Mrs. Gauld had no idea what kinds of things lurked beneath the surface of Olivia's calm and smiling demeanor.

Alicia returned a few minutes later. It was a strained and uncomfortable afternoon tea. I knew Tavia and Fia were dying to know what was going on, and we trusted them completely. I didn't like having to guard my tongue. Unfortunately, that was the reality of the situation.

I drove up to Ranald's the next day. His reaction to the news of Olivia's latest allegations was different than either Alicia's or my own. He took in the news seriously and thoughtfully. The wheels of his brain were obviously turning, though at the time I had no idea what he was thinking.

"What are ye gaein' tae du, lass?" he asked.

"I don't know," I replied. "That's one of the reasons I'm here. I hope you can help me. I wish Iain was here, too, and I could ask you *both* for your advice. Do you still have no idea where he is?"

"I ken naethin', lass," Ranald replied, though with an odd expression on his face. I could not help wondering if he was keeping something from me. Yet I knew that for Ranald Bain to tell a lie,

even a minor untruth, was a complete impossibility. If he said he
did not know where Iain was, then he did not know where he
was.

"Mr. Crathie wants me to mount what he calls a vigorous refuta-
tion of all Olivia's charges," I sighed, "fight fire with fire, he says. But
I'm not sure I am comfortable with that, or that it is the right thing
to do."

"Ye're instincts are nae sae far wrang, Marie, lass," Ranald said,
nodding, "an' I'm aye prood o' ye for feelin' sich like."

"Why do you say that?"

"Because faniver we're facin' ony dilemma in life, there's but ane
way tae ken fit we're tae de—by spierin', *What did the Master say?*
an', *What did the Master du?* Gien we can lay haud o' his *command*
an' his *example*, we're weel on oor way tae findin' the trowth o' ony
situation. I think the discomfort ye're feelin' in yer hert comes on
account o' ye've been spierin' those twa questions."

"I wasn't thinking consciously about it."

"Maybe no, but whan a body sets himsel' tae follow the Master,
his subconscious is spierin' ilka day—*What wud ye hae me du, Lord
Jesus? . . . What wud ye hae me say?* Ye're orderin' yer life by his command an' his example whether ye're thinkin' o' it ilka second or no."

"So what did the Lord say and do about something like this?" I
asked. "Jesus never knew Olivia Urquhart!"

"Ye're in the richt there, lass!" Ranald chuckled. "But when he was
hault tae court, the lees agin' him were jist as egregious. He didna
ken Olivia Urquhart, 'tis true. His enemies were men called Caiaphas
an' Herod an' Pontius Pilate."

Ranald's words sobered me.

"As for what he said, we hae his words, *Bi réidh ri d' eascaraid
gu luath, am feadh a bhitheas tu maille ris's an t-slighe—*"

He began laughing as he saw the look of utter perplexity on my
face.

"Ye'll hae tae forgive me, lass," he said. "The auld Gaelic's always
the first way my mind hears the Scriptures as gien it's comin' straight

oot o' my granfather's mouth. I maun mak a conscious effort tae translate it intil the English. What the Lord said, in the lowlan' tongue, was, *'Settle matters quickly wi' yer adversary wha is takin' ye tae court. Du it while ye are still wi' him, aiblins he may hand ye o'er tae the judge.'* Aboot the Master's ain example, 'tis a wee bit mair complicated. In Luke's Gospel, the Lord is spiered twa questions, an' he answers baith wi' straightforward honesty. He's spiered, *'Are ye the Son o' God?'* an', *'Are ye the King o' the Jews?'* Jesus answers the first, *'Ye say I am,'* an' the second, *'Ye hae said so.'*

"Those were twa o' the charges broucht agin' him—bein' the Son o' God an bein' the King o' the Jews—an' though he didna exactly defend himsel', he answered those twa. But there were ither charges as weel. In Mark's Gospel, Pilate spiers anither twa questions, *'Hae ye no answer tae mak? Dinna ye see hoo many charges they bring agin' ye?'* But tae that question, listen tae what Mark says—*'But Jesus made nae further answer.'* In ither words, he wud answer wi' a statement o' trowth, but he wadna refute the charges agin' himsel'. Matthew says it wi' e'en mair force. Whan Pilate spiers, *'Hae ye nae answer to mak? What is it that these men testify agin' ye?'* Matthew says, *'But Jesus was silent.'*

"Div ye hear, lass? *Jesus was silent.* So there's yer twa examples—speik for the trowth, an' remain silent in the face o' accusation. Isna always easy tae ken which tae obey, an' my ain feelin' in the matter is that we're mair likely tae be called tae the defense o' anither nor oursel's. Defendin' oorsel's is a dangerous sort o' thing in the speeritual realm. Defendin' anither for the sake o' trowth—that may be required o' us. It has aye been my experience that in maitters where trowth itsel' is at stake, we may speik oot, though we are nae compelled tae du so. But in maitters where we are personally bein' attacked, we maun be very wary o' makin' defense. Gien Alasdair's guid name be attacked, ye may be called on tae speik oot for him. Gien yer *ain* guid name an' reputation be attacked, ye may be called on tae be silent as was oor Lord, an' let the Father o' lichts be yer defender an' witness. A body will almost ne'er gae wrang tae be silent in the face o' accusation, an' alloo God tae be oor shield. Beyond that, I canna tell ye what ye oucht tae du. But I haena doobt the Lord'll show ye weel enouch."

I thanked Ranald and left.

What I would do in court, I could not yet know. It was what he had said about Jesus' words about *pre*court negotiations that weighed most heavily on my mind.

Chapter Forty-three

Fruitless Attempt

Confide ye aye in Providence, for Providence is kind,
And bear ye a' life's changes wi' a calm and tranquil mind;
Tho' press'd and hemm'd on ev'ry side, hae' faith an' ye'll win through,
For ilka blade o' grass keps its ain drap o' dew.
—James Ballantine, "Ilka Blade o' Grass Keps Its Ain Drap o' Dew"

The very day Olivia returned from London, I again sought her out.

"Olivia," I said, "we need to talk. I promise, I will listen to whatever you have to say and will not argue. I just want to talk to you. Would you like me to come in, or would you prefer to come down to the Music Room and talk to me there?"

"I will be down in ten minutes," she replied.

I turned and walked back down the corridor the way I had come. I went straight to my studio and sat down at my harp to calm myself as I waited.

I played and sang along softly:

> Be Thou my Vision, O Lord of my heart . . .
> Be Thou my Wisdom, Thou my true Word . . .
> Thou my great Father, I Thy true son;
> Thou in me dwelling, and I with Thee one . . .
> Heart of my own heart, whatever befall,
> Still be my Vision, O Ruler of all.

Olivia walked in, slowly, calmly, her steps, her whole demeanor measured. I rose from my harp and went over to the sitting area and sat down. She took a chair opposite me.

"Thank you for coming," I began.

She nodded without expression.

"Obviously I know about your new affidavit," I went on. "I'm sure you knew that Mr. Crathie would share it with me immediately."

Again the slight nod of acknowledgment.

"You also knew of Alasdair's affidavit and the document I showed to you and Mr. Warmington. So we both have documents which, if this thing proceeds, the court will consider in trying to resolve the issues before us."

I paused, drew in a breath, and tried to collect my thoughts.

"But we are both Christians," I resumed. "We see one another in church, we have listened to the same sermons. It doesn't seem right that we should be adversaries in court. Jesus said that we should try to agree with our adversaries *before* going to court. So I would like to see if we cannot do that—discuss this, including our differences, and try to reach a resolution between ourselves as mature and reasonable women . . . as Jesus said Christians ought to be able to do."

"What kind of *resolution* do you have in mind, Marie?" asked Olivia, her voice soft.

"Something that can be good for us both," I answered. "Why could we not both continue to live here, perhaps even share in the administration of the affairs of the estate? You were Alasdair's sister; I was his wife. We both have legitimate legal claims. Why not put the rancor behind us and seek common ground?"

"Forgive and forget is what you are suggesting?"

"I don't know, maybe not exactly, but something like that. I suppose it cannot be helped that we will always have our differences over what happened in the past, with Gwendolyn and other things. But why could we not accept the fact that those things are behind us, and move forward? We both probably made mistakes. I will admit that I have. I was not always as gracious to you as my sister-in-law as I might have been. I am sorry. But I would like to move on. I would like to have a relationship with you, Olivia. I would like to be able to work together. I am willing to reassess what Alasdair left you in his will. Perhaps that amount should be increased. I see no reason why we cannot find some way to comanage the estate, as partners rather than adversaries."

I stopped and drew in a deep breath. It was silent a moment or two.

"You are *willing*, you say, to reassess what Alasdair left me?" said Olivia at length.

"I am."

"That is an interesting way of putting it, Marie. It implies that the estate is already in your control. If I win in court, I will have everything, and you will be left with nothing. Are you not getting ahead of yourself?"

"But that is exactly my point—why should we go to court at all?"

"Because I *will* win. Why should I settle with you when I can have it all?"

Her words, though softly spoken, were blunt. They brought me up short.

"I guess," I said hesitantly, "because it is the right thing to do."

Olivia smiled a condescending smile, as if she were talking to a child.

"Do you remember when we first met, Marie?" she said, her voice enchanting, hypnotic, numbing. "When you asked me about Alasdair and about much that had taken place in the past, before you knew him, and I told you that there was much you did not understand, that you could not understand?"

"I remember," I replied.

"Yet you chose not to take my advice. You chose to believe the lies he told you—some of them lies about me."

"If I have believed wrong things of you, Olivia," I said, "I am sorry. Please forgive me. But about Alasdair, I chose to believe in his character rather than what others told me—not you alone but others, too. Everything was too confusing, so I decided that I had to know him, as a person, as a man, and judge him by the character of his manhood, judge him for nothing more than just who he was *himself*."

"But what if you were reading him wrongly? What if all along he was deceiving you about who he really was?"

"I do not think he did. I do not think he *could* deceive me. He was too honest and real and humble for that."

The word *humble* must have grated on her sensibilities like fingernails on a chalkboard. I saw her almost visibly wince as I said it. A momentary flash of anger followed, but she contained it. I wonder if humility is the *last* possible attribute of character human nature is capable of recognizing in one with whom they have a difference.

"There is still much you do not understand, Marie," she said, calm again. "His power to deceive and manipulate the truth was greater than you were able to perceive—greater than you are *still* able to perceive. Because you did not choose to believe me, and chose to believe his lies, I have no choice now but to rescue the estate from his clutches, and now from yours as well. It is your own stubbornness and pride, Marie, that have forced matters to this end. You have never been out for anything but your own gain. You thought only of yourself. It is for the good of our family name, for the good of the community, certainly not for any thought of gain to myself, that I have undertaken this action. Indeed, I am sacrificing much for the sake of the estate and the community. I could take what Alasdair designated for me—small sum though it is—and travel and live in luxury. But no, Marie, instead I knew that it was my duty to take my rightful place, as Alasdair's sister, as the duchess, and do my duty to the people of this area."

"Then you would be willing to work with me and lay aside our disputes," I said, "for the good of the community?"

"I don't know that I could do that, Marie."

"Why not?"

"You have believed too many lies. You are deceived. Don't you see—how could I work alongside one who was incapable of recognizing the truth? I tried to help you understand, Marie. I told you that

I could help you understand. But you rejected my help. You even insist on calling *yourself* the duchess. Now, unfortunately, you have left me no choice."

"I am willing to let the court decide that," I said. "If the court determines that you are the rightful heir to the title, I would never dream of contesting it."

"Ah, but you see it is too late for that. The wheels are already set in motion. It must be seen through."

"But, Olivia, you know as well as I do that nearly everything claimed in your affidavit is untrue. You know I had no affair with Iain Barclay. You know Alasdair and I did not kidnap Gwendolyn. You are fully aware that I knew no one here before coming to Scotland. I had never even heard of the Duke of Buchan, much less had my eye on him. You *know* all that. Yet you told your solicitors otherwise."

A subtle smile crept over her lips.

"But only you and I know it, Marie," she said. "My solicitors and barristers believe every word of the affidavit. I have made them believe it. I have shed tears of grief in their presence for my poor brother being taken in by the opportunist from Canada. They feel so sorry for me, for the way I have been taken advantage of by you. They will fight tooth and nail on my behalf, they feel so badly for me. I will make the judge believe it, too. I can make *anyone* believe me, Marie. So you see, there is really nothing left for you if you hope to save face but to return to Canada. You cannot possibly win against me."

I was stunned by such an open confession of deceit.

While I still sat gaping in shock, trying to think how to reply to such a thing, she rose and left the room.

Chapter Forty-four

Courtroom Climax

Time went on.

The wheels of justice ground slowly forward toward my date with destiny.

All the while I dragged my feet about a response to Olivia's charges, and the humiliating and damning affidavit she had filed in London. Despite Mr. Crathie's persistent urgings, I could not summon the wherewithal to refute each of them. He wanted to prepare an extensive brief answering in scrupulous detail every point, explaining all the circumstances of Gwendolyn's yacht trip and her subsequent move to the castle to live out her final days with Alasdair. Yet knowing Olivia's uncannily persuasive ability and that, as she said, her solicitors and barristers believed every word she told them, I questioned whether it would do any good. All I could do was give him names of others he could talk to. The more time that passed, the more settled I became in my decision not to offer up a defense. If I could not follow Jesus' example for something as difficult as this, how much would it mean to try to follow it for something easy?

Word obviously spread through the community about the lawsuit. To what extent its details became part and parcel of the rumor mill of local gossip, I didn't know. I cringed at the thought of what might be being said. It was difficult to keep my head held high. Mr. Crathie's words were ever with me—*"She will be able to seriously damage, if not completely ruin, your reputation throughout Scotland."* I imagined suspicious looks coming my way. Whether they were real or based on my own fancies, I don't know. Going to church with regularity was painful. Having been informed that Olivia had taken to sitting in the laird's loft herself, and not wanting to create a scene, I crept in a few times right on the dot at 10:30 and sat in a pew toward the back. But it was intolerable knowing that Olivia was there above us all, now and then descending to help take the offering or read one of the morning's passages of Scripture. She never once glanced my way or displayed the least hint of recognition.

Mr. Crathie was beside himself at my hesitation to mount a defense. More legal documents continued to arrive from Olivia's London barristers. Two months went by, then three. I spent a great deal of time up on the hill in Ranald Bain's cottage. Ranald's reaction to the whole thing was a little odd. He often became strangely quiet, in a way that wasn't like him. He seemed to be turning things over in his mind in a way he could not share with me.

Finally a court date was set. Mr. Crathie insisted that there was nothing he could do if I did not take steps to defend myself. By then, however, answering the charges with silence had become a matter of principle.

Like all long-anticipated days that seem as if they will never come, the day of reckoning came at last.

I walked into court accompanied by Mr. Crathie and Mr. Murdoch. We sat down at our places. The spectators' gallery was full. I glanced around and saw Alicia, Fia, Cora, Tavia, Mr. McDermott, Mrs. Gauld, Adela Cruickshank ... before the sea of faces faded into a blur. Olivia walked in with Mr. Warmington and their legal team of four London solicitors and barristers. They looked imposing. Mr. Crathie was fidgety and, I thought, a little nervous.

The judge came in with his white wig and robe, and after preliminaries reviewed the charges. He looked at Mr. Crathie and asked how the defendant pled. Mr. Crathie opened his mouth, but before he could begin the door at the back of the courtroom opened. A few heads turned toward the sound, including mine.

Ranald . . . There was Ranald walking through the door!

Though his beard and unruly crop of hair could never be made to look entirely civilized, in all other respects no one would have taken him for a lowly shepherd. He wore a perfectly groomed dark blue suit and waistcoat, set off with a bright red tie and leather dress shoes. The sight took my breath away. That he carried no briefcase no doubt alerted the judge to the fact that he was not a late-arriving solicitor. Otherwise, he had no idea who the man was.

Ranald walked forward down the center aisle. He glanced toward Olivia, who had also turned around to look. Their eyes met but for an instant. I thought I saw Ranald's lips silently form a single word. A look of horror crossed Olivia's features and her face went ashen.

"I am sorry to come into the proceedings late, Your Worship," said Ranald, turning to face the judge, shocking me with the perfection of his English. "If I might be permitted a word of—"

"What is the meaning of this interruption?" barked the judge. "Who are you?"

Olivia quickly leaned over to Mr. Warmington. He jumped up the next instant to voice his protest and objection.

At the same time, Mr. Crathie leaned toward me. "Do you know that fellow?"

"Yes, he's one of my closest friends," I whispered. "I'm sure he is here to help."

"What can he do?"

"I don't know, though it would not surprise me if he intended to expose Olivia as a liar."

"What kind of information would he have?"

"I don't know, but he has known her all her life."

"That's good enough for me. Please, Your Worship," said Mr. Crathie. "This man is known to my client and may have key information pertaining to the veracity of Mrs. Urquhart's allegations. We can vouch for his credentials. He will be called as one of our witnesses."

"Then call him when his time comes," said the judge, "and tell him to sit down and keep silent. I will tolerate no more interruptions of this kind."

During this brief exchange, however, a hubbub had been mounting in intensity at the other table. Olivia was growing heated and her solicitors were trying to calm her.

" . . . out of here, I tell you. He must be . . . Throw him out . . . no right to be here!"

"Mr. Bygraves," said the judge. "Now I will have to remind you to keep *your* client quiet."

Suddenly Olivia jumped to her feet and pointed a long arm at Ranald where he was making his way toward one of the few empty chairs of the gallery.

"That man is a fraud and a liar!" she cried. "I demand that he be removed. He has no right to be here!"

"Mr. Warmington, please, I must insist that you control your client!" said the judge angrily.

"But, Your Worship, you do not understand!" cried Olivia toward the judge. "There is a curse on him . . . a curse, I tell you. A curse of madness over the house of Bain!" she shrieked. "Nothing he says can be trusted."

The gavel pounded loudly and repeatedly, at last silencing the court.

"This court is in recess!" said the judge angrily. "I will see all counsel in my chambers immediately!"

He rose and left the courtroom. Slowly the attorneys also rose. Mr. Crathie, Mr. Murdoch, and three of Olivia's team followed the judge, while the fourth escorted Olivia, nearly hysterical, outside to wait in the corridor.

I didn't dare turn around and look at anyone in the gallery.

A few minutes later, a court official reentered the court. He nodded to one of the officers, who went out into the corridor and returned a minute later with Olivia and her solicitor. "Mr. Ranald Bain," he said, "you are instructed to follow me."

Behind me I heard Ranald stand and walk forward. Olivia looked daggers at him as they both followed the official and Olivia's solicitor from the courtroom in the same direction the judge and the others had gone.

Again the courtroom was silent. I could not imagine what might be going on.

Six or eight minutes later, a door opened. Olivia's solicitors returned to their table and sat down. Olivia was not with them. Mr. Crathie, Mr. Murdoch, and Ranald were behind them. The two lawyers came and sat down again beside me. Ranald returned to the gallery.

Finally the judge walked in and resumed his seat. He pounded once with his gavel on his desk.

"This case contesting the disposition of the estate of Alasdair Reidhaven, Duke of Buchan, has been dropped, and the accompanying affidavit withdrawn," he said.

He turned to the desk where Olivia was no longer present. "Gentlemen, you may inform your client that charges will be brought by Her Majesty's Crown Court against her in the amount of all costs incurred by this court, which is hereby adjourned."

Mr. Crathie turned to me and rose with a smile. I couldn't believe it. Before I knew what I was doing I had given both him and Mr. Murdoch great hugs.

I jumped to my feet and turned around. But all I managed to catch was a glimpse of Ranald's back disappearing through the door.

"Congratulations, Mrs. Reidhaven," said Mr. Murdoch. "It would appear that at last you are the uncontested Duchess of Buchan."

"I have you to thank," I said, "for taking such care to be deliberate in your investigations and procedures before anyone knew anything about Alasdair's Edinburgh affidavit."

"Including me!" Mr. Crathie laughed. "I understand now why it was best it remained silent until it was settled. I believe we would have won even had this case of Mrs. Urquhart's gone forward. Which, by the way, Mrs. Reidhaven, you were right about what you whispered to me—that fellow Bain had something on your sister-in-law, something extremely persuasive. Have you no idea what it is?"

"No, none. What happened when you were alone with the judge?"

"The man Bain said he had information he could not make public but that he was certain would result in the suit being dropped. He asked for a moment alone with Mrs. Urquhart. The judge, very annoyed by this time, was barking at us all. But he granted the request. The two of them were shown to an adjoining room and left alone. They were not together more than a minute. When they came out the woman's face was white as a sheet. She whispered amongst her solicitors a moment, then they informed the judge that her contest of her brother's will was being dropped. It was a remarkable turnaround."

"I can see I must pay a visit to Ranald Bain!" I said. "Though knowing him, if it is something he feels his conscience requires him to keep secret, nothing I say or do will induce him to tell me." I couldn't help remembering Iain's private exchange with Olivia about Gwendolyn, and wondered if that had any connection to what had just happened in the courtroom.

"I still maintain what I said to you before—I think there is every likelihood that the woman is clinically mad. I've never seen anything like her wild performance in there. I would be extremely careful of her, Mrs. Reidhaven, and get her out of the castle without delay."

"Don't you think it would be better for her to leave on her own?" I said.

"I suppose so. With such types, it is always best not to rouse their anger. Just keep me apprised of the situation. If she doesn't leave cooperatively, you let us handle it."

"I promise, I will."

"Oh, and by the way," added Mr. Crathie. "You asked about the minister Barclay. I managed to turn up some information. It just came through yesterday. He is no longer with the church."

"What— I can't believe it. What is he doing, then?"

"I cannot say. All I have been able to learn beyond that is that two months ago he was in London."

Chapter Forty-five

Dangerous Olive Branch

The nicht had been rainy, but fair was the mornin',
Bright shone the sun, comely Nature adorning,
Sweet bloom'd the daisy yon bonnie simmer mornin'
An' fragrant the green dewy plain;
Saft to their minnies the wee lambs were moanin',
Fond 'mid the flow'rets the wild bee was dronin',
As Katie sat milkin' her kye i' the loanin',
Yon bonnie mornin' after the rain.
—James Smith, "The Bonnie Mornin' After the Rain"

By then everyone in Port Scarnose knew of the lawsuit. And now knew also of its peremptory dismissal. Speculation ran rampant as to the reasons. No one knew anything for certain, only that Ranald Bain must have *something* on Olivia Urquhart, and that whatever it was must be powerful and secretive.

I called on Ranald the very next day. He was back to his normal self—dirty dungarees, plaid wool workshirt, and thick Scots accent.

"I scarcely recognized you!" I said. "You looked like an MP! I didn't imagine you owned such a dashing suit."

"'Tis only for special occasions—'twas either the suit or the kilt."

I thanked him profusely for what he had done—whatever it was!—but not to my most persistent entreaties would he divulge one word of his secret. The expression on his face, however, told me that whatever it was that he and Olivia shared, it was personal and painful.

When I returned, a familiar car sat in front of the castle. I recognized it immediately as Mr. Crathie's. I wondered how long he had been waiting for me, and if he had more papers for me to sign.

I walked inside and found him standing in the entryway.

"Hello, Mr. Crathie," I said.

He returned my greetings, though he struck me as unaccountably nervous.

"You could have waited for me in the Drawing Room," I said. "Have you seen Alicia? She would surely have—"

Footsteps coming down the stairs behind us interrupted me. I glanced behind Mr. Crathie to see Alicia descending toward us. The moment she saw me, a blush spread over her cheeks.

"Actually, Mrs. Reidhaven," said the attorney, "I didn't come on business. I hoped that Alicia might be free to take a drive with me along the coast."

"Oh, of course. That's wonderful."

"You don't mind, do you, Marie?" said Alicia. "I wasn't sure how long you would be gone."

"Not at all."

"If you don't need me for anything, Nigel asked if we might have dinner together at the Banff Hotel."

"Certainly—take the rest of the day, and the evening!"

Alicia walked past me, a faint fragrance of perfume following in her wake. I must say, she looked radiant. I had never seen her with makeup on. As she and Mr. Crathie reached the door, she turned her head to cast me a momentary smile, and mouthed the silent words *Thank you*.

I was very happy for her.

Olivia went into a self-imposed exile. I assumed that she returned to Aberdeen. Neither was Adela Cruickshank seen in the village after that. After two weeks we thought we had better check the room where she had been staying. We found it empty of any sign that anyone had occupied it for years. When she had come to move her things out, we hadn't an idea.

I wasn't quite so eager to investigate Olivia's private domain to see whether she, too, had somehow moved out without our knowing it. I would wait until I was certain all remnants of her temporary occupation of the castle were gone before I would again take up residence in my former apartments. Eventually, however, I had to know. I went to the room and knocked, then again, and called loudly. I knew she wasn't there, but I didn't want to go in without giving a warning just in case. When there was no reply, I tried the door. It was locked. I tried every key in my possession, but none opened the lock. I asked both Nicholls and Farquharson if there were keys I didn't know of. Both men examined the large key ring I had in my hand and said that as far as they knew, those were all the keys since the changing of the locks several months before.

At that point I had no choice but to call in a locksmith from Buckie to pick the lock and have a new key made.

It was strange to invade Olivia's private domain, even though it had once been mine. All her things were still in place. Nothing appeared the worse for her presence. I did not look around extensively. I only wanted to determine the status of the apartments. I did have one additional motive. During all the months since my return, when either Alicia, Nicholls, or myself had methodically examined every nook and cranny of the castle in search of my pedal harp, there remained one set of four rooms we had *not* ventured into—the former apartment of the duke, which had then been mine and Alasdair's, and more recently had been occupied by Olivia during her brief tenure. I secretly hoped that she might have hidden my harp in her own rooms, knowing it was the one place I would never dare look.

Now I *did* look, and with great disappointment saw nothing whatever that interested me, certainly no harp.

I could be patient to wait for her to collect her clothes and the furniture that was hers. My eyes did fall on one item, however, that instantly made my blood boil. An old rusty iron ring lay on her bureau containing a dozen equally old and equally rusted giant keys—

each four to six inches in length, one notably of brass that was greening rather than rusting.

I grabbed it, left her rooms and locked them behind me with the new key, and again went in search of Harvey Nicholls.

"Have you seen these before?" I asked, showing him the ring.

"They look like more keys to the basement rooms, my lady," he replied.

"Just as I thought!" I said. "Olivia specifically told me she had *no* basement keys. She was lying through her teeth the whole time. Take these, Nicholls—see if there is *any* lock you could have missed, even a small storeroom, a closet, a room within a room, an unobtrusive recess or panel or movable wall . . . anything. You know how these old places are, with mysterious passageways and alcoves and storage rooms and stairways hidden behind walls. I don't know if there's anything like that. How I wish Alasdair was here. These keys would not have been in her room unless she was hiding something from me. I simply do not believe her story about my harp being stolen by some man she hired whom you never saw. It's got to be here . . . *somewhere*."

Alas, even the new search produced nothing but dead ends. And still no sign of the *Queen*.

A week and a half later I was asonished to receive in the post a note from Olivia saying that she would like to talk to me about Alasdair and Gwendolyn. She apologized for the misunderstandings about the will and the estate. She added that she hoped we could put all that behind us. As the weather had been nice, and knowing how much I loved the sea, perhaps we could take a walk together. She loved the coastline, too, she added, as it reminded her of happy times when she and Gwendolyn used to walk together. She asked me to call and gave a telephone number. I recognized it as that of her former house where I had first made her acquaintance and spent so many happy hours with dear Gwendolyn. She also thought she might have an idea where we could locate my missing harp, about which she felt just dreadful.

Overjoyed at the prospect of this olive branch of reconciliation, I went to the telephone immediately. Olivia's tone, as I had gathered from the note, was warm and friendly. I could hardly believe the change. Even as sisters-in-law, we would never become friends. Yet I hoped we might be something other than adversaries. We made arrangements to meet that same afternoon at three o'clock at the Scar Nose promontory. It had rained the night before and was bright and clear and promised to be a lovely day for a walk.

I had already planned to have lunch that same day with Ranald at his cottage. Because of Olivia's call I drove rather than walked up and we had a nice visit. We enjoyed a simple cold lunch with egg mayonnaise on softies. With the court case behind me and my future now clarified, we talked about the difficulties and decisions now facing me. I told him about my father and his work in the States, which I also felt a responsibility to attend to.

"So you see, Ranald," I said, "I've lost two men in the last year, and now find myself wanting to do what I can to further the works of both . . . yet they are six thousand miles apart!"

"Ye'll du what the Lord gies ye tae du faithfully, o' that I haena a doobt. But it may tak time for him tae mak yer way clear. Jist be nae in a hurry, lass. God's best things tak time tae unfold."

Ranald gave me good counsel, but mostly was just a wise and willing listener. We prayed together. Then he asked if I would like to play. I glanced at my watch. It was about two. I said that I was a little short of time and that maybe we ought to get together again soon. He said that was fine and that he understood.

As we were cleaning up the lunch things, a fighter jet suddenly screamed by overhead. Though it was a common occurrence here, I nearly leaped out of my skin. It prompted Ranald to tell me about his days as a young man in the RAF during the early years of the Cold War.

"I had no idea you were in the RAF—so was Alicia's father."

"She an' I need tae swap stories. Div ye ken whaur her father was afore they came tae Lossie?"

"I don't know that she told me that. She did tell me that she would like to learn to fly one day herself."

"Did she noo? She maun be an adventurous lass!"

I don't know why, but the thought of bearded, white-haired Ranald Bain as a young fighter pilot flying secretive missions over the Soviet Union of the 1950s surprised me. He asked if I would like to see some of his old photos, both of his RAF years and of the croft and of he and Maggie and their Winifred.

Suddenly I again remembered the time. Again I looked at my watch. It was 2:40.

"Oh, I would dearly love to see them," I said, quickly rising. "But I have to go. Believe it or not, Olivia Urquhart wants to get together with me. It's an opportunity I can't pass up. After all that has happened, I am hoping that at last she is going to bury the hatchet. I am encouraged that this might be the beginning of a breakthrough. She and I agreed to meet at three for a walk."

"A walk...whaur?" said Ranald, his voice suddenly grave. He stood and followed me slowly toward the door.

"I don't know," I replied, "probably along the coast. She said she has always loved walking along the headlands, as I do."

Ranald's expression turned yet more serious. "I sud say she does," he mumbled. I had no idea what he meant. Then he reached out and placed a hand on my shoulder. "Dinna gae oot wi' her alone, lass," he said. His tone was so commanding, it frightened me.

"But I have to, Ranald," I said. "You were the one who told me of the Scripture about agreeing with your adversaries. I tried and it wasn't successful *before* she took me to court. Perhaps now, after the fact, she might at last be ready."

"Marie," he repeated, "*dinna* gae. E'en after a' that has ta'en place, ye hae nae idea fit she is."

"I think I have some idea."

"Ye dinna ken a'."

I stared back at him, then slowly nodded. "I understand," I said. "I'll be careful."

I turned toward the door. He walked outside with me. I faced him again, tried to smile, and thanked him for lunch. But his face remained somber. I knew he wasn't satisfied with my response. He gave me a warm, fatherly embrace, then stepped back.

"God gae wi' ye, lass," he said, "an' protect ye."

I must have had a puzzled expression on my face. His words sounded far too much like a benediction for comfort. I nodded, and got into my car and drove back down the hill toward Port Scarnose.

Chapter Forty-six

The Cliffs of Findlater

Wha will be a traitor knave?
Wha can fill a coward's grave?
Wha sae base as be a slave?
Let him turn, and flee.
—Robert Burns, "Scots, Wha Hae"

I was standing on the overlook above the Scar Nose at five till three. I was surprised to see Olivia drive up in her car. I had expected her to walk. She greeted me from the open window with a friendly smile and asked if I would like to go for a short drive. She would show me one of her favorite walks, she said. I nodded and climbed in on the passenger side.

We drove east, through Crannoch, turned off the main road and into the farmland, where Olivia parked in a small obscure wood. We got out and began walking along a path out of the trees, through cultivated fields, toward the sea. I wasn't exactly sure where we were. Being east of Crannoch, I should have known. I knew most of this coastline intimately. But a mental fog was invisibly settling over me. The path was a little muddy in spots from the rain, but there was mud everywhere in Scotland. It was something you got used to. Olivia talked about Gwendolyn's harp playing and how happy she was that I had given Gwendolyn that opportunity and had taken such an interest in her. Again she expressed regret that the situation between us had been so awkward and had caused so many misunderstandings. But she hoped this could be a new beginning. I kept waiting for her news about the *Queen*, but I didn't want to appear too anxious.

We reached the promontory probably a mile or two east of Crannoch beyond Logie Head.

"Have you seen Findlater Castle?" Olivia asked.

A chill swept through me.

"Oh, Findlater," I replied. "Yes... I, uh... Alasdair pointed out the ruins to me one time from the sea."

"Would you like to see it close up?" she asked.

"I, uh... Maybe this isn't the best day," I said hesitantly. "I remember Alasdair saying it was dangerous."

"Nonsense—he was afraid of his own shadow. I want to show it to you."

I continued to follow. I was afraid of alienating her. We walked along the top of the cliff east from Logie Head, single file in spots where the path was narrow, occasionally side by side. I had to watch my footing because we were at the edge of the headland where the cliff rose straight up from the sea.

"There are the ruins," said Olivia, pointing ahead some two hundred yards. I knew well enough by now where we were. Ranald's and Alasdair's cautions rang in my ears. But I could not stop. A dreamy inevitability had come over me. My brain was sleepy. Ahead was the spot where we had found Alicia standing in the rain as Ranald and I approached the ancient castle from the other direction.

I saw the ruins now more plainly from this angle. They were still not so easy to see as they had been from aboard Alasdair's yacht. A little grass-topped promontory jutted out into the sea, on the side and top of which what remained of Findlater Castle appeared from this vantage point like great piles of rocks and fallen stone walls. A steep narrow path went down over the edge of the promontory, along a narrow sort of land bridge, then up to the ruins. From the path the cliff extended almost straight down to jagged rocks where the tide swirled and splashed and beat against them. What an inhospitable place to have built a home to live in, even if it was a fortified castle.

We walked on to the point where the path veered out onto

the promontory and down in the direction of the ruins. There we stopped. We were almost exactly at the place where Alicia had been standing. By now I knew I was in a precarious situation. But I was walking in a dream. I had become just like Alicia, under a spell. The wind was blowing strongly up from the sea, howling and whipping my hair across my face.

"How did they come and go when they lived here?" I said in a monotone of disinterest. "It looks so dangerous."

"There was a bridge from the mainland here over to the castle," said Olivia. Her tone had changed, too. I glanced toward her. She was staring across to the ruins with a far-off look in her eye. "Come, I will show you," she said.

She began to follow the narrow path that led steeply down from the edge out along the top of a narrow and uneven slice of earth that had apparently, over time, been built up between castle and headland to take the place of the bridge. She made her way across it with the confidence of a Highland sheep. She obviously knew the way well.

"Olivia," I called after her, roused a little by the wind. "I don't... I mean... It's slippery, and so windy."

"It's fine," I heard her say. She did not turn around as she spoke. "I'll show you the way down inside the castle. There are rooms still remaining. Don't you want to find your harp?"

"My harp?" I said, taking a few tentative steps after her. "What does Findlater have to do with my harp? It can't be here."

"One never knows. Findlater holds the key to the mysteries—why not your harp?"

"What mysteries?"

"All the mysteries. The mysteries and the curses. Do you know the curse of Bain, my dear? Everyone knows the curse: *The curse of madness will be the stain, of all who enter the house of Bain.* The curse of Bain lives on at Findlater. It will always live on because the curse of Bain does not die. Winny still lives. She has become the curse."

She was talking gibberish. Frightening gibberish!

"Olivia, where is my harp?" I said again.

"Your harp? All in good time, my dear. You will be united with your harp again. Winny will show you the way. Perhaps Winny will play for you."

"But, Olivia, my harp is not here. These are only ruins. You are confusing the two castles."

Suddenly she stopped and turned to face me. Her face was wild, her eyes full of strange light.

"Don't be too certain, my dear," she said. "You think I am crazy, but there are mysteries you know nothing of. There is a secret tunnel. No one knows of it now. It is blocked by the sea. No one knows how they escaped during the Viking rampage. But I know. And Winny knew. That's how she escaped, too, escaped from the sea. Maybe it was Winny who took your harp where no one could find it. Ha! Ha! Maybe she took it to play for her own funeral. Ha! Ha!"

I trembled as I listened. Then Olivia began to chant horrifying rhymes. *"Winny Bain was not drowned by the sea, she hid from the Vikings and now is free.* Ha! Ha! *Her thin bony fingers pluck harp and lyre, as flames rise around her funeral pyre.* Ha! Ha! Ha!"

This was becoming creepier by the second. I shook myself awake.

"Olivia!" I called. "I want to know what you did with it."

She stopped and turned. She had reached the ruins at the end of the precipice and stood staring down into a hole among the rocks.

"Olivia," I called again.

She did not answer or show in any way that she had heard me. Still she stood, peering into the blackness below.

"Come here. I will show you."

I crept tentatively ahead, careful of my step and by now wanting to keep my distance. Olivia was sounding like a lunatic!

Gradually the hole she was looking down came into view, the decayed remnants of an ancient circular staircase spiraling its way straight down through the rock into the interior of Findlater. It was steep and so many of the stones had fallen that it was clearly impassable.

Was it possible . . . *could* she have somehow contrived to bring my harp here? Horrible thought! It would be ruined along with the ruins! How could she possibly—

My thoughts were interrupted by the sound of her voice, calm again.

"This is where Maggie Bain died, you know," said Olivia, walking slowly toward me. Her voice was low, expressionless.

"No, I didn't know," I replied.

Her eyes glassed over and her voice sounded strange. "The old crow—she came here and left flowers for poor Winny. What good do flowers do? Nothing would bring Winny back. Winny had followed the hidden path. She had gone where they would never find her. They tried to find her. But they did not know the secret. She was gone where not even the Vikings knew where to look. So she brought flowers, always flowers, because she thought Winny had been swept away. Every time I came along the path I saw one of her silly bouquets of dead flowers. And the way she spoke to me— she had no right. Blaming *me* for what happened, spreading it about that I knew more than I was telling. Who was she to accuse me?! She won't blame me again, that's what I told her. Now they bring flowers for her, the old witch."

I stood paralyzed. Olivia's voice was harsh and rasping and low.

"And Winny, the goose! Everyone loved Winny. All the boys loved Winny. Once she got pretty and her hair grew long and her breasts filled out . . . none of them looked at me again. It was Winny this and Winny that. Where is Winny Bain now, the goose! Taken by the sea, sailed on the tide, they all think. But she is hiding. She must preserve the curse of the house of Bain."

I couldn't make heads or tails of what she was talking about. But I knew enough to realize I didn't want to be on this dangerous cliff with Olivia acting so strangely.

Cora's words came back to me: *"Welcome, O death, thy warm embrace, on the cliff at Findlater's face."*

I shivered and suddenly realized my incredible folly. How stupid could I be?! Slowly I turned and began creeping back the way I had come. I had seen enough of this place!

Suddenly Olivia shouted after me. "Where do you think you're going!" she cried.

"It is too steep for me," I said, though I did not stop. "I felt myself getting light-headed. I thought I should go back up onto the mainland."

"What about your harp? Don't you want to see your harp?"

"I'll look for it later."

"You're not going anywhere!" cried Olivia. "I want you to see the ruins. I told you I wanted to show you the rooms inside, down the stairway."

I glanced behind me. Olivia was following.

"I don't think I'm up to it today, Olivia," I said, hurrying on. I felt genuine terror now.

"Oh, Little Miss Opportunist isn't up to it today!" she spat back derisively, coming rapidly toward me. "You have certainly been up to everything else. Up to ensnaring my brother and laying your greedy hands on his fortune. Oh, you have been up to it all right, turning him against me so he would cut me out. Oh, yes, Winny—you have had your way, and now you will get what you deserve."

"Olivia—I'm not Winny. I'm Marie . . . Marie Reidhaven, your sister-in-law."

"Of course you are," she said, walking quickly to me, reaching out and laying hold of my shoulder to stop my retreat. The feel of her hand clutching me paralyzed me with dread. She forced me around to face her, then stared into my face with a wicked smile.

"Who else would you be? My dear, dear sister-in-law who has taken everything that should be mine. I am the rightful duchess. You wormed your way into Alasdair's affections. I warned them about you. I told them your music was but the allure of a charlatan. *Though her music seems soft and sweet . . . in her heart lies only deceit.* Yes, Marie, my dear sweet sister-in-law, I saw your scheme for what it was from the start."

"Olivia, there was no scheme. I was as surprised by everything that happened as you were."

"Surprised!" She laughed bitterly. "Ha, ha! Surprised that Alasdair left you the fortune that should be mine! Ha, ha, ha! Surprised!"

"You admitted that you know all those things you said about me aren't true."

"*You* are a liar!" she cried. "You are nothing but a deceiving, scheming tart."

Suddenly she lunged at me.

I shrieked and jumped back, slipping as I did. I screamed as I recovered and tried to run toward the safety of the top of the headland. But she knew the path better than I. She caught me within two seconds, grabbed my shoulder again, and yanked me backward with such force I fell to the ground.

I screamed in terror. She was standing above me, such a look of hatred in her eyes as I had never seen on a human face. She lifted one foot and brought it down on my chest, then slowly began to shove me toward the edge.

"Olivia, please!" I cried. "You can't get away with it. They will know it was you."

"Who will know? No one saw us in town together. No one saw Winny, and no one saw you. Soon you will join her. You and she can play your harp together."

"I told Ranald I was going to meet you."

Another horrible laugh burst from her lips. "That old fool—no one will believe him. Where do you think the curse comes from? *He* is its source, his Highland blood from generations gone by. The curse from the ancient sorcerers of the Highlands. He is the curse from which the madness comes. You wanted me to show you Findlater. I warned you. I told you it was dangerous, that the path would be slippery. But you wouldn't listen. You insisted that you had to see it. You set out on your own. Frantic for my poor sister-in-law's safety, I followed. But I was too late. I arrived just in time to see you lose your balance and to hear the forlorn sound of your final cries as you fell to the rocks below— Right down there, Marie. They will never find you. They will think you were taken by the tide. No one will know, dear Marie, that you are with Winny. You and Winny and your idiotic harp—making music with the angels . . . or the devils. Ha! Ha! Ha!"

She began to kick me violently toward the cliff. Frantically I grabbed all about me for anything solid.

Suddenly a voice cried loudly behind us. It was only ten or twelve feet away from the direction of the cliff.

"Olivia, stop!" it said. "Stand awa'!"

Shocked but not cowed, Olivia's foot relaxed as she turned toward it. I knew the voice instantly as that of Ranald Bain. I had never heard him speak with such command.

"You old imbecile!" she spat. "Do you really think you can stop me? I will send you to join your wife."

"Ye will do nae mair evil at this place, Olivia Reidhaven. I ken who ye are. Ye hae deceived mony, but ye hae ne'er deceived me. I willna alloo ye tae hairm anither. Ye hae killed here afore, an' I dinna doobt twice afore though I canna prove the first. But I aye saw ye push my ain Maggie doon wi' my ain twa eye, though I followed too late tae stop ye, as I told ye in court tae stop yer lyin' schemes. But I learned my lesson that time, an' I'm nae aboot tae let ye repeat yer evil deed. Ye willna kill again. *Imich uam a Shàtain!* Noo, Olivia Reidhaven, I command ye in God's name—stand awa'!"

The sound of her former name and the Gaelic command seemed to jolt Olivia like a dousing of cold water.

For a tense moment all was silent.

All at once, she let out a dreadful shriek and kicked and flailed at me with terrific power. I screamed again in terror.

"The grass, Marie—grab the grass. It'll haud ye!" yelled Ranald.

Even as he spoke he rushed forward, swinging his great shepherd's staff mightily in a great arc. It caught Olivia at her knees. She cried in pain and toppled to the ground. Two or three solid hits to her body followed until she scrambled up and out from under the torrent of blows. Limping and shrieking the foulest of obscenities, she hurried along the path and away.

Had it not been for Ranald's last words, I would surely have been dead by now. I was probably four feet over the side, legs scrabbling frantically for something to cling to, clutching with my hands and elbows at the roots of the tough wiry shore grass covering the rocky projection of the cliff.

"Hang on, Marie!" called Ranald. "I'll git ye. Here's the staff. Take haud o' the crook, ane hand, then the ither. 'Tis good for pullin' mair tae safety nor jist wee lambies! Haud till it wi' a' yer life!"

I don't know how he kept his balance on the precarious path. Nor had I imagined a man of his years could be so strong. I grabbed desperately as he lowered his staff, and held it till my knuckles were white. Once I had a tight grip, Ranald pulled, kneeling and leaning back to balance himself. Slowly I struggled up to safety. I climbed to my feet and fell into his arms weeping in relief.

"I'm so sorry, Ranald. I was so stupid. I should have listened to you."

"Dinna fret, lass," he said tenderly. "She's weaved her spells ower many afore ye came along. But I dinna think we'll hae't fae her again. The spell o' her lies is finally broken."

Chapter Forty-seven

Waking Dormant Seed

When lambs and calves upon the meads in mirth and gladness bound,
When loud the mavis and her mate make woodland vales resound;
When she prepares her cozy nest adown the leafy grove,
The vision brings to mind again, my first and early love.
—Neil MacLeod, "My Love of Early Days"

The following day a small lorry appeared at Castle Buchan. Two men asked to see me. They produced a list of possessions they had been instructed to remove on behalf of Mrs. Olivia Urquhart. They also had a key to the apartment Olivia had occupied. I was relieved to know that I would not have to tell Olivia in person that I'd had the lock changed. After the trauma of what had taken place, I had no interest in seeing her again.

I looked over the list, saw nothing I was not eager to be rid of, and happily showed the men upstairs. Within two hours they were done. It was with a tremendous sigh of relief that I watched the lorry pull away, and with it the last remnants of Olivia's occupation of the castle.

Olivia was not seen in Port Scarnose again. Within days a sign from "Stewart & Watson, Estate Agents," appeared in the front window, notifying all interested parties that the former Urquhart home was for sale.

It would seem that nearly every frayed end of my life's tapestry had at last been woven into its proper place. All uncertainties and doubts had been resolved.

All but one.

The moment the words *Banff Hotel* had sounded from Alicia's lips as she was leaving for her date with Nigel Crathie, my subconscious mind began stirring an unexpected corner of my being into renewed wakefulness.

Thought of dinner at the Banff Hotel reminded me of one of *my* memorable dates in Scotland, too.

It had not been with Alasdair.

They say ancient houses and castles such as Buchan often possess gardens that come and go and change with time. One owner or mistress or gardener plants and cultivates a certain area or plot of ground with prized species of flowers or trees or bulbs and shrubs. In time, however, these may become neglected and overgrown in favor of another plot fashioned elsewhere by another gardener, who then cultivates new and different varietals. Then a later descendant does the same yet again. And thus many changes over the centuries are made from ever-shifting needs of space, causing gardens and their locations and contents to adapt to the passage of time.

It is likewise said that nothing from the past is lost. Nothing dies out. Life endures. It may change its form, but because it originates in love, life continues on. As the snows and frosts of winter send the earth into a season of dormancy, so also do the shifting and changing circumstances of life cover once-thriving plants and send them into seasons of periodic hybernation. But the pods wherein is contained the life-germ of such plants are not dead. They only await new sunlight and fresh rains to bring them out of their sleep into renewed vitality of life and reemergent growth.

One of Scotland's greatest men, Huntly's native son of the nineteenth century whose books I had discovered since coming to Scotland, phrased this truth in this way:

> Many of the seeds which fall upon the ground and do not grow, strange to say, retain the power of growth. I suspect myself that they fall in their pods or shells and that before these are sufficiently decayed to allow the sun and moisture and air to reach them, they get covered up in the soil too deep for those influ-

ences to get at them. They say fish trapped alive and imbedded in ice for a long time will come to life again. I cannot tell about that. But it is well known that if you dig deep in any old garden ancient—perhaps forgotten—flowers will appear. The fashion has changed, they have been neglected or uprooted, but all the time their life is hid below.*

And thus it was that a seed, not long-neglected but long-dormant, began to come to life again in the deep, hidden, invisible garden of my heart. When he had first shown me the rose garden at the castle, Alasdair had said that the secret of a good garden was the gradual revelation of its mysteries. Was the same true of the garden of the human heart?

At first I feared the quiet whisperings of the germ-cell urging the chrysalis awake.

I pretended it was other than it was. I refused to look at it, refused to acknowledge that some unseen force was stirring in my innermost depths, reluctant to ask if God, the master Husbandman, was wielding an upturning spade and shifting the ground so that light fell again on the dormant seed.

Yes, I admit, it was a little fearsome.

But with the fear came also a tingling thrill of excitement. And the question: Can love ever be a bad thing?

Is it not what we do with any God-gift that distinguishes the good from the bad, the self-centered from the selfless, the temporal from the eternal, the earthly from the holy?

Fear is not intrinsic to the equation of life, only right response.

At last, when I could no longer ignore the inevitable whispering reminders of what had once *been*, and now seemed to be a new *becoming*, the question arose again that had driven me back to Canada after my first sojourn in Scotland:

---

* From George MacDonald's *Paul Faber, Surgeon*, chapter 41.

Can a woman love two men?

Discovering the answer to that question five years before, and making the choice between them, had set me on the path to a destiny I could never have foreseen. But the question had now changed. No *choice* now confronted me. Only the question of whether love might still exist . . . or, if dormant, was it reviving again into life, rebirthing itself from out of the past?

If so, what was I to do about it—flee again to Canada to escape its consequences, to escape where it might lead? Or meet it with honesty, even courage, and find out—yet again—what the future might hold?

I had run from it before. But my running had only presented me with the inevitable conviction that I had to *know* what my heart was saying.

Even as many questions posed themselves again, questions I thought I had put behind me forever, I knew that again there could be no resolution without knowing.

I had to know.

Many long walks followed. Much prayer. Time with *Journey* sitting on my favorite bench, reliving many special moments, playing the melodies that probed the depths of Scotland's historic melancholy soul, thinking of Alasdair, wondering what he would want me to do.

Yet could Alasdair, could the Lord himself, help me *know* what lay in my heart?

Chapter Forty-eight

Fear and Confusion

Why should I sit and sigh when the greenwood blooms sae bonnie?
Lav'rocks sing, flow'rets spring, and all but me are cheery,
Ah! But there is something wanting. Ah! But I am weary.
—"Why Should I Sit and Sigh?"

The knowing I sought contained no speculation of outcome. As yet I was building no aerial fantasies of renewed romance. At first I did not even envision a meeting. It was simply the waking *within myself* that I had to understand. *I* had to come to terms with it so that my own personhood would be whole and complete in its self-knowledge.

But is it possible for love to sprout in the human heart without the desire to meet its accuser face-to-face?

If so, surely it is rare. For love, by its very nature, is *compelled* to make itself known. I was not thinking consciously in such terms. Yet even then, surely my subconscious had already begun impelling itself toward the inevitable desire to *see* him again.

In inquiring about Iain Barclay's whereabouts, and after Nigel Crathie had successfully tracked him to London, my initial response had been excitement at the possibility of locating Alasdair's friend. But with the words *Banff Hotel*, and the flood of memories and emotions that began infiltrating my senses like an incoming tide, I became tentative, afraid of pursuit, afraid of what it might imply about me...perhaps afraid of what it would look like, of what people would think or of what *he* would think.

Women did not pursue *men*. It was supposed to be the other way round. Especially widows in their mid-forties did not do so.

Iain left Port Scarnose four years earlier for reasons of his own. He had not shared them with me. They were not for me to know. I couldn't go chasing after him to fulfill some selfish need to know whether my feelings were those of a friend or something more. To attempt to find him again, if it was only to satisfy my own selfish ends, would be wrong.

What about *his* thoughts and feelings? He obviously did not want to be found. Otherwise, he would not have gone to such lengths to keep his whereabouts secret.

The largest and most obvious uncertainty hanging over my conjectures was the huge question of whether Iain was now married. How could he not be after so long? I couldn't lose myself in a ridiculous whirlwind of thoughts about *love* if a married man was involved!

And no matter from which angle the sun shone on the long-buried soil that was being cultivated anew, my love for Alasdair complicated everything tenfold. The question was constantly with me: Was I somehow being unfaithful to that love by allowing myself to think of Iain? Did this hidden sprouting reveal a betrayal of Alasdair's memory?

I tried desperately to examine the other side of the coin. I tried to convince myself that Iain was a good friend. *Only* a friend. He had been Alasdair's *best* friend. What if he didn't know about Alasdair? He *needed* to know, *deserved* to know. It had nothing to do with me. As Alasdair's widow, it was my duty to contact Iain. His probable marriage had nothing to do with it. I still needed to contact him . . . for Alasdair's sake.

This was not about romance or love. It was about friendship with a man with whom Alasdair and I had once been very close.

At last I convinced myself that such was the right and honorable perspective. I came to terms with it on the basis of the friendship that Alasdair had cherished and had missed during the final years of his life. I came to terms with it by keeping Alasdair in his proper place in my memory. Yes, I had once loved two men. I had married one of them. Those two men had been friends—good friends, close friends, best friends. The one deserved to know about the other. To tell him was my responsibility. It was a debt I needed to discharge on Alasdair's behalf.

I must try to find Iain Barclay to tell him of Alasdair's passing, and that Alasdair had loved him to the end.

I telephoned Nigel Crathie to ask if there were any additional details concerning what he had learned about Reverend Gillihan's predecessor.

"None," he said. He had contacted Church of Scotland headquarters in Edinburgh to make inquiries. He had been told that Rev. Iain Barclay was not listed among the church's active clergy. Thinking it a dead end, he did not pursue it immediately. On a hunch, some time later he wrote to the church offices requesting a list of all living *retired* Church of Scotland clergy. He had received the list only two days before the trial was set to begin. On it was the name of Iain Barclay, residing in London.

"But no address?" I said.

"No, only the city."

"Surely it could be found with an Internet search."

"Probably . . . but London? It would not surprise me if there are two hundred Iain Barclays in the greater London area. Both are common names."

"Unless he is still using the *Rev.*," I suggested. Even as I said it I knew it was a stupid idea. "Forget it," I said. "Iain always hated the 'Rev.' in front of his name, even when he was the curate of a church. He would certainly not be using it now."

"Do you know his middle name?"

"Actually, come to think of it, I don't even know if he has one."

"We can find out. He was born in Deskmill Parish, I believe. It will be in the records. What about other family?"

"All I know is that he has a married sister. It seems she may have married an American, but I could be wrong. I really know very little about his family. Both their parents are dead, I believe."

"Not much to go on. Would you like me to pursue it?"

"If you don't mind. Maybe I will, too—though I'm not very Internet-savvy."

"What about Alicia's friend Tavia Maccallum? Isn't she a computer whiz? As I recall, she does Internet research for some firm in Sydney—all by e-mail and online."

"That's right."

"She probably knows how to track folks down. People who know what they're doing can practically google a picture of someone walking along the pavement in front of their house."

"Really!"

"Well, maybe not quite—but it's amazing what people can do these days."

"I will talk to her."

I would have been reluctant to mention such a request to anyone else in town. Can you imagine what Mrs. Gauld would do with a tidbit like my trying to track down Iain Barclay!

But Tavia had faithfully kept our plans and movements secret when Alicia came for me in Canada, and then when she and I had snuck into the castle without Olivia getting wind of it. I knew she could be trusted to keep it confidential.

When I went to visit her and told her of my request, she did not seem to think it so difficult an assignment.

"Sure," she said. "I can find him. Knowing he is in London is the main thing. If Nigel—Mr. Crathie—is certain of that, I can do the rest. In a worst-case scenario I should be able to narrow it down to two or three possibilities."

She glanced toward the window a little nervously.

"Are you expecting someone?" I asked.

"Actually . . . well, yes, but it's fine. I'm all ready."

"Whoever it is, it must be special—you look very nice."

Tavia dropped her eyes in embarrassment.

I stood. "Well, I'll be going then. So you will see what you can find out . . . And have a good time," I added with a smile.

Tavia nodded.

I left the house. As I walked toward the Volvo parked on the street, a familiar car drove up and pulled in behind me. It was the BMW with the *Buchan* license plate. Harvey Nicholls got out and greeted me with a sheepish look on his face.

Confused for a moment, I turned back toward the house. There stood Tavia at the window.

The light dawned. *How intriguing*, I thought, smiling to myself. I wasn't the only one around here with secrets!

Chapter Forty-nine

London

And when he came to his true love's dwelling,
He knelt down gently upon a stone,
And through the window he whispered lowly,
"Is my true lover within at home."
—"The Night Visiting Song"

Even as I boarded the plane for London, I was still convincing myself that I was doing this for Alasdair, for the friendship, for the past, to tell Iain that his friend was now with God...that it was my duty to bring all things full circle, including the relationship that had been so pivotal in my life and Alasdair's.

By the time I landed at Gatwick, however, I was far more keyed up and excited than duty as a widow could account for. After all the fuss I had made over packing for the trip, the little glances at my hair in the airport bathroom, wondering what dress would be best to wear, those were not the signs of someone on an errand motivated by a sense of duty!

London was big, loud, overwhelming, confusing, tumultuous. As I really did not know much of the city, I thought about trying to do a little sightseeing. Alasdair and I had come down once for a play, but that was my only visit. Now that I was here, I was far too distracted about what I had come for to be able to enjoy even so much as a bus tour. I walked a little that afternoon, gathering my courage, and spent the whole evening in my room pretending to read. But all I could do was think about what awaited me.

Over and over I rehearsed what I would say:

"*Hello, Reverend Barclay,*" I would begin, preserving the formal note and extending my hand.

"*Why, Mrs. Reidhaven,*" he would say, "*what brings you to London?*"

"*Some sad news, I am afraid. I have come to inform you of the passing of my husband. You and he were such good friends, I felt you deserved to hear it from me.*"

"*Thank you. That is very kind of you. May I extend my deepest condolences.*"

"*Thank you.*"

"*Would you come in and have tea?...I would like you to meet my wife...*"

And so it went as I played out every possible scenario in my mind, so that I would not act like an idiot and fumble over my words when the big moment actually came.

As I left my B and B the next day, I took a good long look in the mirror, adjusted a few strands of hair, then sprinkled on a dash of perfume. I hesitated, then went back into the bathroom, wet a washcloth, and gave my face and neck a quick scrub to remove it.

Perfume...This wasn't a date! What was I thinking?! Get a grip, girl!

The address I gave to the cabdriver supplied by Tavia landed me in front of a row of old but respectable brick flats on a pleasant and quiet street in Holborn. Once I had the street located, I asked the man to drive slowly by number 716, then drop me a block away.

Slowly I got out and began to walk toward it.

A postman was coming along in the opposite direction, stopping at each house in succession. I watched as he made deliveries to 714, 716, 718, and 720. As he then approached, I walked toward him.

"Excuse me," I said, "that house you left back there, number 716—is that the Barclay home?"

"Yez, mum, 'at's right," he replied in thick Cockney.

"Iain Barclay?"

"Yez, 'at's it, mum—Mr. Barclay an' Miz Barclay."

"*Mrs.?*" I repeated.

"'At's right, Miz."

I had expected it, assumed it, planned on it. Yet suddenly knowing it stopped me in my tracks. I stood like a block of granite as the postman continued down the pavement on his appointed rounds. I had tried to prepare myself for every contingency. I told myself over and over that Iain was *sure* to be married. Yet somehow I had not quite managed to thoroughly convince myself. Suddenly all my energy drained away.

This had all been a mistake! What a fool I was. I couldn't go through with it!

I turned and began to walk away.

I had taken only half a dozen steps when I heard a door open behind me. A rush of adrenaline surged through me. My heart began to pound. What if it was *him*?!

I stopped, and slowly looked back. Huge disappointment dashed my momentary hope.

A woman was coming down the steps of number 716. She turned onto the pavement and began walking toward me. I stood where I was, staring as she came. She approached. I tried to speak but could find no words.

She glanced at me with a questioning expression, then continued along the pavement.

"Please...excuse me," I said after her. "Are you Mrs. Barclay?"

She turned back toward me.

"I am *Miss* Barclay," she answered. I thought I detected a hint of the Scots tongue.

"I don't...I mean," I said, fumbling for words, "is Iain Barclay your husband...Rev. Iain Barclay?"

"He's not a reverend just now." She laughed lightly. "I'm sorry for laughing, but it always sounds funny in my ear to hear him called that. And no, he's not my husband...he's my brother."

"Your brother!"

"I have been living with him since my husband passed away. I went back to my maiden name."

"Is your brother...married?"

"No," replied Miss Barclay, then hesitated. "He says he once met an angel," she added. "After that, he said, he had no interest in marrying."

The dormant seed suddenly exploded into flower as a full-blossoming plant!

"Go in and see him if you like, ma'am," she said. "He's home. He's just working on his book."

She turned and walked on, leaving me standing on the pavement gasping for breath. At last my legs began to move. I numbly walked toward the house, turned from the pavement, and climbed the steps.

How long I stood in front of the door—five minutes, ten, two hours. All proportion of time lost its meaning.

Finally I raised my hand, then lifted the brass knocker. The sharp echo as it dropped sounded like a gunshot in my ear.

After an interminable wait, steps approached. The handle turned...the door swung open—

Suddenly there he was!

Orange hair...wild and gloriously uncombed...those pale blue eyes just like I remembered them...his face uncharacteristically stubbly and unshaven.

He stared at me as if gazing upon a specter...expressionless, stunned, awestruck. I stood trembling, mouth half open in an agony of joyful terror, afraid to utter a peep.

His head slowly began to shake...his lips quivering for speech. He blinked several times. His eyes, now red, flooded with tears.

"*Marie!*" he whispered in disbelief. "I can't believe...Is it really you?!"

At the sound of his voice an electric tingle swept from my head to my toes.

He opened his arms. I rushed forward, bursting into sobs, and fell into his embrace.

Time stood still. My eyes gushed a river of pent-up release and relief. Iain trembled as he held me. I knew he was crying, too.

I was the first to speak.

"Alasdair is dead, Iain," I said in what was scarcely more than a whisper.

"Yes, I know," replied Iain softly. "I am so sorry, Marie."

I nodded, my head still leaning against his chest.

"The dear, dear man," he went on. "Did he...Was it prolonged? Did he suffer?"

"I don't think so," I answered. "It was slow but peaceful—exactly like dear Gwendolyn. He was listening to her harp music when he went."

"How wonderful—the music of the angels...and his own little red-haired angel."

A moment more we stood. At last Iain stepped back and gazed deeply into my eyes. His face was wet but aglow. He wiped several times at his eyes, then chuckled.

"I forgot I hadn't shaved for two days!" he said as his hand passed over his face. "A luxury I allow myself on my days off—not a very presentable picture for a reunion. Oh, but it is *so* wonderful to see you! As often as I have played out this day in my mind, it is even better than my imaginings. You look so beautiful, Marie—radiant, at peace. Marriage to Alasdair obviously agreed with you."

I nodded. "Oh, I have so much to tell you," I babbled, "about Alasdair...about everything. You won't believe all that's gone on with Olivia. And I have been back to America...My father was also dying and I took care of him, too."

"Is it over...Is he gone?"

I nodded. "He died about eight months ago," I said with a quiet smile.

"Oh, Marie, I *am* sorry," he said tenderly. "You have had to face much grief."

"Yes, but I think I am stronger for it. I hope so. It is all still fresh. It takes time to put it into perspective."

"Tell me everything. I want to hear it all, every detail, though it take days! Come in— Oh, this is so wonderful! I still cannot believe you are here—Angel Marie in my home again!"

I laughed at his exuberance. I couldn't believe it either!

Chapter Fifty

Alasdair's Song

I think of thee when spring wakes smiling nature,
When birds sing sweetly and when flowers are bright,
When pleasure gladdens every living creature,
And sunshine bathes the earth and sea in light.
And when the rainbow springs, its glory throwing
O'er cloud and storm, to bid their darkness flee;
And all is bright and beautiful and glowing,
Like one that I could name—I think of thee.
—Alexander Hume, "I Think of Thee"

I followed Iain inside and into the kitchen.

"I don't know if this will be quite the same as having tea in your house in Scotland," I said, glancing about, "and having water from the kettle poured down my back, but it is charming in its own way."

Iain laughed. "You would bring that up!"

"Whenever I think of you making tea—what else would come to my mind?!"

"Maybe you're right—clumsiness . . . my cross to bear! But you're right about the flat—everything in central London is old. Housing here is unbelievably expensive. You can't be particularly choosy."

"Do you own this house?" I asked.

"No, just rent. You've got to be independently wealthy to *own* in London."

"Your sister—" I began.

"You met my sister?"

"Yes, outside on the street. I thought she was your wife. I was so afraid. I almost left."

He laughed. "She told you about losing her husband?"

"Only briefly. It is good of you to take her in."

"She is great. We are good friends. It's wonderful to have someone to share the house with...and share expenses with."

"Where does she work?"

"She's a clerical assistant for one of the banks in the city. Nothing fancy, but it helps keep bread and potatoes on the table. We grew up in humble circumstances and both have simple tastes. We manage fine."

"Does she have children?"

"No. Her husband died young and they never got around to it. She's only thirty-eight."

"She's attractive. Do you think she'll marry again?"

"Possibly. She's not 'looking,' but you're right, she's an attractive, capable girl—er, woman, I mean. Once a younger sister, always a younger sister."

"What did her husband do?"

"He was involved in finances, though I was never sure in exactly what kind of role. That whole world remains a mystery to me."

"For me, too," I said. "Though I am learning. I had to take care of my father's estate—I've got his house up for sale now in Oregon. My house in Calgary is in limbo...and now Alasdair's huge holdings are apparently mine to administrate. I'm still pretty overwhelmed. As a Nashville song might put it, I'm just a simple country girl!"

"I doubt if you're really all that simple," said Iain. "You may find you like being a tycoon."

"A tycoon? That's hardly how I would describe it!"

"You're a duchess."

"A reluctant one."

"You will grow into it, of that I have no doubt."

"What about you?" I asked. "I understand you are no longer in the ministry?"

Iain nodded as he poured boiling water into a pot and gathered a few things onto a tray. He carried it across the room and we sat down at the small kitchen table.

"Is it permanent?" I asked. "Have you, I don't know, had some change of belief or—"

"No, no, nothing like that," replied Iain. "If anything my faith is stronger than ever. As to the duration of my present circumstance, one never knows about such things. I think of it as a season of recharging my spiritual batteries, to live awhile in the real world working for a living, which all pastors and clergymen ought to have to do at least one month of every year."

"A radical idea," I said. "But then as I recall, you rather thrived on finding the unusual edges of gospel practicality to make your Christianity real."

Iain roared with delight. "You have me pegged to perfection—the gospel's unusual edges . . . Well put!"

"It's true. That's exactly what you do."

"I just hate stale, rote, formula religion. Jesus employed none of that in his methods. If those who attach themselves to his name don't wake up eventually to the imperative of being real *followers*, not zombies parroting back the clichés of their pastors and priests, or fractious political and theological zealots bickering with those of differing outlook, Christianity as a spiritual force in the world is finished."

"No wonder you are not in a church," I said with a laugh. "No church would have you!"

"You're probably not far wrong."

"But what does all that have to do with working?" I asked.

"Because the professional clergy, so called, is an enormous part of the problem. Have you ever seen such antithesis to the lifestyle of Christlikeness or the example of the apostle Paul than as represented by the Catholic priesthood or the Evangelical ministry? The thing is positively a joke. Jesus wearing robes or waving incense about . . . Paul wearing gold jewelry and expensive suits and motoring about in luxury cars! That's why I say that one of the qualifications for any form of the pastorate or priesthood ought to be the ability to work and make a living doing something *else*. Any man or woman who cannot sweat and groan hard alongside the working class is not fit for ministry. Otherwise they get completely insulated from life. They ought to have to *work*. Depending on donations from *other* people for your salary—it's such an artificial means of supporting oneself. A man ought to be able to make a living by the sweat of his brow. Only if he can do that does he deserve periodically to take donations so that he can minister more effectively. But to enter the so-called *ministry* as a lifetime vocation and *career*, to me seems a travesty against truth, profit-mongering from the gospel."

"Will you go back into the church, that is, on the assumption that anyone would have such a radical?"

"I don't know," replied Iain reflectively. "I think so...I hope so. But I am in no hurry."

"I can just hear Ranald saying that. He told me not so long ago that God is never in a hurry."

"Oh, dear Ranald!" he exclaimed with affection in his tone. "I can hear the exact words from his mouth. How is the precious man?"

"Well...very well. I now know why you revere him so."

"I take it that you and he have become well acquainted?"

"I would say *very* well acquainted," I said, nodding. "As you say— what a precious man. He has become for me exactly what he was for you—a spiritual mentor. And for Alasdair toward the end as well. They had amazing talks at Alasdair's bedside. I only heard bits and pieces, but it brings tears to my eyes whenever I think of it."

"I am so glad. Among all the reasons for my leaving, that was primary among them—the hope that those two men would draw together in a way I do not think could have happened while I was present."

Iain's words rubbed open my own perplexity about his leaving. But I did not pursue it.

"What *are* you doing in the real world, then?"

"You see before you a humble construction laborer . . . pouring cement and framing new buildings. See?" he added, lifting his palms
toward me. "I've got the rough, blistered hands to prove it!"

"Your sister said you were writing a book. That's great. I always
thought you should."

"It's slow going," said Iain. "I am not a natural writer, but I am
writing about something I feel strongly about. So I try to give quality
time to it on my days off, which usually come in two- to three-day
chunks. That helps me achieve a little continuity."

"What is it about?" I asked.

A sheepish look came over Iain's face. "It's funny you should ask,"
he said. "Actually, this whole thing is amazingly coincidental."

"Why?"

"Because it is a book about Alasdair, about his life, about the principle of growth and change and regeneration in the human heart."

"That is amazing. I would never have guessed it, given, you know,
how we completely lost touch with you."

"Don't read too much into that, Marie. My deep affection for you
both remained unchanged. Indeed, my admiration for my friend has
grown so mightily since I last saw the two of you that finally I had
no choice but to try to write about it. People don't usually change.
Alasdair did. He changed because he wanted to *grow*, to become
better than he was. I just find his story amazingly inspirational. I'm
thinking of calling it—I hope you won't mind, I took the word *song*
from *your* musical talents—*Alasdair's Song*."

"I don't mind at all." I smiled. "I think it's a lovely title. I can't wait
to read it."

Iain's words warmed my heart and set so many things to rest. I
was so proud of *both* men I loved.

"How long are you staying?" asked Iain. "What else brought you
to London—do you have business, or—"

"No, nothing else," I said, "only to tell you about Alasdair. I would
have come or written sooner—but I didn't know how to find you."

Iain nodded. "I know, I am sorry— I'm sure it must have been confusing for you at first. Hopefully I will have the chance to explain one day, if and when the time is right. But right now . . . I can still hardly believe you are here. It is just so great to see you! We can do London together—that is, if you have time. If not, of course . . . I mean, I understand. I'm sure you are busy. You are a duchess, after all . . . an important lady now—many responsibilities, people depending on you—places to go, things to do, people to see, situations to evaluate."

I couldn't help laughing at his characterization of my life. I couldn't believe how refreshingly good it felt to bask in Iain's zestful, energetic outlook, his sense of humor, his exuberance for life.

"Have no worry about intruding," I said. "There is nothing I would love so much as to have you intrude on my time as much as *you* have time for. I have so much to tell you!" I said.

"And I want to hear it all," rejoined Iain. "I told you—every detail."

As we walked through Kensington Gardens two days later, the initial mood of excited and exhilarating reacquaintance had given way to a quiet sense of contentment merely to be in each other's presence. I think we both felt the same. It was different than it had ever been between us. There were no issues to contend with, no distractions, no people to worry about, no village gossip, no reminders of the past, no church politics or disputes or personalities, no watching eyes, not even any spiritual issues.

Just us.

Two people walking along. Two friends . . . a man and a woman.

We must have walked an hour without a word. All around bustled the life of London—horns and traffic in the distance, ducks and families and lovers scattered throughout the massive park. In the midst of it all we walked in peaceful silence.

We *had* talked. Almost nonstop for two days as we could find the time, late into both evenings, till almost midnight the first, till ten-thirty the second after Iain had been at work all day. Then today he had taken off from his job. If they fired him, he said, so be it. Being with me was a higher priority. We had talked about everything that had taken place in our two lives during the past four years.

Everything. Thus the silence between us now was the silence of *fullness*, not the silence of emptiness.

We had spoken of everything . . . except the one thing.

At length Iain broke the silence.

"When will you go?" he asked softly.

The question dropped like an anvil of inevitability on my head. In that instant I realized that what I had come to London for had been accomplished. To prolong it now could only lead in directions I wasn't sure it was supposed to go.

I drew in a long sigh and slowly exhaled.

"I think probably tomorrow," I replied.

He nodded.

"I had a feeling," he said . . . then said no more.

As my plane lifted off from Gatwick the following morning and slowly banked north, I felt quietly at peace. Sad but at peace.

Whole.

Full circle.

Duties discharged.

Friendships fulfilled.

A good, quiet, melancholy sense of completion.

I didn't know whether I would ever see Iain Barclay again.

Chapter Fifty-one

Uncertain Return

There lives a young lassie far down in yon glen;
And I lo'e that lassie as nae ane may ken!
O! a saint's faith may vary, but faithfu' I'll be;
For weel I lo'e Mary, and Mary lo'es me.
—John Imlah, "There Lives a Young Lassie"

Now began one of the difficult interludes of my life since first coming to Scotland.

Suddenly I had nothing to look forward to. Truly now everything was wrapped up, every loose end tied off. All I could think was, *Now what?*

Did my future at this point consist solely of becoming a businesswoman and administering the affairs of the Buchan estate? I can't say the prospect thrilled me.

I would begin adding harp students, of course. But was that all... Was that *enough*?

What did I have to *hope* for, to look forward to? What new challenges, adventures, opportunities awaited me? I could think of none. It was a little depressing.

I had even put the disappearance of my pedal harp behind me and filed an insurance claim. I wasn't particularly hopeful that I would receive anything. Its theft couldn't be proven, and in all likelihood Olivia had contributed to it, too—sort of an "inside job," as they say. But in a way filing the claim was my way of bringing proverbial closure to Olivia's tenure in the castle. Of course I could afford to buy a new pedal harp. But a harp studio is like a library—

you can't just go out and blindly purchase a collection of harps any more than you can a collection of books. Both have to grow and develop over time. A library is built on love of books that are obtained one at a time, savored as their truths make unique contributions to the whole. My little collection of harps had come into my life the same way, one at a time, each unique in both appearance and tone, each adding something special to the studio family. I had bright-sounding harps, mellow-sounding harps, some with incredibly rich bass notes. There were those with light airy tones, others with subdued mysterious timbres. In Canada I had needed a pedal harp for the symphony and for weddings. But in Scotland the *clarsach*, or folk harp, was the harp of choice. Therefore, I couldn't know if another pedal harp would ever join the family again. At the right time, perhaps. Only time would tell.

For some of my friends, on the other hand, the next few months were gloriously exciting. Alicia and Nigel Crathie were now seeing each other seriously. I had a pretty good idea where that relationship would lead. The romance between Tavia and Harvey Nicholls, while a little slower to develop, had also nevertheless begun to attract the notice of many of the village auld wives. I thought it was absolutely delightful.

Alicia had a birthday coming up and I planned a day together, with a surprise present to climax the day's outing. When the morning arrived, we left about ten. We drove to Nairn first, then to Logie Steddings south of Nairn where we visited their bookstore, which specialized in books of interest to the northeast of Scotland. After spending a hundred pounds on books, we lunched at the Logie Steddings Tearoom. From there we drove the rest of the way into Inverness, walked the river, went into some of the shops, then spent an hour in the magnificent Leakey's used-book store and spent more money than we should have there, too. For all Alicia knew, when we drove out of the city on the A98 about three in the afternoon, we were on our way home. But I had one more stop planned. As I turned into the Inverness airport, Alicia asked where we were going.

"I thought you said you liked airplanes," I said.

"I do."

"Did you know they give private flying lessons here?"

"You remembered!" Alicia exclaimed. "This is brilliant—I'll go in and find out what the procedure is. I've been wanting to look into it anyway. Thank you, Marie."

"You don't understand, Alicia," I said. "You're going to do more than find out about it."

"What do you mean?"

"Your first lesson starts in fifteen minutes."

Alicia gasped in astonishment.

"You don't . . . you really—"

"It's all arranged. You're paid up for ten lessons. All you have to do is go into the office and sign a few papers. Happy birthday, Alicia."

Beside herself with excitement, it was all I could do to bring the Volvo to a complete stop before she was out of the car and running toward the private hangars.

"The office is this way, Alicia!" I laughed after her.

Twenty-five minutes later I stood watching Alicia, excited beyond words, taxiing away in the passenger seat of a little Piper Cub. They took off as I watched from the ground. After about fifteen minutes circling around and flying back and forth in the general vicinity of the airport, I saw the plane take a sudden dip. My heart leaped up into my throat. The pilot must have given Alicia the controls! Almost immediately the plane righted itself, then flew straight again for a while, then dipped again, though not so badly, then leveled off, then suddenly arced upward sharply.

Alicia! I said to myself. *What are you doing up there?!*

But all ended well. The little blue Piper finally swooped down for a smooth landing. Alicia got out and ran toward me, absolutely radiant and more thrilled than I had ever seen her. She gave me a great hug and thanked me at least twenty times before we were back at Port Scarnose.

"That was so fun!" she said over and over. "That was *so* absolutely entirely fun! Can we stop by Nigel's office in Elgin?" she said. "I've just got to tell him!"

"It's your birthday!" I laughed. "We can do anything you like."

That evening we gathered with a group of Alicia's friends, including Nigel Crathie, of course, and Harvey Nicholls at Tavia's for fish-and-chips. Alicia even invited crusty old Farquharson, whom I had kept on at the castle and who was gradually warming to the rest of us. Alicia regaled everyone with tales of her exploits over the airfield in Inverness, as if she had been flying a dangerous mission with a secret military cargo onboard. The two of us had all the others laughing so hard tears were flowing even from the men.

The lessons continued. The ten went by, I bought her ten more. Alicia went to Inverness every chance she had. For the next few months, flying lessons dominated her life. Before long she was going for her license. With every spare minute she studied books and rules and codes and maps and charts and radio and radar and navigation protocols and flight plans. We went to Ranald's frequently and kept him posted on her progress. I think he was almost as excited as she was.

Alicia had to log forty-five hours in the air and pass a rigorous series of tests, both written and in flight. She was making day trips all over Scotland, practicing the routes and gaining familiarity with all the airports. She was actually going to do it! And she was determined to do it in record time.

The day she passed her final test, she asked Ranald and me to accompany her on her maiden flight as a qualified pilot—to Perth, she suggested.

"I've never been up in a little plane," I said, not particularly eager.

"You'll love it," insisted Alicia. "There's nothing like it. I feel like a bird up there. It's so peaceful."

Finally I agreed, though still with more than a little trepidation.

She and Ranald had the time of their lives as we flew down to Perth a week later. Speaking for myself, I was scared out of my wits.

My knees were wobbly when we landed and I staggered into the airport reception room. We had lunch in Perth—a very light one for me!—and then had to fly back. I wasn't sure I could make it.

I sat in the passenger seat behind Alicia and Ranald, my knuckles white the whole way as I clutched the hold-bars beside me, listening to them laugh and talk airplane lingo and compare their RAF stories. Ranald took the controls for part of the flight home. Even though he said he hadn't flown an airplane in thirty years, in all honesty I have to say that I felt a little more secure. Alicia was entirely competent. But somehow when you get into an airplane, you feel better seeing a man with gray hair at the controls.

We returned to Port Scarnose and I remained wobbly and airsick. We had been home about an hour when Alicia came to find me. I was lying on one of the couches in the Great Room, still feeling woozy.

"You have a visitor," she said.

"Oh, do I have to?" I groaned. "I'm not sure I'm up to it."

"I think you will want to see this one," said Alicia. Her eyes sparkled with a strange light and her lips wore a mysterious smile.

I looked up at her with a forlorn expression.

"You really have to, Marie," she said. "Trust me."

I dragged myself to my feet and followed Alicia downstairs. She disappeared somewhere en route. By the time I reached the front door, I was alone.

I drew in a breath to steady my nerves, then opened the door. A sharp gasp of surprise escaped my lips.

There stood Iain, two dozen yellow roses in his hand.

"Duchess Reidhaven!" he said exuberantly, "a bouquet from Aberdeen, the city of roses, delivered by special messenger, just for you."

"Iain!" I exclaimed. "Now it is my turn to ask— What are *you* doing here?"

"What do you think? I am here to see you. We have to talk, Marie."

Chapter Fifty-two

Spey Bay

When dew drops load the grassy blade, in summer's rising morn;
What time the flow'rs with regal garb, the verdant fields adorn—
As shines upon the varied scene the golden gleams above;
The vision brings to mind again, my first and early love.
—Neil MacLeod, "My Love of Early Days"

If I was light-headed and weak-kneed on the bumpy little plane flight over the Grampians to Perth, seeing Iain at my door with flowers in his hand certainly didn't help my precarious mental equilibrium. I'm surprised that a full-fledged attack of emotional vertigo didn't lay me out flat in a faint.

My knees, I confess, did buckle slightly and my head swooned. Before I could put my swirling thoughts in order, Iain had whisked me to his car. The castle entryway passed in a blur, as did the village of Port Scarnose. I didn't even possess sufficient wits at that point to worry that Mrs. Gauld would see us and immediately send a new round of gossip over the invisible wires of town chatter.

I suppose some small talk must have passed between us, though I can't remember. I was in a sort of waking stupor. When I began to come to myself, we were driving along the coast road through Port Gordon. The salt air of the sea through the open window had revived me.

"Where are we going?" I asked.

"Oh, I don't know," replied Iain. "I thought perhaps Spey Bay. I understand the dolphins have been running."

"That would be fun. I haven't been there in ages."

352

"It seemed a safe place to have a talk, far enough away that we might not be recognized."

"It's only fifteen miles—we *might* be recognized. Everyone knows the crop of red hair of Deskmill's former curate."

"And the face of Buchan's lovely duchess. But we'll risk it!"

By the time we parked at the mouth of the river Spey and walked through the sea grass across to the rocky shore, I was feeling invigorated and at last over the effects of the plane ride earlier in the day.

"You'll never guess where I had lunch today," I said.

"Where—Puddleduck...Linda and Eddie's?"

I laughed. "Not even close. The Highlander in Perth."

"Perth—that's a three-hour drive."

"But only an hour by plane. We flew down for lunch and back. That's why I haven't been feeling well."

"*We?*"

"Alicia and Ranald and I."

"What, alone? Who was flying the plane?!"

"Alicia just got her pilot's license—it was her first solo with passengers."

"No kidding. What an adventure."

"I was terrified." I laughed.

"And Ranald?"

"He flew part of the way himself. He had the time of his life."

"That's right—he was an RAF pilot."

Gradually it quieted as we walked away from the river mouth and the dolphin crowd thinned.

"I haven't yet answered your question about why I am here," Iain began at length.

"Or said for how long," I added.

"Actually...," replied Iain slowly, "my sister is with me. We came back to Scotland to stay."

"Oh, I'm so glad!" I exclaimed, looking excitedly into Iain's face. "You're really moving back! Why that's...that's wonderful!"

The gush of words poured out of my mouth before I could moderate my enthusiasm with the proper decorum of a duchess.

"Oops, sorry!" I said sheepishly. "Maybe that was a little over the top."

Iain laughed with good-natured delight.

"No bother at all," he said. "Suddenly our roles are exactly reversed from the last time. In London it was me falling all over myself at seeing you again. Actually, that's what I want to talk to you about—that reversal of our roles."

"What do you mean?"

Again it was quiet. Iain was thinking. Whenever he had something to say, he took his time to collect and organize his thoughts.

"I had been praying for some time for leading, even for a sign of what I was supposed to do," he began. "I knew neither Katie nor I were content in London. We were marking time. We were fish out of water. Scotland always beckoned. But making a change had to be right—at the right time and for the right reasons. We needed to return north. It was where our hearts were. But I couldn't make a move too soon, given the circumstances. I had to let you and Alasdair establish your lives together."

"What if he hadn't died, would you ever have come back?"

"I don't know—perhaps after I felt enough time had passed. But when that might have been, I cannot say. Obviously Alasdair's death changed the dynamics of what a return to Scotland would mean. But it didn't make a decision any easier. Actually, just the opposite. In one way, it made me even more reluctant than ever."

"Why would that be?" I asked.

"It is hard to explain. Don't you see—how could we not have drawn closer together during a time of vulnerability for you?"

"I suppose I can see that. And people would have talked."

"It ties in with why I left; it ties into everything. I was very protective of Alasdair, even of his memory. I had come to realize how alike the two of us were as boys . . . and also as men. To fall in love with the same woman—twice! That's a little unusual. As different as were our backgrounds and outlooks, we were somehow wired inside similarly. I think that's why we were close."

"Alasdair felt it, too," I said. "I knew there were times, though he said nothing, when he literally ached for missing you."

An expression of pain passed over Iain's face. "If only there might have been another way," he sighed. "Yet, as close as I felt to him, somehow I realized that this time Alasdair would have found a way to be the selfless one, and would have encouraged you and me to be as close as we wanted to be. I just couldn't let that happen, even though it would have been a testimony of Alasdair's growth and maturity as a man. I could not do *anything* that might in the slightest way come between you and him, even your memory of him. I had to know beyond doubt that you still loved him and would always love him. I *want* you to always love him...even if, at any time and for any reason, I were to have a role in your life again."

"I will, Iain," I said. "Have no worry about that. My love for Alasdair is secure in my heart."

"I know that," he said and nodded. "I know it *now*. But I wasn't absolutely certain about it before you came to see me. I had seen neither of you in four years. I could not know how things might stand. After the time we spent together in London, as wonderfully close as I felt to you, I knew beyond a doubt that you loved Alasdair in death no less than you had loved him in life. That is when I realized that nothing I ever did would, or even *could*, diminish that love. It was a great burden lifted from me. I no longer had to protect Alasdair from anything I might do."

I smiled—sadly but contentedly—with reminders of Alasdair, as well as to be reminded how much the two men esteemed each other.

"In time," Iain concluded, "I recognized *that* as the sign I had been waiting for, the sign that I was finally free to return to Scotland."

"What were you talking about before," I asked, "about the reversal of our roles?"

"Only that I had waited for *you* to come to see *me*," replied Iain.

"I waited for you, as the saying goes, to make the first move, though I mean nothing beyond that than that you were the one to take the initiative in a relationship that I had basically cut off—and cut off completely."

"At first, I admit I was angry with you for leaving without a word," I said, "and even a little upset that you didn't get in touch when Alasdair was dying."

Iain did not reply immediately. Much seemed to be passing through his mind.

"It was difficult to know how to handle," he said at length.

"*Why* didn't you contact him or come?"

"It was a complicated situation, at least for me. I don't know if I did the right thing or not. I agonized in prayer. As I said, my reasons, right or wrong, were to make sure I did not place either of you in a vulnerable position, or in any way complicate what you were having to face. After your visit, as I reflected on the courage it took for you to come to me, having no idea why I had left or knowing whether I was married, I began to reevaluate the whole thing, even wonder if I had, in fact, handled it wisely. I still think it was the right thing to do. However, I began to think that perhaps it wasn't right of me not to contact you after I learned of Alasdair's death. I had my reasons—"

"I would like to hear them."

"Perhaps there will come a time for more than what I have just told you. But since you came to London, I have done a great deal of thinking. *Soul-searching* would be the more appropriate term. I realized that I had put you in an awkward position, having to come *to me* to tell me about Alasdair. I'm sure that was hard for you. Yet with that behind us now, whatever were my reasons, once I saw how secure your love for Alasdair truly was, and how you and he had grown together, and what a fine, noble woman of dignity you had truly become, suddenly things changed for me. I began to realize not merely that I *could* return to Scotland, but that I *must* return. If some further destiny, some further plan of God's lay in the future for me, for *us* ... I had to find out, and be willing to find out ... have the courage to find out ... even trust you enough to find out."

"Trust *me*?" I said. "I'm not sure I follow you."

"Perhaps my former reluctance stemmed from thinking you weaker and more vulnerable than you were," replied Iain. "If so, I apologize for that. Yet once I saw how you had grown, saw your strength, saw your security in who you were, I realized I could trust you enough to handle seeing me again, and to know what to do with me in the larger picture of your life."

"I see."

"And now, whatever there is between us," Iain went on, "whatever there might be, whatever there is supposed to be, it would not be fair or right of me to wait for you again. After that walk in Kensington, I knew I had to come to you. It was time for *me* to take the initiative. There was so much that remained unsaid that day, so much I wanted to say. But I was hesitant, still protective of Alasdair's memory and your feelings. As time went by and I realized that your love for one another was eternal, I was liberated for the first time to admit that my own feelings for you had never died. I knew that I had to find out what was in my heart, and what might be in yours. Maybe it is too soon. If so, I will turn around and leave. But I have to give us the chance to say what we couldn't say before, and to feel what maybe we couldn't feel before."

At the words *find out what is in my heart*, my own heart leaped. Iain was using exactly the same words to describe what I had been thinking for myself.

"But your moving back ... ," I began, fumbling for words. "What are you going to do? ... Where will you live? ... How will we—"

I didn't even know what I was asking. Suddenly I was feeling very much like a schoolgirl!

"I mean ... the church ... Reverend Gillihan—"

"I have no designs on his job," said Iain. "Nor am I ready again to occupy a pulpit. I know there are many unanswered questions.

The last thing I want to do is complicate your life. I will keep my distance, if you like."

"No, no, it's not that. I just—"

"As far as the daily logistics of the move," Iain added, "I've taken a job in Huntly—a construction job. Actually, I like construction. It's out of doors, it's physical, there's a sense of accomplishment—you see visible and tangible results of your work every day. It's a rewarding way to make a living."

"Huntly, but that's so far," I said, obviously a little disheartened.

"Not far, really," rejoined Iain. "Only half an hour. I seriously contemplated Aberdeen and Inverness."

"Oh, Iain, that would be way too far!"

"We don't want to make it any more complicated than it already is."

"I don't mind a *few* complications," I said with a smile.

Iain laughed, then grew serious again.

"Marie," he said, "I don't know where this will lead. I only know I had to come north to give the Lord a chance to do whatever he might want to do. But we cannot engineer it. If there is something between us, Marie, *God* must do it."

Iain stopped and looked over at me with the most tender childlike smile, almost a smile of wonder.

"What am I saying?" he said. "*If*...It is obvious that *something* is happening between us. It is clear to me, I don't know about you. It was obvious to me five years ago. It was obvious to me when I saw you standing at my door. It was obvious to me when we were walking through Kensington Park. My heart feels things when I am with you that I feel at no other time."

I listened with a full heart. Of course I knew.

"But just because something is happening between us," he went on, "doesn't mean we are to pursue it. It doesn't mean it is necessarily right. That's why we have to wait to see what God says. As great as is my love for you, it will always be a love that must be subordinate to my love for and obedience to God. That's what's wrong

with the world—people think that feeling love is the only justifica-
tion for pursuing it fully. But that's a wrong perspective. *Feeling* love
doesn't mean love is to be pursued. Some loves are to be denied
so that they contribute to greater purposes, even higher loves. I was
privileged to deny my love for you for the greater good of Alasdair's
love. It is one of the great joys of my life—a bittersweet joy, but a
joy nonetheless—to have been given the privilege of loving you and
to sacrifice my love in order that Alasdair's might flower in its fullness. So love may exist—but we may be called upon to deny it, to
relinquish it for a greater good."

He drew in a long breath and exhaled slowly.

"I don't yet know where it is leading," he said. "But I had to come
back to find out."

"*Do* you think we will be called upon to deny it?" I asked. I was
almost fearful of what might be Iain's answer.

"I don't know, Marie. Honestly, speaking from the depths of my
heart, I have to say I hope not. But long ago I ceased to rule my
own affairs. I am under orders. Until those orders come, my motto
is . . . to wait."

I smiled. I hoped not, too. But if Iain was now trusting *me*, I knew
that I could likewise trust *him*.

"We will be watched and scrutinized," he went on. "How we
handle this—for Alasdair's sake, for the sake of the community,
for the sake of our witness of Christ—I as a curate, you as the
duchess . . . everything must be absolutely scrupulous. We must walk
in complete transparency and integrity. Your reputation will be my
highest priority. With my living in Huntly we can be open, we can
see one another as often as we like, while still preserving our lives
in separate communities. I cannot think that it will strike anyone as
untoward for two former friends to reestablish their friendship in full
view of the community."

Again came a brief pause.

"I don't know what we are to do," Iain added. "I know that I
love you, Angel Dawn Marie Buchan Lorcini Reidhaven. I will never

love another. When the angel who is beside me appeared in my life, she was the only angel for me. Yet we must walk slowly and carefully . . . and give God time."

I slipped my hand through Iain's arm and we walked along the sea for another mile without a word. I don't think I have ever been so at peace in all my life.

Chapter Fifty-three

Interlude of Peace

Where the roses blush and bloom mid the waving trees and broom,
And the busy bees are gath-ring in their store,
I would sent me in the glade, mid the green and gold array'd,
And breathe the breeze of heav'n ever more.
—J. S. Skinner, "Where the Roses Blush and Bloom"

Things obviously changed dramatically with my knowing Iain was now living in Huntly. The fact that he made no secret of his return made it easier. Within a week everyone knew he was back in the north, knew that I had gone to London to inform him of Alasdair's death, knew that he was no longer in the active ministry but was working in construction, and knew that we were unembarrassed about our friendship and that we intended to see as much of each other as we wanted.

He visited the Deskmill Parish Church regularly, was often asked to read Scripture by Reverend Gillihan, and substituted for him when he was away. Though he and his sister Katie lived in Huntly, he was often seen in both Port Scarnose and Crannoch. He had no intention, he said, of slinking about or of trying to hide himself from view. Let people say what they wanted, he would live in the light. He would likewise visit me in full sight of the community.

On Iain's first Saturday back, we lunched together at Puddleduck at the busiest time of day. Then we walked through Crannoch's streets, popped into Crannoch Collectibles and Abra Antiques and Slorach's Hardware, and the Crannoch Ice-Cream Shop for two ice-cream cones before heading on foot along the viaduct to Port

Scarnose. After that day, news about the return of the former curate was out in the open in full view of everybody.

The tide was out as we walked along, the golf links stretching a gorgeous green below the viaduct all the way to the equally gorgeous blue of the sea. It was a warm summer's day. The beach was filled with children and dogs and swimmers and walkers.

"Why is that rock down there called Florimel's Rock?" I asked, pointing out to the elongated black mussel-encrusted rock that stretched a little way out into the water opposite the towering red boulder at the shore called the Bore Craig.

"Its traditional name is the Black Foot," replied Iain. "But the name Florimel comes from George MacDonald's classic that was set in Crannoch and Port Scarnose."

"The Victorian novelist—yes, I know about MacDonald. I've read some of his books that are in the castle library. "

Iain nodded. "Did you know that he stayed in Crannoch in the 1870s when he wrote his novel set in this region?"

"I'd heard that. But I haven't read that one. I couldn't follow the dialect."

"One of his characters, the daughter of the local marquis, was sitting on the Black Foot reading a book as the tide gradually came in and engulfed her before she realized it."

"Was she in danger?"

"Possibly of being swept off the rock, but hardly of being drowned. The water wouldn't have been higher than her waist. But it took her by surprise. You can always tell where the tide is with a quick glance at Florimel's Rock. At high tide it is invisible, completely submerged. At low tide its base is visible on the sand and you can walk all the way out to it."

"I had almost the same experience once," I said. "It was the day when I was thinking about your sermon about the prodigal and about the meaning of God's Fatherhood. But I got off the rock I was on before it got that high. So what happened to the girl Florimel?"

"The hero of the story, a young fisherman called Malcolm, ran through the water, scooped her up in his arms, and carried her back to the beach."

"Sounds romantic. Did they fall in love?"

"Uh...a difficult question to answer." Iain smiled mysteriously. "Not exactly. Florimel thought Malcolm rude—and he smelled of fish."

"I can tell I will have to read it," I said, laughing. "I will have to keep working on trying to read the dialect."

"Findlater also comes into MacDonald's tale. A terrible accident takes place there and the marquis, Florimel's father, is badly injured. It really is a dangerous place. There's also a witch-lady in the story who knows of a secret passage to Findlater."

"Is that true?" I asked.

"Some say so," replied Iain. "The story goes that the first inhabitants of Findlater, for it was the first of the three castles or great houses of the region—"

"Which three?" I asked.

"Findlater, then Deskford, then Castle Buchan. The Picts who first occupied this coastline were particularly exposed to the attacks of the Vikings. When the Viking onslaught began it was especially fierce in the north of Scotland. It is said the Picts contrived to escape by means of the tunnel they had discovered, which led inland. When the castle was later built on the site, perhaps it served some other purpose, or was used in the same way against threats from the Danes."

"Was it a natural tunnel?"

"I don't know. Perhaps they excavated it to lengthen what the sea had carved out naturally through time."

"Why doesn't anyone try to find it?"

Iain laughed. "Actually, Alasdair and I did. But we found nothing. Everything about Findlater now, its inner rooms and vaults and broken staircases, is much too dangerous and far beyond the stage of decay where exploration is possible. Any tunnel that might once have existed would surely be caved in and filled with stones by now anyway."

"Are there really ghosts at the castle?" I asked.

"*Your* castle?"

I nodded.

"It depends on who you ask." Iain laughed. "My friend Leslie Mair says he has heard strange noises when working there. The years are full of stories of sightings—the green lady, she's called. But then Fyvie Castle has its own green lady, too, as well as a secret burial crypt where legend says a mad earl trapped the green lady, then sealed her tomb from the outside, leaving her to die where no one would ever find her. She takes her revenge by roaming about haunting the place. The similarity of the two stories would seem to diminish the likelihood of either being true, in my opinion."

"It all sounds spooky!" I said with a shudder. "I'm glad the sun is shining. What about the crypt beneath the church?"

"That much of it apparently is true," said Iain. "No one knows how to get there, because, like the mad earl's hidden tomb at Fyvie, the descent to the crypt from the church was entirely covered over by the floors of the church that were built on top of the original structure. The present floor now contains tombs of the Ogilvies and Grants and Sinclairs and lords and ladies of ages past, including some portion of the entrails of Robert the Bruce's wife, Elizabeth."

"Ugh!"

"She died while visiting this region, you know. This whole area, including your home, is very historic. But the long and the short of it is that no one will ever find the way to the crypt because the graves and tombs beneath the church floor are not only historic, they are a sacred part of Scotland's legendary past. No one would ever get permission to excavate and potentially disturb the bowels of one of Scotland's queens."

By this time we had arrived at the end of the viaduct and into the streets of Port Scarnose. We made our way down to the promontory at the end of town where Bow Fiddle Rock was visible, then through the village, past the harbor, and eventually all the way back to the entrance of Castle Buchan.

Gossip, of course, in the weeks that followed raged like a wildfire. The tongues of the auld wives wagged indeed.

But it died down soon enough. Our obvious unembarrassed and unabashed enjoyment of each other, Iain's perfect decorum as a gentleman, and that we gave not the slightest appearance of being other than good friends was evident. And as word got around that Iain was writing a book about Alasdair, which would obviously involve me, people got used to seeing us together. As there was no talk of marriage, there ceased to be much to fuel the gossip. People spoke of "the curate and the duchess" as not scandal, but as one of the many facts of interest that surrounded the life of Castle Buchan and its environs. I didn't mind the talk. I liked having Iain back in the area. Simply knowing he was nearby, as Alasdair's friend and mine, gave me a sense of security and safety.

Meanwhile, Sunday open-castle gatherings resumed. I encouraged both Iain and Ranald to participate as much as they were able, as my twin spiritual advisers and male authority figures, whom I now depended on with my husband gone. I took comfort in knowing I had two strong men close to me and watching out for me. Gradually a few mothers began asking about harp lessons for their youngsters. My harp studio slowly began to fill with the happy sounds of young musicians. Intimidated at first by taking lessons at the castle, by the time of our first recital, the Music Room was filled with parents and friends and grandparents of the young harpists, as comfortable in their surroundings as if we had been in the town hall.

Nigel Crathie and Alicia Forbes were married by Reverend Gillihan the following spring at the Deskmill Parish Church, with a great reception on the castle grounds. By then Nigel had become such a friend to us all and such a fixture around the castle, I approached him with an offer. He had already decided to relocate his office to Port Scarnose from Elgin. He did not want to take Alicia from her friends and roots, he said. He could conduct his business anywhere.

I proposed to him to inexpensively let he and Alicia as many rooms of the south wing as they might need to feel comfortable—even to remodel to suit their needs—if they would like to establish a home in the castle to begin their marriage.

"The place is huge," I said. "I want it filled with people. I know it may not fit into your permanent plans, but you are welcome to be part of the castle family as long as you like."

Nigel took my suggestion one step further. In the end we not only remodeled for their living accommodations, he set up his legal offices in the south wing as well.

"It will be the most prestigious solicitor's address in Scotland," he said proudly.

Alicia continued to act as my part-time housekeeper in charge of the day staff. I hired Cora as her assistant, and she moved into Alicia's former apartment. As confidentiality was so important in his work, Nigel set up his offices such that he and his clients were free to come and go through a separate entrance without disturbing or being seen from the rest of the house.

Chapter Fifty-four

Surprise Visitor

Hoo, O! Soon shall I see them, O; Hee, O! See them, O see them, O;
Ho-ro! Soon shall I see them, the mist-covered mountains of home.
There I shall visit the place of my birth, and they'll give me
a welcome, the warmest on earth;
All so loving and kind, full of music and mirth,
in the sweet-sounding language of home.
—John Cameron, "The Mist-Covered Mountains of Home"

When Alicia came to me with a repeat of the announcement she had made the day Iain unexpectedly appeared, I was naturally curious when I saw her expression. I was not able to read what she was thinking.

"You have a visitor," she said.

I returned her statement with a look of question.

"You will want to see this one," added Alicia. "Trust me."

"Iain again . . . with flowers?" I asked as I rose.

"Just wait and see."

I followed her downstairs. At the door stood Adela Cruickshank. It was a greater shock than seeing Iain.

My mouth fell open. Suddenly I understood Alicia's expression.

The expression on Adela's face, however, was much different than I would have expected. She was obviously embarrassed and a little intimidated, perhaps almost fearful. She could not meet my eyes.

"Adela!" I exclaimed. "How nice to see you! Won't you come in?"

"I dinna ken gien I sud . . . I came only . . . That is . . . I jist—"

"Adela, please," I said, reaching out and taking her hand. "The past is forgiven—please, it would mean a great deal to me if you came in."

She smiled sheepishly, still embarrassed and averting her eyes. Alicia stood in the entryway. I could read her face like a book. I knew it might be more difficult for her to forgive than it was for me. She was eyeing our visitor with a cold stare.

"Alicia," I said, "tell Cora that Adela is here. Why don't the two of you fix us a great tea. This is time for a celebration. It's like Adela has come home, isn't it? We will be in the studio."

Slowly, Alicia turned away.

"Come, Adela," I said. "You remember the way!"

Hesitantly, still not quite sure what to make of my welcome, Adela timidly followed. She was obviously shy about entering the regions where she had herself been housekeeper for a season.

"I don't know if you knew," I said as we went, "but Alicia is married now—to Nigel Crathie, my husband's friend and solicitor."

"I had heard somethin' aboot it," said Adela.

"They are actually staying here, in the south wing," I went on. "And you remember Cora; she is working for me, too. She is staying in Alicia's former rooms . . . and yours, too, of course. She will be delighted to see you."

We entered the studio. I led Adela to one of the couches and sat down opposite her. She glanced about at the familiar surroundings, but remained uneasy.

"I . . . wanted tae see ye, mem . . . Duchess—" she began.

"Please, Adela. We know one another too well for that!"

She smiled nervously.

"I didna ken fit I sud call ye. But I've been workin' . . . ye may hae kennt . . . I went tae Aberdeen, ye ken, wi' Olivia—"

"Yes, I knew." I nodded.

"I dinna ken hoo tae say't . . . er, uh, Marie . . . 'tis a sair thing, ye ken . . . but I see noo . . . that is . . . I ken noo that I was mair nor a mite foolish an' . . . I sudna hae believed all o' the things she said aboot ye . . . I ken . . . that is, I think I kennt they werena true, but . . . I, that is...she could mak me sair confused like, that I believed onythin' she told me...She has a way, ye ken, a way o' makin' people believe her...an' I dinna ken—"

She glanced away. I stood and walked over and sat down beside her and placed my hand on her arm. She sniffed a time or two. I reached for a tissue from the low table in front of us and handed it to her. She was struggling with tears. Knowing Adela as I did, I suspected that it was difficult for her to cry.

"I see noo...she was sae full o' anger an' hate...why I didna see't afore...I dinna ken hoo she cud mak me hate jist like her...She blint me een, I believed things I sudna hiv believed...I am sorry, Marie—I sud hae kennt ye werena what she said."

"Oh, Adela," I said, "she could make us all terribly confused. She confused me, too. I understand how difficult it must have been for you."

"But I sud hae kennt...I am aye sorry—"

She glanced away and wiped at her eyes.

"I didna want tae face ye, Marie," she struggled to continue. "I didna ken fit ye might say. Ye hae ilka right tae be angry wi' me for all the mischief I caused ye. Div ye think Alicia will e'er forgive me? She was sich a frien', but I was dreadfu' tae her, too."

"I am sure she will," I said.

Just then Alicia and Cora came in, wheeling a cart with a spread of finger foods and two pots steaming with tea. Their expressions as they entered were obviously a little mixed, with hints and reminders of the past. But one look at Adela on the couch with me, my hand on her arm, and she wiping at her eyes with a tissue, was enough to begin thawing both their hearts. Most people—not all, but most—I believe are ready enough to forgive in the light of a humble and repentant heart.

"Adela has apologized to me for misunderstanding many things before," I said, breaking the ice. "She says that Olivia was able to confuse her and make her believe things she knew weren't true. Is that right, Adela—have I represented accurately what you meant to tell me?"

"Aye . . . 'tis jist it, ye see."

That was all it took. We had all suffered from the same fate. With Adela's contrite admission unlocking the dam, the floodgates broke open wide. Within minutes the three friends of youth were chattering away like schoolgirls about their memories of their time together under Olivia's control. Alicia and Cora shared how they had struggled to break free from it in recent years. Adela explained how her eyes had at last been opened to the truth of what Olivia had been doing to her for so long. As they chatted, with the harps of my studio around us, it occurred to me, as much as it represents the music of heaven, the language of the harp is the language of forgiveness. It was obvious—among her friends, forgiven, at last at peace with them and herself—that Adela felt at home.

After an hour or so, the conversation took an unexpectedly serious turn.

"I dinna ken gien ye heard," said Adela after Cora had just returned from the kitchen with fresh hot water, "but Max was killed on the rigs a year syne."

The news stunned Alicia and Cora especially. They had grown up with Max and had once known him well. As often as I had been in the Urquhart home, however, I had actually never met Olivia's husband. He had always been a mysterious shadow-man lurking behind the scenes.

"We knew nothing about it," I said. "Is Olivia alone now, or—How is she handling it? I didn't have the idea they were especially close. Has it been difficult for her?"

"Na, they werena close," Adela went on. "I dinna doobt she did the same tae puir Max she did wi' ilka body she met. She hadna shown him muckle o' the love o' a wife these mony a lang year, I'm thinkin', gien ye ken my meanin'. But nae lang after that I began tae see a change in her. At first I thocht 'twas jist on account o' losin' Max, ye ken, but as time gaed on, she was pale an' weak—no' like hersel'. She went till the doctor an' that's fan we learned she had the cancer."

The dreaded word fell like a bomb. Again, we all took in the news with momentary silence.

"She went for treatment," Adela continued, "but it only made her mair an' mair angry an' bitter, an' I couldna bide it. She had nae right tae gae blamin' me for her ills, me wha's stood by her these lang years mair nor I sud hae dune, an' I regret it noo. She blamed ilka body, especially yersel', Marie . . . an' Alasdair, the duke, I'm meanin', God rest his soul. She e'en blamed ye for her cancer. 'Tis whan it began tae dawn on me— Did I want tae become like her—a miserable bitter wretch o' a woman? She was sick, but I didna pity her for that, but for bein' sae decrepit an' lonely an' accusin' the whole rest o' the worl', but ne'er lookin' intil her ain sel'. Nae, I said tae mysel'—I didna want tae become like her. 'Tis whan I gie her my notice. I suppose it may hae been an ill thing o' me tae du, but jist bein' aroun' her was drainin' the life right oot o' me. I couldna bide it nae mair. She was angert mair nor I hae seen in man nor beast—cursin' at me, accusin' me o' desertin' her in her time o' need, callin' me dreadfu' names—me, after a' the years I gie her, an' she ne'er gie me no' so much as a brass farthin' extra, nae on Christmas, nae fan I was sick, an' then she refused tae pay me my last week wages on account o' desertin' her, she said.

"She's like ane o' them fa's got mair siller nor maist folk, but is always frettin' ower't like she was a pauper. Always talkin' aboot siller, she was, as gien she had nane, angert that she didna git mair o' the duke's, ken. I dinna ken whaur it went, but I dinna think she had muckle left at the end, an' she wadna e'en gie me fit she owed. Then she shouted ane o' her evil rhymin' spells at me like I hadn't heard oot o' her mouth in mony a lang year, spittin' the words at me like she was shoutin' oot fae the veery pit o' hell itsel'. It made me shudder wi' a chill colder nor the snaws on Ben Nevis, an' filled me wi' dread. But no' for mysel' . . . 'twas like her words was a curse on her ain sel'. Her cancer isna in her banes, 'tis a cancer in her soul. She's aye dyin' twa deiths, an' I didna want tae dee wi' her. An' I left an' ne'er looked back. She showed me fit she was, an' I saw hoo wrang I had aye been aboot the rest o' ye."

We all were sitting with mouths open and eyes wide.

"*Is* she dying, Adela?" I asked.

"I dinna ken," said Adela, shaking her head. "I left her four month syne. I went tae Glasgow tae live wi' my sister for a spell, ken. I lost touch wi' Olivia. I didna want tae ken a thing aboot her. But I kennt I had tae come back. I had tae tell ye a' hoo sorry I was, an' I thocht ye maun ken aboot her gien ye didna on account o' her bein' the duke's sister, ye ken."

Chapter Fifty-five

Difficult Decision

Nae partin' words were spoken,
That nicht, lang syne,
But twa aged hearts were broken,
In the lang, lang syne.
—J. S. Skinner, "The Lang, Lang Syne"

I went to the Elms in Crannoch that same day and told them that Adela would be staying with me at the castle, and paid them for the night she had already booked.

Adela remained with us a week before returning to her sister's. It was as if the past had never happened. Cora and Tavia, and Fia and Alicia as well, took her back to their hearts with complete forgiveness. The five together found great healing simply in being able to talk freely with one another about their own experiences and the different ways Olivia had been able to control and influence their thought patterns and how they had each learned to overcome its effects in their own lives. She spent a good deal of time in my studio, too, playing quietly on the *Shamrock* and humming softly to herself.

Something else, however, was on my mind. I mentioned it to Iain, then he and I went to consult Ranald. He took in the news of Max's death and Olivia's cancer soberly, sadly, and with grave concern.

"The puir woman," he said. "I only haup she hasna waited too lang."

"Too long for what?" I asked.

"Tae repent," replied Ranald. "I haup she hasna burned the veery life oot o' her conscience wi' the flames o' her ain selfishness an' evil."

"I can hardly imagine Olivia *repenting* of anything," I said. "The idea of it would be hateful to her. She would resist it with the last ounce of her strength, I hate to say it, but right up till her dying day."

"Aye, but repentance is the only door tae life. We maunna call ony time too late."

"Do you think," I said, "I mean, could there be a chance that Olivia might at last...Maybe it is wishful thinking, but *could* she be ready to be reconciled with us—with me, with you, Ranald...and to put her animosities behind her?"

I could tell my question struck deep in Ranald's heart and mind. Iain and I waited.

"I wud tak the puir woman straight intil my arms," said Ranald at length. "I wud sit at her bedside an' spoon the milk o' kindness intil her wi' my ain hand. I wud sooth an' stroke her hair wi' the love o' a father till his child, e'en kennin' as I du that she took the life o' my ain Maggie— I'd du my best tae love her wi' the love o' God the Father o' us a'...*gien* she'd only luik intae her ain soul tae see fit God wants us a' tae see. But wi'oot repentance, there's nae place tae git a haud, nae place tae drop the anchor o' forgiveness intil the harbor o' love sae that the Father-hert can find its way intil her. A body's got tae repent. She *maun* face the evil's she's dune tae sae many. She winna git aff wi'oot payin' the last farthin' o' the debts o' conscience, nae mair nor will I, an' woe till her gien she winna du't. But tae repent's an ill thing for ane such as her. There's mony a consequence tae be faced, mony a debt tae be paid. Whether she'll see the need o' it in this life, nae livin' man can say."

As he had been listening, I noticed a strange look on Iain's face.

"Do you mind if I ask you a question, Ranald?" he said.

"We've a' been through too muckle ower the years, laddie, for ye tae be spierin' sich a thing."

Iain smiled. "Don't answer if you would rather not," he said. "But your forgiving heart toward Olivia is such an example to me. If it's not presuming too greatly, I would like to know what happened to Maggie."

An expression of deep emotion passed through Ranald's eyes. He sat for some time, obviously reliving what was a very painful memory.

"I ne'er told anither livin' soul," he said at length, "aboot what took place that day. But perhaps 'tis time at last wi' the twa closest frien's o' my hert."

He drew in a deep breath and exhaled slowly.

"I had suspected ill motives afoot," he began, "all that day lang. I kennt Olivia's evil, an' I kennt that my Maggie couldna leave weel enough alane, bless her. 'Tis why I followed her, but I reached Findlater too late. They were already arguin' an' yellin' at ane anither fan I was still a long way aff. I heard the curses fae Olivia's foul mouth ower the wind. 'Twas like naethin' I hae heard syne my days in the military, which isna a place whaur pureness o' hert is athegither honored. An' the instant I heard her sweerin' wi' sich abandon, I kennt the evil had grip o' her. I couldna rin like I once did for I was gettin' auld in the knees for it wasna sae lang syne, but I hurried as fast as I could. But I was too late. I saw them scufflin', then my Maggie screamed an' disappeared ower the cliff. My hert smote me wi' terror. *'God, oh God,'* I cried. *'Dinna let it be! God, preserve her!'* I ran on, wi' tears pourin' doon my face an' cryin' oot tae the Lord, hardly noticin' that Olivia was nae mair tae be seen. Whether she had fallen hersel', or had gone after Maggie tae help her, I didna ken.

"I reached the cliff an' Olivia was jist disappearin' alang the path doon tae Sunnyside. She ne'er looked back nor once kennt what I had seen. As for the thocht o' helpin', 'twas clear she wasna thinkin' ony sich thing. An' straight below me on the rocks at the water's edge I saw my puir Maggie, lyin' still and lifeless."

I gasped in shock. "Oh, Ranald!" I said as I began to cry.

"Aye, lass—'twas the moment o' truth o' my life, whan I had tae see what I was made o', an' gien I really believed in the goodness o' oor Father's hert. Weepin' an' crying oot till her, I scrambled doon the lang way roun', winnin' my way at last doon till the rocks near the Doo's Cave. She was jist breathin' her last whan I reached her, moanin' but faintly wi' her dyin' breath. I didna ken gien she was in pain or no, but her een were closed an' she seemed at peace. Babblin' an' weepin', horror-struck at the sight, I sat beside her an' took her gently in my arms an' kissed her face an' whispered till her a' the words o' a lifetime o' a man's love.

"*'I was right, Ranald,'* she said, sae, sae saft. *'She did it . . . jist like I said. She kennt a' aboot Winny.'* Her voice was jist a whisper. *'Aye, but 'tis nae maitter noo,'* I said till her. *'Winny's waitin' for ye.'* My Maggie sighed and seemed to smile. *'Aye, ye're in the richt . . . There she is . . . she's comin' oot o' the licht, jist there . . . I can see her, she's aye been waitin' for me . . .'* But her voice was already too saft for me tae hear mair. And those were her last words tae me. She was gane tae Winny."

I burst into sobs. I couldn't help it. What the poor man had endured!

"I carried her in my arms back tae Crannoch. 'Twasna easy, for I wasna a yoong man. But I wasna aboot tae leave my Maggie alane, no' then. All the way the anger o' man battled wi' the Speerit tae git the upper hand. An' anger an' guilt to mysel' for no' gaein' sooner. I kennt weel enough that one word fae me wud put Olivia in jail, an' I was sair put upon by the de'il tae tell what my een had seen. But afore I saw anither human face, the word o' the Lord had burned intil my soul—*'Vengeance is mine,'* the Lord said. *'Dinna prevent me doin' my ain wark wi' yer sma' revenge o' the flesh. My wark's bigger nor ye ken nor can see. Keep yer ain hand awa' fae her; Olivia's mine tae du what I can wi' her.'*

"An' so I told naebody what I had seen, only that my Maggie had fallen an' I had foun' her on the rocks. An' by-an'-by, oot o' that obedience, the Lord softened my hert e'en toward Olivia hersel', an' I grew tae pity the puir woman, for I began tae see what was in store for her gien she didna repent. An' I said nae word tae her nor onyone aboot it, until that day in court, ye min', Marie, lass, whan I

kennt the Lord was givin' me leave t' speik at last till her an' tell her
what I saw, tae mak' her stop her lies aboot yersel'."

Iain and I sat listening, more moved than at anything we had
heard in our lives. Iain's eyes and cheeks were as wet as mine. And
after all that, Ranald was now suggesting going in search of Olivia,
to extend forgiveness and compassion toward her!

Much more serious discussion and prayer passed between us.

"None of us can know Olivia's heart," said Iain. "But we know that
it is often the Lord's way to use sickness to probe the conscience
in areas that have not before lain open to the heavenly light or yet
yielded themselves to the divine scalpel. Who can say—perhaps it
might indeed finally be time."

"I hate the thought of her suffering with cancer alone," I said,
shaking my head sadly. "I wish we could do something for her."

"Maybe we can, lass," mused Ranald thoughtfully.

"It is probably the last thing anyone would expect of me, but if
she is dying, and if *you* can forgive her a sin far worse than anything
she has done to me, I cannot hold a grudge," I said. "It's not easy,
but I know that God wants us to have compassion for her. Especially
after what Adela said—that she is frail and bitter and lonely. In spite
of what you've told us, I do feel sorry for her. She is Alasdair's sister,
and I owe her my forgiveness in the way that you have forgiven her.
I am the only family she has left. Why could we not bring her here
and nurse her—who knows, maybe back to health, or, if not, help
ease her dying if that is where it is leading?"

I thought a moment more.

"I wonder if I should go to Aberdeen and try to see her," I suggested.

"It winna be enouch tae see her, lass," said Ranald. "She maun be
confronted wi' what she is an' has dune. Dinna forgit, it wasna sae
lang syne that she tried her best tae kill ye, too. Invitin' her back an'
tryin' tae minister tae her's a fine thing, an' I honor ye for it wi' a'
my hert. But the Lord's aye got her *complete* healin' in mind. The
prodigal's got tae come a' the way back."

"Do you think I shouldn't go look for her, then?" I asked.

Ranald thought again. He was obviously turning many things over in his mind. At length he began nodding his head as if in decision.

"Her chief antagonism has always been wi' me," he said slowly. "'Tis me that maun gae till her. I'm the one she's sinned agin' wi'oot repentance. Gien she's tae return, it maun be by comin' tae terms wi' her sin toward me an' her hatred o' *me* first. I'll gang tae Aberdeen."

"What will you do?" I asked.

"I will gie a' oor condolences aboot puir Max. Then I will tell her 'tis time, that she has waited lang enouch, an' spier gien she's ready tae repent o' what's in her hert. Gien she's aye facin' deith, there's nae sense playin' games wi' her soul. She's *got* tae repent. Ilka body's got tae repent. Then I will tell her that I've come on a mission fae the duchess, her brither's wife, tae spier gien she'd be happier in the hame o' her childhood, an' tell her that she's welcome an' that there's mony hands waitin' tae love her an' serve her."

Iain listened seriously, nodding all the while as Ranald was speaking. When he was through and we had prayed and reached a consensus, both Iain and I offered again to go ourselves, or drive him into the city. But Ranald insisted this was something he had to do alone.

"Then go, Ranald," I said. "Go and bring her back to us. This is her home. We need to try to minister life and God's love and forgiveness to her."

Ranald left on the Bluebird two mornings later for Aberdeen. He was gone three days.

On the afternoon of the second day, Ranald telephoned me from his hotel.

"I need tae confer wi' ye, lass," he said, "an' see what ye'll be thinkin' I ocht tae du."

"Did you find Olivia?" I asked.

"Aye. It took me mair nor a day—she wasna at the hoosie nor a sign o' her. But spierin' aroun' wi' neighbors an' wi' visits tae a handfu' o' hospitals an' clinics finally led me till her at a private ward for cancer patients fa canna tak care o' themsel's but fa's got siller tae pay for private care. But her siller's maist gane an' hoo lang they'll keep her, I dinna ken."

"How is she?"

"She disna luik good, lass. I hardly kennt her wi' her yellow skin an' sunken eyes an' shrunken frame. She luiked older nor me."

"What did she say?" I asked.

"She jist luiked up at me wi' her dark een wi' nae sign o' feelin'. 'What div ye want?' she said. 'Gien ye came tae ease yer conscience, ye can leave me be. I dinna need yer pity.'"

"She said that!" I exclaimed.

"Aye, lass. For a' her sufferin', she isna humbled for't."

"What did you say?"

"I spiered gien she was ready tae repent."

"And what did she say?"

"She jist lauched in my face, a bitter, hard, cold, raspin' lauch—it was the lauch o' the veery de'il himsel'. 'Repent!' she spat back. 'I'll repent whan I stand on yer grave an' curse yer soul! What hae I tae repent o'?'"

"She said that!" I repeated. "I can't believe it. What is she thinking? Didn't she care that you had come to visit her?"

"It meant naethin' till her. She's still full o' the venom o' hate."

"Did you tell her I would like her to come home?"

"Aye. That silenced her. She sat glowerin' doon at the floor, staring wi' her dark, sunken een intil whate'er cesspool o' memories sich like stare intil. I saw that she was revolving the thing ower in her mind fae ilka direction."

"What did you do?" I asked.

"Finally I left her wi'oot anither word an' cam tae talk tae ye an' spier what ye want me tae du."

"How do you mean?"

"Div ye want me tae try tae bring her?"

"Will she come?"

"I dinna ken. I left after tellin' her fit ye said, an' she was thinkin' hard."

"Do you *think* she might come?"

"I dinna ken, lass. 'Tis a dangerous thing tryin' tae coax the prodigal hame afore he's ready. Wi'oot repentance there's nae hame-comin'. 'Tis like tryin' tae befrien' a snake fa's still got its fangs an' its poison. The prodigal's got tae repent, an' *then* arise an' gang till his father, no' jist gang hame till his warm bed an' meals an' a' his comforts fan there's been nae change in his hert. Sae we maun tak care o' takin' her in an' thinkin' we're helpin' her gien the viper's still in her."

"Do you think she is dying, Ranald?" I asked.

"Deith is written all ower her face, lass. But no the right kind o' deith, no the deith that brings life."

I thought a few minutes.

"I can't turn my back on her, Ranald," I said. "I just can't. If she will come, bring her home."

Chapter Fifty-six

Guest from Aberdeen

Let worldly worms their minds oppress
Wi' fears o' want and double cess,
And sullen sots themsel's distress
Wi' keeping up decorum.
But for the discontented fool,
Wha wants to be oppression's tool
May envy gnaw his rotten soul,
And discontent devour him.
—Rev. John Skinner, "Tullochgorum"

When Ranald arrived back in Port Scarnose two days later, the shrunken, weak, feeble lady beside him with thinning white hair and stooped shoulders, a mere forty-nine alongside Ranald's seventy-three, was recognized by no one as he helped her off the bus. What might have been going through the woman's mind as her eyes fell upon the village over which, in a manner of speaking, she had once ruled, both as a girl and, for a season, as the presumed duchess? Now she was being helped off the bus by the very hand of a man she had despised all her life, a man whose wife, and maybe whose daughter she had also killed if Maggie's dying words were right, yet who had never brought charges against her, and who was now doing his best to minister the compassion of mutual humanity to her. Is such a one even capable of grasping the first elemental principles of such a forgiveness as had been sitting at her side for the past two hours?

Ranald had telephoned ahead. Iain and I were there to meet them

381

and take Olivia directly to the castle. Nicholls and Tavia, Alicia and
Cora, and most of the day staff were on hand, standing in the entryway to welcome her, if not with open arms, certainly with smiles
and greetings and handshakes and well-wishes.

I had moved out of my apartment so that Olivia could be in as
familiar surroundings as possible. A banner proclaiming "Welcome
Back to Castle Buchan" stood above the door as Alicia and I escorted
her down the corridor. Flowers and a bowl of fruit sat on the table
as we entered.

Up till then, Sarah Duff had continued as a day maid, though she
had been on the castle's full-time staff for a year prior to Alasdair's
death. She was twenty-three now and had been a particular favorite
of Olivia's. I made Sarah Olivia's personal attendant and offered to
have her come live at the castle for a substantial increase in pay,
and occupy a room of her own across the hall from the entrance
to Olivia's new apartment and adjacent to Cora. She'd had nursing
training when she worked at Leith Home as a caregiver for dementia
and terminal patients. She was not intimidated by the more difficult
aspects of extreme care. Her only assignment would be to see to
Olivia's every need, and to summon me if those needs were beyond
her.

I made arrangements for a specialist from Dr. Gray's Hospital in
Elgin to come to the castle to evaluate her, give me a thorough
assessment of her condition and prospects, and to take over her
treatment and medications from the clinic in Aberdeen.

All this—from the greeting, banner and fruit, to a personal attendant, to the medical care—Olivia took in stride as if it were
expected.

Not a word of gratitude once passed her lips.

You would think that having one more person in a castle as large
as Buchan, with as many people as were coming and going, and as
much activity as was constantly about the place, would not make
a great difference. But when that person is a malcontent, a divider,
a spreader of division, never was a truer word spoken than "A lit-

tle leaven leavens the whole lump." The effect of Olivia's presence was noticeable immediately. An invisible cloud settled over the castle. Tiny grumblings could be heard. A different spirit was about the place. I even noticed it in my harp students, who knew nothing of what was going on. Their usual exuberance was subdued. They were uncharacteristically snippy at one another, occasionally irritable toward me.

I must say I was gratified that not a single person on the staff, to my knowledge, succumbed to any of Olivia's subtle divisiveness. Even her former favorites—from Sarah, her attendant, to Farquharson, who had now become my indispensable and loyal handyman—found themselves repulsed by her negativity, grouchiness, and spirit of constant complaint. They say old age and sickness bring out the traits a person has been invisibly building into the soil of his or her character all their lives. Those lifelong flowers at last blossom—either into the beautiful and fragrant petals of a sweet and humble spirit of grace, or into the bitter weeds of rancor, regret, and complaint. We are all preparing throughout our lives for the character that will emerge during our gray-haired years. In Olivia's case, though it came earlier than expected, for she was not yet fifty, that character garden bore the foul aroma of selfishness. No one found any joy being near her. A seventeenth-century monk once said that a sour old person is one of the crowning works of the devil. That there was no change in Olivia was certainly clear evidence of that truth.

Olivia rarely went out in the first week, but gradually could be seen around the castle or out on the grounds with Sarah. She had a wheelchair, a walker, and canes all at her disposal, but was not reduced to quite such a level of infirmity yet. Though she occasionally allowed herself to be wheeled from her room and down the elevator to the ground floor, she was still able to walk about and get outside when it was warm. I thought I saw signs of a slight improvement in her condition, a strengthening of her walk, slightly less pallor in her cheeks. We were feeding her well, though she did not take meals with those of us who usually ate together—Cora and I and Nicholls and Farquharson and whatever of the staff were on duty at meal-time. She showed no interest in going into the village.

Iain came to the castle more regularly after Olivia's arrival. He seemed watchful and anxious.

"Iain, what is it?" I finally asked one day.

"What's what?"

"You are different, quieter. You seem...I don't know, a little on edge."

"You noticed. Sorry."

"What is it, then?"

"I am concerned about Olivia."

"In what way—about her health, you mean?"

"Her *spiritual* health, not the cancer," he replied. "I don't alto-gether care for the look in her eyes. I have not spoken with her. But even from a distance I catch a glint that makes me nervous. I am concerned that we may have opened the door to something I am not sure I like—the prodigal coming home before repentance has taken place, before he is ready to say, 'I will arise and go to my father.'"

"What harm can she do now? She is dying of cancer."

"Being an unrepentant prodigal whose stock in trade is division, who derived her power from a satanic stronghold of matriarchy and control, without a change, she will be able to work evil literally until the day of her death."

"Do you think it is that serious? None of the staff but Sarah will have a thing to do with her."

"I do think it is serious, though I have no idea how it will manifest itself."

"Actually, I think she is regaining a little strength."

"That may be. Yet it might also increase the danger. Be wary, Marie. I do not think her fangs have yet been drawn. I do not say it was a mistake to bring her into your home because it was done in love and out of a heart of service. We all participated in that decision. But having a contrary spirit under your roof is a matter of grave spiritual concern. Something is wrong. I can feel it. All I say is, remain wary. Remember the Lord's words, *'Be watchful and on guard.'* I do not believe the demon has been thoroughly exorcised."

Chapter Fifty-seven

Bumps in the Night

Fearfu' soughs the boortree bank,
the rifted wood roars wild and drearie;
Loud the iron yet does clank,
and cry o' howlets makes me eerie.
—"O! Are Ye Sleeping, Maggie?"

Iain's words chilled me.

It probably didn't help that since Olivia's coming I was occupying a little-used set of rooms on the third floor of the east wing. Not knowing how long she might be with us, I wanted to relocate myself into quarters where I could be comfortable and carry on my affairs and conduct my business, along with my continued use of Alasdair's office between the library and the Great Room, for an extended period of time.

The apartment was one that had been used by the dowager countess of Buchan a century earlier after the death of her husband. She had been a great local favorite during her life, but in her final years, so the legends said, had gone mad. I thought little of it, knowing that today's dementia was the so-called madness of a century before. The countess's apartment was spacious, actually more luxurious than the apartment Alasdair and I had considered our home and retreat within the huge expanse of the castle. It had a private staircase leading to the ground floor easily connecting to the labyrinth of corridors binding the rest of the great house together like an internal spider's web, and also an outside door at the base of this staircase leading into the central courtyard. It seemed like an ideal place for me—far enough from Olivia that my presence would not be an annoyance to her, but still accessible if I happened to be needed.

Thus far, however, Olivia had shown not the slightest inclination of needing me! After two weeks, Olivia had still not spoken a word to me.

At first it was fine. Moving into new quarters is always fun, even if just a hotel or B-and-B room for one night, and I enjoyed myself for the first couple of weeks.

But then a misty wind blew in from the east—an "eastern haar," as it's called. Then the skies cleared, but the wind was bitterly cold and blew every wisp of smoke from every chimney on the coast of the Moray Firth straight over at ninety degrees. To try to walk while the gale lasted took maximum effort. Great blasts attacked the trees of the castle grounds as if they would whip the tops right off them. Their trunks swayed and creaked. With an occasional loud crack a branch tumbled to the ground now and then. It was an exciting, wild, frightful display of the power of the elements.

The night the haar hit was the first time in my new quarters so far from everyone else, and I found myself jittery with sleeplessness. I heard the wind whistling and howling through every crevice and tile and around every chimney stack and corner of the castle. I imagined no end of banging about outside. The frenetic east wind brought with it dozens of strange sounds I did not like.

It was at such times I really missed having a husband!

Alasdair would have simply said, "It's nothing, go back to sleep." That would have been enough.

Or he might have said, "It's only the Buchan ghosts . . . they won't bother us." Or even, "It's just the green lady roaming about. She's harmless." With him beside me, I would have been fine.

Reassuring myself with such palliatives, however, only made matters worse. The very act of telling myself the Buchan ghosts and the green lady *wouldn't* bother me heightened my own terror that maybe they were lurking in the darkness after all! Remembering my strange dream with the flakes of straw on my bed the next morning didn't help either.

I imagined all sorts of things going on—from assorted Buchan ghosts to the green lady coming to haunt my room, to Viking marauders fooling about in hidden passageways trying to sneak in and whisk me away and hold me for ransom. I tried to keep a fire going in the fireplace, but it was so windy the smoke kept blowing into the room.

But the fireplace, even cold, continued to whistle and moan, as if the wind were blowing down and up from the basement regions out into the wild and tumultuous night sky.

Morning eventually came. Everyone else had experienced their own battles with the imaginary wind-ghosts of the night. Sarah said Olivia had been awake and restless, adding that she had followed her up and down several corridors convinced she was sleepwalking before she eventually returned to her room and settled down without knowing Sarah was watching her.

Oddly, I continued to hear sounds in the night long after the wind spent itself and moved across toward Iceland. That's when I began to have second thoughts about my new accommodations in the dowager countess's apartment. I wasn't especially superstitious, but why torment myself listening to distant banging and clattering from the depths of the castle? Even when there wasn't a breath of wind, I was certain I heard sounds coming from the fireplace. It was okay during the day, but it could be really unnerving at night. I told myself crows were scratching about on the chimney. But even crows I found a little creepy at two in the morning!

I certainly didn't believe there was any green lady haunting Castle Buchan. But I didn't want to meet her either!

Equally peculiar was the fact that the series of windstorms seemed to fill Olivia with more strength, almost as if the wind brought with it some otherworldly source of life that spoke to her depths. The more the wind blew, the more she seemed determined to go out in it, turning to face the gale, her white hair blowing wildly, occasionally shouting into the wind or raising her fist against it.

Observing such peculiarities, I heard Nicholls mutter more than once, "The loony woman's madder than a March hare."

According to Sarah, nighttime only made such behavior worse. Olivia became positively animated, awake half the night, rummaging about in her rooms, talking to herself and opening drawers, searching through closets, and taken to somnambulism on a more extensive scale. Sarah listened with her ear to the door, not knowing what Olivia was up to, afraid of disturbing her, but also more than a little anxious. She was enough a Scots lass, raised on tales of Highland superstitions and the second sight, and knew enough about what was whispered of Olivia among the staff, to find such nighttime peculiarities more than a little fearsome.

On one occasion Sarah followed Olivia down to the kitchen where she also rummaged about, apparently looking for something and muttering strange things to herself. Several nights later Sarah lost track of her wandering somewhere in the east wing for almost an hour. Beside herself and afraid for what I might say, she was about to rouse me, when suddenly she heard Olivia back in her own rooms.

This went on for some time. As Olivia grew more and more strange, Iain grew more and more concerned. I feared dementia or even the onset of Alzheimer's, though neither had the least connection to the advance of her cancer. I also recalled Nigel's conjecture that she was schizophrenic or delusional if not outright insane. If asked, I would have said I believed no such thing. I continued to convince myself that dementia met the case adequately. Yet Nigel's diagnosis was not easily dismissed.

Neither Cora nor Alicia would have anything to do with her.

Chapter Fifty-eight

Soothing Dream

Hush ye, my bairnie, my bonnie wee dearie;
Sleep! come and close the een, heavy and wearie;
Closed are the wearie een, rest are ye takin'—
Soun' be yer sleepin', and bright be yer wakin'.
—"Hush Ye, My Bairnie"

Then came the strangest occurrence since Olivia's arrival had begun to upset the peaceful equilibrium of life at Castle Buchan.

With the rising of the sun one day again came another terrific wind from the east. The crows and gulls flew overhead, squawking and shrieking in the tempest as if heralding the end of the world. Their frenzied tumult seemed to bring upon the castle a visitation of apprehension. Everyone was unaccountably on edge, nervous, jittery, as if a spiritual plague had blown in with the wind. I longed for Iain's calming and strengthening presence. But he and I had had supper together the evening before and he was to work late on this day. I did not expect to see him for several days.

Sarah came to me frantically in the early afternoon.

"I canna find her, mum," she said. The look on her face was one of terror that she was about to lose her job.

"Who, Sarah?"

"My mistress, mum . . . Mrs. Urquhart. She's gone missing."

"She must be around somewhere."

"I've searched high and low, mum. 'Tis two hours now. I'm worried she might have fallen, mum, and it'll be my fault."

"Don't worry, Sarah," I said, following her from my studio where I was

390

getting ready for my afternoon's series of lessons. "I am sure we shall find her. Whatever happens, no one will blame you. My sister-in-law is lucky to have someone as devoted as you. I am very thankful, too."

"'Tis kind of you to say, mum."

Sarah and I went to Olivia's rooms and conducted a quick search. Sarah was right. Olivia was not there.

We set everyone in the castle looking, but no one turned up a trace. At three I returned to my studio for my four students, leaving Nicholls and Farquharson to continue the search. By then the ladies were getting squeamish about what they might stumble onto if they did happen to find Olivia.

I finished lessons about five-thirty. By then the darkness of mid-October was setting in. Still Olivia had not turned up. If she was taking walks and getting lost, as now appeared the case, a diagnosis of Alzheimer's began to loom as a real possibility. I notified the police in Buckie. They came, briefly interrogated Sarah, then drove all the castle entryways several times, looking into the surrounding woods and shrubbery as best they were able in the darkness.

By the time we retired for the night, worse than a harmless walk was on everyone's mind. We all feared that Olivia was in genuine danger and, wherever she had got to, that she might not live through the night. Nicholls speculated that she might have wandered to the village or the sea. She was clearly not strong enough to walk the rocky coastline or keep her balance on the cliffs in the darkness.

The possibility also existed that she was still in the castle, but had fallen and was unable to move. We would just have to wait to see what the morning brought.

In the middle of the night I had the strangest yet most wonderful dream. I dreamed of harp music playing through all the chimneys of the castle. I dreamed I was on the roof somewhere and that all the chimneys were filled with the harmonies of all my students, and more besides, playing on all my favorite harps. The chimneys blew soft windy mysterious harp-melodies coming from deep below. Singing to the music was the softest most lovely voice, though I could make out no words of the mysterious song. It sounded like Gaelic...soft, soothing, mesmerizing, weaving upon me a spell of enchantment as if coming down from the very Highlands on the wind, somehow being drawn into the chimneys of the castle, where it mingled with the music of the harps of my studio.

Just as I began to come awake, even as the dream and the music and the mesmerizing voice began to fade, suddenly I recognized the tune and I knew the familiar words of the ballad I taught all my students. But I was able to catch only the faint ending dream-fragment: *"Over the sea from Skye...over the sea from Skye...over the sea...over the sea...from Skye."*

And then it was gone. I awoke and all was still. I didn't know whether I'd dreamed the sound or actually heard something.

When again I slept, it was peacefully and soundly, until the light of morning shone in through a high window facing south. I dressed and hurried down to the kitchen where I could depend on Farquharson to have water on for his own strong coffee and for those who followed to prepare their own beverage of choice. It was a few minutes after seven. Cora and Sarah were sitting with him waiting for a pot of tea to steep.

"Any sign of Olivia?" I asked.

"No, mum," replied Sarah. "I hardly slept for worrying about her."

"You are certain she did not return to her room?"

"We jist came fae there, Marie," said Cora, "baith o' us. Nae a hint—the bed's no' been slept in."

I glanced toward Farquharson.

"Harvey an' I's been oot since daybreak," he said. "We been all ower the groun's, 'neath the brig, the gardens, the path doon alang the burnie."

"And nothing?"

"No' a footprint tae be seen."

The day advanced. The police came again. The search was expanded to both villages. By midday everyone in town knew that Olivia was missing.

Chapter Fifty-nine

The Sea's Claim

I sit on a knoll and I view the ocean; Ho ro la-heel o,
My bosom is swelling with keen emotion;
Ho riun-een ail-a Na hee hook o, kook ho-riun an.
—Angus McEachearn, "I Sit on a Knoll"

A cloud hung over Buchan Castle all day, and deepened as the morning of the fruitless search advanced.

Dozens of men and women from both villages joined in the search, which by silent accord began to focus on the rocky and jagged coastlincs between Findlater and Crannoch. The sound of the police helicopter whirring back and forth along the shoreline, hovering here and there for a closer look, was a constant reminder to this coastal community that, more often than not when someone went missing, it was the sea making one more claim, serving notice again that these waters were not to be tamed.

Not a few of the older men and women among the searchers found themselves reliving the disappearance of Winny Bain thirty-five years earlier, and noting the eerily similar circumstances. Among those who had helped conduct that search it was well known that Olivia was the last person to see her alive. Now, some said, she seemed destined to the same fate. Though few had voiced such thoughts during her life, more stories gradually began to circulate from garden to garden, clothesline to clothesline, over fence and across street, from one to another to another until all Port Scarnose and Crannoch were abuzz. By midafternoon the entire coastline was covered with men and women scouring the paths and rocks and promontories and coves for some clue that might point to the duke's missing sister.

The activity stemmed not so much from the great love in which Olivia was held so much as that now at last it was out in the open how strange had been everything connected with the brother and the sister, their father and grandfather and his strange witch-wife from Skye. Everyone was suddenly talking about the queer happenings, the second sight, Olivia's curses and hexes, even poor little Gwendolyn's peculiarities. All the superstition held in check for decades by Olivia's presence was now loosed on the gossip-winds of hundreds of prattling tongues. The most valuable currency of the day came to be the possession of some yet spookier or more bizarre tale that one might parcel out piecemeal to ears hot with curiosity. The search was thus driven not by love but by the fearful thrill of the dark unknown, everyone lusting to be the first to proclaim to the community, becoming an instant celebrity by the discovery—*"Here, over here ... I've found her body!"*

The boys of the villages, the instant school let out and informed that the search continued with nothing yet found, dashed for the shore, no thoughts on this day of donning wet suits and swimming off the harbor pier. It was the lure of a dead body to be found, and possibly one with unknown connections to the dark forces of the underworld, that drew them, and that would keep them scouring the coastline till dark.

All the while, the older women who kept counsel together agreed that the body of Olivia Urquhart would never be found. Fate ordained it. She was with Winny now, they said. They had suspected more to the story of Winny's disappearance than was commonly known, though none had breathed a word of their suspicions to a living soul. But they had known. And now fate, or the gods of the deep, or the call of an ancestor's past, had decreed that Olivia, like Winny before her, would join the legions of the dead without a trace. The men and the nickums were wasting their time, they said. The tide had claimed her by now, every trace of blood washed away by the salty sea. Her body was floating miles away, and would eventually sink to rest in the middle of the Firth, if the sharks allowed it, to rot off its bones and lie with Winny's awaiting the last trump when they would rise together out of the sea and into the clouds.

Such was the justice of fate, they said, that Olivia should go missing in exactly the same way, and never be heard from again.

Could it be suicide? asked a few. Others merely nodded with significant looks that hinted at inside knowledge but betrayed nothing, and clicked their tongues.

If they wanted to know where Olivia's final minutes had been spent, they said, though they would find no trace of her, the searchers would do well to concentrate their efforts between Logie Head and Findlater. It was there that Winny had last been seen. The same stretch of lonely headlands and cliffs had always exercised a lurid fascination upon Olivia Urquhart since her earliest girlhood.

The auld wives were right. Not a trace of Olivia turned up, either at the base of Findlater or anywhere else. Eventually even the most enterprising of the searchers were compelled to admit the case hopeless until another day of light came. By then two more tides, one predicted extremely high, would sweep the coast clean twice more of what evidence might possibly remain.

The police gave up their search as evening fell. A pall of gloom settled over Port Scarnose and Crannoch like a descending black cloud of death. Not a few went to their beds that night more attentive to locked doors than was their custom, and lay listening for strange sounds outside, and thinking of ghosts. As Castle Buchan retired for the night, it was with a sense of sad inevitability, perhaps a few regrets, sober reflections, along with the sense that, whatever Olivia had been to us all in life, we would now have to come to terms with what she would be to us in death.

Most of the women of the castle household, however, were, if anything, even more agitated. Those who came in by day were glad enough to return to their own homes. I noticed that both Farquharson and Nicholls fortified themselves a little more heavily than usual

through the evening with doses from the traditional medicine cabinet of Scots through the ages—the amber brew called *aqua vitae*.
Sarah refused to sleep alone and pulled a rollaway into Cora's room
for the night. However imaginary the green lady may or may not
have been, Sarah's fear of Olivia's ghost was real enough. She had
no doubt that if her mistress had indeed passed out of this world,
Castle Buchan was the first stop she would make on her way to the
next.

As I laid my head on the pillow, I must confess almost to a sense
of relief that it was finally over, that Olivia and Alasdair would finally
somehow be reconciled on the other side.

My last thoughts before drifting off to sleep were wondering what
kind of service we should plan for Olivia, and how long the authorities would wait, without a body, before declaring her officially dead
so that we could proceed with a memorial.

Chapter Sixty

Another Dream... and Not a Dream

O bright the beaming queen o' nicht shines in yon flow'ry vale,
And softly sheds her silver light o'er mountain, path and dale.
There's nane to me wi' her can vie, I'll love her till I dee;
For she's sae sweet and bonnie aye, as kind as kind can be.
—W. Cameron, "Sweet Jessie o' the Dell"

Again came the dream of the harp music from the chimneys, with the same peaceful effects. I cannot imagine any more-soothing music to sleep to than that of the harp. I lay dreamily, soaking it in, almost as if listening to myself, or to Gwendolyn, or to the angels. Who can tell in a dream? All your sensations mingle together in a weird blend of reality and fancy. I was no longer on the castle roof hearing the music coming from the stacks, but lying in my bed as the sound came from the cold hearth in my room. Contentedly I lay with the sounds of my harp emerging faintly out of the fireplace as if its strings were the parallel blackened iron bars of the grate.

I could hardly distinguish between waking and sleeping, dreaming that I was actually awake, yet somehow knowing that the wakefulness was part of the dream.

Slowly the music began to change. It became less melodic. I no longer recognized songs or tunes, only notes. Fingers strummed up and down the strings without regard for melodies or chords...random sounds as if one who knew nothing about the harp were plucking and strumming the strings to create *noise* rather than music.

397

Still I lay, gradually coming awake without realizing it, trying to recapture the exquisite roof harmonies of earlier in the dream.

But it was no use. Finally I realized I was drowsily awake... *really* awake. The music had gone. I lay for several seconds. The night was pitch black.

Suddenly my eyes shot open wide and a chill swept through my frame. Or... *had* the music entirely gone?

I strained to listen. I could still make out faint sounds from a harp!

It was the merest whisper, but there could be no doubt. Surely I was too far away from my studio to hear anything if Cora or Alicia were trying to cure insomnia with a little music in the middle of the night. Yet... was it possible that the sound could somehow travel through the interior of the castle for greater distances than I realized?

I lay a moment more. Suddenly I was feeling very strange.

I threw back the duvet, shivered briefly, and crept toward the fireplace. I knelt down and bent my ear toward the open hearth.

I gasped. The sound was coming from inside the chimney! It was a sound I would recognize anywhere, even though the notes emanating from it were faint and random and the sounds dissonant and musicless.

I was listening to the *Queen*!

My heart was pounding. My entire body crawled with goosefleshy tingles.

I sat back on the floor, thinking hard. I glanced at my clock. It was 1:47 a.m. No other sound disturbed the night... but the faint plucking of the *Queen*'s strings continued.

I stood, turned on the light, and hurriedly dressed.

Five minutes later I opened the door into my studio, fully expecting to find the light on and Cora or Alicia sitting at one of the other harps whose tone my sleepy brain had mistaken for the *Queen*'s.

But the room was dark and empty. All hint of sound was gone.

Bewildered, I slowly returned to the countess's quarters, chalking the whole thing up to the fragmentary remnants of the dream left behind after my waking. Obviously I had not been as awake as I thought.

But the moment I walked in, an even deeper chill seized me than before. The sounds were still there! I dashed to the hearth and knelt again in front of it, with an exact repeat of the same sensations.

Notes *were* coming from deep inside the wall, through the fireplace chimney. They were definitely from the *Queen*!

I jumped up and moments later was flying down the private stairway, flashlight in hand, to the second floor. There I turned along the corridor to a series of onetime guest rooms that sat directly below the apartment I now occupied. Not locked and never used, I ran into the first, listened . . . then another . . . and finally a third. As I cocked my ear in front of its hearth, again I detected the sounds. I must be standing directly beneath my current sleeping quarters; the two fireplaces apparently shared a common chimney. The same weird disharmonious conglomeration of notes came from both!

Again I ran down the stairs to the first floor . . . with the same result . . . then to the ground floor, where I hurriedly investigated the storage rooms. I continued to hear sounds from one chimney on each floor. I had to find my way lower still! The chimney carrying the sound obviously originated in the basement.

I rose from my knees from the last hearth and ran, hardly caring who might hear me now, to the kitchen and pantry where Nicholls kept the keys he used to access the rooms of the basement. The ring of keys was not on the peg where I had seen him place it.

I turned again and ran to the stairway that led to the regions below, hoping to find the door at the base of the staircase unlocked. Obviously Nicholls had been down there during the day's search for Olivia. He must have inadvertently left the keys in the lock.

Reaching the lower level, I found no sign of the keys. Just as I hoped, however, the door into the main basement corridor was open.

I hurried through it and along the corridor. There were not so many passageways on this subterranean level. By now I had a pretty good idea what I was looking for. The complete absence of noise in the studio and elsewhere indicated that the sound was being carried through the chimney, perhaps amplified in the narrow confined space like a megaphone. I had to find whatever room lay directly beneath those I had just examined and shared their chimney cavity.

I came to a joining of two halls. Judging as best I could, after having come so far and made so many turns, which way led west, I turned to my right and hurried along. I was certain that at last I was about to locate the *Queen* in one of the basement rooms where she had somehow eluded our most persistent searchings, a room that must coincidentally lie below the countess's chambers and whose hearths shared a chimney. Whatever had unaccountably set the *Queen*'s strings vibrating—whether gust of wind or tremor of the ground—at the moment I did not stop to think that though we might have earthquakes in North America, they were utterly unknown in Scotland—the random sounds had drifted up to me where I slept. In its frantic attempt to explain the thing, my feverish brain almost imagined that the *Queen*, now that she had me in a place where I could hear her, was making music of herself, beckoning me to come rescue her at last.

Reaching the end of the hall, I saw a door to my left. In its lock, a key was inserted, with Nicholls's ring of keys hanging from it.

Suddenly a horrible thought occurred to me. No wind could possibly vibrate the strings of the *Queen* with enough force to be heard several stories above me.

The green lady!

A terror of dreadful foreboding nearly drained my bones of courage. But I could not stop now. I swallowed hard and approached the door. Reaching out a trembling hand, I turned the key, slowly opened the door, and sent my flashlight around the cubical enclosure.

The room was empty. I had been so certain I was about to lay eyes on the *Queen*, with perhaps an ethereal form in green faintly visible beside her. Relieved to see no ghost, nevertheless my heart sank.

Across the room was an empty fireplace, long disused. I ran to it and knelt down.

Again came the unmistakable, random, dissonant nonmusic of the *Queen*'s strings! If possible, slightly louder than before.

Was I still dreaming?! Was I still lying upstairs in my bed, the music of the chimneys having now become random notes from imaginary dream-fireplaces in abandoned rooms in the bowels of the castle?

I stood and gazed about the room again.

No, I thought. *This is no dream. I am wide awake!*

But I was in the basement. I was at the bottom of the castle. Where could the sounds *possibly* be coming from? The *Queen* could not be on the roof—there was no way to get her there. She *must* be inside the castle. Surely this room held the clue!

I dashed back to the door and fumbled with the ring of keys and yanked the key from the lock. I looked them over one at a time. Why had Nicholls left them *here*? I ran back inside and scanned every inch of the room with the beam from my light. The stone walls, some damp, some mossy and grimy with age, seemed devoid of life... except for a tiny alcove cut into the wall about chest height with what appeared a perfect semicircular bowl cut into the flat vertical bottom stone.

Of course... a holy water font!

I spun around and examined the walls again. My eyes began to detect here and there an ancient carving cut into the stones. And—how could I have missed it?—a single decaying wooden cross with tarnished silver crucifix attached. This room was part of the ancient monastery!

Yet nothing else was here, other than... there, a small broom leaning against one corner. As I had with the crucifix, in my haste before I had missed it.

What an odd thing—a *broom*. Why here?

I set the light on the stone floor and reached for the handle. It was ancient with age and nearly falling apart, the ends of the clumped conglomeration of thin twigs bent almost to ninety degrees from years of use.

I set aside both key ring and flashlight and absently began gently sweeping at the dirt and dust from the corner where it stood. I swept back a foot, then two feet from where the two walls joined. Instead of the larger paving stones with which the rest of the room was tiled, those nearest the corner, I now saw as I swept the dirt from them, were smaller stones only six to eight inches square, perfectly shaped and set in place, yet covered with dirt and dust so they would not be noticed as distinct from the rest.

My curiosity aroused, I swept the smaller stones of the corner clean until the grooves between them appeared with greater clarity. The grooves surrounding one center stone appeared cut deeper than the rest. I knelt and probed with my finger. This center stone was held in place by loose dirt, not mortar. I scraped harder and harder, loosening the dirt to a depth of about half the length of my finger, then tried to grab the stone by its exposed edges. It was loose, held in place only by dirt swept over it to hide it from view.

I jiggled and pulled and after a little effort the stone gave way. I lifted it up and out of its resting place.

Beneath it, set in a bed of perfectly cut stones mortared in place beneath the level of the floor, was a six-inch oval brass plate, green and tarnished with age. I examined it with my light, then reached into the cavity and probed with my hand. The plate seemed intended to swivel, though with difficulty, from a small pin at its top. I pushed harder to pivot it sideways. As it swung away, below it my eyes fell upon a keyhole in the center of an ancient complex mechanism of brass.

I stared in disbelief. It was *so* old, how could it possibly still work? The next instant I had the ring of keys in my hands and was fumbling with one after another. The matching key was not difficult to find—it was the mysterious decorative key of brass. It fit the hole perfectly. I inserted it and turned. A dull clank sounded somewhere above me. The sound came from the adjacent wall, as if invisible pins, probably also of brass, had just given way inside it.

I stood and began examining the wall, pushing and probing with my free hand. Suddenly a portion of the wall gave way an inch or two. I gave a great shove with my shoulder and gasped in astonishment again as a door three feet wide swung back out of the wall, revealing a stone staircase behind it of equal width leading down into a chasm of blackness.

A rush of damp air met my face, almost—though it could hardly be—with reminders of the sea.

Without thought, I probed the tunnel yawning before me with the light of my torch, then began a new descent into unknown regions below.

I found myself walking down a long stairway. When I reached its base, a small blind alcove to the left led a short distance where, curiously, nothing was to be seen but a small air duct, which I could only assume supplied draft air for the system of chimneys.

I paused to allow the echo of my footfalls to die away. There could be no doubt. The sound of harp notes was more clear and pronounced now. This tunnel and duct could be none other than the source by which it had made its way above, there to invade my sleep with the harp-dreams that had instigated my search. The sound no longer came from the chimney duct, but from the corridor itself!

In the opposite direction from the alcove, a narrow tunnel led in the opposite direction into darkness. There were no rooms or doors. Its walls and ceilings were of dirt and stone and of about six feet in height. Alasdair would have had to stoop, but I could walk upright without banging my head. Even shining my light straight along its length, I could not see any end to it.

Heedless of what it all might mean, or the potential danger, not once thinking that not a soul knew where I was, I hurried into the tunnel toward the weird sounds.

The way before me was long and straight at first, then gradually curved a little left and then right again, though the turns were gradual. I came at length to where a wall of stones had at one time been erected to block the tunnel and prevent further passage. The stones had not been mortared in solidly but set in place dry, in the manner of a dry-stone dyke. I paused to assess what to do. At some later time, perhaps a third of the stones had been removed and were now stacked and strewn along the tunnel to one side out of the way.

The way through the conglomeration of random-shaped stones was passable, though not easily, just possibly wide enough that a pedal harp might be gotten through it, though the very thought of the damage that would result made me cringe. I crept through the opening and, once beyond the barrier, hurried on. The floor was now strewn with stones and debris and, if I dared look carefully, possibly bones. Alasdair's spooky stories flooded my mind, and I did *not* look carefully. I couldn't lose my nerve now!

Ahead, after another long walk of probably fifty or seventy-five meters as the way seemed to curve more noticeably to the right, the tunnel came to an end. In front of me, a great oak door, with massive rusting iron hinges still stoutly embedded into the surrounding stone, stood slightly ajar.

Behind it—there was no doubt now—I heard the *Queen*.

I drew in a deep breath as if summoning the final measure of courage, then set my hand to the door and pushed.

Creaking and groaning as if wood and hinges together might disintegrate from the strain, the door swung slowly back.

Chapter Sixty-one

The *Queen*

Oh, the sweetness that dwells in a harp of many strings,
While each, all vocal with love in a tuneful harmony rings.
But, oh, the wail and discord, when one and another is rent,
Tensionless, broken and lost, from the cherished instrument.
—L. B. Cowman, *Streams in the Desert*, January 28

The room I beheld was dimly lit with assorted flickering candles. The thought flitted through my brain that I had stumbled upon a druidic or cultic séance. Immediately I remembered the monastery that had originally occupied Castle Buchan. The candles were more likely reminders of ancient Catholic liturgical ceremonies. Perhaps this was a storeroom for its chapel supplies. Such thoughts flashed past in a split second.

Across the room, my eyes were drawn instantly to the magnificent form of the *Queen*. The blond hues of her wood shone golden in the light of the candles. From her strings continued randomly plucked notes and an occasional grating glissando.

Behind it like a specter of white stood Olivia Urquhart, her fingers stabbing at the strings without pattern or purpose other than to make sound. I recoiled at the blasphemy of seeing *her* at my harp, she who had always despised both me and my music.

The flickering light of a nearby candle lit her face not golden but a ghastly yellow. For a moment it occurred to me that she was already dead and that I was imagining the sound. I was so transfixed by the horror of her form that for several seconds I did not see below her what was a far *more* grotesque sight.

As I entered, Olivia ceased plucking and stepped out from behind the harp. I could not take my eyes off her, though the sight was appalling. The grin on her thin white lips was so repugnant it made my stomach lurch. It was the look of death itself.

"You could not resist the sound, I see," she said in a voice that sent chills through me. "You have come to rescue your *Queen*."

I stood like a statue. I had stepped into a dreadful horror movie.

"Is it really worth your life, Marie?" she went on. "For that is what finding your harp will cost you. Yes, Marie, you have just given your life into my hands. *Neither you nor your precious queen . . . by mortal eyes will again be seen*."

Hearing the rhyme awoke me from my terrified reverie with reminders of Ranald Bain and his strength in battling the demons of Olivia's control. Could I be as strong? My eyes slowly accustomed themselves to the light, and the room filled with odd shapes and apparent furnishings and carvings and stone benches. My vision drifted back to the *Queen*. An object, a figure of some kind, was seated low below where Olivia had stood, seemingly leaning against the soundboard for support, with fingers on the lower strings. There was no movement, no sound. The bony fingers were still, as if being held in place by the strings themselves.

As I gazed, a horror spread through my frame, chilling my blood to ice.

The fingers were *not* fingers, but bones! The form was a human skeleton propped against the *Queen*, its fingers hooked grotesquely to the strings to mimic play, its skull partially obscured by the harp's post.

As she saw my eyes at last taking in her ghoulish exhibition, Olivia burst into a revolting death rattle. The whole room echoed with a frightful laugh of insanity. The ring of keys I had carried from the house fell from my hands and clanked as they hit the stone floor.

"My God, Olivia!" I exclaimed. "Oh, Lord...help me...Lord Jesus...Olivia, what have you done?!"

I crept closer to the abhorrent grisly display that could have been imagined only by a psychopath.

A silver chain and locket hung from the neck beneath the skull of the hideous form. Grimacing in terror lest my eyes should drift to the two vacant sockets where once human eyes had been, I reached to pull it closer. On the locket was engraved, *Winifred Bain, From Mummy and Daddy.*

"Good Lord...Oh, God...Olivia...what have you done?!" I repeated, unable to distinguish between prayers, outrage, and terror. "In the name of Jesus...Oh, what did Ranald say—you lying devil...Olivia, what kind of madness—"

"Yes, it is Winny!" Olivia laughed repulsively, moving slowly across the floor. "Now you and she shall make music together...the music of death! Ha! Ha! You have your precious harp, but now at last the castle will be mine!"

"Olivia, you are dying," I implored, not even noticing her movements, paying no attention as she slowly picked up the keys and moved away from me. "You need help. This is insane. What are you—"

"Ha! Ha! You are the one who is dying, Marie! They will never find you. They have not found Winny all these years. This is your burial tomb, Marie...you and Winny and all the dead monks to console you just like they kept Winny company when I brought her here— to show her a secret, I told her. Ha! Ha! Their bones and their skulls will keep you company as darkness falls around you, and you slowly lose your mind. Ha! Ha! You can play to your heart's content! *Make music if you can, while life remain...you and the silent Winny Bain.* Ha! Ha! Ha!"

Suddenly, and with a speed I did not imagine her capable of, she dashed for the door. Before I could recover myself, I heard the clank of a massive bolt, followed by a faint laugh from the other side.

I ran to it and tried the latch, pushed and shoved and called after her, but the door was fast. Like a tidal wave, the terror of my predicament overwhelmed me.

I was locked in what I now realized was no storage room but the ancient monastery crypt with Winny Bain and my *Queen* and what I did not doubt were more dead men's bones from ages past than I could imagine.

Chapter Sixty-two

Trapped

Now farewell light—thou sunshine bright,
And all beneath the sky.
May coward shame disdain his name,
The wretch that dare no' die!
—Robert Burns, "MacPherson's Lament"

How long I stood facing the solid-oak door of my prison in stunned disbelief, I have no idea. I still couldn't fathom that Olivia would *really* leave me to die. The thing was beyond comprehension. Yet behind me as I stood, I knew the skeleton of Winny Bain was all the proof I needed.

When and how the reality of sheer horror fully sinks in to the point when you realize you are *not* dreaming, that you may actually be about to die . . . is a slowly dawning consciousness of finality, of inevitability. What words can describe what goes through your mind? Your brain is overflowing yet weirdly empty and numb, every thought bound up in denial.

Olivia was obviously not coming back. I had no doubt that even now, summoning some final measure of devilish strength, Olivia was shoving and lifting the stones into place to block up the walled portion of tunnel through which she had lugged the *Queen* and lured me to my own tomb. Help would not come from behind the oak door.

After an interminable time, slowly I turned and shrank down, leaning against the wood as I stared at the stones of the floor. I still didn't dare look into the candlelit crypt. I began to cry.

I sat and cried for what seemed hours, petrified with fear, chilled to the bone.

Eventually my brain began to function, hardly at full strength but at least with an attempt to think. I told myself I *had* to get a grip on myself. Summoning whatever minimum of courage I possessed, slowly I lifted my head, climbed to my feet, and began to look around.

Not only did no one know where I was, no one even knew this place existed. I was obviously in the legendary crypt beneath the church. Ranald was two miles away, Iain thirty. No one would find me unless Olivia divulged my whereabouts. That was clearly not going to happen. What story she would tell to account for being missing, I could not imagine.

I turned off the flashlight to conserve batteries. I then walked about and extinguished all but two of the candles and began a search of the place for more, and also matches.

I tried desperately to avoid looking at Winny's remains, though I would eventually have to deal with the fact that I was trapped with her bones.

I saw a pole whose purpose I could not determine leaning against a wall. I grabbed it and beat and whacked on all the walls and ceiling, but everything was solid. There was obviously no communication with the church above. However the crypt had once been reached from the church had been blocked up long ago. I was at least thirty feet belowground. No one could possibly hear me.

There was, however, a faint smell as from the sea. With it came an occasional flicker from the candles. *It must be just as Iain said, there must be a tunnel from here to the shore*, I thought to myself. It was obviously my only hope of a way out.

I located its entry easily enough, a small opening through a portion of wall. Through it came a faint breeze. As I put an ear to the opening, I imagined that I could just hear the sound of waves. They must have been a mile away, perhaps two. The smell of the salt water gave me hope. Whether the tunnel behind the opening was passable, and whether it was possible to get through to the other side, and then to the shore without drowning in some tidal pool, was another matter. One thing for sure, I needed to protect the candles from a sudden draft. If I lost light, I would *really* be in trouble!

The opening to the tunnel wasn't more than six inches square, a tiny window through a former door or passage. It had been blocked and bricked up with stones not dry-set, but securely mortared in place. It seemed utterly unlikely, but what other explanation could exist but that Olivia herself had done so after luring Winny into the crypt, sealing her into her own grave, with just enough opening to give her air to breathe until she died of starvation. The thing was too gruesome to think about. But *how* had she blocked it up from the seaward side, with Winny probably screaming for her life, when Olivia was no more than a teenager herself? It was beyond fathoming, and indicated hideous premeditation. Or had the whole story about seeing Winny along the shore before her disappearance been a fabrication? Had Olivia lured her down through the castle just as she had me, and then made up the other story?

I would never know. And how long had she been planning to kill me in the same way? What story might she be telling about where *I* was?! What if they were searching for me . . . but miles and miles away?

I examined every inch of the area surrounding the little window from top to bottom. It was of solid stone at least fourteen inches thick. It would take picks and tools and hammers to chip out an opening large enough to squeeze through. There was nothing resembling such a tool anywhere.

The silence was deeper than could be imagined—awful, terrifying, even if for a moment I happened to forget who—or what!—I was entombed with. Finally I lay down in a corner, crouched into a ball and cried again, and eventually fell asleep.

Chapter Sixty-three

Above Ground

Och, och mar tha mi! here so lonely,
Despair has seized me and keeps his hold.
Oh were I near thee in Islaw only,
Before tho'st taken that man for gold.
—"The Islay Maiden"

In the castle no one had an inkling I was missing until well into the morning. It was not until about noon that Cora, then Alicia, then Nicholls began to wonder aloud to one another that no one had seen me. When I did not answer their knocks at my quarters and the studio showed no sign of my presence, still they did not worry, assuming, it being a fine day, that I had gone for a walk, perhaps up to visit Ranald Bain. But when one student, then two, then three all appeared for lessons that afternoon, and still there was no sign of me, they began to worry.

Nicholls drove up to Ranald's. He had seen nothing of me. A call was placed to Iain and a message left to telephone the castle as soon as he was home from work.

The mystery was all the more peculiar in that Sarah reported finding Olivia asleep in her bed that morning, insisting that she had never been gone at all. She had not felt well and had remained in bed the entire previous day and through the night. The police were notified and the search for her called off, but the mystery remained. Sarah did say that Olivia seemed more fatigued and wild-eyed than normal.

By the time Iain arrived at the castle about eight that evening, panic about my absence was setting in. He tried to calm everyone, but Cora and Alicia were beside themselves. Both were convinced that Olivia knew more than she was telling. Her reappearance at the exact time I had gone missing could not be coincidental. But no information could be extracted from Olivia, who played the soft-spoken concerned invalid to perfection. The fact that she was too weak to get out of bed even to go to the bathroom without Sarah's help seemed to confirm the impossibility of her having harmed me.

Iain, Nicholls, Farquharson, Campbell, and Nigel searched high and low through the castle till after midnight, Nicholls even taking the ring of basement keys from its peg in the pantry and opening every room below ground knowing full well they were empty, while Alicia and Nigel and Iain scoured the third floor and attic rooms a fourth time. Farquharson, meanwhile, conducted one more search of the garages and outbuildings with the most powerful lanterns he had at his disposal.

Iain spent the night in one of the castle guest rooms. By morning everyone was seriously worried. Again the police were summoned, with again a similar tale but different missing person. Iain did not go to work but remained in Port Scarnose. His first item of business was a drive up the Bin to notify Ranald that I was missing. The day passed, the police and some villagers again searched the coastline. But whether it was the boy who cried wolf syndrome, or the fact that I wasn't so fascinating a potential victim, the crowd and enthusiasm involved in the search was not so great as for Olivia two days before.

As the search turned up nothing, serious but mystified anxiety set in for my safety. In Olivia's case, illness and dementia had offered reasonable explanations for her unaccountable behavior as well as her going missing for a time. With me there were no such simple solutions.

There could be no *good* reasons why I had disappeared, only bad ones.

Chapter Sixty-four

Desperation

Who would dare the choice, neither or both to know,
The finest quiver of joy or the agony thrill of woe?
Never the exquisite pain, then never the exquisite bliss,
For the heart that is dull to that can never be strung to this.
—L. B. Cowman, *Streams in the Desert*, January 28

I awoke freezing, then had to battle the progressive stages all over again—disbelief, thinking myself dreaming, the sight of Winny, renewed terror, hopelessness, and the final realization that I was going to die.

There was no sense of time, only the light of a lone flickering candle. How many times I dozed, waked, and dozed again, I had no idea. Time passed in a blur.

Suddenly it dawned on me that only *one* candle was still burning...and it was flickering low and about to reach its end. Quickly I held one of the others to it and lit a new wick.

They were burning too fast! I would have to use only one at a time. And be more watchful. I had been careless to use two at once.

Slowly I became aware of a physical sensation other than the cold—I was thirsty.

A lightbulb came on in my brain. I was *thirsty*. I would get thirstier and thirstier. I had no water. It was a simple enough truth, but it brought with it a string of further realizations.

Neither did I have food. Without water and food, I would soon weaken. How long could people live without water? Surely not longer than a few days, maybe a week. Even if it was two weeks, it didn't matter. However long it took, no one could possibly find me, and I would eventually die. It felt like I had already been trapped for days.

I still was trying to make myself believe that eventually, against all logic, I would hear sounds of the door opening and Olivia would return and let me out. But if that didn't happen, I had only a limited number of hours when I would have the physical strength to break out myself.

Whatever I was going to do, I had to do it *soon*, while I still had strength.

That realization woke me up. I stood and began examining the room again. There were no tools. Only stone containers sitting around the floor against the walls, some stacked on top of one another. Even if I could remove their stone lids, they were not tool chests but *coffins*! I knew well enough what was inside them. Almost feverishly I set about examining the crypt more carefully. All that lay about me were a few odd chunks of stone and granite. My eyes fell yet again on the door.

I couldn't waste time sleeping and freaking out that the skull of Ranald's poor daughter was staring lifeless at me from across the room. I had to get on with it, or I *was* going to die!

I turned on the flashlight and examined the door. This door was my only hope. It had seemed so old and dilapidated when I first saw it. Surely I could make a hole through it.

I grabbed the pole and banged the stoutest end of it against the wood, hoping to find a weak spot. But it jarred back with surprising force, stinging my hands with an electric jolt. The door was as solid as a wall of granite.

I banged and whacked and beat on it but only succeeded in shattering the pole into three pieces after twenty minutes. I tossed the wood aside and picked up a six-inch-square piece of stone and set about bashing it against the door for another half an hour, then whacked at the area around the hinges until my arms and shoulders were so spent I couldn't even lift the rock for another blow.

I had accomplished nothing.

I could beat on this door for a week and it would not give way. In desperation I grabbed one of the pieces of wood and flailed and beat and yelled again, more like a child throwing a tantrum than for any good I accomplished. At last I collapsed in a heap at the base of the door in an agony of hopelessness. I hadn't put so much as a dent in it! There wasn't an inch of rot anywhere.

When I came to myself, my arms and shoulders ached. I looked at my hands. I hadn't even known what I was doing—rubbing and picking at the door with my fingers, now half rubbed raw with blood and full of splinters.

"God, what should I do?!" I cried in complete exhaustion. "I don't know what to do!"

I broke into sobs, which, with the extreme fatigue, soon put me to sleep. I woke again, lit another candle, yelled and beat on the door and prayed and cried once more . . . and fell asleep again.

Chapter Sixty-five

Interrogation

Sad am I and sorrow laden, for the maid I love so well;
I adore thee, dearest maiden, but my thoughts I dare not tell.
Why deny my heart is rending, for the fair one of the lea;
After all my careful tending, she has now forsaken me.
—"Farewell"

As night fell on the second full day of my absence, Ranald and Iain spoke seriously, each probing their memories for *anything* I might have said, hoping against hope that *some* explanation would present itself. The Volvo unmoved, perhaps I had for some reason taken the bus into Aberdeen and Cora or Alicia had forgotten my mentioning it. Something had to turn up to explain it... *anything*. In their growing uneasiness, however, they found their thoughts increasingly hovering about the person of Olivia Urquhart.

Finally Iain and Ranald told Alicia that they intended to speak with Olivia. She wished them luck but wanted no part of it.

The evening was advanced. It was probably about nine of a dark, moonless night. A terrible sense of gloom had settled over the castle as its inhabitants prepared for their fourth night in a row with one of their two mistresses missing.

Sarah had just finished getting Olivia ready for the night when the knock came to the door of my former apartment.

Sarah saw the two men standing in the corridor. Her eyes widened with question and apprehension. She seemed to sense from their expressions that it wasn't a social call.

"We need to speak with your mistress, Sarah," said Iain, "alone. You may return to your room."

Though Iain was not an official member of the household, Sarah knew well enough how things stood between him and me. He spoke with such quiet command, she did not hesitate but left the room.

"Who is it, Sarah?" croaked a weak voice from the bedroom.

Iain and Ranald entered the apartment and walked to Olivia's sleeping quarters where the door stood open. Iain paused and knocked on the doorframe.

"It is Iain Barclay, Olivia," he said.

"What are you doing here?" she spat back. The volume of her voice was weak, but not its intensity.

"I would like to ask you a question or two."

"Go away. I have no interest in seeing the likes of you."

Iain now walked into the room. Ranald followed.

Lying in bed, Olivia glowered at them as they entered, her eyes aflame at seeing her wishes so rudely ignored.

"I told you, go away. Get out, I tell you. Get out and leave me in peace."

"Olivia," said Iain, approaching and standing beside her bed, "I want to ask you one more time if there is anything you can tell us about where Marie might be."

"Why would I know anything? I told them I had nothing to do with her. She can go to the devil for all I care, and take the two of you with her."

"Where were you when no one could find you?"

"Where I was is none of your affair, Iain Barclay. I was nowhere. I told them I was here the whole time."

"Sarah says otherwise—that your bed was empty for two days."

"She's an imbecile, a goose, a lying vixen! Who would you believe, a fool girl like that or me?"

Iain did not answer.

"Marie said nothing to you about going anywhere," he said, "about taking a walk, about anything?"

"What she and I said to one another is none of your affair. But she will insult me no longer, nor will I put up with your insinuations. Get out of here before I tell Sarah to call the police and have you thrown out!"

"It would hardly go well for you if you tried," rejoined Iain, growing a little heated, "seeing as you are here at the goodwill of the duchess, and we are trying to locate her."

"The duchess! Ha! Ha! She'll not long—"

She stopped abruptly, seemingly drawn by an invisible spiritual force. She turned toward Ranald where he sat staring straight into her eyes, his lips moving imperceptibly. She cast on him a glance of undisguised scorn.

"We shall see what song you sing," she went on, forcing her attention back to Iain, "when I bring charges of trespassing against you after I am restored to my rightful position."

She stared daggers at him for another moment, then they turned and left without another word. A shrieked volley of imprecations and curses followed them. It still sounded as they emerged into the corridor, finally ending in loathsome laughter that sent chills through the bones of both men.

They notified Sarah to return to her mistress, and to let one of them know if there was any change.

When they were alone again they held private counsel.

"She aye kens somethin'," said Ranald. "Fan she cast upo' me that glance, the luik o' her een spoke evil. That moment I kennt wi'oot doubt that she's seen Marie."

Iain nodded. "My thoughts exactly. She is far too confident in being reestablished without Marie to contend with. She is not a woman in any sense of the word preparing to die."

"I ken fae Marie's ain words that afore she went missin', nae a word had passed atween them."

"That's right. She told me the same thing the last time I saw her."

"An' noo Olivia's hintin' they hae spoken nae lang syne."

Iain nodded thoughtfully.

"She knows something," he said. "I'm sure you are right. We must keep careful watch. Is there any chance of a secret way out of Alasdair's apartment, where she now is, that could account for the time she was missing and might also explain, I don't know, where she has perhaps hidden Marie . . . drugged her . . . or worse?"

"I dinna ken, laddie. 'Tis mony a tale o' secret passageways in the auld hoose, but I dinna ken."

The result was an organized watch all night—the women who were willing taking turns in Olivia's apartment outside her bedroom door, kept ajar, listening for movement, and the men taking shifts in a chair with strong coffee in the corridor. Their hope was that, after being unsettled by the interrogation, Olivia would try something in the middle of the night that would offer a clue to what she knew. However, morning arrived with only a universal sleepiness to show for the night's watchfulness. Olivia had not once stirred from her bed.

The morning brought, if possible, a greater sense of urgency and the feeling that if they didn't find me today, they probably never would. No one had seen me in two and a half days.

The police had by now widened their search and were everywhere. My disappearance may not have brought out the village nickums in such numbers, but a missing duke's wife was noteworthy and had begun to be reported on the Scottish national news.

Chapter Sixty-six

Hallucinations

Straight the sky grew black and daring,
Through the woods the whirlwinds rave;
Trees with aged arms were warring,
O'er the swelling drumlie wave.
—Robert Burns, "I Dream'd I Lay Where
Flow'rs Were Springing"

When I awoke again, I was cold. *Very* cold. I had gone to sleep in a sweat and was now dreadfully chilled. I thought it must be night again, or the same night...or maybe day. Why would it be any warmer at one time than another? My mouth was parched and dry, my lips beginning to chap. I was so famished the hunger had actually diminished.

I tried to stand. My head swam a moment with light-headedness. It had begun. I was growing faint! I had been stupid to beat at the door so long. It had sapped too much strength. I had probably shortened my life by a day.

Yet what difference did it make? No one was going to find me. A few hours, a day, seconds...why not get it over with?

At least it would not be long before I saw Alasdair again.

Oh, and Gwendolyn! Dear Gwendolyn. She and I could play together again and—

No, what was I thinking? I wasn't ready to die.

I ran to the opening to the sea, unsteady on my feet, and screamed desperately into it.

"Help ... help ... anyone ... Can somebody hear me? ... I'm beneath the church ... Help ... help!"

Crying out made me hoarse and more light-headed. I coughed and choked from the effort. The echoes of my frantic screams died away. A faint whistling breeze caressed my face. There again was the distant far-off whisper of the sea.

I remembered, as from a former life, the happy times of my first weeks and months in Scotland ... wonderful conversations with Iain as I discovered the reality of God's love. I remembered feeling for the first time the sensation of God speaking to me ... of the revelation that the ocean's tide was like the great Fatherhood of God, lifting and swelling and filling all humanity.

After those wonderful times, how had I become so involved with such evil? How could it have happened?

How long had I been here? I was weak. I was starting to go crazy, just as Olivia had said I would. Suddenly an even more odious thought occurred to me.

How did Olivia know I would go crazy?

Because she had listened to Winny, too, as she slowly died. She had seen it all before! Olivia probably crept back and was listening to me even now, smiling in evil pleasure as I slowly went berserk ... without water ... without food ... soon without candles ... losing hope by the hour.

I ran across the room to the door.

"Olivia, Olivia ... please ... You can have the castle, you can have all the money! Please, you can have everything ... just let me out!"

Only silence met my frantic cries.

The candle flickered low.

I struggled to it and lit another. Only two left. What would I do then?

I crossed the room again to the little opening.

"Olivia," I said through it. "Olivia, I know you're there. I know you're listening. Just tell me what you want. Please ... I will do anything ... please, Olivia."

Again silence...only silence. If Olivia was listening to my dying pleas, she was keeping her laughter to herself.

I crumpled to the floor.

"God...please," I whimpered. "God, please don't leave me...help me."

Chapter Sixty-seven

The Ancient Castle

"Look ahead, mates," o hee,
"Without dread, mates," o ho,
Those that danger would flee,
Let them sneak down below.
—"A Boat Song"

Ranald returned to his cottage in the morning to tend his sheep and dogs. He appeared again at the castle about nine and immediately sought Iain.

"I hae a thocht, laddie," he said. "'Tis an evil thocht, but whan Olivia luiked at me that gait when ye was speikin' till her, 'tis whan I kennt somethin' wasna unco richt, an' all the night lang I cudna help thinkin' o' my Winny. 'Twas almost a luik o' warnin'. An' jist the noo whan I was ben my hoosie prayin', a word came till me—whate'er Olivia kens, I'm thinkin' *Findlater* may hold the clue til't. She tried tae harm Marie ance there, an' 'tis well kennt that she was always fascinated wi' the auld spooky tales o' the place. An' dinna forgit my ain Maggie, an' Alicia's troubles at the same spot. Gien she's dune Marie harm, it may be there we maun luik for a clue."

Iain listened seriously. His mind was spinning rapidly. Slowly he began to nod. *What better place to lure or hide Marie where she was bound to come to danger?* Ranald's worries had prompted memories of his own.

"Then we must get to Findlater, Ranald," he said after a moment more, "without delay!"

Within an hour, two police speedboats had deposited Iain,

Ranald, and half a dozen volunteers from the coastal rescue team in Dove's Cove at the base of Findlater's cliffs. The men immediately spread out in all directions to thoroughly scour the coastline for any sign or evidence that might indicate foul play. An unusually low spring tide, corresponding to the series of high tides of recent days, aided their efforts. An hour's search turned up nothing. Iain, however, was reliving another incident from his past and was thinking along different lines. He went to the skipper of the police vessel.

"Do you have a tide book onboard?" asked Iain.

"Don't need one, mate," the man replied. "I can tell you—today's the lowest tide in six years . . . two hours from now."

The words lit Iain's brain on fire.

"Then get me all the ropes and flashlights you can put your hands on, and a pick-ax and a shovel and a helmet."

"What for, mate?"

"I'm going inside Findlater."

"Are you daft? The place is too dangerous."

"I *am* going in," replied Iain. "It can't be any more dangerous than an ordinary cave, except getting trapped by the water and drowned. You said yourself the tide is low. This may be our only chance. Now get me to the top of the cliff, with enough rope and light to lower me inside, or else I'll do it on my own. It's the one place we haven't tried. Hurry—we have no time to lose. We have to move before the tide turns."

Chapter Sixty-eight

Visions

Angel voices, ever singing, round Thy throne of light.
Angel harps, for ever ringing, rest not day nor night;
Thousands only live to bless Thee, and confess Thee, Lord of might.
—Francis Pott, "Angel Voices"

Again I slept...dreaming...thinking myself dead...half waking...crying...sleeping and dreaming again.

Then came a vision of Gwendolyn...a dream...a vision...I didn't know...I didn't care. It was wonderful.

I was out on Alicia's hillside of heather...her musicians making heavenly music of harmonies complex and beautiful...the red-haired conductress...It *was* Gwendolyn...I knew it now.

She greeted me, welcoming me to her orchestra!

She led me to a great harp standing at the head of a vast congregation of lesser harps—the most magnificent harp imaginable.

"There has been no one to play it," said Gwendolyn. *"It has been silent all this time, just waiting for you, Marie. I have been waiting for you ever so long. See how much older I am already? But time goes by fast here, and every moment is full of happiness and joy and music, Marie! Such music. I cannot wait to share it all with you. Now that you are here, I have ever so much to tell you and show you! You can meet my mummy, and of course Daddy is waiting for you, too. I am grown up to be the same age as them, but I still call them Mummy and Daddy. And your daddy is here, too. He is a nice man and asked me if I would be his daughter for a while—until you came. Do you remember—it is just like when I asked if I could call you Mummy for*

426

a while. But first, I want you to play for my orchestra. You will not need music. You know the song already, for you taught it to me and I taught it to my orchestra. It is called 'Heather Song,' but in my heart I call it 'Marie's Song.' And there is Winny, too, Marie. I have taught her to play the harp. She is sitting next to your harp waiting for you, Marie."

Gwendolyn took my hand and led me to the great golden harp. A girl was sitting next to it. I recognized the harp in front of her as my own *Journey*, though larger now, as though it had grown into its perfection in the same way that Gwendolyn and Winny had theirs. What a happy smile the girl wore, her hair golden, a locket around her neck. She was the same age as Gwendolyn, which was the perfect age, but no age.

"Hello, Winny," I said. *"I am Marie."*

"I know who you are," said the beautiful girl. *"Everyone knows you. Gwendolyn has told us all about you. We have all been excitedly waiting for you. You know my father."*

"Yes, I do. He is one of my dear friends."

"Gwendolyn lets me play your harp, I hope you do not mind. She said you were so kind you would be happy for me. She said this is the same harp you played with my father."

"Yes, it is. I recognized it immediately. And your father played with me on his grandfather's harp."

"Oh, yes—my great-grandfather. He told me. He sometimes plays here, too, on his harp. But he and my mother are playing with the angels. They were sent somewhere else to play I think."

"How long have you and Gwendolyn played together?"

"Ever since she came here. I have been playing in Gwendolyn's orchestra all this time, but we have all been waiting for you to arrive because the big harp is for you alone. Gwendolyn says only you can play the big harp, because it is your music we are playing. But do you mind . . . could I make just a few notes on it, just to see what your big harp sounds like?"

"Of course not, Winny . . . I would be happy for you to."

She reached out from where she sat, reached a long arm toward the strings, then her fingers bent to touch them, and again I heard my voice saying her name. "Winny... Winny... Winny..."

But the sound that came as she touched the strings was scratchy and dissonant, like picking at rusty wires rather than harp strings.

My eyes opened and I heard myself croaking Winny's name in my sleep. I was lying on the floor staring at the *Queen*, with Winny Bain's bony fingers still attached to its strings.

I whimpered and began to cry. If only I could go back to the dream!

All I wanted was to go be with Gwendolyn and Winny and play the "Heather Song."

If I was going to die, I thought, and play with Gwendolyn's heavenly orchestra, why not die at my harp, doing what I loved best? What a wonderful way to die. Why not die to the sound of my own music? Maybe my music could linger in the air long enough to go with me as I drifted away from life here to be greeted by everyone there.

More voices filled my consciousness. I grew warm and happy again. The voices were far away, not like Gwendolyn's and Winny's... but the voices of my father and mother, aunts and uncles, my first husband... and Alasdair. They were coming, I could hear them now. They were all together, waiting for me... waiting to greet me. I was about to see them all again.

A great joy of anticipation filled me. I was so happy.

I pulled myself to my feet and walked slowly toward Winny and the *Queen*.

I was no longer afraid. I had met the real Winny Bain, and I did not think it was a dream. This skeleton wasn't really her, she had only used it awhile. But she wouldn't mind my touching it. She was playing real harps now with Gwendolyn.

I approached, stumbling once and nearly sprawling onto the stone floor. I knew I was weakening.

I stooped down. Gingerly I took Winny's hand, hardly even squeamish at the touch. Very slowly I began to extricate Winny's fingers from the strings. She was so fragile, the poor thing.

"I will be careful, Winny," I said. "I know you are in heaven now. Still I do not think you would find it pleasant for me to break your bones. Maybe you don't care about this old body, but I will be careful anyway. I know you would be gentle with me."

Slowly and easily I gently laid what had once been Winny Bain on the floor with the same care I would use handling a baby rather than a gruesome skeleton.

"There, Winny. You can rest now. I will play you some music. I will practice for Gwendolyn's orchestra. Then we will play side by side, together on our harps."

I pulled my harp across the floor next to a coffin of stone. The light was so dim I could not see all the dings and scuffs and scratches from Olivia's rough treatment, or where she had dropped it once and put a great ugly gash across the soundboard.

Then slowly I began to play. I didn't even care whether it was in perfect tune. I played softly at first. I was weak. My senses became sluggish, as if my brain had gone into slow motion. For all I knew I wasn't even making music but was just plucking randomly at the strings as Olivia had done. Maybe I was making no more music on it than had Winny. But to my feverish mind, it sounded like the songs I knew and loved.

I played mostly Scottish songs, sometimes only phrases of a song.

I was forgetting how they went. Then my fingers, sore and raw as they were, would remember something and play it for a while, then drift into something else. My fingers and ears weren't connected. I played and I listened, but they were two different parts of me.

Then I heard hymns playing.

I recognized the hymn. Someone had taught it to me . . . told me a story about it. Now I remembered, it was about harps!

> Angel voices, ever singing
> Round Thy throne of light.
> Angel harps, for ever ringing,
> Rest not day nor night . . .

Maybe it was time for church. Could it be Sunday? It was the church organ! And voices raised in song. I could hear them...they were singing in the church!

They must be able to hear me, too! If I could only cry out, surely they would hear me.

I tried to call. But no sound came from my mouth. I was too weak to utter a peep.

In dismay I realized the music was coming from me—it was *my* harp playing, not hymns from the church organ.

I had already forgotten the hymn.

I glanced at my fingers as they played. Would I die here...right here...lying against my harp...my fingers turned to bones on its strings just like Winny's...silent forever? No one would find me like I had found Winny. I would be here with my harp forever.

My eyes grew heavy.

"No...not yet, Marie," I said weakly to myself, urging myself to keep awake. "Not yet. Play, Marie. You must practice. You don't want to disappoint Gwendolyn."

Chapter Sixty-nine

In the Footsteps of the Picts

This dearest of Isles is so fertile and fair,
That no other island may with it compare;
Here Gaelic was spoken in ages gone by,
And here will it live till the ocean runs dry.
—M. MacLeod, "The Isle of Heather"

By means of the boat's radio, a helicopter was dispatched to Findlater with all necessary rescue equipment. From the shore Iain and two volunteers were lifted by pulleys up the cliff and set down at the vertical entrance to the interior of Findlater.

With exceeding care, wearing a cave helmet with attached light, and outfitted with ropes and picks and water bottle and a powerful transmitter and flashlight and extra gloves all slung about his shoulders, Iain was lowered into the black vault. The two men eased down the rope inch by inch while Iain shouted instructions up to them.

Six or eight minutes later, he stood, as far as he knew, where no man or woman had stood in at least two centuries, possibly longer, and began a search of Findlater's lowest portions made possible only by the retreating tide.

As the volunteers waited above for the result of his preliminary search, Iain made his way toward the interior of the castle. Debris and fallen stone cluttered his way as he moved deeper into the hillside upon which the castle had been built. As he probed possible passageways with the strong beam from his light, silence began to envelop him, though still with faint rhythmic reminders of the sloshing tide behind him.

After ten or fifteen minutes of exploration, Iain paused. He had come a good way inland. A retreating wave in the distance left a deeper silence than he would have thought possible this near the sea.

He was stooped low, the passage no more than four feet high, yet clearly passable. The walls around him, even the ceiling of the tunnel, were wet throughout, dripping from the recent high tide a few hours before. At any normal time, this tunnel, even at low tide, would be completely filled with water and unreachable. Only now, today, it communicated again with the interior precincts of Findlater and bored its way straight inland.

As he stooped, then at last was forced to his knees on the wet, sandy, gravelly tunnel floor, he had no doubt that he had at last discovered what had eluded him and Alasdair so many years before, the legendary escape route of the coastal Picts from the Viking attack.

With the light attached to his helmet bobbing about, he continued ever deeper into the interior of the coastline. After twenty more minutes he realized his two-hundred-meter lifeline connecting him to the men behind him on the headland had come to an end.

Disconnecting it from the buckle at his waist, he crawled on.

He advanced by slow degrees farther from the shore. The silence deepened as he inched incrementally upward in elevation.

All about him was a silence as of death.

Suddenly Iain stopped all movement. A sharp intake of breath jolted him as one struck dumb.

Could it be?! He listened again. A faint rustle of water far behind him momentarily muffled the sound he thought he had heard. He waited for the wave to retreat and again listened with superhuman effort.

Yes...there could be no mistake! It was the faint melody of his favorite hymn! He had never told another soul about his love for that song! Only one person! An Angel!

Angel voices, ever singing...Angel harps, for ever ringing...

It was not mere music itself. He heard the music of a harp!

Chapter Seventy

Voices

I wish I were now in that Isle of the sea,
The Isle of the Heather, and happy I'd be;
With deer in its mountains, and fish in its rills,
Where heroes have lived 'mong its heath-covered hills.
—M. MacLeod, "The Isle of Heather"

As I played, I was hardly aware what sounds were coming from my harp or my voice. I was talking to myself, and also to Gwendolyn and Winny, in the way people do the closer they get to insanity. The vision of them was so real, so warm, so pleasant. I wanted to live in the vision, not in a cold dark dungeon whose only purpose was to hide bones of the dead.

Winny was alive beside me. We were making beautiful music. We were not lying dead in an underground crypt. We were playing the "Heather Song" on a beautiful hillside where everything was light and bright and fragrant and warm.

"Listen, Winny," I said, *"let me teach you this song—unless Gwendolyn has already taught it to you— It is a hymn I learned...I learned it from someone...I think it was someone's favorite hymn, but I've forgotten. Do you forget things, Winny? I am getting forgetful, but it will be all right, won't it? I will remember when I am with you in heaven. Someone taught it to me, I cannot remember who, but I remember that it was someone I loved. You will like it, Winny; it is about God and angels and harps... We will play it together—you on* Journey *and me on the* Queen. *You have such thin delicate fingers, Winny—that is why you can play the harp so well."*

"But, Marie, I do not think I will ever be as good as you and Gwendolyn."

"Oh, but you will, Winny. Your fingers are perfect for the harp . . . There is plenty of time. We have all the time in the world to play together."

"But it is too dark, Marie—I can't see your fingers to help me . . . I need to see to play— Please, Marie . . . Marie . . . I can't feel the strings . . . Someone grabbed my fingers and took the harp away. Help me, Marie . . . help . . ."

"Marie!"

"Marie . . . Marie . . . it is too dark . . . Marie . . . Marie . . ."

The light from my last candle was flickering to its death. But I was scarcely aware of it. Slowly it faded, then in a final tiny death-burst was gone. I was left in utter blackness. I hardly knew it. The music from my harp somehow drew all my senses into it. I could no longer distinguish between seeing and hearing. Neither had I been able to hear the sea for some time. But I didn't notice that either. I continued to babble and play.

"It is all right, Winny. We can play in the darkness."

"But I am afraid, Marie. Please, Marie . . . help me . . . help me . . ."

"Marie!"

"It is all right, Winny. Just lie where you are—you are safe there. I will take care of you."

"But, Marie . . . Marie . . . Marie . . ."

"Sleep, Winny . . . just sleep . . . You are safe now."

"I don't feel safe. I am cold and it is dark . . . I am afraid, Marie. I don't think anyone will ever find me. I have been lying here ever so long and it is not a nice place, Marie . . . Marie . . . Marie . . ."

I was growing weary of playing. I wanted to sleep. But Winny kept calling my name.

"Marie . . . Marie!"

"Not now, Winny. Go back to sleep . . . We will play later. Let me sleep."

"Marie!"

But it wasn't Winny's voice. It was a strange voice...a deep voice...a frightening voice. I kept hearing my name...How long had the voice been calling my name?

"Marie...Marie...is it you in there? Marie, wake up!"

Panic seized me. What was going on? Someone was after me! I was lying on the floor. How did I get here! I was playing my harp. How had I fallen on the floor! Strange flashes of light blinded my eyes. Terror consumed me.

"Winny...Winny...where are you, Winny?!"

I began to lose consciousness. The time had finally come when I would not wake up. I imagined voices...I grew warm and happy again. The voices faded into the distance...They were all waiting for me.

The voices grew louder again. I was getting closer and closer...but it was only one voice. Where had everybody gone?

"Who are you?" I tried to call back. "Where are you...Where am I?"

"Marie...Marie!" called the voice. "Marie, are you there?...It's Iain! Marie, it's Iain."

A stab of blinding remembrance shot through my brain. From a time long ago! Somebody...a name...red hair...a kind smile...

"Marie!"

"Iain!" I tried to scream. Only a tiny croak escaped my lips. Was I dreaming? What kind of terrible nightmare to pretend someone was there.

"Iain—" I tried again. My mouth was too dry!

"Marie!"

"It's too dark...I can't see...Iain! What is— Are you with Alasdair and Gwendolyn?...Tell them not to worry, Winny's here with us...It's dark. All the candles went out. But we are here. Tell them we are coming to them. Tell Gwendolyn I have been practicing."

"Marie, it's Iain! You're not dreaming. I am here."

"Iain!" I shrieked. Reality began to penetrate my brain.

I squinted as a sharp beam stung my eyes.

"Marie...I see you! Can you follow the light with your eyes? I am over here...there is an opening. It's me, Marie! It's Iain. Can you stand and come to me?"

"Iain...Iain...Oh, God...is it really—"

I struggled to my knees, hardly conscious what I was babbling.

"Iain...I'm here...Are you still there?...Help me! God...oh, God—is it really Iain?!"

"I'm here, Marie. Come toward me."

I staggered toward the light, then fell on my knees a few feet away.

"Iain...Iain...I was so afraid!" I cried as I broke into uncontrollable sobbing. "How did you get...But where are you, Iain?...The hole is too small. I can't get through."

I collapsed in a heap on the floor.

Iain waited a few seconds.

"How did you get there, Marie? Tell me how to get to you."

I struggled to stop crying and get a breath.

"Olivia...," I whimpered. "I'm in the basement."

"Basement...What basement?"

"I don't know...below the church. I forgot where."

"The church has no basement, Marie."

"Not the basement...the crypt...the old crypt."

"But where, Marie?"

"In the crypt...the basement...somewhere in the castle."

"How can I find it?"

"The keys...Nicholls has keys...Iain, help me!" I said, struggling to my knees and to the little window that now had light coming through it.

"I will come to you, Marie. But you must be brave awhile longer. It will take me an hour, maybe more. But I will come to you, Marie. Tell me where to go. You must tell me how to get there."

"From the basement...a long corridor beneath the castle...a tunnel...It's blocked up...Nicholls has keys. Get the keys...a big brass key. Unless Olivia hid them. She is not nice to me,

Iain. She said terrible things. She left me here, Iain. She is not nice."

"I know, Marie. But when we have the keys, where do we go?"

"There's a room...in the old monastery...at the end...on the right, I think...or is it the left, I don't know...and a broom, find the broom...holy water font in the room...There's a lock in the corner...it's hard to see...under a stone in the floor...You have to sweep the floor to find it...An old lock under the floor opens the door...a stair leads down the crypt...Olivia may have blocked it...Get through the stones to the oak door...behind the oak door. That's where I am. I tried to break it but wasn't strong enough. Please don't leave me in the darkness. I can't find my torch. Oh, Iain, I'm cold and afraid."

"Here, take mine. Try to find yours."

He handed his flashlight through the opening. My fingers fumbled for it and met his hand reaching through. I clasped it with mine and held on for dear life, sobbing again.

"Is it really you? It feels like you—is that your hand, Iain? Don't let me go...Please, don't let me go."

"I have to, Marie. But just for a moment."

He pulled his hand away. "Find your light, Marie."

I turned frantically back into the room. I found the light over beside the *Queen* where I had dropped it. Its beam was weak. I staggered back.

"Give it to me," said Iain. "Hand it through the opening. You keep mine. It will be brighter."

"Iain, Iain...I can't believe you came. I was so afraid. Thank you. Oh, Iain...I thought I would die."

"Here is a bottle of water, Marie," said Iain, handing it through the opening. "Drink it slowly, very slowly. You have had nothing in almost three days. Only sip at it. I will be back before you know it."

"Please don't go. I don't think I can bear it."

"Be brave, Marie. You can do it. I know you can. You are a courageous woman. Be brave, Marie. God is with you. He was with you all the time. He led me to you. Don't despair. I am coming. I will bring Ranald; he will help me find you."

"No . . . no, Iain. Ranald mustn't come. Winny is with me, Iain. Ranald mustn't see her. It would break his heart."

"I understand, Marie. I am going now, but only for a while. Be brave. Play for me again, so I will hear you when I find the basement. Play the hymn about angels' harps."

"Oh, yes . . . I can do that. I will play for you!"

Chapter Seventy-one

Light of Day

Wi' thousands to adore her
She loves me only surer;—
An angel may be purer,
But not mair sweet than Mary, O.
My blessings on thee, Mary,
my bonnie blue-eyed Mary;
The love I bear my fair one,
Is all my heart can carry, O.
—"My Blessings on Thee, Mary"

I can hardly say what was worse, to have been losing my mind talking to the bones of Winny Bain and playing my harp in the darkness, or the two hours that followed, my senses awake again, full of hope, invigorated by a few drinks of water, yet aware more keenly than ever that I was trapped in a crypt with dead people's bones...and that *if* something happened to Iain in the meantime, my plight would be worse than ever.

I went to my harp. Weak though I felt, still talking to myself, I began playing again. I was determined not to stop until Iain returned.

It seemed like days, not hours. My hands and fingers grew so tired I could barely hold them to the strings.

Eventually I heard sounds, muffled at first...the tromping of feet...then a great metallic clank...and the room flooded with light.

I tried to stand. My head swirled...I saw Iain...I think Nicholls, Alicia. Everything was a blur.

439

Iain hurried toward me and I dropped in a faint. I knew nothing as he ran back through the tunnel with me in his arms, followed by the others. Neither did I remember being hurried up stairs and through corridors and outside into the waiting ambulance summoned by the frantic call from the policeboat as it sped Iain back to the harbor. I vaguely recall hearing its siren, and being faintly aware of Iain at my side holding my hands and speaking into my ear. But all went black again.

I woke up several hours later at Dr. Gray's Hospital in Elgin.

When at last I opened my eyes, I actually felt surprisingly good. The IVs in my arms had been pumping fluids into me long enough to have stemmed the worst of my dehydration. My hands were bandaged and I was conscious of tremendous weakness. They had feared mild hypothermia as well as dehydration. My temperature in the ambulance was only 94 Fahrenheit, but was now climbing steadily back. I was hungry enough to eat a horse, though I had to settle for gelatin and Popsicles and broth the rest of the day.

I glanced around the room and tears flooded my eyes.

Mrs. Gauld stood there crying. I couldn't believe it. And around the bed stood Alicia and Nigel and Cora, Nicholls, Farquharson, Tavia, Fia, Ranald, several of the other maids, Reverend Gillihan . . . and of course Iain.

I tried to say something. But only a croak came out. The entire room burst into chatter and tears and laughter, some cheering, hugs and hand squeezes, everyone talking at once and more joy than I would have thought one small room capable of containing. I smiled so big my chapped lips began to crack. When at last I succeeded in finding my voice, my first words surprised me as much as anyone.

"Does she know?" I asked weakly.

No one doubted who I meant.

"No one has breathed a word," replied Iain. "We thought you ought to have the privilege of telling her yourself."

"I can't imagine what I will say," I said.

"I have the feeling words won't be necessary," rejoined Iain.

I glanced around and realized that there was one other face missing. "And Sarah?" I said.

"She cudna stand no' comin' wi' us," said Cora. "She's been sair upset aboot ye. But somebody had tae stay wi' *her*, ye ken. We *cudna* hae her gae wanderin' off agin', ken. Sarah's got orders fae me that her mistress isna tae leave her rooms, no' for the rapture itsel'!"

"There'll be unco little worry o' that, I'm thinkin'," mumbled Nicholls.

From his side, Tavia now stepped close to the bed and held out her hand to me. A diamond sparkled from her fourth finger.

"Look, Marie," she said. "Harvey celebrated your being found by asking me to marry him."

"Tavia, it's lovely!" I said. "Congratulations, both of you!" I turned to Harvey. "I must say, Nicholls, I am honored to have been able to help push you across the line. I was wondering how long it was going to take you."

Everyone laughed and was treated to the rare sight of seeing Harvey Nicholls's face go red.

I now looked sadly at Ranald. He nodded with a knowing expression. He had obviously been told.

"I am sorry, Ranald," I said with a smile. "If it is any consolation, in a strange way she was good company and may have helped keep me alive. I had a vision of Winny with Gwendolyn in heaven. I hope it was real. I think it was. They were both playing harps."

"What ither kind o' music cud they be makin' than the music o' the angels?" said Ranald.

I looked over at Alicia. She was smiling and tears were spilling down her cheeks. "They were playing your 'Heather Song,' Alicia," I said. "They invited me to play, too. I almost did . . . but I guess it wasn't quite time for me to go be with them yet."

Chapter Seventy-two

Home

They kept me in hospital two days. I felt fine after one. But it was precautionary, they said.

I was still weak, but I ate and drank as much as they allowed. I quickly felt on the way back to being my real self.

The men had already seen to the removal of the *Queen* from the crypt. Not knowing whether I would want to see her again so soon, with whatever emotional trauma the sight might cause, they did not bring her to the studio. But she was now safe inside the library until I decided what should be done about the damage to her. Winny's bones had also been removed before I arrived home. She was placed in a small coffin and now lay in the funeral home in Buckie awaiting a further decision by Ranald of what to do.

All this took place outside the ken of Olivia Urquhart, who, not surprisingly considering the physical and emotional strain, had taken a turn for the worse since her own return from the crypt. She had scarcely left her bed since.

Upon returning to the castle, a visit to her room was one of my first items of business.

I asked Cora to go to Olivia's apartment and relieve Sarah so I could greet her. She came flying down the stairs and into my arms, weeping like a child for happiness. I think she still more than half-way blamed herself for what had happened. Her relief was profound and the gush of tears humbling. To be loved is a wonderful thing. If possible, she was thereafter even more devoted to me than ever.

I left her and went upstairs. I nodded to Cora where she sat outside Olivia's bedroom. She left the apartment and closed the door behind her. I walked into the bedroom.

Olivia glanced up. Her eyes fell upon me, seemed to flicker momentarily as if she were having a dream. I stood staring down at her. To describe my feelings would be impossible. I must say, I was pleased that I did not hate her. Neither can I say I loved her. I think I pitied her. Whether I could forgive her, that was not a question I was yet prepared to face. I hoped when the time came I would be capable of forgiveness.

Olivia took me in as if I had now become the ghost. She seemed unable to determine whether she was seeing things or imagining them. Maybe she thought I was dead. She showed no sign of recognition or response. She just stared. I returned her stare expressionless.

After a few more seconds, I turned and left the room.

If the episode in the crypt and the two days before it had weakened Olivia's frail system, my brief visit to her—as ghost or real hardly mattered—taxed her remaining strength to the limit. She began to fail almost immediately. Whether the cancer was invading her organs more rapidly, or whether my appearance sapped her of the will to live, not even the doctors could determine. Her face thinned yet more in the coming days, she ate little, and left the bed only when Sarah or I helped her to the bathroom.

Sarah remained devoted to her service, for my sake, and one or the other of us was nearly constantly at her side. What nourishment and water we managed to get into her came from our hands. When we were unable or needed sleep, Ranald sat beside her, now and then holding a cup of water and straw to her thin wrinkled lips. I played *Journey* at the bedside, mostly Gwendolyn's music. What Olivia thought of thus being ministered to by Ranald Bain and myself, no word or gesture ever revealed.

Chapter Seventy-three

Confrontation of Conscience

Fareweel my ain dear Highland hame,
Fareweel my wife an' bairns.
There was nae repentance in my hert,
When my fiddle was in my airms.
I've lived a life of sturt and strife;
I die by treacherie:
It burns my heart I must depart,
And not avenged be.
—Robern Burns, "MacPherson's Lament"

For several weeks, we took turns sitting by Olivia's bedside, feeding and helping her drink. It was clear the strength was ebbing out of her. She showed no interest in anything nor sign of softening.

A day came when Iain was at the castle. By common consent, we all felt it was time we three—as a threefold cord representing the past, present, and future—looked Olivia in the eye to see if she was ready for what God desired to make of her.

We went to her room and sat down in three chairs around the bedside.

She was wide awake but displayed no response at seeing us invade her shrinking private domain.

Ranald was the first to speak. Even after all this time, as well as I knew him, his words stunned me. The depths of the man's reservoir of godliness continued to astound me.

"I forgie ye, Olivia," he said.

I glanced at her pallid face. The faintest motion flickered at her eyelids.

Again it was silent. My heart was stirred. God was speaking to me. I knew I was ready.

"I forgive you, too, Olivia," I said at length.

"And I, too, Olivia," now added Iain. "I also forgive you with the love and forgiveness of God."

Again her eyes flickered and now slowly moved around the bed, resting a moment on each one of us.

"You . . . *forgive* me?" she whispered in a faint, rasping snarl, as if the idea were too huge to comprehend. She lifted her head an inch or two, and struggled with great effort to look at each of us again. "You forgive me . . . for *what?*"

"For yer sin, Olivia," said Ranald. "Ye've lived a life o' selfishness. Ye've hurt mair folk nor ye hae ony idea. 'Tis but ane way oot o' the pit o' hell for ye, sae that ye can lay haud o' the forgieness o' yer God an' Father. We a' forgie ye. But for the Father tae git *his* forgieness intil ye, intil yer verra hert, ye maun spier for't. Sae I spier o' ye agin, afore ye meet yer Max agin, an' afore ye meet yer brither an' oor dear Gwendolyn, an' afore ye meet my Maggie an' my Winny . . . I spier ye once mair, Olivia Reidhaven, what I spiered o' ye afore—are ye ready tae see yersel' for what ye are . . . Are ye ready tae repent?"

With what little life was left in her, Olivia turned her head toward Ranald, her eyes gleaming with the fire of what the Scots call "the ill place" itself. The words that came through clenched teeth of determination—slowly, arrogantly, barely audible as she clung to the lifeless thread of pride and independence—chilled me all over again like her horrid laughter in the crypt.

"But I've done nothing wrong."

We sat in stunned and silent disbelief. Olivia laid her head back on the pillow and closed her eyes, satisfied to have haughtily denied to the end the claim upon her dead conscience.

They were the last words she ever spoke.

Ranald rose from the bedside, shaking his head in sad disbelief, and left the room. Iain and I followed.

"I may hae jist come ower tae yer view o' the thing," he said to Iain with great seriousness as we walked along the corridor. "I think at last I unnerstand Geordie's Lilith. I hae seen her wi my ain een. This can nae be the end o' it."

By nightfall, Olivia was dead.

Chapter Seventy-four

Closing Chapter

The settin' sun, the settin' sun,
How glorious it gaed doun:
The cloudy splendour raised our hearts
To cloudless skies aboon.
The auld dial, the auld dial,
It tauld how time did pass;
The wintry winds hae dang it doun,
Now hid 'mang weeds and grass.
—Lady Nairne, "The Auld Hoose"

Olivia's death was the final closing of the Reidhaven chapter in the long saga of Castle Buchan and its storied history. It was a sad realization that reconciliation does not, even in the end, find a home in every human heart. It is possible to resist the call of Fatherhood's voice till death, and beyond.

It was a bittersweet end to know that Alasdair, Olivia, and Gwendolyn were all gone. The family line was at an end. Whatever future lay in store for this proud castle, and proud family, now rested with me. I may always be an incomer, but I did not want to be an interloper to my historic Scottish name whose future, for good or ill, was now bound up in my own.

I vowed to do my best to discharge faithfully the duties and responsibilities that had, by so many twists of fate and destiny, thus fallen to my shoulders. Planning Olivia's funeral was one of the first of those responsibilities I had to face. Given the circumstances, it was a very difficult one.

The simplest solution to an obviously awkward dilemma was to let Reverend Gillihan conduct a minimal ceremony, without fanfare, according to the standard form. He knew little of Olivia's history. None of the controversy needed come into it. I asked him to consult Iain for details about her life.

The church was packed. There were no testimonials, no procesional, no gathering afterward. Olivia was buried in the Reidhaven family plot at the Deskmill Parish Church. Few people spoke, though I heard tongues clicking as the somber crowd walked away from the grave. What tears were shed by some who had been the friends of Olivia's youth seemed to be tears of relief.

In the weeks that followed, I did not want to press Iain about any aspect of the future—his . . . mine . . . or ours—even to the point of wondering what his vocational plans were. I was interested, of course. But I knew he would tell me when he was ready.

"I had a most enlightening conversation with Reverend Gillihan yesterday," he told me one evening as we enjoyed tea together at the castle.

"What about?"

"My future in the church."

"Hmm . . . does he think you are angling for his job?" I asked.

"Not at all," Iain said with a laugh. "Just the opposite, in fact. He was most gracious, said that he appreciated how I had handled the delicate situation of returning to a former parish, and that I had been so supportive of his ministry. Then he asked me if I hoped to occupy a pulpit again, specifically the Deskmill pulpit. I must admit, the question caught me off guard."

"How did you answer him?"

"I said that my prayers had not been so specific as that, and that all I could say at this point was that I did not feel ready to resume a full-time curacy. He then explained himself. He said that as much as he loved it here, and loved the people of the parish, he was not a native as I was and could be happy anywhere. Essentially he offered to step aside and move elsewhere if I felt inclined to resume my former position."

"That is a remarkable offer for a clergyman."

"I thought it entirely remarkable." Iain nodded. "I was moved by his consideration. I told him, however, that I have been enjoying the part of supply minister upon occasion. So much so that I have been considering reinstating myself with the Session as a permanent fill-in and supply minister for north Scotland. That way I can keep my feet firmly planted in both worlds—the workaday world of manual labor, which I find fulfilling, and the spiritual world of church life, where I feel I can have a voice and make a contribution. I enjoy visiting different churches, sharing what God has shown me about practical Christian living, yet without the burden of administration that goes with the occupation of a permanent pulpit. I especially find fund-raising odious—so antithetical to the gospel...one more reason I believe the clergy ought to work—at least part of the time."

"There you go again with your controversial notions!"

"I can't help myself. But don't you think supply and fill-in preaching would suit me?"

"Perhaps. But the ministry so desperately needs men like you—men who understand the life Jesus truly calls us to, and who aren't afraid to challenge people to live that life."

"True, yet I question whether the pulpit is the best place for setting out that challenge. So much of what the organized church both represents and emphasizes seems to produce the opposite effect in people's lives from what I believe God intends."

"Shouldn't you be in the church as a pastor to make sure that doesn't happen?"

"That is certainly one view of the pastorate. I believe Reverend Gillihan is just such a positive influence. And I am open and willing to move back into it full-time. If and when that time comes, I will take up again the mantle of the pastorate with eagerness. But at this point in my life, I do not feel so led or inclined. You cannot imagine how I look forward to getting up and going to work every day—to get my hands dirty with the things of God's world, to sweat, for my muscles to feel the strain of hard labor. Nor do I have the least ambition for clerical advancement—a thing even more antithetical to the gospel than fund-raising. It seems like what I have proposed might be a perfect balance."

"It sounds ideal, Iain," I replied. "But you mustn't mind if a certain local duchess follows you about occasionally from church to church, trying to glean all she can from your vast store of wisdom."

Iain laughed with delight. "I will not mind," he said. "But people might talk."

"Let them!"

Chapter Seventy-five

Witness to a Threat

We'll join our love notes to the breeze
That sighs in whispers through the trees
And a' that twa fond hearts can please
Will be our sang, dear Mary.
—W. Cameron, "Meet Me on the Gowan Lea"

In keeping with Iain's decision to take up preaching again on a regular but part-time basis, Reverend Gillihan secured official sanction from the Session to name Iain Barclay his assistant. Iain would resume the title of curate and would again be listed on the role of active church clergy. At his insistence, however, he would remain unpaid.

On the Sunday after the new arrangement had at last proceeded through its necessary channels, Reverend Gillihan conducted a brief reinstallation ceremony, then officially welcomed Iain into his ministry, which he said he was privileged to share with him. He then turned over the pulpit to Iain for the morning's sermon.

The church was packed. People were hoping, I suspect, that Iain might say something publicly that would hint at where things stood between him and me. There were so many present that I invited some of the overflow to join me in the duke's—now people were calling it the "duchess's"—box. Thus began a tradition that I continued, of opening my private pew to anyone from the village who wanted to use it.

Iain uttered not a word about me or Olivia or the past, other than

451

some kind remarks about his friend the former duke, adding that he felt refreshed in mind and spirit from his time away and the work in which he was engaged, and that he looked forward to what God would be doing among them in the days ahead. He was also very appreciative of the opportunity to serve alongside Reverend Gillihan. He then preached on the practical obedience of the Sermon on the Mount as comprising the essence of what he called life in the center of God's purpose.

As we filed out of the church a short time later, with Reverend Gillihan and Iain standing side by side, Iain surprised everyone—especially me!—by embracing me and kissing me lightly on the cheek, totally unconcerned with who might be watching. "With your permission," he said as he stepped back, "I would like to call on you this afternoon."

"Of course," I said, smiling happily. "I will look forward to it."

"About two?"

"Perfect."

When Iain appeared at the castle that afternoon, he asked if I would like to go for a walk.

We drove out of town where we parked at the new cemetery, then walked to the path along the top of the headland that led from Port Scarnose to Findectifeld. We sat down on the familiar bench where we had first met.

"That was a bold greeting you gave me at church," I said. "I doubt people have stopped talking about it."

"I believe in keeping gossip out in the open." Iain laughed. "Do you remember my telling you about my secret hiding place," he asked, "down there over the ledge, where I first heard you playing your harp?"

"Of course."

"Would you like to see it?"

"Am I allowed? I thought it was your own special place."

"It is. I am inviting you to share it with me. "

Iain stood and took my hand, and we scrambled down over the

grass and heather. He helped me down a few steep spots until we were safely out of sight from the trail above.

"Be careful of the gorse," he said. "It's more than prickly—it's lethal. I often say that if the Lord had appeared in Scotland instead of Palestine, his crown of thorns would have been woven of gorse. It is one of the reminders I believe God gave the Scots of the great sacrifice of the cross. I never look at the gorse without being reminded of the Lord's *not my will* prayer of relinquishment."

Within moments we were seated in a little alcove of grass and heather looking out upon the sea below. The only sounds were of the waves crashing into the rocks, and the gulls flying about everywhere.

"I see why you love it here," I said. "It's lovely. So peaceful and cozy. You can shut out the whole rest of the world."

"Now do you understand why I was so surprised to suddenly hear harp music?"

"No more surprised than I was to see your red head!"

Iain became thoughtful. We sat for probably five minutes looking out over the sea.

"I almost feel I owe you an apology," he began at length.

"For what?" I said.

"I know you would not expect it. Perhaps that is the wrong way to say it, but I feel that what happened with Olivia was partially my fault."

"How could that be? You had nothing to do with it!"

"I might have seen it coming," replied Iain. "I *should* have seen it coming. I cannot help but feel that I let my spirtual guard down, that I should have been more wary and careful."

"You warned me about her."

"Perhaps. Even so, I did not perceive the full scope of the danger. I should have been more attentive even when I was in London. Seeing how things developed after Alasdair's death—with Olivia trying to take everything—I regret my long silence, and my absence from your life."

"Honestly," I said, "I would not have minded too terribly losing the castle and everything. If she only hadn't resorted to such tactics, I probably would have given her half of it in the end anyway."

"That would have solved nothing. Nor would it have been the right thing to do. I know the wealth means little to you. But Alasdair's memory does. He knew who and what Olivia was. You must be faithful to that, and do good with what has come to you. Alasdair knew that she would have been incapable of using her position to do God's good, as you will do. Truth must prevail. What Olivia sought was personal gain and power. She was motivated by greed, avarice, duplicity, and untruth. Believe me, even half of everything would not have satisfied her . . . Having it *all* would not have satisfied her. There was evil in Olivia. Now I question whether my silence about what I knew of her was for the best."

"Silence . . . about what?"

"There was another incident. I should not have forgotten the lesson from it. My silence accomplished nothing toward repentance. It only deepened Olivia's self-righteousness. It did not humble her. And it nearly cost you your life."

"Is the incident you mentioned something you can tell me about?"

Iain paused and thought a moment, then drew in a deep breath.

"Alasdair told you about our adventure in the cave," he said, "and the little dinghy we capsized?"

"Yes." I nodded with a smile.

"There was another incident involving the dinghy and a second cave—a secret we shared that we never knew what to do about."

"I assume it involves Olivia."

Iain nodded. "The three of us often played together on the castle grounds when we were young, and she was able to bend us completely to her will. She possessed almost a hypnotic power. We didn't dare cross her for the terrible threats she made of what would happen to us if we did.

"Gradually Alasdair and I grew older and braver and had adventures of our own. Yet still Olivia was a powerful influence in our lives. By then Winny Bain and she were friends, as were Alasdair and I. Winny was about Olivia's age. All the children for miles were terrified of old James Bain, Ranald's father. Stories ran rampant about the Bain croft and what happened to children who ventured too close. But everyone loved Winny. When she was twelve or thirteen and began to take on a woman's form, she was stunningly beautiful. Even at such a young age, the older boys for miles talked about nothing else."

"Were you in love with her?" I asked.

"Good heavens, no." Iain chuckled. "I think I was thirteen at the time, about the same age as Olivia and Winny, Alasdair about a year older. We were still mere boys. We were fascinated by boats and caves and pirates and forts and castles and swords and all the exploits of Scotland's heroic past. Our thoughts were filled with the Wallace and the Bruce and Bonnie Prince Charlie, not girls. But Winny Bain's hold on the older lads of the village did not escape Olivia's notice, and she became dreadfully jealous of the attention.

"You know now about the caves near Findlater. The tide comes in and out, swirling with great force. The passageway which led me to you has had all sorts of legends associated with it, of a hidden room where all the old Sinclair gold was hidden, as well as artifacts reputed to have originated with the Knights Templar that were brought to Findlater when the Templars were escaping Jerusalem in the fourteenth century. The legends involve Henry the Navigator, himself a Sinclair. I don't know if there is a grain of truth in any of it. But as boys we were fascinated with the legends. We lay awake at night dreaming of finding the gold for ourselves.

"It was before the other cave incident, the one Alasdair told you about. I told you that Alasdair and I had tried to find the tunnel but never did. But I didn't tell you the whole story. We were determined to get into a certain cave called Dove's Cave and look for the secret passageway. We knew our fathers would never allow it, so we made our plans in secret. We contrived to attach our dinghy to an old plow horse of my father's and lug it overland and down to Sunnyside Beach. There we launched it. We were careful of the tides and made our approach to the cave at low tide. We knew we would have an hour at the most to explore and get out. We were well enough aware of the danger of being trapped inside. Even then it wasn't so low as the low tide that allowed me to find you.

"We managed to get the boat launched and then began maneuvering our way toward Findlater and Dove's Cave. It was about an hour before the lowest point of the tide. We had to struggle a little against the outgoing current. But we made slow and steady progress and gradually saw the mouth of the cave yawning before us.

"But then an unexpected surprise interrupted our schemes. Suddenly on the promontory above us we saw two figures walking along toward the Findlater ruins.

"'Look—it's Olivia and Winny!' said Alasdair.

"'I wonder what they're doing here,' I said.

"'I don't know, but if they see us, we'll be in for it.' We were terrified that Olivia would betray us and that our fathers would whip us and probably burn the dinghy. 'Quick, we've got to get out of sight!' yelled Alasdair.

"Frantically we kept rowing, hoping they hadn't seen us. We managed to get the dinghy behind a projection of rock that formed one of the walls of the cave. Once we were out of their sight, and seeing the cave opening up before us, we forgot about the girls. Our thoughts immediately turned to Templar gold. In another ten minutes we were inside and beaching our gallant craft on a slope of sand exposed by the low tide. We climbed out and looked around. We were awestruck, hardly able to believe that we had actually done it. We were inside Dove's Cave! We pulled out our torches, switched them on, and crept into the blackness of the interior.

"What met our eyes was enough to fire the imagination of any boy. The cave went straight into the side of the rock and we were able to walk with ease. After twenty or thirty feet, the sand beneath our feet gave way to rock as the cave floor began to slope more steeply upward. We kept on, trembling with excitement, yet also afraid that any moment we might stumble across some old pirate's bones, or worse. As I now know from my recent exploration, however, we had *not* on that day discovered the way into the inner portions of Findlater. We were in one of a hundred other coastal caves that wouldn't have led us anywhere. But at the time we thought we had found the ancient treasure cave and were excited beyond words.

"Then we heard voices. We stopped and listened. They were girls' voices. It was Olivia and Winny up on top of the ruins. We could hear them as clearly as if they had been beside us, their voices echoing straight down through some opening above us into the cave.

"'There is a passageway up into the castle!' I whispered. 'Listen, Ally. Can you hear them?'

"'I hear them, but I don't want Olivia to hear us,' Alasdair replied. 'We can't make a sound till they're gone.'

"We sat down to wait. By then the voices were clear enough and coming from directly above us. The two girls were arguing. We both knew what Olivia could be like when she was angry. Then we heard her taunting Winny. That's when she was at her worst. Her taunts were terrifying and dangerous.

"'Olivia... Olivia, watch out!' Winny said. 'It's steep.'

"'Are you afraid, Winny?' said Olivia in her taunting voice.

"'A little... yes. I don't want to go down there.'

"'Why not, Winny?'

"'I just don't. I'm afraid, Olivia. Please... can we go back now?'

"'Go back?... You're not going back, Winny.'

"'Why... What do you mean? I want to go back. I want to go now... Olivia—ouch... Olivia, please stop!'

"We heard what sounded like scuffling. Winny screamed. The sound of rocks falling echoed down the hole. Alasdair and I looked at each other in dread. We both still had our torches lit, which made our faces appear grotesque against their beams of light.

"Then a terrifying shriek sounded above us. We sat paralyzed, afraid one of them had fallen. When we heard Olivia's voice again, we were filled with relief, but also with dread.

"'Next time, Winny dear,' she said, 'it will be you tumbling down the hole with those rocks. So don't you say a word to him, or he will never see you again. If I bring you here again, Winny, no one will ever find you.'

"'Please, Olivia,' we heard Winny whimpering, 'please . . . don't hurt me. Please let me go . . . I am afraid.'

"'Afraid? Are you afraid, Winny?' mocked Olivia. *Then tremble, Winny, when I look in your eye . . . and know our secret—it is here you die. Ha! Ha!'* She laughed to see what fear she could cause in her friends. She was so cruel to them, yet they remained with her. We were all afraid to stand up to her, though Alasdair gradually did."

"Who were they talking about?" I asked.

"I don't know. Some boy Olivia was keen on. She was insanely jealous of Winny and all her other friends."

"What did you do?"

"We waited awhile, then explored some more. But what we had heard took the fun out of it. We knew what it was like to be afraid of Olivia. And though we might not have been in love with her, we liked Winny. We were furious at what Olivia had said to her, but afraid at the same time. We left the cave and returned to our boat and shoved off. By now the tide had about turned.

"As we rowed into Sunnyside Cove, we looked up. There stood Olivia on the top of the cliff—alone—staring down at us. She had heard our voices, too, coming up from the cave below. Winny was far ahead of her along the headland by now, hurrying back toward Crannoch, probably thinking Olivia was chasing her and running for her life.

"We hauled the boat in and started up the path. When we reached the top out of breath, Olivia was waiting for us. The look on her face was sinister and malicious.

"'Olivia,' said Alasdair, 'is Winny all right? It sounded like she fell.'

"The only answer she gave was a cold stare first at her brother, then over at me. 'You will tell no one what you heard, or that you were here, or that I was here—do you understand?' She stared at us with an evil look. 'If you do not vow silence, I will run back and tell exactly what I saw—the two of you here with your boat...the two of you and poor dear Winny Bain. Everyone will believe me, because I will make them believe me. I will be crying and sobbing and begging them to come help, telling them that you tried to hurt her and throw her off the cliff and tormented her until she promised to make up a story about me.'

"As she stared at us, she began to mumble the words of some incantation or other that paralyzed us both. 'Vow here and now,' she said, 'under penalty of death, that to none other will you divulge what you heard.' Then she pointed a finger straight at us and spoke one of her rhyming curses—*'Speak no word of what you have seen— take heed...or you will be blamed for the evil deed.'* Then she turned, walked a few paces to the field of wheat alongside the cliff, tore off a handful of stalks, walked back, and tossed them straight into our faces. Alasdair stood like a statue.

"We knew well enough that if anything happened to Winny, blame would naturally fall on us. Alasdair and I were already viewed as nickums and scamps. She had such a way about her—she could make *anyone* believe *anything*. In the end she extracted a promise from both of us not to tell, then stared at us with the look of the evil eye and chanted a few more incantations that held us spellbound.

"A few minutes later we watched Olivia walk slowly away as if she hadn't a care in the world. At last we retrieved the horse and the boat and made our way back in silence. Of course, as nothing came of it, and Winny was fine, we gradually forgot about it...until four or five years later when Winny disappeared. Then we remembered."

"But you said nothing?"

"What could we say? There was no proof."

"Did you ever tell Ranald?"

"I did, later. He said the same thing, that we could not accuse Olivia knowing nothing for certain. And despite the circumstances, my promise haunted me. As a man who has made truth my life, I wrestled with what a promise to someone like Olivia meant. More times than I can tell you, I chastised myself for being so weak, even as a boy, for not having the courage to stand up to her threats. Ranald's Margaret suspected from the first that Olivia was responsible for Winny's disappearance, and was a little too outspoken about it."

"Was your threat of revealing what you had heard the reason Olivia allowed Gwendolyn to see Alasdair?"

"More or less. I did not go into detail. I only asked her if she wanted the community told of the Findlater incident and the curse she had spoken, now that I was a curate and Alasdair a duke. I said that she might not be able to quite so easily manipulate the story as when we were lads. She was full of threats. But I told her I was willing to put my curacy on the line and reveal what I had heard that day. If she pressed the matter, I would take my chances in the court of public opinion. She was furious, but she backed down. I thought that was the end of it. I didn't dream that her evil would come after you. That's why I say I now wonder if I should not have stayed away so long."

Iain let out a long sigh.

"I also find myself wondering about Fiona's death. Alasdair once hinted that he suspected Olivia might have given Fiona something."

"I never heard a word of it from him," I said.

"He said that Olivia always knew he was sickly. She always resented him—resented his being a man and knowing he would inherit. But she knew also that she would in all likelihood outlast him and that the castle would come to her eventually. But then Fiona threw a spanner into her plans. The moment Alasdair married, Olivia had to get rid of Fiona. At least that's what Alasdair wondered."

"What about Gwendolyn?"

"It would also explain why Olivia took Gwendolyn. Even if Gwendolyn should inherit, Olivia would still possess control. Once Gwendolyn's condition became known, all Olivia had to do was be patient. Thus she made certain that rumors about Alasdair circulated freely—even haunting him and coming to him at night with curses and potions—"

"I can still hardly believe that. What exactly did he tell you abut it?" I asked.

"Alasdair said that Olivia would sneak into the castle and come right into his bedroom and threaten evil things. He was convinced she was trying to make him go insane. She had done so even in their childhood, chanting the words of the old druidic curse while beating a blood-soaked rag—"

"What were the words?" I asked.

"Just an old Morayshire curse...nothing you would want to hear."

"I do want to hear it. Tell me, Iain, please."

"Are you sure?"

"Yes, tell me."

"All right. It's just this... *I beat this rag upo' the stane, to raise the win' in the de'il's name. It shall nae fa' till I please again.*"

"But what does it mean?"

"It's just mumbo-jumbo. The Highlands are full of such from ancient times. That curse, I think, originated with some druid calling on his power to raise the wind. Later it became a chant used by witches to invoke the curse of insanity. Coupled with it was the old tradition that a wisp of straw flung in the face of an enemy along with the curse caused raving madness. That's what the straw in our faces was about. She literally thought she had the power to make people go mad. It was all calculated to get Olivia what she wanted in the end, which was complete control of the Buchan estate."

I shook my head as I listened in disbelief.

"What is it, Marie?" Iain asked.

I told him of the similar experience and dream I'd had after Alasdair's death.

"I thought I was dreaming of a ghost haunting the castle," I said. I shivered briefly. "I never did understand the scraps of straw on my duvet the next morning. Do you think...I mean, is it possible?...Could she have actually snuck into my room, too?"

"It would not surprise me. She may even then have been hatching a plan to get rid of you for good."

I shuddered at the thought.

"Did Alasdair tell you about their grandmother—the witch woman from Skye?" I asked.

"No, I know nothing about her."

"It ties into all this," I said. I went on to relate to Iain the story of their visit to Skye as Alasdair had recounted it to me.

Iain shook his head as he listened. "That is undoubtedly where the curses and many of the family strongholds originated. Or, if not originated, she must certainly have given them added power. I have little doubt that is where Olivia learned it, from the old woman, especially the straw and chant about the rag. It is straight out of old Highland superstition. As it turned out," he went on, "as in God's economy I think may always be the case, all her curses, even the chant invoking insanity, ultimately came back on Olivia's *own* head. She always tried to bind others to her secrets and maintain a hold over them with her rhymes. Yet, one by one, most have been freed from them, thank God, while it turns out Olivia's prophecies came back against her. There is one I remember vividly, though I cannot recall the circumstances when she spoke it: *'Do not forget, nor heed the curse . . . lest your own fate become far worse.'* What she was actually doing without knowing it was speaking curses down on her *own* head. Alicia and the others, they are living lives of wholeness. They have broken those bondages. But poor Olivia's fate did indeed become worst of all. One even wonders if some physical ailments have origins in such demonic strongholds out of the past."

"Iain," I said, "what *do* you think happened to Winny?"

"I honestly don't know." Iain sighed, shaking his head. "She was never able to escape Olivia's wiles. Somehow, through one of the two tunnels, either through the castle or from Findlater, Olivia must have lured her into the crypt. The way to the sea blocked up as it is, it seems they must have snuck in from the castle, where Olivia trapped her just as she did you. But we will never know for certain."

"With all those terrible curses swirling so close," I said, "and all Olivia's schemes against her father, why wasn't Gwendolyn affected when she was with Olivia most of her life?"

"I have thought about that," said Iain reflectively. "I believe her very innocence was her protection. There is no discounting the Lord's hand in it as well. Though she was raised by Olivia, God protected her spirit and kept her pure. As she grew, I believe she contributed her own share to the resisting of evil within her. There are many ways to break demonic strongholds. Coming against them by the power of God's Word is certainly one. A stronghold of the enemy has only the power we give it. If we stand against it, and repudiate it by whatever means, it has no power over us. You have to look it in the eye and rebuke it, break it, grind it under your feet, and boldly say, *You have no more power over me.'* Obedience accomplishes that. Humility accomplishes that. Innocence accomplishes that. In a way, Alasdair broke it by love for you, and by his own determination to grow and change. There are many weapons God gives us to fight evil and produce wholeness. Gwendolyn broke the power of the family stronghold in her life by simple humble innocence and obedience."

We sat another few minutes in silence, allowing our minds to return to more pleasant things by gazing out over the sea. Finally we rose and left Iain's private sanctuary in the side of the hill.

"I'm sorry, but I have one more question," I said as we walked back to Iain's car. "Don't answer it if you don't want to. I trust you, but knowing of his possible condition, why did you never contact Alasdair again? I think it would have meant so much to him to have heard from you before he died."

Iain smiled a little sadly.

"Actually...," he answered slowly, "I did."

I looked at him with a puzzled expression.

"I sent a letter to Ranald," Iain began, "to be given to Alasdair if ever he should be taken sick. I said nothing to Ranald or Alasdair that hinted at my whereabouts. I did not want them able to contact me."

"But why, Iain? I don't understand why."

"Because had they known where I was or been able to get in touch with me, so would you eventually have known. I did not want to have such a secret with either of them, or place upon them a promise not to tell you."

"But why didn't you want *me* to know?"

"Because you *would* have contacted me."

"What would have been wrong with that, especially with Alasdair dying?"

"You would have asked me to come. And I would have."

"I wish you had, Iain."

"I know. But I couldn't. Even Alasdair's death was something I felt you and he had to share together...*alone*...to cement your love for one another forever. I could not be part of it. It would have turned it into something between all *three* of us. I was not about to do that to Alasdair. Even in his death, I would not put him in the position of having to share you with me. Nor did I want to be part of that process in your heart. Painful though it was, I knew that you and God and Alasdair had to live through it together, and then Alasdair to die...without me."

"I think I begin to understand. You did it out of love for Alasdair, not because you were ignoring him?"

"I hope so. That was certainly my intent. As I had comforted Fiona at her death, I knew that if I came I would find myself in a similar position. The circumstances were, of course, totally different. Alasdair had become a completely different man. I knew that Alasdair would even have encouraged me to comfort you. But I could not do that to my friend, knowing that he would see you and me leave the room together, would hear us talking in quiet tones. I could not again be in the position of comforting the woman he loved. What comfort was to be realized had to be derived from *your* love for him—not my words of consolation. That love was sufficient to see the two of you through without my help. I had to know that even your *memory* of Alasdair's death would be untainted by anything but love for Alasdair, without *anything* to do with me. I hope you can see that. I loved and trusted you both enough to know that you and Alasdair would be strong and able to endure it together without my presence."

"Why didn't you write and just tell us?"

"I could *say* none of this, without undoing the very thing I felt I needed to do. To say it would hint that there might be something between you and me that could make my presence awkward. I couldn't raise that idea without, as I said, intruding myself into both of your thoughts. Your thoughts had to be only of one another. I was pretty sure Alasdair would understand, though I knew you might not. Silence was the only avenue open to me. I asked Ranald to be attentive to Alasdair's spiritual needs, to give him my letter, but not to tell you."

"I should have known," I said, smiling, "that there would be love at the heart of it, even if I couldn't see it or understand it. Do you mind if I ask what you said in the letter to Alasdair?"

"I don't mind," replied Iain. "I told him there wasn't a day that went by that I did not think of him with the love of a cherished friend and lift him in prayer to God. I told him that he had always been a friend to me and that I loved him. But as much as I wished I could be there with him at this time, given the circumstances and the past, it was not something that I felt would be best. I hoped and trusted he would understand and know that I would do nothing to diminish the happiness he had come to realize in recent years."

As he spoke I remembered the blue papers I had seen Ranald take into Alasdair's sickroom.

"And now that you and I are together, so to speak," I said, "what do you believe he thinks now? You obviously no longer feel a constraint about being with me."

"Circumstances change. As I told you before, once I knew that your love for Alasdair was secure, I was free to love you, too. True love diminishes no other love. To answer your question, I think he is happy for us."

"Do you think that is really possible, for a man to happily to see his wife with another?"

"Do you resent that Alasdair and Fiona are together now?" asked Iain.

"Of course not. I am happy for them."

"In the same way, don't you think Alasdair would be happy for us?"

It was a wonderful thought. And I did think so. I *knew* he would be.

Chapter Seventy-six

Knotted Strands

Love whispered to the nightingale—"Sweet minstrel, tell to me,
Where didst thou hear that melting tale of matchless melody?"
The bird replied, "From dawn of day to ev'ning's dewy hour,
I ofttimes licht to learn a lay o' love in Mary's bow'r."
—Alexander Maclagen, "Mary's Bower"

My harp studio grew. I had to buy more harps to keep up with all the children who now wanted to take lessons. Many families bought instruments of their own. But I needed practice harps available for those who couldn't. Eventually Tavia showed such an aptitude, both in the rapid advance of her own abilities and also demonstrating a wonderful gift for teaching, that she began the initial instruction of most of the young beginners.

After they were married, she and Harvey also took up residence in apartments at the castle.

After a return to Portland, and in further consultation with my father's lawyer and friend Mr. Jones, my involvement in my father's foundations increased to the extent that I returned once a year. I decided to take my father's Oregon home off the market, and thereafter used it whenever traveling to the States. I did, however, arrange for the sale of my house in Calgary, and for my remaining possessions there to be shipped to the Portland address that I used when I was in the States. It was clear by then that Scotland would always be my home.

After being feared by so many of Olivia's generation, Ranald Bain became so endeared to the children of Port Scarnose and Crannoch that on weekends half a dozen or more youngsters could always be

467

found at his cottage, busy with his sheep and his dogs and ducks, and bottle-feeding whatever wee lambies happened to be on hand. Ranald kept a good supply of oatcakes and milk and a wide variety of home-bakes and sweets in his cupboard for the constant flow of young guests. He conducted hikes up the Bin and taught the children about plants and animals and Scottish history, as well as fascinating the boys with tales of his days in the RAF during the Cold War.

At Iain's request, a weekly Saturday afternoon Bible study and discussion was begun at Ranald's cottage as well, open to any and all from the community who desired to probe the deeper aspects of the Christian faith. According to Iain, Ranald was the host and Bible teacher. According to Ranald, that role fell to Iain. Suffice it to say that, sitting at the feet of both these remarkable men of varying doctrinal viewpoints, all of us who participated were enriched in our spiritual lives by continually growing in a deepening understanding of the nature and character of God.

In the twilight years of his life, Ranald Bain thus became not only Castle Buchan's official fiddler for all events, at which he appeared in kilt and regalia, but also one recognized as spiritual bard to an entire community, esteemed and beloved by all.

I set out to use Alasdair's fortune for the good of the community and for all of northeast Scotland in what ways I could. That I would have no children meant that I had difficult decisions to make regarding the disposition of the estate for the future.

With an eye to that future, I set up a governing board from among members of the community to administer the estate. If something should happen to me, I wanted to ensure that the entire community would own and benefit from the holdings and business activities of the estate. The castle itself I arranged to turn over to the National Trust for Scotland after my death, with a stipend to provide for its maintenance and care. Nigel helped draft the legal documentation for these changes, as well as being one of the initial members of the governing board. He was joined by Iain Barclay, David Mair, Alicia

Crathie, Leslie and Morag Mair, and local businesspersons Moira and Alex Legge, Harry Harshaw, Tom and Judith Johnston, Steve and June Rush, and Alan and Marian McPherson.

I had the gates and signs installed by Olivia removed. All roads into the property were kept open. Gradually I sold some of the estate's land in order to allow the town to expand in the direction of the castle, hoping that in time, if it would not exactly become part of the town, the castle would be less isolated. I started harp classes in all the primary schools of the area, at which Tavia and I both taught. Iain and I went on a drive together every Sunday afternoon and stopped somewhere different most every time for a tea, a snack, supper, and sometimes for a thorough high tea.

I set in motion an attempt to locate any of Alasdair's cousins, however distant, who might be traceable. I wanted to be certain that whatever obligations might exist toward them were faithfully fulfilled. Alicia and Tavia also helped me locate as many of Max Urquhart's relatives as we could. They were, after all, in essentially a similar position to mine, in-laws to the Duke of Buchan and his family. I felt a responsibility to make sure they were provided for financially. We established contact with Max's brother and two sisters, as well as his elderly mother, who was living in pensioner's housing in Port Scarnose, a positively delightful woman. She had been devastated at Max's marriage to Olivia and the treatment she had received at the hands of her daughter-in-law. Though initially suspicious of me, we became the best of friends, and she took Alicia to her heart like one of her own daughters. When her health began to fail, we brought her to the castle to live so that we might care for her. She lived with us until her death at age ninety-three.

Iain completed his book. It had become in the writing much more than a book about Alasdair, but about growth, healing, and reconciliation in personal relationships. It was not the kind of book to become a bestseller, though it enjoyed modest success throughout northern Scotland.

About once every month or two, whenever Iain had the occasion to preach in the Deskmill Church, he paused in walking down the center aisle, waited for me to descend from the laird's loft to join him. Then we both stood on either side of the door outside, greeting people as they left. The functions of church and castle, standing so close for so long with a wall between them, were now truly one, the dividing wall of separation broken by the truth of reconciliation Iain had explored in his book. The priesthood and aristocracy now functioned as one, fulfilling the purpose for which both ought to have been intended all along—to serve the people.

Alicia became an accomplished pilot, flying Nigel wherever in the UK his business took him. Much to his delight, Ranald Bain was also a frequent passenger. I have to admit, however, that I never went up with her again.

In afteryears, dear Ranald's step began to slow. It was clear to all his closest friends, and to Ranald himself most of all, that, in his mid-eighties, his earthly days were gradually coming to an end. Never having forgotten her own unkind words to him when under Olivia's influence, and his response of gentle forgiveness, Alicia's tenderness toward Ranald as he declined was wonderful to behold.

When he could no longer care for himself, Alicia and Nigel temporarily moved up the hill into the Bain cottage. It was their desire to be his caregivers in order to allow Ranald to continue tending his sheep until he joined his great Shepherd, and, if his health permitted it, to enable him to die at the end in his own bed.

Chapter Seventy-seven

Hearts as One

Happy maiden! Long ago life to me was full of beauty,
Guided by the radiant glow, diffused by Hope o'er Love and duty.
Slowly through the scented wood passed the maiden, smiling sadly,
But afar impatient stood one whose arms would fold her gladly.
—J. S. Skinner, "Maiden by the Silver Dee"

Three years had passed since Olivia's death. I was forty-eight, Iain forty-nine.

It had been a gradual process in which we had both grown into the realities and complexities of our situation. At last Iain allowed himself to gaze into my eyes in a way he had not done in years. His face that afternoon as we walked along the sea wore an understanding, tender smile. It was a peaceful, quiet, unobtrusive, yet radiant smile full of light. Out of the deep emerald green of his eyes, almost as if emerging from two bottomless mountain sapphire pools, shone again *the look*.

My eyes met his. I walked a little timidly toward him. His hands spread wide as I approached. The next thing I knew I was in his arms. It was the day he told me he loved me, really *loved* me in the full sense of all the word can mean between a man and a woman.

"It is still difficult to understand," I said softly, "how you can love me, after . . . when my heart was being pulled and torn by love for Alasdair and you . . . when it was Alasdair I chose, and you I rejected."

"You did not reject me," rejoined Iain in the most tender voice imaginable. "You gave yourself to a man who needed your love. As much as I may have loved you, I respected you for your choice. You *loved* Alasdair, and that made me love you all the more."

"But how could your love be so unselfish as not to be hurt or jealous that I married him?"

"Jealous?" repeated Iain, as if the word were a defiling poison he did not want to touch. "Why would I be jealous? How could I *possibly* have been jealous? I loved you both. Jealousy has no place in love."

"That is hardly the way the world sees it when two men and one woman are involved," I said.

Iain smiled. "It has not been my practice to adopt the ways of the world as my standard."

He paused thoughtfully, weighing carefully what he was about to say.

"I think you knew," he said at length, "that I loved you. I did not say it before because I would do nothing to interfere with what God was deepening between you and Alasdair. I had to wait for God's purposes to unfold. When you and Alasdair told me of your love and your plans, of course, on the level of my humanity, I felt pain. But it was not the pain of jealousy or rejection, but the pain of sacrifice— a good pain, a cleansing pain. Therefore, I also rejoiced in the midst of my tears—rejoiced for Alasdair, and for my abiding love and respect for you."

"You shed tears after learning about Alasdair and me?"

Iain nodded.

"I had no idea. You never gave a hint of it."

"I usually keep the door to my prayer closet closed."

"But why . . . if you rejoiced in it, as you say?"

"Why did I weep?"

I nodded.

"Don't you know? Because I loved you, too. I knew that you cared for me. But in your choice, and in my tears, I came to love you more deeply."

"This is all hard to believe," I said. "It is not the way I expected things to turn out."

"Real life rarely follows a script. But here we are. This is the way life has come to us."

It was silent several minutes. I knew I loved Iain. I had loved him almost from the beginning—first as a friend, and now . . . yes, as more than a friend.

"Did you suspect that Alasdair was going to die?" I asked at length. "Did you know I was making myself a widow even as I said my vows to him?"

"No," replied Iain. "I wondered, of course, especially after Gwendolyn's death. The disease never affected him, at least that I ever knew, as a child. Maybe I was simply unaware of it. So I tried to hope for the best. I always thought his health was fine. Obviously I knew there was a possibility it could strike him, which was the basis for my letter. But I always hoped my letter would never be read at all, and that eventually I would return to you both. Did he tell you of his condition?"

I smiled nostalgically. "He tried to," I answered poignantly. "He told me that he had been diagnosed years ago and that his life expectancy would always be in doubt. He wanted me to know before accepting his proposal. I dismissed it without taking his precautions as seriously as perhaps I should have."

"Would you have done anything differently had you known?"

"No," I answered. "Love is careless and blind to the future. Now that he is gone, I am so glad for the few years I had with him."

"I, too, am glad. I think you are right—even had you known, you would have done the same. You were thinking of a greater good than the security of your own future. The least I could do was follow your example."

"What are you saying, Iain—you following *my* example? You are the one who awakened faith in me."

"Perhaps. But you awoke love in me."

Chapter Seventy-eight

"Gwendolyn's Song"

For auld lang syne, my dear,
For auld lang syne,
We'll tak a cup o' kindness yet
For auld lang syne.
—Robert Burns, "Auld Lang Syne"

Late one summer while Ranald was still strong and full of vigor, I began what I hoped would be an annual outdoor open-air concert at the Bain croft, with local musicians, crafts, food, and a community celebration inaugurating the coming of the harvest.

It was a Highland games festival without the games.

Of course, harps were featured. Some drove up to bring tables and instruments and food and other supplies, but most of the villagers gathered with me at the castle, there to trek as a festive throng of two or three hundred up the slope of the Bin on foot. By the time we reached Ranald's, our voices were booming out the robust strains of "Scotland the Brave" with such power that it was reportedly heard all the way to Buckie.

The heather was in bloom. I couldn't help thinking of Alicia's lovely vision as the inspiration for the gathering. People were walking about, some hiking to the top of the Bin and back down to the cottage, families and dogs and blankets and sheep and kilted lads and lassies all spread out over the hillside in such colorful array. The gray towers of the castle rose amid the canopy of trees below us, the blue of the sea and coastline of the Moray Firth spreading out east and west as far as the eye could see. Pipers and fiddlers played from the makeshift stage between Ranald's cottage and barn, the skirl of the pipes drifting over the countryside for a mile in every direction.

As I glanced around at the panorama of people and families and music and activity, I was suddenly overwhelmed by a stunning thought—what if I had never come to Scotland! How would this scene before me on this wonderful day be different? Would all these people ever have known Alasdair? Would he and Gwendolyn ever have known each other? What would have happened to the castle, the estate, the community?

It was too overpowering a thought to take in. You never know what the future might hold, or what will be the impact of your life in ways you cannot anticipate. And you never know how God might use the simple decision to pursue a dream.

Midway through the afternoon, when most had eaten and drunk their fill, the ladies of my harp ensemble—twelve in number now—took the stage, with Ranald at his grandfather's harp in a place of honor at the center. We played four pieces, ending with my favorite save one, "Wild Mountain Thyme."

Then came a great scurrying and moving and shuffling and re-arranging, as the ensemble gave way to the twenty-two young students of my studio. When their nervousness and fidgeting and glances about at the sea of watching faces at last settled down, we began our program. We played a variety of Scottish and pop tunes, including, in Alasdair's memory—though no one but me knew the story behind it—"Eleanor Rigby." We finished, as did all the recitals with my students, with what I introduced as "Gwendolyn's Song."

With the brief concert and recital over, proud parents and grand-parents clustered about their young musicians, with congratulations and thanks to me, and exclamations of relief from my students to have completed the performance. Harps and cases and chairs and music stands were gathered and moved about, a few of the parents handing me flowers and wanting to have a few words, a general air of pandemonium indicating that many of the day's revelers were gathering their things and readying to begin the walk back down to the two villages.

As a break in the string of visitations came, I walked to the stage area where Ranald was just picking up his harp to carry it back into his cottage.

"It was wonderful, Ranald," I said. "Thank you for hosting such a memorable event."

"Oh, aye," he said enthusiastically. "'Twas a happy time for a', I'm thinkin'. 'Tis love o' yersel' that's brought the fowk o' the toons thegither this gait."

I smiled and was about to reply that he was as much a part of the changed atmosphere throughout the community as I was, when I felt a tug from behind.

I turned to see a sweet little girl of about six, standing and gazing up at me with the most gorgeous light blue eyes. Her hair was bright orange.

"Please, Duchess," she said sweetly, "may I spier a question o' ye?"

"Of course, dear—what is it?"

"Div ye think I cud learn tae play a wee harpie like the ither lassies?"

"I am sure you could," I said. "Perhaps you will come to my house and I will teach you. We will see what music you can make. What is your name?"

"Maisie, mum."

"That is a lovely name. Do you know where I live, Maisie?"

"Fowk say ye bide in the castle."

"That's right. If you want to play the harp, that's where you will come to learn."

"Wha is Gwendolyn, Duchess? Ilka body's talkin' aboot her, but I dinna ken wha she is."

I knelt down and gazed into the girl's huge innocent blue eyes.

"She was the very first little girl from Port Scarnose who learned to play the harp," I said.

"Whaur is she the noo? Is she still playin' the harpie, Duchess?"

I smiled, with the most wonderful images of heavenly music filling my mind's eye.

"Yes, sweetheart," I said. "She certainly is."

As I said in the beginning, it can be a terrible thing when dreams die.

But mine had taken wings I could never have imagined.

Perhaps my dreams were like the seeds Jesus spoke of: "Unless a grain of wheat fall into the earth and die, it remains alone. But if it dies, it bears much fruit."

My dreams had certainly borne fruit. Even though they had contained sadness, the reality turned out even better than the dream.

Is that not the way it is with all God's realities? They are better even than we can dream them.

As for the duchess and the curate, there was little doubt in anyone's mind, still less to either of them, that they loved each other with an eternal love. What was to become of that love, however, they were not yet prepared to say with certainty, though their lives would forever be joined in a oneness more lofty than the world could understand.

They were growing in their love, that much they would say. And when a man and a woman love God, such is perhaps the best thing that can be said of their love for each other.

Appendix

Scots Glossary

A': all
Abody: everyone
Aboot: about
Abune: above
Ahint: behind
Aiblins: perhaps
Ain: own
Ane: one
Anither: another
Athegither: altogether
Aye: yes
Bairn: child
Bin: hill/summit
Bonny: pretty
Burn: creek/stream
Caw canny: be careful
Coo: cattle
Dee: death
Deid: dead
De'il: devil
Dinna: don't
Disna: doesn't
Div/du/de: do
Doon: down

Dune: done
Een: eyes
Fa/wha: who
Fae/frae: from
Fan: when
Fit: what
Fleyt: afraid
Gae: go
Gait: way
Gang/gaed: went
Gar: make
Gie: give
Gien: if
Greet: cry
Gude/guid: good
Hae: have
Hame: home
Heid: head
Hert: heart
Ilka: every
Intae/intil: into
Isna: isn't
Ken: know
Kennt: knew

Lang: long
Lauch: laugh
Luik: look
Mair: more
Maun: must
Mirk: dark
Mony: many
Muckle: much, big
Nae: no
Naethin': nothing
Nickum: ruffian
Nor: than
O': of
Ocht: ought
Oot: out
Ower: over
Po'er/pooer: power
Puir: poor
Richt: right
Roon: round
Sae: so
Sanna: shall not
Sicht: sight
Siller: money

Spier: ask
Sud: should
Sudna: shouldn't
Syne: since/since then/ago
Tae/till: to
Thocht: thought
Toon: town
Trowth: truth
Twa: two
Unco: great/much/a lot
Upo': upon
Verra: very
Wad: would
Wadna: wouldn't
Wark: work
Warna: weren't
Weel: well
Whan: when
Whaur: where
Whiles: sometimes
Wi': with
Winna: won't
Wis: was

For information about Michael Phillips and his other books, including The Eyewitness Bible *and other nonfiction, as well as his many bestselling fiction series, you can visit FatherOfTheInklings.com.*